"You're trembling like a leaf."

He stepped closer, taking in her pale face and shadowed eyes.

"It's nothing," Ty mumbled, refusing to look at him, suddenly feeling too close to the edge emotionally to withstand his scrutiny. It must be the stress, the nerves, the fatigue. "I'm just cold all of a sudden."

The force was magnetic, drawing him to her, thoughts careening inside his head, blaring commands for his body to follow. *Kiss her. Touch her. Hold her.* His movements were slow, unhurried, but thrillingly certain nonetheless.

"I'd really like to kiss you," he whispered, and took her faint indrawn breath for a yes. Their lips met in a clinging caress, and Steve felt a jolt of recognition race through him. The taste of Ty was unlike anything he'd ever experienced. He needed more.

A heart-stopping smile spread slowly across his face. He leaned into her, the warmth from his body enveloping her. "Still cold?" he asked in a husky voice. "Let's see whether together we can't warm you up."

Books by Laura Moore

Ride a Dark Horse
Chance Meeting

Published by Pocket Books

LAURA MOORE

Chance Meeting

POCKET STAR BOOKS

New York   London   Toronto   Sydney   Singapore

This book is a work of fiction. Names, characters, places and incidents are products of the author's imagination or are used fictitiously. Any resemblance to actual events or locales or persons, living or dead, is entirely coincidental.

An *Original* Publication of POCKET BOOKS

A Pocket Star Book published by
POCKET BOOKS, a division of Simon & Schuster, Inc.
1230 Avenue of the Americas, New York, NY 10020

ISBN: 0-671-04293-9

First Pocket Books printing October 2001

10 9 8 7 6 5 4 3 2 1

POCKET STAR BOOKS and colophon are registered trademarks of Simon & Schuster, Inc.

For information regarding special discounts for bulk purchases, please contact Simon & Schuster Special Sales at 1-800-456-6798 or business@simonandschuster.com

Front cover illustration by Gregg Gulbronson

Printed in the U.S.A.

for my father

PART 1

1989

1

Lake Placid, New York

"*O*migod! Omigod! Ty, Ty, it's *him!*" The force of Lizzie's elbow into her ribs sent Ty stumbling, smearing a thick coat of mint chocolate chip ice cream across the front of her nose.

"Jeez Louise," Ty muttered in aggravation. She looked reproachfully at her perilously lopsided cone, now in imminent danger of landing on her beige breeches. Recognizing this as a crisis situation, Ty wiped with the back of her hand at the sticky green mess coating her face. Then she carefully brought the cone within range of her mouth once again and gave it a long, hard sweep with her tongue, righting the precarious lump.

Unfortunately, the sharp mint flavor no longer tasted quite so refreshing, even in the heat wave that was currently roasting the Northeast. It was barely nine o'clock, and already the thermometer was in the upper eighties. The forecast predicted a weekend high of a hundred and one degrees, practically unheard of in upstate New York. A wholly unanticipated side effect of the stifling heat wave, and an especially low blow for Ty, was how it destroyed her enthusiasm for one of her favorite foods.

Now the ice cream treat was little more than a sticky, melting mess clasped between her fingers. She wanted to get rid of it. Normally, Ty loved the liberty on show days to eat the most improbable foods at whatever hour caught her fancy. Pizza at eight, a hamburger with the works at ten, ice cream—who was going to argue that it was still breakfast time when she'd been up for hours already? And if her father bothered to come and watch, he wouldn't arrive a minute before her classes were scheduled to begin, so she never risked his chilly disapproval at the sight of his only child doing something so vulgar as eating ice cream before lunch. This morning, however, it was simply too darn hot to eat—even ice cream.

Appetite gone, Ty spotted a trash can a few feet away, still three-quarters empty, with only a few bees buzzing around its rim, as very few of the spectators or competitors who'd arrived this early had begun eating in earnest. Ty dropped the offensive cone into its gaping mouth. Glancing down at her hands, she wished that earlier, back at the concession stand, she hadn't so hastily declined the offer of a napkin from the man scooping ice cream out of the enormous ten gallon cardboard drums. Now, she thought gloomily, she was doomed to walk around the show grounds with a patina of green goo all over her.

Recalling what had caused this catastrophe, Ty glanced over at her best friend, Lizzie, who was still standing transfixed, apparently struck dumb by whatever had caught her attention. That set warning bells a-ringing far more effectively than Lizzie's linebacker's shove of a few seconds before. Lizzie was constitutionally incapable of keeping quiet, as their eighth grade teacher, Mrs. Brockhurst, loved to proclaim at regular intervals. As this was about the cleverest thing Mrs. Brockhurst had ever said, the teacher was tickled pink each and every time she found an opportunity to repeat this insightful comment. Poor Mrs. Brockhurst.

But who in the world could possibly have her best friend acting as if she'd just caught a glimpse of Tom Cruise right here in the flesh? Tom Cruise . . . Wait a second, hadn't she read an article about him and horses in one of those glamor magazines she'd flipped through while waiting her turn for the orthodontist to torture her mouth? Ty's eyes lifted, scanning the crowd.

All thoughts of Tom Cruise vanished.

When at last she remembered to breathe, Ty had to force air past the lump that had taken residence in her chest. It was a lump of longing, formed by countless articles clipped from *Equus*, *Practical Horseman*, and other horse trade magazines she read, mentioning the man standing twenty yards away. She'd even videotaped interviews he'd given on ESPN, allowing Ty to replay the sound of his voice, his Kentucky accent wonderfully exotic to her ears, watch that quick grin of his flash across the TV screen, and then sigh wistfully whenever the camera lens happened to catch those twinkling blue eyes as he replied to the sportscaster's questions with clever, insightful quips about his fellow riders and their mounts.

He was her idol.

Steve Sheppard. Could it really be him?

She'd dreamed of seeing him so many times now, at the bigger horse shows she competed at, always wondering, as she lay in her bed the night before, whether he might just possibly be there, too. Maybe he'd happen to see her ride and would be wowed by the exceptional talent of this young rider. He'd want to meet her, and there'd be this instant attraction that would flare up between the two of them. They'd get to talking, and . . . he'd understand her.

"Do you see him?" Lizzie's voice carried an urgency appropriate for the occasion.

"Yes," Ty managed to whisper, still staring, drinking in the sight of him as he stood, his blond, close-cropped head bent at an angle as he listened to whatever the woman next to him—also a competitor, judging from her rust-colored breeches and sleeveless rat-catcher— was saying.

Ty looked on, filled with awe and longing as Steve Sheppard and the woman turned and began to walk around the perimeter of the schooling area.

"Come on," Lizzie urged, grabbing Ty by the elbow and dragging her along, "We've got to follow him."

"But we can't! We can't just follow *Steve Sheppard* around the show grounds. It's not right, I mean, he's Steve Sheppard!" Ty finished desperately, as if that were all the explanation needed.

"Yeah, and you've had a humongous crush on him for how long now? Since fifth grade, that's when. Remember when we first saw him at Madison Square Garden, when your dad gave Sam permission to take you to the National Horse Show, and you begged and pleaded until Sam let me come, too? Come *on*," Lizzie repeated impatiently, pulling the reluctant Ty after her. "We're not runty fifth-graders anymore. We're women."

Oh sure, retorted Ty silently. Lizzie might have acquired all the physical equipment necessary to make the boys drool every time she passed by, but Ty was sadly stalled in prepubescent limbo. Her body was just one embarrassing joke. A few months ago, she'd thought she was at long last growing breasts. *Hah!* All she had to show for herself were two puny bumps where her nipples were, sort of like the floppy end of a balloon where it hasn't been inflated fully. Only with Ty there were no balloons to parade around with.

But Lizzie had balloons, hips, and a lovely rounded bottom. Not too big, just right. The boys swarmed around her like bees in clover. Older guys, too. Not that Ty minded, she loved Lizzie too much to be jealous of her best friend's beauty. It was just that by comparison, Ty was a walking, talking stick and generated as much interest as a mushed sandwich among the few boys who mistakenly spared her a passing glance.

And Steve Sheppard wasn't a mere teenage boy. He was twenty-three, almost a whole decade older than her, and the most exciting American rider to grace the show circuit in many years.

Again, her eyes feasted on the sight of him.

He was dressed in jeans and a cobalt-blue polo shirt. His casual attire stood out in sharp contrast to the multitude of tan, fawn, and white breeches, black field boots, short-sleeve shirts, sleeveless rat-catchers; nobody was going to put on their hunt jackets until the last possible second, not in this heat. Ty suspected that splash of bright blue was what had caught Lizzie's eye. It was a cinch to identify him after that. Steve Sheppard's golden good looks, combined with his aura of quiet authority, made him a man people had a hard time forgetting.

Lizzie was still pulling her along in his direction, when Ty saw the young woman who'd been walking alongside Steve Sheppard stumble slightly, her body brushing his side. He paused, looking down at her with mild concern. His lips moved, the question obvious, his hand supporting her elbow. In response, the woman's slim form stretched as she rose up on her toes and planted a kiss on the corner of Sheppard's mouth.

Ty's heart lurched as she caught the fleeting smile of triumph cross the woman's face as the pair turned, heading off in the direction of the parking area, jam packed with vans of different sizes and colors.

Lizzie, too, had witnessed the kiss but dismissed it immediately, refusing to let such a minor incident deter her from her mission. Any woman in her right mind would be tempted to give a dreamy guy like Steve Sheppard a kiss. He probably got accosted by little old ladies crossing the street, so it was stupid to blow what had been a mere peck out of proportion. Ty might not see it that way, but then Ty hadn't had a whole lot of experience with kissing. Lizzie had done her level best to help out in that area, pointing out boys from the private school across the street who might prove worth her while as candidates, if Ty would only give them half a chance. So far, Ty hadn't seemed interested, which Lizzie considered a terrible waste. What were boys for, after all? But she knew Ty would give the moon to meet Steve Sheppard. So Lizzie was bound and determined to arrange it. Like a bloodhound on the scent, she followed Steve Sheppard's retreating figure, dragging along a protesting Ty.

When Ty dug the heels of her black field boots into the grass, again forcing Lizzie to slow down, Lizzie shot her a look, impatient to keep their quarry in sight.

"What?"

"Lizzie, stop! We can't do this. First of all, we've got to go warm up, and second, do you really think Sam is just going to stand around with a big, happy smile on his face while I go chasing after someone like Steve Sheppard? *For sure*," she finished heavily.

Sam Brody had been with the New York Police Department, a detective or something, before Father had hired him to protect her. It was yet another huge embarrassment in her life—she didn't need a bodyguard, for heaven's sake. No one would ever know her from Adam; she looked like anyone, normal. It wasn't as if there was some sign attached to her that read, "Hi, my father's mega-rich, kidnap me!" At least Sam was kind enough not to make it totally obvious he was watching her every move, as well as everyone else's who came within ten feet of her.

A small frown moved the freckles sprinkled over Lizzie's forehead and the bridge of her nose. Shoot, she'd forgotten all about Sam. It was kind of cool, the way he could be only a few yards behind Ty and be so, well, invisible that you just forgot his presence. That is, unless you were Ty Stannard. She figured she'd think it was a major drag, too, if her father were paranoid nutso enough to hire a personal bodyguard for her. Then again, her folks didn't have billions of dollars, either.

"Okay, so we lose Sam. And we'll warm up *after* we've met Steve Sheppard. There's still gobs of time before our first class. If we pull this off fast enough, Sam probably won't even realize we slipped away."

Ty's jaw dropped at the outrageousness of her friend's suggestion. Fourteen-year-old girls didn't just lose bodyguards like Sam Brody.

"You don't really believe we can lose him, do you?" she croaked.

"Of course we can." Lizzie's voice rose with excitement at the daring of her idea. "See, we'll pretend we're going to the toilets over there. Steve Sheppard's heading that way, anyway. Then we'll kind of duck out behind them and run real fast. I'll be watching which way Steve goes the whole time. I'm betting he's going back to the van to change or something." A small giggle escaped her. "Maybe he wants to show Miss Lips his tack. What's the name of the stable he rides with? Golden Club?"

"Gold Crest Farm," Ty replied automatically, realizing a second too late that Lizzie was teasing, as if she weren't perfectly aware he was still riding with that private stable in Southampton, even though the latest buzz was that Steve Sheppard had recently bought a farm in Bridgehampton, New York. She wondered whether he was planning to open a stable of his own soon. But Ty knew she'd never get the chance to ask him.

She knew it; the trouble was, Lizzie didn't.

"For Pete's sake, Lizzie, I hope you know this is not going to work. What've you been watching lately? Marathons of *Miami Vice?* 'Lose' Sam, 'shake' him off? We're setting ourselves up for a major grounding, and I'm not even going to mention how embarrassing it's going to be when Sam catches us."

Somehow, despite her objections, Ty found her feet moving in the direction of the bright blue row of plastic portable toilets. Lizzie had that kind of effect on people.

"Yeah, well, you'll never know until you try, will ya?" Lizzie shot her a wicked I-dare-you smile and then, in a pathetic imitation of Groucho Marx, wiggled her strawberry-blond eyebrows exaggeratedly. "You know, Ty, sometimes a girl's gotta do what a girl's gotta do."

Lizzie was totally ridiculous. Totally.

Laughter abruptly bubbled up inside Ty and erupted. She stood, clutching her sides, laughing hard enough that tears trickled from the corners of her eyes. Her braces flashed in the bright sunshine as she continued to laugh, heading off toward the toilets. This was just another reason she loved Lizzie Osborne more than anyone else in the whole world.

Lizzie's incredible zest for life drew everyone in, Ty included. It enabled Ty to imagine that she, too, could do wild and stupid things, like any kid. Her life didn't have to be perfect, deadly boring, something from the sterile pages of *Town and Country*.

Lizzie was the best friend she could ever have. Had

been, since that first day in third grade when Ty had come to the private girls' school as a new student. It was a class in which all the girls had been together since kindergarten. Out of the seventeen pupils seated behind their plastic and metallic desks, Lizzie had been the only one to smile at her. She'd won Ty's heart and steadfast loyalty when, in the middle of second period, while their teacher droned on about a multiplication problem Ty had already finished and checked by herself, Lizzie swiveled around in her chair and whispered to Ty, asking if she wanted to play jacks at recess. At Ty's shy nod, she'd grinned and uttered, "Great!" loudly enough to receive a warning from the teacher.

When the bell rang for dismissal at the end of that first school day, the girls from her class watched the way hawks would a field mouse as Ty was greeted by a solidly built, forbidding man who was clearly much too young to be her father—they distinctly heard him address Ty as "Miss Ty"—standing beside a chauffeur-driven Rolls-Royce. The girls also noted the significant absence of a mommy or a nanny waiting to greet the new kid; they'd hung around just so they could peer into the open doors of the Rolls, the tinted windows previously having blocked their view. Every single suspicion they'd nourished throughout the day was confirmed. Ty was different. Ranks closed, excluding her from friendships or cliques.

Given time, Ty might have been able to win those other girls over by inviting them to her house, but her father wouldn't permit it. It had taken considerable courage to screw up her nerve to ask her father again and again over the following weeks. He never provided Ty with a satisfactory answer. Just: it was impossible, and she shouldn't bother him right now, anyway, because he had some important papers to read, because he was waiting for a conference call or had an urgent meeting at the office, or because the helicopter was ready to take him to the airport where his private jet waited.

Ty stopped asking, realizing her father's response would never change. But she thought about it a long time, turning the problem over in her mind, and came to the conclusion that her father must not believe the other girls at her school were good enough for her. Even then, at age eight, Ty understood that *good enough* meant, according to her father, having enough money. As Ty came to understand the extent of her father's vast wealth, she realized, too, that if her father truly felt that way, then only about sixty families in the entire world were *good enough* to be considered friends of Tyler Stannard's daughter. And not one of those other families had a daughter in Ty's third-grade class.

Luckily for Ty, Lizzie had never cared about any of that. She'd never been put off by the large, shiny black car that pulled up in front of the school steps every afternoon at dismissal. She didn't think it unusual or creepy that Ty was never picked up by a family member. Nor did she appear offended or become standoffish when months passed and Ty didn't invite her over after school or accept any of the invitations Lizzie herself extended. Day after day, Lizzie simply waved good-bye to her best friend, calling out cheerfully, "See ya tomorrow, Ty," before skipping down the street, her mother's hand clasping hers.

In the wake of her father's refusal, Ty turned to Sam Brody, her bodyguard. It took quite a bit of hard campaigning before she persuaded him to discuss with Lizzie's mother the possibility of an afternoon's outing for the two girls.

Or perhaps it was eight-year-old Ty's visible loneliness, her poignant need for companionship, which ultimately swayed Sam. Throughout that period, he watched the pattern unfold. Ty waving good-bye to the only girl who called out to her. Ty waiting beside the Rolls as Lizzie skipped down the street until at last she turned the corner and was out of sight. Only then would Ty reluctantly slide into the darkened leather and hand-rubbed mahogany splendor of the car's interior. After he'd witnessed this daily drama repeat itself one too many times, Sam sided with Ty and became her ally. Willingly risking the wrath of Tyler Stannard, should he discover what had transpired without his express permission, all so that Ty could spend some afternoons with her best friend, eating popcorn, working on homework together, and laughing hysterically over nothing at all.

Ty knew she owed Sam a lot, for he had recognized how important it was to have a friend who liked her for herself, rather than because she was Tyler Stannard's only child.

But the plan Lizzie was concocting right now was an entirely different matter. That Sam understood her need for friendship didn't mean he was about to let her run loose over the Lake Placid show grounds, chasing after Steve Sheppard like some deranged fan.

Nevertheless, she was going to do it. Somehow, she'd reached the point where she had to test the strength of the gilded cage her father had constructed around her. Her father, the real estate king, who excelled at building things. She wanted to see whether she could break free, if only for a little while. Surely Sam wouldn't be too angry.

Quickly, before she lost her nerve, Ty grabbed the metal handle on the molded plastic door of the portable toilet, resisting the urge to glance over her shoulder and see how far back Sam was standing, waiting. She opened the door wide, moving her body behind it so that she was blocked from view.

Yuck! The stench of cherry-scented cleanser liberally mixed with fermenting urine assaulted her nostrils, about a hundred times more awful in this heat. She held her breath and pulled the door after her. Praying that Sam's eyes had strayed momentarily as she'd stepped inside, she abruptly reopened the door, slipped out from behind it, and dashed around the back of the tall, rectangular toilet. Lizzie was already there, flushed with excitement.

"Quick, hurry! I saw which way they went!"

"This is crazy!"

"Yeah, isn't it fun?" Lizzie grabbed Ty's hand. Giggling, breathless adolescents, the two girls ran, weaving in and out of the tall metal alleyways of the parked vans.

2

"*Uh*, Allegra, could you please hold on a minute . . ." Steve's hands pulled at Allegra Palmer's elbows, in the hopes of loosening her manacle hold. He stepped back, creating as much space as he could between himself and Allegra's hungry mouth.

What was up with these rich girls? Allegra had pounced on him as soon as they reached the van. It felt as if she'd smeared crazy glue on top of her lip gloss. To make things worse, she had arms like an octopus on amphetamines. It was a bit scary, actually. He didn't really want to be devoured in the back of a horse van, at least not by Allegra Palmer.

Christ, his pop had warned him to steer clear of rich men's daughters. Especially if he happened to be working for the rich man. Those girls were always more trouble than they were worth. Even if Steve didn't always take it, Pop's advice was worth listening to. In this instance, Steve had recognized the wisdom of his father's words and had been keeping a safe distance from Allegra for some time. Unfortunately, since returning home for summer vacation from her first year away at college,

Allegra seemed even less perceptive than before she'd left. She refused to understand his polite refusals and gentle rejections for what they truly were: a complete lack of interest. It was a real problem. How did one come right out and tell the daughter of the man who was giving Steve a quarter-of-a-million-dollar horse to ride that she was becoming a royal pain in the butt and that all that suction-cup kissing and mad grinding of her body wasn't quite the turn-on she imagined?

Steve hadn't yet figured out the answer to that one.

Hell, he didn't want to hurt her feelings. She wasn't so bad, though definitely too pushy. And oversexed to boot. Generally, Steve didn't mind oversexed. But he liked to be the one to choose. At this point he was feeling like a hunted animal, with Allegra hauling around an arsenal that would do Rambo proud.

And now she was at it again. Relentless. She'd taken advantage of his momentary distraction to wiggle her way closer, her breath all catchy, her fingers moving up the sides of his polo shirt. She was planting little kisses along his jaw, her hands reaching around his neck, pulling his mouth down to hers. He stiffened, holding his neck rigid, but to his chagrin, Steve realized she'd backed him up against the inside of the van. Dear God, she was trying to have her way with him.

A burst of high-pitched giggles saved him. His only thought, *hallelujah!* Allegra heard them, too, spinning around to locate the source of uncontrolled mirth, no doubt ready to give someone utter hell.

Two girls stood on the wooden ramp leading up to the van. Framed by the sun, only their silhouettes were distinct. Steve didn't know whether he knew them; he was just damn glad they were there, for whatever reason. Allegra, however, didn't share his point of view.

"What are you doing here?" she demanded shrilly.

"Don't you know this is private property? Who do you think you are, trespassing like this?"

Since first laying eyes on Steve Sheppard, Allegra had been making her attraction for him crystal clear. He was a real catch. All the girls in her set were after him. He was so handsome, with those amazingly bright blue eyes. And she loved how that strong jaw ended in a square chin; his lips curling so easily into a sexy grin. And then there was his thick golden hair. The fact that he'd recently cut it so it was cropped close to his head didn't deter Allegra from fantasizing about running her fingers through it. Thoughts of Steve occupied Allegra for hours at a time.

A few months ago, she'd been flipping through a magazine and had come across photographs taken of Paul Newman when he'd been in his twenties. She'd been completely bowled over. Steve Sheppard could have stood as his double. And if that weren't enough to set a woman's pulse fluttering, Steve had a Kentucky accent and a dimple when he smiled that could cause a total meltdown.

An entire year had come and gone, with Allegra virtually throwing herself at him. To no avail. It was supremely frustrating, the way Steve constantly brushed her off and avoided her. Today, however, represented a major breakthrough, finally getting him alone for long enough to prove just how exciting a woman she could be. She'd do anything for him, she wanted him so bad. Now two idiotic kids had burst in, ruining everything. Allegra wanted to spit, she was so mad.

At her angry questioning, one of the girls had frozen. The other seemed incapable of controlling her fit of giggles.

Actually, Ty hadn't been laughing at all, but as her hand was clamped over her mouth, neither Steve Shep-

pard nor Allegra Palmer could tell. Ty had instinctively
tried to hide her expression of astonishment, embarrassment, and, worst of all, envy. She was fourteen and
had never in her whole life witnessed two people in the
midst of an intimate embrace. Sure, she'd seen stuff
happen in movies and on TV, but that was nothing like
seeing the real thing. She was still somewhat stunned,
dazedly wondering whether she, too, would behave
that way, if given the chance—would she plaster herself
recklessly against the body of a man, kissing and kissing and kissing? Her eyes strayed to Steve Sheppard,
and she blushed hotter than the ovenlike air around
her.

Allegra didn't like being ignored. These obnoxious
little twits still hadn't answered her, and she hadn't succeeded in scaring them away, either.

"Steve." Her voice was whiny, petulant. "Make them
leave. They shouldn't be hanging around here, anyway.
No one who doesn't ride with Golden Crest is supposed
to be in the vans." To hear her, one would think Allegra
owned the stable.

"Lighten up, Allegra," Steve replied with barely
veiled impatience, disliking her attitude. Back home in
Kentucky, it took far longer when talking to strangers to
reach the level of rudeness Allegra so easily attained. "I
don't think these girls are planning on stealing any
equipment, are you?" His gaze narrowed on them, trying to make out their features. All he could tell so far
was that one of them was quite tall and thinner than a
twig on a sapling. The other was perhaps four inches
shorter and had lovely, eye-catching curves in all the
right places. Both were wearing breeches and field
boots. Their hair was pulled back tight and flattened
smooth. A dead giveaway that they had on those thin,
nylon hair nets trapping each strand of hair in place.

Wildly unattractive, those hair nets, but the judges were extremely picky about proper attire. No loose hair flowing out from under hunt caps accepted. So the girls had to be riding today, they weren't merely spectators, and both of them were young.

He saw the shorter one nudge the skinny one, forcing her to step forward up the ramp. By his side, Allegra stiffened, as if ready to pounce, perhaps strangle them with their hair nets if that's what it would take to get rid of them.

No way did Steve want to be left alone with Allegra again. He might be forced to say something so brutal it would send her running off to Daddy Palmer. "Allegra, why don't you go see whether Show Me is ready yet. I still have enough time to watch you school him over some fences before I have to warm up myself. Just got to find my chaps. Why don't we meet outside in a few minutes at the warmup ring?" He dangled the carrot in front of her, sure Allegra would grab it. It wasn't that she cared terribly much about preparing properly for her classes. As a matter of fact, she was one of the laziest riders he'd ever seen, the hugely expensive horses bought by her doting parents an utter waste, except that those horses were so "made," so well trained, they probably could jump the courses all by themselves. They might even do better without Allegra messing around with their mouths all the time.

No, it wasn't that Allegra wanted to learn anything from Steve. If she did, it was in the sack and not on a horse's back. She'd agree to his suggestion because having other people see Steve Sheppard coach her conferred a huge cachet. Furthermore, it reinforced Allegra's thoroughly misguided impression that she was actually a decent horsewoman. He was willing to foster the pretense just to get rid of her.

A disgruntled Allegra breezed past them, her nose high in the air.

The shorter girl giggled again. "Man, is she ticked off!" This time, he saw the taller one nudge her companion warningly. "Oh, sorry about that," the shorter one offered, not sounding sorry in the least. "We just saw you and wanted a chance to say hi. You're Ty's idol." Steve saw her elbow the tall girl in return. These two were going to end up with bruised ribs if they continued the mutual nudging much longer.

"You know," the shorter one was still chattering away, as if she'd known Steve for years. "Ty's taped all the big shows that have been aired on TV, just so she can watch you ride."

At that, the tall girl dropped her head, the toe of her shiny black boot an object of intense fascination. Now all that was visible of her head was her dark brown hair, twisted into a long, flat knot at the back of her head. Steve felt kind of sorry for the kid; she was clearly awfully shy. He stepped forward, sticking out his hand close enough that it entered her field of vision.

The girl lifted her head, her eyes meeting his. Steve was close enough now to see the details of her face. High cheekbones that jutted sharply. Dark eyebrows arched in delicate wings. A straight, thin nose that ended in a flared bump. Lips pressed together, hiding what looked like the uncomfortable bulge of metal braces.

Steve supposed if one were being charitable, one might label the girl's face attractive, but really it was too much like the rest of her: awkward and bony-looking. Not yet fully formed. When he saw her eyes, though, Steve couldn't deny their beauty. A soft gray, speckled with black, they were huge, framed by thick, dark lashes. And they were fixed on him, filled with a wealth of emotion. The expression in them too grown-up, too passionate for someone so young, at odds with her wraith-like, undeveloped body. For a moment, Steve was taken aback.

Then, suddenly, she smiled. A quick, shy smile that lifted her lips, revealing the flash of steel wire and metal tracks. Vastly reassured by the sight of a mouth crammed full of braces, rubber bands, and God knows what other painful junk, Steve's momentary unease evaporated. *It's cool, Shepp,* he said to himself. *She's just a young kid with a big teen crush. Nothing more.*

Ty gazed into Steve Sheppard's sparkling blue eyes and wanted never to look away. It was hard to believe that at long last her dream had come true. She was finally getting to meet him, stand close to him. He was everything she'd expected. He was kind, he was understanding. He was *so* good-looking. Already, he'd proven his innate chivalry by not kicking Ty and Lizzie out of the van and now, once again, by so courteously extending his hand to her.

How would it feel to touch him, feel his skin against hers? Would that spark of electricity, that shock of recognition, run through them both? Her eyes still fixed on his, she lifted her hand, meeting his, clasping it. A rush of absolute horror flooded her as the sugary coating of melted ice cream stuck to his warm, dry palm.

She wanted to die. She wanted to be vaporized and blown away, out of this universe. Where were black holes when you needed them?

The poor kid. Steve didn't want to make her feel any worse by asking what exactly it was she'd just rubbed off on him, but Holy Mother of Christ, it was really sticky. He could still remember, though, what it had been like at her age, when every little thing could strangle him with embarrassment. The girl, Ty, was beyond embarrassment, moving on to the tears phase, her face kind of crumpled into itself. Maybe talking would snap her out of it, maybe cheer her up enough that he could send her and her friend on their way and get a few moments of blessed peace.

"Well, uh, Ty," Steve said as cheerfully as he could, while surreptitiously wiping his palm against the leg of his jeans. "It's a pleasure to meet you. Who's your friend?"

At the sound of his voice, Ty struggled to find her composure. She'd lost it some time ago, back when she and Lizzie had walked in on Allegra kissing Steve. That Steve Sheppard was still willing to talk to her, Ty, a total idiot who couldn't even keep her hands clean, was nothing less than a miracle. She wasn't going to make a fool of herself a second time.

"This is Lizzie, Mr. Sheppard. Lizzie Osborne."

This girl, Ty, was certainly unusual. Sticky, gummy hands and now this. Speaking so properly, her tone so polite and formal, she could have been the hostess at a tea party. Real proper. The kind of girl his Granny Polly would like.

He nodded, giving the other girl an easy smile, careful not to shake her hand. "Pleased to meet you, Lizzie, and both of you can call me Steve. How old are you, by the way?"

"Sixteen." "Fourteen." They replied simultaneously, drowning each other out. Ty shot her friend a cryptic look. Lizzie shrugged carelessly.

"Uh, Ty's fourteen, but she'll be turning fifteen *really* soon. I'm sixteen," Lizzie said, smiling confidently, knowing he'd believe her. She refused to feel guilty about stretching the truth. She knew enough about guys to realize Steve Sheppard wasn't about to stick around and shoot the breeze with a couple of fourteen-year-olds.

So Lizzie was sixteen, Steve thought. Still jail bait,

though, which was too bad. She was already a real eye-ful. As sweet-looking as a Georgia peach. Lovely reddish-gold hair, bright blue smiling eyes, and a mouth shaped like Cupid's bow. Her body looked as tempting as a summer peach, too. Had she been a few years older, Steve would have been two steps away from asking her out, but he knew better than to go down that road. He'd had enough female trouble for one morning.

"You girls riding today?" A no-brainer.

"Medal, Maclay, and a couple of other classes, too," Lizzie replied. She shot Ty an impatient look. If Ty would only speak up! But she was probably still in shock over Lizzie fibbing about her age.

It worried Lizzie that Ty might blow her big chance if she didn't start talking soon. It wasn't as though Steve Sheppard was just going to hang around all day! Well, if Ty was too shy, Lizzie was more than willing to do a little bragging on her best friend's behalf. "If Ty wins her classes today, she'll be qualified for regionals in both the Maclay and the Medal. Isn't that right?" She gave a hard nudge.

Ty just nodded, a blush staining her cheeks.

"What about you, Lizzie, you close to qualifying?"

"Not yet." Lizzie grinned, unconcerned. "I mostly come in second or third. You see, Ty and I go to practically all the same shows, and she's tough to beat. I'm hoping she'll win today so I won't have so much competition." She laughed as Ty made a sound of protest.

"And if you win, Ty, what'll you show in afterward?" Steve asked in an effort to draw the kid out of her shell. Though he'd never competed in them himself, having gone straight into jumper classes, the Medal and Maclay events represented the top level of equitation and hunter classes for riders under the age of eighteen. After that, one usually chose either to follow the jumper route or to show primarily in the hunter division.

"I'm hoping to persuade my father to let me start riding in Junior Jumper. Then one day, if I get that far, I'd like to compete in Open Jumper, maybe even Grand Prix. Like you. Will you be riding Soirée and Palomar today?"

Steve nodded. "And tomorrow I'll be entering another horse, a new one, Jasmine. Allegra, that girl you saw a moment ago, her family owns the mare."

"I hope you win. You deserve to," Ty offered softly.

Steve smiled. The kid was definitely suffering from a hard case of hero worship. It was funny. In the insulated world of riding, he didn't run into all that many fans. His life was pretty much restricted to the company of his fellow riders or that of his wealthy sponsors, like Allegra Palmer's family. The kind of attitude Allegra displayed was different, more like that of a demanding groupie. Basically, she just wanted a guy to toy with, and as she spent a lot of time with the horsey crowd, Steve was the one she'd selected. Steve wasn't under any illusions; he knew he was basically interchangeable as far as someone like Allegra was concerned. This girl Ty, however, looked at him as if he were Superman on horseback. He had to admit to being a little flattered. It hadn't occurred to Steve that his abilities as a horseman were known, let alone admired, outside his own circle.

"Well, good luck to both of you. I'd better go and catch up with Allegra. If you start riding in jumper classes, Ty, pretty soon you'll be competing against Allegra. Bet you'll beat her, too." He winked, smiling at the awestruck expression on her face. Right, time to grab his chaps from his tack box and get the hell out of there. But Ty's voice had him glancing at her one more time.

He'd winked at her. How personal, intimate. Surely it meant he liked her somewhat. The thought gave her the courage to ask, "Mr. Sheppard . . . I mean, Steve, do you think . . . could I please have your autograph?"

The request came out a hushed whisper. Man, she really had it bad. He'd known her for all of, what, three minutes, and already he could sense how much a request like this cost her. Steve gave her a warm smile, utterly unaware of how handsome, how wonderfully dashing he appeared. Quickly, he scanned the back of the van, searching for a hidden pen. Nothing, only saddles and tack boxes. He patted his jeans pockets on the off chance and felt it.

"Hold on a sec. I have something better than an autograph I can give you. Here, take this." He dug his hand in his jeans and fished out something round and flat. "Here, let me give you this instead. My pop gave it to me. It's from a race he won way back when, as a young jockey just starting out. Go ahead, take it," he encouraged. "It'll bring you luck." Resting on his palm, a flat silver medallion glinted in the soft light.

"Oh, no, I couldn't possibly. Your father . . ."

"Really, take it. It's what Pop would want, I promise."

Hesitantly, Ty reached out and accepted it, bringing it close. She held her palm flat so that Lizzie could look, too. The medallion was roughly the size of a quarter, perhaps a tiny bit bigger. Engraved on its surface was the image of a running horse, legs stretched out in a full gallop, mane and tail flying in the wind.

Ty's fingertips traced the horse's outline slowly, reverently. Her lips were pressed tightly together. It didn't stop them from trembling. As though she felt Steve's gaze on her, she looked up. The moisture in her eyes made them shine as brightly as the silver medal she held.

"Thank you so much," she whispered. "This is the most beautiful gift I've ever gotten. I'll keep it forever."

Already in her fourteen years, Ty had received far too many expensive presents, the majority of them devoid of meaning. She didn't have the words to express how much this gift touched her, one spontaneously and generously offered.

Thanks were unnecessary. It was all there in her face, her eyes sparkling so bright, making her almost pretty. Steve was pleased he'd thought of the medal, knowing that he'd done the right thing, that his father would approve. Pop could have been talking to him right now, that voice roughened by a lifetime of cigarettes easily conjured. "Steve, son, don't you ever forget this. Never be afraid to pass the good fortune you have on to someone else. You share it, it'll stick around. You try to hoard it all to yourself, it'll go sour, as bad as rotten milk. You remember that when you're out in the world, trying to make your way."

These days, things were going about as well for Steve as they ever had. If he kept riding smart, if his horses remained injury-free, he might win the American Grand Prix Association Rider of the Year award, given to the competitor with the highest points won in the jumper division. Winning that might bring him one step closer to his goal of being selected for the United States Equestrian Team. And that would provide him with the opportunity to compete internationally, to experience the challenge of riding in Europe against the seasoned and formidable foreign competition. The Olympics were just around the corner. Although it would be great to compete at the Olympic trials, and a dream come true to make the Olympic team, Steve was realistic about the likelihood of that happening. He hadn't had the kind of experience he needed yet, riding against truly great equestrian teams or tackling the bigger, tougher European courses to be able to compete at the highest level, which the Olympics represented. He was getting closer, but he still needed to put in a lot more hard work, to learn from the horses he rode, and to be blessed by Lady Luck.

In the meantime, he'd share his good fortune, and happily, too. He'd follow Pop's advice and help out a young, star-struck kid. And who knows, maybe that would give her self-confidence a little boost, win her a few ribbons that she could pin up on her bedroom wall. Because, with the exception of those spectacular eyes, it was hard to imagine her ever being anything but the way she was now: thin, plain, and awkward.

Both girls were studying the medallion intently, whispering excitedly to each other, when, without warning, a man stormed in, startling them all. And total hell broke loose.

At six feet, Steve Sheppard considered his height respectable. Hell, he positively towered over his mother, father, and two sisters by seven inches and more. But coming face-to-face with a guy like this was like coming nose-to-nose with a professional linebacker whose main goal in life was to squash his opponent flatter than a pancake. An ambition that might become reality, since the guy had Steve shoved up against the side of the van and was breathing a little too close for comfort.

The sight of the human gorilla pinning him against the wall had turned Ty's face white as chalk. She'd rushed over and grabbed hold of the guy's arm. A nice gesture but utterly ineffectual; she might as well have been trying to uproot a tree. Lizzie's face had paled visibly, too, her freckles standing out prominently as she joined her friend in the effort to free Steve. Finally, Steve managed to get his arms up and shoved, hard. Unfortunately for his ego, his attacker didn't fly across the room as Steve had envisioned but merely stepped back, the promise of murder still in his eyes.

Everyone began talking at once.

"If you've so much as touched these girls, you son of a bitch, you're dead meat."

"No, Sam, no! Sam, please, it's all my fault. I dragged Lizzie here to meet Mr. Sheppard."

"Who in hell are you? Girls, do you know this guy?"

"Sam, I'm so sorry! I won't do it again. Please don't hurt him," Ty cried, her voice high, near hysteria.

"Don't believe her, Sam! I mean, she *is* sorry, but it's all my fault," Lizzie cut in hurriedly as she gave Sam a nervous, shaky smile, hoping it might sway Ty's angry bodyguard. She'd never seen him like this, never realized that he could actually hurt someone. It kind of put him in a whole new light, one she didn't particularly want to think about. Then Lizzie reminded herself of how much Sam liked Ty. And Lizzie was convinced he had a soft spot for her, too. At least, he always laughed at her jokes.

She wished she could think of a good joke now, settling instead for "Really, Sam, we just wanted to say hi to Steve, so we snuck away. It was only for a minute. You won't tell on us to her father, will you?"

Sam's eyes locked on Lizzie. Eyes that had always seemed a warm, indulgent brown suddenly transformed into tawny flecks that cut, slicing you to ribbons. Eyes that made his face suddenly hard and ruthless. The Sam Brody staring at her now was not a man to be messed with. Lizzie swallowed nervously, savvy enough to realize this was not a reassuring sign. Meanwhile, Steve Sheppard was looking angry as anything. Who wouldn't be after being mauled and then forced to listen to some girls' desperate pleas?

Well, at least she could clear up *that* mess, thought Lizzie as she slipped into the role of interpreter with a great deal more pluck. She gave Steve a bright smile.

"Sorry about all this, Steve, but, you see, Sam is Ty's bodyguard. Sam, you do realize who this is, don't you? This is *Steve Sheppard,* Ty's favorite rider. Now you understand why we had to come, don't you?" Her question ended on a note of pure bravado, convincing only herself that everything had been explained most satisfactorily.

Bodyguard? Steve heard Ty's soft gasp and glanced over at her. She was the picture of unhappiness. Like a puppy with no one to love it. *Bodyguard.* The word echoed in Steve's mind, too bizarre to believe. He'd assumed Gorilla Man was her older brother. "Wait a second, I don't get it. Who are you, anyway?"

"I'm Ty . . ."

But before she could finish, Lizzie interrupted her. It never took long for Lizzie's buoyant good spirits and thirst for adventure to rebound. As Sam hadn't done anything to them yet, she figured he wasn't really going to punish them. He was just glaring like that for effect. After all, it was his *job* to look really scary. "Oh, she can't tell you her last name, Steve, her dad's too important. Super, super rich. Sam here would be forced to kill you with his bare hands." She barely suppressed a grin, thrilled by the hint of James Bond romance in her answer, and the way it made Ty sound so mysterious. She knew Steve would never ever forget Ty now.

"*Lizzie!*" Ty wailed, too mortified to continue.

Oh, God, Lizzie was so impossible when she let her imagination run wild. What would Steve think if he were to recognize her name? Perhaps he'd even think she believed the silly junk Lizzie had been spouting.

And now it was over. Ty felt as if her heart would break.

Sam stepped forward, his strong hands encircling both Ty's and Lizzie's arms. "Let's go, Miss Tyler." Ty shrank inside. Sam never called her Tyler. He knew how much she hated it. "You, too, Lizzie, before you concoct any other foolishness. The three of us are going to have a little talk before your classes start." He didn't have to speak loudly to have Lizzie's smile fading and the two girls following meekly, not daring even a backward glance at Steve Sheppard. But Sam Brody did. A final, lethal look in Steve's direction as he hustled the girls outside.

Jesus Christ, Steve thought, shaking his head as he watched them depart. He rubbed his face hard as though awakening from a bad dream. *Save me from rich girls.* There was an incident he'd just as soon forget. Quickly, Steve located his chaps and set off to meet Allegra, who had just skyrocketed in his estimation. At least she didn't wander around with personal thugs ready to tear you apart, limb from limb. A shame he'd given that girl, Ty what's-her-name, Pop's medal. Girls that rich didn't need his help, or any luck. They just opened their alligator-skin purses.

3

"*I*m not a baby. It's not right, it's not fair to be treated this way."

With any other girl, reflected Sam Brody sadly, he would have been subjected to the earsplitting strains of a young teen on the verge of a full-blown tantrum. But never with Ty. Sure, the desperation was clear in her voice, but the words came out low, their want of theatrics lending all the more power to her plea. *Christ Almighty*, he thought. Why wasn't her father here to have this talk with her? But only a fool would go looking for help from that corner.

Tyler Stannard had telephoned half an hour ago, leaving a message with the driver that his breakfast meeting had gone on too long. What with the weekend traffic, the airport was so busy he'd lost his takeoff slot, and the next one available wouldn't get him into Lake Placid in time for Ty's classes. He'd check on how his daughter was progressing another day. At least Tyler Stannard's absence relieved Sam from having to inform his employer of his daughter's dangerous escapade right away. He could use the time to figure out the best way to present the thing to her father and spare Ty as much of her father's wrath as possible.

Sam's blood still ran cold each time he thought of it. He didn't blame Ty—or Lizzie, for that matter (he knew full well the stunt had Lizzie's fingerprints all over it). They were good kids, great kids, and they were only fourteen years old, for Christ's sake, full of budding independence and impossible dreams.

No, it was his fault. It was pathetic. Here he was, barely thirty years old, and already he'd grown soft, playing nursemaid and watchdog to Ty. The way he'd sat, minutes ticking by, waiting for her to reemerge from that goddamned portable toilet, was a far cry from the hard-nosed cop he'd been six years ago in New York. God, if she'd really been grabbed, the kidnappers would have been miles away by the time Sam wised up enough to realize she was missing. Sam cursed again.

"I know you're angry, Sam. But don't you see, I have no life. I'm like a puppet on some stage; every time I want to do something, I get yanked back. Am I supposed to have a bodyguard forever? If my father prefers to be constantly surrounded by a security detail, that's fine, it's his money, but *I* don't want to live that way."

"Ty, after all the years we've been together, you know as well as I that it's not up to me to decide on the degree of your protection. Your father says, 'Twenty feet back, and never out of your sight, Brody.' Well, then, that's what I do. And though you may choose to ignore it, Ty, there *are* creeps out there who would love to get their hands on you. Ones who know down to the last shiny penny what you're worth as Tyler Stannard's only child and heiress to his billions, and the ones who don't, who'll hurt you simply because they can. *Because they like to.* That stupid stunt you pulled just now could have gotten you raped, kidnapped, or killed. Perhaps all three. Don't ever do it on my watch again."

It was so rare to see her cry. If anything, she had a tendency to dam all her feelings up inside. He felt like an ogre for making even one tear fall, knowing he'd caused the floodgates to open. She flew into his arms, choking on a sob. "I'm sorry, Sam! I promise I won't!"

He enveloped her in a bear hug. "It's okay, Ty," he soothed gruffly. "Come on, don't cry, you'll be all blotchy for your class." He looked down into her tear-streaked face, trying to coax a smile from her. "Remember, you've got to go out and win those two classes today. You won't be able to memorize the course if your brain's all waterlogged." He patted her awkwardly, his strong hands seeming even larger, completely out of proportion, juxtaposed against the slenderness of Ty's back. And though he loved Ty as though she were his kid sister, Sam knew he shouldn't be the one doing this, his anger rekindling at the callous indifference Tyler Stannard showed with respect to his daughter's emotional needs. Was the guy dead inside? What did all that money mean, what was it worth, if a child didn't feel loved, if the only hug she got was from her bodyguard?

It took too long, seeing how awful it made him feel, but eventually her tears ceased. A shy smile flitted across her face as she stepped back, her eyes brightening as she drew something from the small inside pocket of her breeches.

"Look, Sam, I forgot to show you. Steve Sheppard gave this to me." She held the medal out to him. "He said it would bring me luck. Isn't it beautiful?"

Sam dutifully inspected the small coin decorated with the image of a running horse. His gaze lifted, taking in Ty's features. The tip of her nose was slightly reddened, her eyes still shining from tears and, Sam suspected, the effects of her first crush. He was fully aware of Ty's infatuation. She worshiped the ground Steve Sheppard galloped over. He knew about the file she kept in her dresser drawer, bursting with pictures and articles about him. Ty had very few secrets she could hide from her bodyguard. Hell, he knew things he didn't want to know, for instance that she'd started getting her period at the end of seventh grade. He'd been the one to accompany her to the drugstore so she could buy the feminine stuff she needed, discreetly looking the other way as she carried her purchases to the counter, a stack of magazines camouflaging the boxes underneath.

Once again, Sam feigned ignorance, allowing her the thrill of a secret crush. "It's real pretty, Ty. Looks like it would make a nice necklace. Better put it back in your pocket for now, though, 'cause I see the groom walking over with Charisma. You don't have a lot of time left to warm up."

Charisma was a dapple-gray Irish hunter, brought over from County Westmeath, Ireland, for Ty's twelfth birthday. The mare was beautiful: big and strong, with long legs that carried her effortlessly and a coat whose color changed from black to all the shades of gray and then to white as she moved. She was flashy and had a heart of gold. To Ty, she was everything.

Ty was a good, talented rider. Although at first glance her body appeared painfully thin, she was actually quite strong, all sinew and muscle, able to be remarkably agile and graceful astride her mare. What made her an even better rider was that she absorbed her trainer's teaching and comments like a sponge soaking up water. When Ty rode, she demonstrated such focus that a correction rarely had to be repeated a second time. She worked and adjusted, demanding perfection from herself and asking it of her horse. One invaluable lesson she'd already mastered was to center her attention on her horse. Ty had understood early on that the best riders work with their mounts as an indivisible team. For a fourteen-year-old, this level of understanding set her apart from the other young riders, helping her win class after class. Ironic, seeing that Ty wasn't even terribly competitive. It was simply that for her, riding was the only area of real freedom. The search for perfection, that wondrous feeling of moving in harmony with the incredible creature beneath her, gave Ty a chance to step outside herself, to achieve a breathtaking flight that in her normal life was simply impossible.

As she negotiated the twists and turns of the Medal class jump course that afternoon, she felt a heightened awareness, challenging her to do even better, to ride with flawless form, to make the distances at the jumps just right, effortless. Somewhere on the show grounds, Steve Sheppard was present. Perhaps, out of curiosity, he was watching her even now.

To those who indeed watched her picture perfect round, it came as no surprise to any of them, riders or trainers, that Ty Stannard won the Medal class that afternoon. Nor were they particularly astounded that she made a clean sweep and took home the blue ribbon in the Maclay, too. That afternoon, she was just too good to beat.

All three of the horses Steve Sheppard had ridden in the qualifying class held on Friday made the cut for the Grand Prix event on Sunday afternoon. In the world of professional riding, it wasn't unusual to see, in a field of forty, a rider enter the event with more than one mount. That Steve Sheppard had succeeded in getting all three horses he'd ridden past the qualifying round and into the most challenging of all the show jumping events, the Grand Prix, confirmed his outstanding skill as a rider. Most riders were happy enough to squeak into the Grand Prix with two horses under their saddles.

The success Steve enjoyed had a kind of snowball effect, the result being that owners were approaching him more and more frequently with first-class horses to ride, as the Palmers had with their mare, Jasmine. Another reason for Steve Sheppard's popularity with owners was that he had the reputation of being a straight arrow, never throwing away a ride for his own personal gain.

Each and every time Steve approached the course with a mount, he gave it his all. In theory, the same was true for every top rider, but the owners who brought their horses to Steve counted on his never settling for an easy second if there was a chance to win. Even if it meant beating himself, depriving one of the horses Steve himself owned of a win. If Steve thought the horse was up to the challenge, he'd always try to shave off seconds, outdoing his previous performance. Giving each horse its best shot at the trophy, at the first-place prize money, regardless of who owned the horse. The owners loved him for that.

At twenty-three, Steve had a reputation that was already the stuff of legend on the horse show circuit. Almost everyone knew that he'd been raised in the saddle since birth. Horses were in his blood. His father, Steve Sheppard, Sr., had been a successful jockey in his own day, before retiring his silks and becoming a well-respected trainer. His son, Steve, had cut his teeth on the backs of hot-blooded thoroughbreds. By the age of thirteen, Steve was already such an accomplished rider that he was hired as an exerciser for some of the fastest horses in the state of Kentucky. So Steve Sheppard knew about speed. Rumor had it that was why Sheppard, or

Shepp, as his friends called him, was so damned hard to beat whenever there was a jump-off, when riders pulled out all the stops, trying to make the fastest time. Nobody could get their horses moving like Steve Sheppard—and clear the fences as well.

Without a doubt, Steve would have made a great jockey, too, except that at age fourteen, he suddenly shot up half a foot in an alarmingly short period of time. Nobody had expected this kind of a growth spurt from a family whose members barely topped five feet five. His father, though disappointed that his son wouldn't be following in his footsteps, took his son's sudden imposing height philosophically. And, fortunately, Steve Sheppard, Sr.'s connections in the equine world were extensive. He sent his young son to a good friend who bred and trained thoroughbreds and Anglo-Arabs as jumpers. "Teach him everything you can, Clyde, Steve's a quick study. And when you're done, I'd appreciate it if you'd send him on to someone else." And so Steve Sheppard, Jr.'s equestrian education had followed a different path from his father's. Steve quickly became Clyde's protégé, absorbing everything he could learn from Clyde about jumping: distances, angles of approach, lengthening and shortening strides. Two and a half years later, Clyde was sufficiently satisfied.

"You've got it down pat when it comes to flying through the air, Shepp. Now go learn how to make your horse move like magic on the ground. I've just found you a top-notch dressage instructor."

"Hey, Pop, it's me. How's everything at home?"

"Steve! Good to hear your voice, son." His father's own scratchy voice was hearty with recognition. "Everything's fine around here. Your mother and sisters are just washing up. Had your favorite tonight, burgoo, and

Maggie made a chocolate pie good enough to put her in the record books. Kerry took one look at it and almost fainted from happiness. She ran two races earlier today, young fillies. A show and a place. Claimed that justified eating three slices: two for the fillies, one for her."

"Kerry always was lousy at math."

"I wish I'd thought of it. I only got two slices. Still, I guess that's okay. We all made Maggie promise to bake another one after next week's race. How's everything going up north?"

"Did real well today, Pop. I took third and seventh with Palomar and Soirée in the Grand Prix. And you remember that new mare I've been riding, Jasmine, the one I told you about? We won the Open Jumper outright and came in second in the Grand Prix. What an amazing horse."

"Sounds like a good day's ride. You blow your earnings yet?"

Steve laughed. "No, I haven't had enough time. Just got back to the motel, dying for a cold shower. It's been hotter than Hades around here. No, apart from the cut I have to share with the Palmers, Jasmine's owners, I've got a little money to burn. That's what I was calling about. Can you keep an ear to the ground, let me know about any youngsters for sale back home?"

"How much you looking to spend?"

"Well, I think with this year's earnings, I can afford a young prospect going for about ten, fifteen thou. The rest is going into the bank and mortgage payments."

"Sounds like a good plan. Take it from me, son, and make sure you think ahead, figure out where you need to be in ten, twenty years. We're in one of the toughest businesses around. Working with horses is a passion that enriches the soul. But if you're not careful, you'll starve trying to keep your mounts in feed."

"I know, Pop. I'd put all the money back into the place I bought, except I need to have good horses of my own, to bring along from the ground up. That's security, too, not being entirely dependent on other owners."

"I suppose so. Well, I'll keep my ears open for you. You might call Clyde, too, and see what his young crop's like."

"Yeah, I thought I'd give him a ring. I'm pretty sure I'll be able to squeeze in a visit sometime in the next few weeks."

"Your ma will be thrilled to hear it," his father replied. "She's been complaining that since you bought that itsy-bitsy piece of land in the Hamptons, you never come home anymore. You know, she still pesters me to get you into business down here. Actually, we all think that's a fine idea."

Steve rolled his eyes. "Thirty-eight acres here isn't that small, Pop. True, it's nothing compared to the places back home, but I don't want a huge operation. And for the horse show world, New York is a prime location. In any case, it's Kerry who's the jockey in the family. Talk her into coming aboard."

Steve's father laughed. "Don't think I haven't tried! But Kerry's as stubborn as you and still feeling her oats. Too much like her brother in that respect as well. Up to now, she refuses to commit. And don't give me any of that 'I'm not a jockey' baloney. When a person's as talented a horseman as yourself, size is not an issue."

"Maybe, Pop, but I love this racket, show jumping. It's intense. Countless things coming at you that you have to calculate in a split second. Every day I'm learning something new. Racing's your and Kerry's world, Pop, has been ever since I grew past five foot seven."

"Remember how your mother carried on that morning you came downstairs looking like Jack's magic beanstalk?" His father's throaty chuckle came over the line. "You must have grown two inches overnight."

"I'm just glad Ma's over it. Black's not a good color on her."

"Well, you're making a name for yourself in your field, and we're all proud of you, son, even if we do miss your ugly face around here. By the way, you realize Kerry's headed your way? She's spending a few weeks in Saratoga next month."

"Make sure she has my number. I'd love to see her ride. I might even take her out to dinner if she wins me some money."

4

*I*t wasn't until mid-July that Steve made it back for a lightning trip to his parents' house. After leaving the airport terminal, it had taken less than the four minutes' walk to his father's white Cadillac parked in the outdoor lot for his shirt to soak through. With nearly one-hundred-percent humidity, it was the kind of weather that made you feel as if the whole world were one gigantic, steaming shower, and you were bundled in clothes more appropriate for the arctic circle. Real uncomfortable. Even the flies were feeling lazy, buzzing only intermittently, half-heartedly.

It hadn't cooled off appreciably during the night, either. Steve lay on his bed, the sheets twisted into thick ropes under and around his naked body, longing for the cool sea breeze that blew in through his bedroom windows in his house on Long Island.

He flopped onto his back, the weight of his body making the wooden bed frame creak in protest. Linking his hands behind his head, he gazed up at the ceiling and watched the shadows from the pine tree outside his window flicker across it, doing his best to ignore the heat. After all, he'd be back on Long Island in two short days. Even this short amount of time was more than he could really spare, but Steve was filled with a growing anticipation, a premonition of sorts, that someday very soon he was going to come across that special horse. He was hoping it would be here, in Kentucky, where he'd been raised to love horses.

Now it was cool enough to blow back the little wisps of steam rising from the paper cup filled with black coffee that Steve held in his hands. Of course, the sun was barely over the horizon. In an hour or so, the temperature would be back up to sweltering.

Steve took a cautious sip. He'd only just rolled out of bed, pulling on jeans and a T-shirt, skipping lightly down the stairs in his socks, his boots in his right hand, so he could accompany his father and watch the early-morning workout of three of his father's horses. It was always fun for Steve to go back to the track, the memories of his youth washing over him. His sister, Kerry, had met them at the track, having volunteered to do a coffee run at the local twenty-four-hour deli. Passing out identical cups of coffee, she'd jiggled a bag of glazed doughnuts in front of Steve and jauntily challenged both men to a race, claiming they needed to settle the question once and for all of who was really the fastest Sheppard in the family.

"Whoever wins gets the doughnuts."

Both father and brother laughingly declined. Then, unable to resist ribbing his little sister, Steve said, "Come on, Kerry, you know I wouldn't want to shake your self-confidence just before you go off to Belmont. I was planning on betting a few bucks on you. If I go and beat you this morning, you'd be so ashamed, it'd be like kissing my money away."

"What, a big oaf like you beating me? I'd have to be racing on a three-legged nag to worry about the likes of you."

"Now, kids, no fighting, no biting. We've got work to do. I want to see Blue Moon and Coincidence run before night falls, if you don't mind. And don't forget, Steve, Clyde's expecting us in a little while. To listen to the pair of you," their father admonished, "one would think you're still twelve and ten years old."

"Well, Pop, that's 'cause Kerry will always be a brat, and a puny one at that." He grinned down at his sister, who tried unsuccessfully to glare back at him without breaking into an answering grin. The sky light enough now to read the mischief in her eyes.

Steve Sr. looked on as his daughter faked a rabbit punch and then pretended to wince as her fist connected with Steve's rock-hard stomach. He hid a smile, proud as the devil of his children. Despite the fact that Steve towered over Kerry by a foot, the two of them were very much alike, temperamentally as well as physically. Kerry's hair was the exact same hue as her brother's; she even had the same dimple when she smiled. But it was their ambition that truly united them. Both wanted to be the best in their profession, and both were blessed with the talent and drive to get there.

Kerry's short hair, styled casually in a careless mop of blond and gold, flew back and forth as she shook her head. "All right, Godzilla, you just sit here and watch how a real rider earns a living. There better be some doughnuts left when I get back." Leaving them standing by the half-mile track, she walked away, a cocky bounce to her stride.

Clyde Farrell's stable was located about fifteen miles outside Lexington, not far from the state's famous Horse

Park, one of the most impressive showcases constructed for the greater glory of equine jewels. In this region, a true mecca for horses and horse lovers, Clyde Farrell was one of the most sought after breeders of Anglo-Arabs and thoroughbred sport horses, in part because of the extraordinary quality of both Arab and thoroughbred bloodlines found in this area but also because of Clyde's uncanny ability to judge bloodlines, traits, and temperaments.

Clyde met them as father and son climbed out of Steve Sr.'s vintage Cadillac.

"Steve, Shepp," he called out jovially. "Good to see you!"

Grinning, the men shook hands, and Clyde thumped a broad hand across Steve's back. He stepped back and surveyed the younger man. "And how's life up north treating you?"

"Can't complain."

"Looking a mite lean, though. You been growing again, or is the food as bad as they say?"

"Like sawdust," Steve groused good-humoredly, his blue eyes twinkling. "It's a crying shame what happens to food once you leave the state of Kentucky. Folks have no idea how to make a decent barbecue. Most of the people I talk to seem to think burgoo is some kind of cleaning product."

"No culture at all." Clyde nodded sagely. "A terrible tragedy."

"That's why I had to come back home for a visit. You know my ma and Maggie's cooking."

Clyde made an appreciative grunt. Olivia Sheppard's cooking was a treat not to be missed, and her elder daughter, Maggie, was following in her footsteps. Maggie'd started a catering business that offered everything from race day picnics to four course dinners. She was saving her earnings to open a restaurant. And as most everyone down here liked to dump on the folks up north in one respect or another, Shepp's pronouncement only confirmed what everyone already knew.

"So, I hear you're in the market for a new horse. Well, you've come to the right state for that, too."

"Might be. At least a good place to start." Shepp knew Clyde well. They were friends, Clyde had been his mentor, but business was business. Clyde would think he'd turned into a fool if he showed too much eagerness.

"Looking for anything in particular?" Clyde asked as the three men began walking toward the white and gray wooden barns.

"A youngster. Barely started or green. Big enough to carry me and still have something left over."

They passed grooms coming and going, leading horses in and out of the fenced pastures. It was still early enough in the morning for many of the horses that had spent the night out in the fields to be led back to their barns, the horses scheduled for daytime turnout taking their places. Quite a few of the grooms walking them recognized Shepp and his father and nodded or called out a friendly greeting. The horse world was an intimate one down here, racing, showing, breeding, all interconnected. The business of horses melded with the passionate love of them.

"So, Shepp, you've been making quite a name for yourself recently," Clyde was saying as the three of them moved in the direction of the main barn. "Not too shabby, getting on the cover of both *Equus* and *Practical Horseman* in the same month. Who owns that horse you've been riding?"

"Richard and Eleanor Palmer. Jasmine is the mare's name. Tell you the truth, Clyde, I'm pretty sure the only reason I made those covers is because of that mare's owners. Not that the horse doesn't deserve it."

"They're rolling in dough?"

Steve nodded. "Unbelievable."

Clyde gave another grunt. "Well, we better find you a horse that's mighty special, then you two'll make the headlines all by yourself."

Steve laughed. "That'd be real nice, Clyde, but remember, unlike most of your clients, I'm operating on a budget."

With horses, Steve was willing to believe in love at first sight.

"Who's this?" Steve tried to keep his voice casual.

"That's Fancy. Fancy Free. Two years old. Out of Belleslettres by Sudden Glory. Belleslettres was European champion three years in a row. Fancy has a bit more to grow, might even reach 16.1 h. Sudden Glory is a big son of a gun." Clyde glanced appraisingly at Steve and his father. "Want me to bring him out?"

Steve hadn't even seen the young horse's body yet. Just Fancy Free's small, black, elegant head watching him over the door of his stall. It had been pure chance that Steve had happened to look into Fancy Free's eyes, which favored the Arab in him, wide-set and huge, and had seen such intelligence there that he'd been unable to look away.

"Sure, why not."

"He's a little temperamental, got loads of spunk, so watch his hindquarters. I'll take him out into the sunshine. You can look him over in a better light. He has a real nice build."

Steve held his breath as Clyde hooked the lead rope to Fancy Free's leather halter. Steve and his father stood to the side as Clyde led him out of the stall and down the barn's wide corridor. The horse's shoes rang out rhythmically against the concrete floor. Father and son followed, neither saying a word. The sound of Fancy Free's hoofbeats changed as he was led into the courtyard. It became the subtler, more drawn-out sound of gravel crushed and pushed aside as the young gelding walked out into the morning sun. The noise stopped, and silence settled over the men studying the horse.

Clyde Farrell certainly knew how to breed a beautiful horse. Fancy Free was black as coal, with only a single white marking: a jagged blaze down the center of his diamond-shaped head. He was a lovely-looking animal, elegant and compact.

"Where is he in his training, Clyde?"

"Just flat work at this point and a few ground rails. He's quick, though. His gaits are real smooth, naturally balanced."

"Would you mind if I try him out?"

"Be my guest. Here, take his lead while I go grab his tack." Clyde gave Steve a broad wink. "We already groomed him for you this morning. Something told me he might catch your eye." He gave the gelding a fond pat on the withers. "You know, I actually had a potential buyer for Fancy last week. Good thing for you this couple was dumber than dirt. Can you believe what the lady told me, in all seriousness? Said she liked him fine, but she was actually hoping to buy a chestnut 'cause then it would match her coloring better." Clyde gave a loud snort of disgust.

"Her coloring?"

"Yeah, you know, her hair color or whatever. I told her in that case, she should think about dyeing her hair black because she wouldn't find a better horse than Fancy anywhere in the state of Kentucky, that meaning the entire U.S. of A. She got all huffy and dragged her husband away." Clyde scratched his chin reflectively. "I probably wouldn't have sold Fancy to them, anyway. He was too good for them."

Steve and his father smiled and shook their heads. Trainers and breeders enjoyed few things more in life than griping about the idiocy they encountered in the horse world. As soon as Clyde had disappeared into the barn's interior, however, Steve Sr. turned to his son, all business.

"Don't go getting all mushy over a pretty face, now, Steve. The gelding's a looker, all right, but for all we know, he might have been born with four left hooves." His father didn't sound as if he believed his words of caution himself.

Steve reached out and stroked the velvety skin between Fancy Free's wide nostrils. His hands and eyes then moved along the graceful curve of his neck. The shock of recognition, when he'd first laid eyes on Fancy Free, hadn't diminished at all. Every instinct told him this was it. This horse was the one. The feeling transcended all logic. But it was as strong and insistent as the beating of his heart. And while his father was right to voice a certain skepticism, Steve knew that he was going to trust his instinct when it came to this young gelding.

"Pop, as one betting man to another, I'm willing to make a wager with you right now, before I even have a chance to hop on his back and see how he moves. I'll wager Clyde's asking price that in seven years' time, this horse and I will be at the top of the show jumping world."

Silently, carefully, Steve Sr. inspected Fancy Free once more. The horse was standing quietly, but even motionless he radiated energy. His head held high, his nostrils flared, his intelligent eyes were fixed on the distant pastures where other horses grazed. His long black tail was extended, individual strands lifting slightly in the warm summer breeze.

Steve's father continued his scrutiny of the gelding's conformation, searching for any hint of weakness or flaw, finding nothing but strength and beauty. His connoisseur's gaze moved up and down the horse's legs. He knelt close, running his hands up and down, his fingers probing for swelling in the tendons, any slight puffiness that might signal injury. Finally, he stood, a small smile hovering about his lips as he gave his son an answer: "Sorry, Steve, but you know I don't take sucker bets."

5

"We'll have to organize a party for after the show at Madison Square Garden. I'll get Smythe to write up a guest list."

"Really, Father, a party's not necessary. Just qualifying for the National is exciting enough."

"Nonsense. We'll need to celebrate your winning the Medal class."

Ty stared at her father. He was standing before her in his library. An interior designer had been hired to decorate it, his mission to underscore Tyler Stannard's immense wealth in this and every single other room in the mansion. Against one wall stood floor-to-ceiling oak bookshelves, filled with perfectly aligned rows of Moroccan leather-bound books which no one ever disturbed. On the opposite side of the room, an enormous fireplace had been built of imported Italian marble. Green, gray, and black marble were inlaid in an intricate pattern modeled after one of the fireplaces in the Palazzo Medici in Florence. Above the massive mantelpiece hung a Picasso depicting a female armed with long, daggerlike teeth and eyes grotesquely distorted, their stare cross-eyed.

Ty hated the painting and always tried to avoid looking at it. She knew, however, that the Picasso hung there for a specific reason. Two years ago, Smythe had been sent to bid for the painting at an auction held at Sotheby's in New York with strict instructions that he wasn't to return to the Stannard mansion without it. The following day, her father's purchase had made the headlines in all the major papers, having set a record for Picassos that had come on the art market. As Tyler Stannard's representative, Smythe had emerged victorious after a furious bidding war that involved several major museums and some Japanese and Arab collectors, too. No one who entered her father's library could fail to recognize the artist, the painting, or the vast amount of money at her father's disposal.

A light scent of beeswax lingered in the air, proof that the staff, before Ty or her father had even stirred from their beds, had performed the daily task of rubbing the mahogany desk, which had once belonged to J. P. Morgan, by the side of which her father now stood. He was as meticulously polished as the room. Although it was a Saturday in August and the temperature had soared to ninety-eight degrees, Tyler Stannard was dressed in a perfectly tailored Savile Row gray wool suit. His white shirt had been sewn in Paris by a shirtmaker near the Ritz who had her father's measurements and details of shirts, pajamas, and bathrobes previously ordered, written down in a black leather notebook he kept with him at all times. Just in case Mr. Stannard should happen to call. The tie, a baroque swirl of navy, gray, and dark green, came from Milan.

He was a handsome man. *Patrician* was the adjective the magazines and newspapers used to describe her father's tall frame, his carefully pommaded hair, his piercing gray eyes. Right now those eyes were regarding her

with impatience, because she'd taken too long in replying. Few people dared to keep Tyler Stannard waiting
for anything.

"But, Father, you don't truly expect me to win the
Medal class at the Garden. The finals are a whole different story from the regional classes. The best junior equitation riders from the entire country will be there. While
it would be thrilling to win a ribbon, I'd be as pleased to
have a good, clean round."

"You aren't talking like a Stannard." It was unnecessary to specify which Stannard she should emulate—he
was the only other one alive. "I didn't spend such a
huge amount of money on that horse of yours to see you
settle for second place. If you truly feel you aren't up to
the challenge, I suggest you call up Meghan and schedule some extra lessons. You can practice until you are,"
was her father's implacable reply. The look accompanying his words told Ty it was pointless to say any more on
the subject.

Indeed, Ty's father was already turning his attention
to the papers that Smythe had organized, lying next to
the dark blue rectangle of his passport. His jet was leaving for Paris in an hour. There were a number of
chateaux as well as a hotel on the Riviera that he was
considering purchasing. He'd be gone two weeks. Ty
watched as he gathered up the papers and slipped them
into his leather briefcase.

"Have a good trip, Father."

The steel-gray head stilled momentarily, catching a
foreign note in his daughter's voice he'd never heard before. It triggered an immediate response. "By the way,
Tyler, please remember the following while I'm away in
Europe. If I should learn of your going off without Sam
Brody for any reason whatsoever, I will make certain
you never see that friend of yours, Lizzie Osborne,

again. I've tolerated her presence far too long as it is. If her bad influence should impair your judgment again, I'll see to it she's no longer in your school or your riding club."

Pressing a finger on the intercom button that would summon Smythe, Tyler Stannard didn't catch the defiant look that flashed across his daughter's face. Before he could, Ty quickly dropped her eyes. She didn't dare risk angering him, for her father wouldn't think twice about using his influence to hurt Lizzie Osborne's family in some way. If not socially, they were certainly financially inferior. Thus, as far as Tyler Stannard was concerned, that made the Osbornes vulnerable and easy prey. It didn't matter to him that Lizzie was her best friend, her truest friend.

It was better to retreat, to let him focus on his business, erasing the very memory of his daughter from his mind. With a quiet, if mocking, "Yes, Father," Ty turned and left the library. Neither father nor daughter considered hugging or exchanging a kiss good-bye.

Once again, Tyler Stannard's head lifted. This time at the quick tapping sound of her footsteps crossing the parquet floor. He watched her slip through the half-opened double oak doors and knew with utter confidence that her destination would be her bedroom, where she'd immediately change into her riding breeches. His wishes had been explicit.

Yet an annoyed frown nevertheless creased his brow. How thin she was, far too frail-looking. And that wasn't her only problem, he reflected. She was fourteen years old. And while she favored his height and his coloring, so far Tyler Stannard had difficulty recognizing even a trace of his character in his only child.

At her birth, his decision to name his firstborn after himself had been made in the hope that some of his indomitable will, his tireless ambition, would imprint itself on the newborn baby, even though she was a girl.

Ordinarily, of course, he'd have waited for a male child to pass his name on to the next generation. But when his wife, Catherine, immediately following the emergency delivery of the baby, was rushed into intensive care, and the obstetrician informed him it was unlikely that his wife would ever be able to carry another child, he decided that the infant would have the name Tyler Montgomery Stannard, after her sire.

His decision proved prescient, for his wife, Catherine, a descendant of one of the founding families in America, died four days later from complications resulting from an obstructed valve in her heart.

He'd loved his wife, as he knew he would love no other human being. She, who had given him so much. Because of Catherine, he'd been able to grasp the wealth, the social prestige, and the power he'd always dreamed of. From that moment on, he'd never relinquished his hold.

Fleetingly, in the cold, dark hours after his wife's death, it occurred to him that he could change his mind and name the tiny newborn girl after Catherine. But he couldn't bring himself to do it. No one could take the place of his beloved in his heart. Above all, he wanted the memory of the woman he'd loved to remain pure, unmarked, and unchanged. There would only be one Catherine Elizabeth Adams Stannard.

Since her death fourteen years ago, Tyler Stannard had made a new marriage, of a different sort: to his company, Stannard Limited, the privately owned international real estate and luxury resort business he'd built with his bare hands and Catherine's money. This new relationship consumed him. And he was amply rewarded for his devotion. According to the rankings of

Forbes and *Money World*, Tyler Stannard was now one of the wealthiest men in the world.

But that his only child should prove lacking, perhaps as weak of heart and will as her mother, filled him with bitterness, a sense of gross injustice, because Tyler Stannard knew he would never remarry. He didn't need to. His sexual urges were tended to by women who flocked to his side, drawn to the immense fortune. He only needed to nod in their direction. And were he ever to fancy himself in love and consider marrying again, the prenuptial agreement alone would kill—with ruthless efficiency—any romantic illusion he might be under.

So he would make do with the only child he had, bending her to his will, fashioning her into the kind of person who could carry on the Stannard name.

PART 2

1991

6

Gladstone, New Jersey

*T*he tableau before Steve filled him with awe, it was so moving, so beautiful. Set against the background of the immaculate, princely splendor of the USET stables at Gladstone, the grooms were leading the small band of horses out in single file into the open courtyard. The horses were dressed for travel: their legs wrapped in identical navy blue bandages, their bodies covered in blue and red quilted blankets, with the letters USA stitched on the corners. He knew that beneath the protection of their blankets, the horses' well-groomed coats gleamed, muscles rippling under silky smoothness. These equine athletes were in peak condition, incredible examples of power, agility, and speed. They were embarking on a voyage to prove just that.

One by one, the horses were loaded into the long silver van that would take them to Kennedy International Airport, where they would then be put on a cargo jet, destination Sweden, where the World Cup qualifier was being held. The qualifier represented the first in a series of long and grueling events leading up to the final championship round. Among the horses chosen to compete for the United States' team was Jasmine. Steve Sheppard would be riding her.

He felt like a kid again, bursting with excitement, jittery with nerves. Frank Delano, the stable manager for Gladstone, had kindly offered Steve a ride to Kennedy so that Steve could rest easy, seeing for himself that Jasmine had been safely loaded onto the plane. It was the first time she'd ever made a transatlantic flight.

"Really, Shepp," Frank said as he turned the ignition. The van started with a loud rumble of engine, and Frank eased it around in a wide circle, giving a signature toot of the horn before heading down the driveway. "It's nothing to worry about. The cargo areas in the jets have these boxes in them that are just like stalls in a horse van. And the ride in the plane, even with the takeoff and landing, isn't any worse than a long trip down a bumpy road. After a couple flights, this mare'll be a seasoned traveler. A jet-setter."

"It's damned hard to imagine, my heading off to Europe to compete. Something I've looked forward to for so long. Now that it's happening, I'm as fussy as my Granny Polly."

"You won't be a rookie for long when it comes to the international scene. Wait till you get to the airport, though. It'll blow your mind. These horses, they're treated like VIPs by the crew and handlers. A helluva lot of money standing on those hooves. Too much to risk injuries." Frank patted the breast pocket of his shirt and pulled out a pack of Wrigley chewing gum. He held it out to Steve.

Steve shook his head, "No thanks. Mind if I smoke, though?"

"Go right ahead," Frank invited with a wave of his hand. "Used to smoke, too, but the wife made me quit. Still love the smell, though."

Steve grinned. "Yeah, so do I. In Kentucky, you learn to appreciate the finer things real early in life: beautiful women, fast horses, bourbon, and cigarettes."

"I guess you must be doing all right for yourself then, Shepp, a true connoisseur—if the gossip floating around is even close to the mark. I've heard all of the above are yours for the asking."

Steve gave a wide smile, his teeth flashing white against his tanned skin. His eyes were exactly the same color as the faded denim jacket from which he withdrew a pack of Marlboros and a miniature box of matches. He stuck the tan filter between his lips and struck the match head with the edge of his thumbnail. The flame flared, small and blue.

After inhaling deeply, he let out a stream of gray smoke, blowing out the flame with his breath. "The good Lord willing, Frank, the good Lord willing."

Even two long years later, Steve Sheppard's gift to Ty remained her most valued treasure. The day after her encounter with Steve, she went to a jewelry store and asked for a small loop of silver to be soldered onto the medallion so that she could thread a delicate sterling silver chain through it. Ty still wore the medallion around her neck, tucked away out of sight, something private that only she knew about. Every so often, she awakened in the morning to find her hand wrapped around it, clutching tightly.

To Ty's great disappointment, especially now that she was riding at the Junior Jumper level, she had yet to run into Steve Sheppard again at any show. Moving up to the jumper division represented for Ty a huge personal coup, a triumph that continued to astonish her. It had taken the combination of winning the Medal class at Madison Square Garden (a stroke of luck Ty more than half believed was caused by Steve Sheppard's medallion) and her trainer's cunning diplomacy in winning over her father.

Observing her father's obvious pleasure in having his daughter beat the national competition, Ty had seized what she recognized as a golden opportunity and asked his permission to move on to a greater challenge: the jumper division. Ty's riding instructor had backed her, stroking her father's ego further, assuring him that with Ty's talent and Charisma's athleticism, they would almost certainly enjoy the same kind of success Ty and her mare had in the equitation classes. That had seemed to clinch it, for there were few things Tyler Stannard relished as much in the world as beating the competition. For herself, Ty was thrilled at the prospect of riding at a higher level. She was having a blast. The jumping events were so exhilarating, the more challenging courses demanding all of Ty's skill.

Still, she wished she might see Steve once again, if only to show him how much she'd matured in the past two years. She was no longer the geeky, ice cream–covered fourteen-year-old she had been. Her braces had come off, and her body had finally gotten some curves. She even had breasts. And while she didn't truly need to wear the bras she'd bought for herself, at least she no longer was as flat as a basement floor. Ty knew she'd never dazzle the opposite sex effortlessly the way Lizzie could, but nonetheless she felt she'd come a long way in the looks department.

But Steve Sheppard was in Europe now, had been for most of the summer, except for quick trips back across the Atlantic to ride at some of the bigger shows with his other mounts. All the while, Ty had read articles from American and European horse journals, scouring them for news of him. He was competing in the major European shows that the USET entered for the World Cup. He and Jasmine were the top scorers among this year's American riders. Back home in the United States, Steve was also doing really well with a horse of his own, a younger horse, Fancy Free, that he was "bringing along," showing at the Preliminary Jumper level.

Ty was keeping her fingers crossed that he'd be at Devon, a show scheduled later in the show calendar, perhaps riding Fancy Free. From the pictures, the gelding looked like a real beauty. It would be thrilling to see them in the flesh.

Devon would be Ty's last show of the season before she had to knuckle down and get back into the routine of school. Not that she really minded school. Academics had always come easily to her; the math that continually stumped Lizzie seemed to her absurdly simple. She often helped Lizzie in the afternoons at the school library during study period. It never bothered Ty that she forfeited the chance to get her own homework finished, for Lizzie was still her closest friend. During the seven years she'd been enrolled there, the other girls at their school had hardly softened toward Ty. She'd learned to block out the cruelty of the ostracism, pretending not to notice the looks they darted at her, the whispers behind cupped hands, as if she were a freak in a side show. At times she could even smile at the irony, the big cosmic joke of it all, that here, in this upper-crust, private school for rich kids where money was revered, the fact that Tyler Stannard had more wealth than the fathers of all other students combined made it so she, his daughter, was stigmatized. It wasn't necessarily true that you can never have too much money.

7

"Hey, Ty, want to grab a bite at the concession stand after warmup?" Lizzie called out as she trotted up on her gelding, Rushmore, a big bay hunter her parents had bought her in the spring. Unlike Ty, Lizzie had chosen to continue competing in the Hunter division, and she and Rushmore had been doing extremely well.

For a moment the two girls trotted side by side, both garbed in matching beige breeches and navy blue riding jackets. As the gray and dark bay horses trotted, the girls rose up and down, posting in unison.

"Sure," Ty replied, nodding. "Can you wait about fifteen minutes? Meghan wants me to take Charisma over a couple of fences before I finish." Meghan Grimshaw was the trainer at the riding club to which both girls belonged. She was the closest thing to a mother figure Ty had. A no-nonsense kind of woman, Meghan had centered her life around the horses she trained and the riders she taught. Extremely perceptive with humans as well as horses, Meghan possessed an uncanny knack for understanding what made people tick, what motivated them. With Ty, she opted for brutal honesty, never offering empty praise, knowing Ty would see right through it. Ty thrived under her tutelage.

"Cool," breathed Lizzie. *Cool* was her new favorite word. She used it about a hundred times a day. "Maybe I'll hang around to watch. Meghan told me to wait until just before my afternoon class to jump Rushmore. Hey, don't forget, it's my treat," Lizzie reminded as she kneed Rushmore forward into an extended trot, slipping ahead of Ty and her mare so that they were once more trotting single file on the rail. A long-standing ritual, Lizzie and Ty took turns picking up the tab for the vast quantities of snacks they consumed at the shows.

Meghan Grimshaw stood by the wooden wings of the jump, her eyes fixed on Ty circling the ring at a canter, urging her mare's pace forward as they rounded the curve and headed toward the fence. Impatiently, Meghan dragged the long strands of fine blond hair that had come loose from her ponytail and were whipping across her face. *Blasted wind*, she muttered to herself as Ty guided Charisma straight to the center of the jump, a large double-oxer with a mass of dusty plastic flowers spreading out from the first rail. Between the horses' hoofprints dislodging clumps of the sandy soil and the strong gusts of wind that were blowing this way and that, it was a good thing the practice fences had artificial flowers and not live ones. Real flowers wouldn't have survived two minutes. Ty was almost at the fence now, about five strides away, her seat still close to the saddle, driving her mare forward with her legs. Her hands were raised slightly, keeping Charisma's hindquarters rounded and underneath her, so that the mare's powerful muscles would be in optimal position to propel them over the fence. They cleared it easily, Ty folding herself over her mare's glossy dappled coat with graceful ease.

The angles they created were just right, a direct line from Ty's elbow to the snaffle bit attached to Charisma's bridle, Ty's torso following the subtly curved arch of the horse's back and neck. Legs folded, knees in tight, horse and rider a pleasure to behold.

"Okay," Meghan called out. "Come at it this time from the opposite lead. I want to see you looking to your left as you clear the oxer, as if you're going to make a sharp turn to the next fence, say right over here, where I'm standing." Meghan walked away from the oxer, counting off the distance in terms of a horse's stride. Satisfied, she came to a halt and looked up at Ty. "Right here, okay? I'd like to see you pick up the tempo a bit, too. Canter right on through, then take Charisma over the in-and-out," she instructed, inclining her head toward the two fences on the other side of the ring.

Ty nodded, gathered her reins, and approached the schooling fence one more time.

"Nice job, Ty. That was a super round." There was a broad smile of approval on Meghan's tanned face as Ty trotted up to her on Charisma. All of Meghan's riders reported directly to her after a flat or a jumping class to analyze any mistakes while they were fresh in everyone's mind.

Ty swung her leg over the saddle and dismounted lightly. One of the girls who worked as a groom for the club and who was responsible for Charisma was waiting to take the reins from Ty. She would rub down the mare's sweat-streaked body with a cloth, place a light cooler over her body, and walk her until it was time for Ty to ride again. In her hand was a bottle of cold water which she held out to Ty.

"Thanks, Caitlin." Ty smiled, exchanging her mare's reins for the water bottle. After giving Charisma a final pat on her sleek neck, she stood beside Meghan, waiting to hear her instructor's comments. Out in the show ring, another rider was already halfway through the jump course. Meghan and Ty watched, standing by the ring's wooden railing as the rider negotiated the triple combination.

"So, how'd it feel?"

"Pretty good. I was maybe a little too hesitant over the water jump, since that was a problem at the last show. But she did fine today."

"Yeah, it didn't cause her any worries. But I noticed she took a good long look at the wall over by the far rail."

"Yes." Ty nodded in agreement. "I'm not sure why. But I remember there were some little fir trees planted at the base of the fence, whipping around in the wind. Maybe that startled her. But I gave her some extra leg, and she responded." Ty paused for a moment, taking a slow sip of the cold water. Only two fences remained, and so far the rider had gone clean. Up to now, Ty had been the only one with no faults, but as her number had been called early in a class of twenty-three riders, she was anticipating a jump-off. Yes, that rider went clear, too.

Ty turned to Meghan. "So what do you think I should do differently in the jump-off?" The abbreviated course for the jump-off had already been posted. Both Meghan and Ty had it memorized.

"After watching your first round, the only thing I can tell you is that you're going to have to dig a little bit deeper. If you feel Charisma's responding well out there, see if you can eliminate a stride as you head from the chicken coop toward the brush jump. That corner to the triple combination might be cut just a little, too, as you head back toward the vertical. If you can keep her balanced and controlled, you'll shave some time. But remember to pay attention to her rhythm. Don't blow it by having Charisma charge the fences off-stride. You'll end up all wobbly, like a badly thrown frisbee." She gave Ty's shoulder a reassuring squeeze. "Other than that, Ty, just stay relaxed and focused, and Charisma will do fine for you."

Ty nodded, eyes directed on the ring, trying to envision a ride taking the jumps as Meghan suggested. She thought she could do it, but the corner from the chicken coop might be tricky. At the thought of chicken, Ty's stomach growled. "You want something to eat, Meghan? Sam, Lizzie, and I are making another run to the concession stand. I'm going to grab a quick bite before the next round."

"Nothing to eat, but get me a can of Dew, okay?" she replied, digging out a crumpled dollar bill from the front pocket of her blue jeans. Meghan had witnessed Ty and Lizzie's eating routine at shows too many times to be surprised that the girls were off to the concession stand for the third time in as many hours. They ate nonstop and indiscriminately. Amazingly, all the extra calories never had any effect on those two; they were just too active. Meghan envied their ability to burn calories at such a high rate, but at age thirty-five, she knew better than to think she could get away with it. "And tell Lizzie to hop on Rushmore again. By the time she's through warming up, you should have finished your round, and I can watch her school him over some fences."

"Sure. I hope my class will be finished before hers starts. I miss watching her ride now that we're competing in different events."

Meghan smiled at the wistful tone in Ty's voice. The girls were so close, they might as well have been twins separated at birth. It hadn't taken long for Meghan to figure out that the girls' horses had to be placed in adjacent stalls back at her barn. Otherwise, Ty and Lizzie would have driven everyone nuts, scurrying up and down the aisle, wasting time that could be spent grooming and riding.

"Maybe the jump-off for your class won't be very big, and you can catch her in the hunter ring."

"I'll keep my fingers crossed." Ty folded Meghan's dollar bill in half. "Back in a bit," she promised with a cheerful smile. Meghan saw Ty's gaze travel over the crowded show grounds, locating her bodyguard with astonishing ease. Sam Brody had been standing off to the side, near a large group of spectators. With all the milling about of horses, riders, and grooms, it would have taken Meghan a good five minutes before she was able to spot him. But not Ty. It was as if she were equipped with some kind of sensor that told her where Sam was waiting, inconspicuous to everyone but her.

What an unnerving existence this girl lived. When you were around Ty, she was nothing if not low-key about herself. Yet there were moments, sudden and illuminating, such as now, when you witnessed her ability to spot her personal bodyguard in a crowd, that it struck home how constant a burden such incredible wealth must be.

Meghan had known Sam Brody for years now, ever since Ty had joined Meghan's private riding club. In Meghan's opinion, Sam was one of the chief reasons Ty had turned out as remarkably unaffected and unpretentious as she was. His presence in her life had helped her avoid the pitfalls Meghan had observed in so many rich kids. She hadn't turned into a spoiled brat or a rebel, intent on getting the world's (or, in Ty's case, her father's) attention by acting up, either with drugs or with wild behavior. She was a good, decent kid caught in a bizarre world of someone else's making.

It was another twenty-five minutes before Ty was back in the saddle, ready to test her skill in the jump-off. The whole concept of the jump-off was still novel to her, for it was markedly different from the way classes were won in the Hunter and Equitation divisions. In hunter classes, horses were judged in terms of their performance, manners, style of jumping, and conformation. In equitation, judges looked for the excellence of the rider's technique, the skill and harmony horse and rider displayed over the flat and over fences.

But the Jumper division didn't rely on the judges' subjective opinions; rather, the challenge lay in completing the jump course itself. In the case of the jump-off, the need for a clear round *and* a faster time than one's fellow competitors increased the challenge that much more.

Intermittent gusts of wind were blowing bits of litter across the show grounds. Leaves on the trees rustled loudly enough to make idle chatter impossible. Which suited Ty fine. She needed a moment to take a deep breath and steady her nerves. Her back ruler-straight as she sat astride Charisma, Ty waited for the show official to give her the sign to proceed into the ring. Her eyes were glued to the jump course in front of her, going over the order of the fences, picturing in her mind what she wanted to do at each point along the course, how her body would bend and shift with Charisma's larger one, helping her horse as much as she could. She lifted a gloved hand to finger her silver medallion hidden underneath the cotton rat-catcher she wore. The official's voice reached her.

"Number 317," the voice called, loud enough to be heard over the group of riders waiting by the in-gate. Seeing Ty's raised hand, the man nodded. "You're up."

"Go get 'em, Ty," Sam encouraged, a smile lighting his tawny eyes as she gathered her reins and headed toward the in-gate. Ty smiled briefly, but didn't say anything, her mind focused exclusively on the task ahead of her.

Charisma trotted through the gate, moving into a graceful, fluid canter as Ty increased the pressure of her leg and softened her hands. She guided her horse down toward the far end of the ring, cantering in a circle large enough for her mare to pass by the first few jumps one more time, reminding her of the job ahead of them. And giving them both a little more time before they triggered the sensors that started the clock.

Out in the open expanse of the show ring, the wind was blowing even stronger. Ty could hear it, the gusts whistling in her ear as she moved Charisma into a strong, forward canter, approaching the first of the eight fences.

Charisma responded beautifully. Up and over, twisting, turning, checking, then thundering forward, they attacked the course with confidence, clearing the first five fences without the slightest hitch. Ty felt their pace was fine: strong and fast but not recklessly out of control. Charisma was galloping, powerful and alert, moving as if she had plenty of energy left for the last three fences: the double-oxer, down to the wall on the far side of the ring, then over to the vertical planks, where they would finish with a fast gallop past the sensors.

They were moving together like clockwork. Ty could taste the sweetness of victory.

Yes! she cheered inwardly as Charisma launched them up and over the four-foot double-oxer. In midflight, Ty was already shifting her body to the left, her head cocked in the same direction, anticipating the sharp turn they'd need to make as they headed over to the other side of the ring where the wall jump towered. As Charisma's forelegs landed, Ty's seat was simultaneously dropping lightly into the saddle, driving her mare around and on, galloping off in the direction of the gray wall, tall and solid, its base decorated with dark green fir trees, their pointed tops dancing in the strong wind.

Remembering her mare's uncertainty from the previous round, Ty dug her heels in, squeezing hard, her crop at the ready in case Charisma needed additional encouragement. Ty was counting off the strides in her head as the distance between them and the jump narrowed. Six, five, four, three, two . . .

In the precious few seconds needed to reach the wall, it happened. In the periphery of her vision, Ty suddenly saw a huge white shape, simultaneously round and pointy, cartwheeling wildly. It was coming directly toward them, far too close for Charisma not to react in utter terror at the unexpected sight. Far too swiftly for Ty to stop her forward momentum as her horse frantically sat back on her haunches, as if slamming on the brakes, sending Ty catapulting, the vertical face of the wall blocking her trajectory. Then Ty knew only black.

The three men hovered near her still body, battered and hidden yet somehow perversely emphasized by the sterile white hospital sheet covering her. Her head was hidden, too, enveloped in layers of gauze bandages, so that she resembled an inexpertly wrapped mummy. The only part of her that was exposed to their collective gazes was her arm, stretched out awkwardly, the clear plastic tubing of the IV sticking into her vein.

Her eyes were shut, her lashes dark and thick against the paleness of her skin. Since the moment she'd crashed into the fence, those gray eyes of hers had been closed. It felt as if an eternity had passed since that awful, terrifying moment, Sam Brody alternately willing, concentrating all his energy in a silent command, *Ty, open your eyes*, and then helplessly praying. She hadn't responded to either.

The doctors, however, were optimistic. The broken collarbone would heal quickly in someone so young and healthy. And though the force of the crash had dislodged Ty's hunt cap and she'd bled copiously from the deep cut on the side of her head, fortunately there'd been no serious damage. The barrage of tests the hospital performed revealed no sign of brain trauma, and the doctors were confident she'd regain consciousness any time.

As for the large gash Ty had received a mere inch away from her eye, which had covered her face with blood, a single telephone call from Tyler Stannard's office had the best plastic surgeon in the country flying in on Mr. Stannard's private jet to tend to it. An hour and change later, he'd finished his handiwork, thirty-nine minute stitches forming a neat crescent-shaped line of black thread holding Ty's lacerated skin together.

One look from Ty's father had quelled any protests the hospital staff might have voiced in an attempt to enforce the rules concerning the number of visitors allowed in a patient's room. They'd scurried off, leaving him, his personal assistant, Michael Smythe, and Sam Brody to their vigil.

Within an hour of Sam's urgent call, the helicopter had landed, depositing Ty's father and Smythe at the local airport. They were met by a driver who rushed them to the hospital, where they arrived to find Ty still undergoing surgery, the plastic surgeon himself having arrived only twenty minutes earlier.

The phone line in Ty's private room had been connected immediately for Smythe's use, the calls continuing uninterrupted as Ty was later wheeled into the room on the hospital gurney. Each telephone conversation was punctuated by rapid-fire instructions from Tyler Stannard.

"Smythe, call London. Reschedule the teleconference planned for this afternoon. Have them set it up for tomorrow morning instead, seven o'clock, our time. Then call the office and tell them to push back the meeting at Hilton Head until tomorrow afternoon. Oh, and make sure the jet's ready to fly us all out of here this afternoon."

"All of us, Mr. Stannard?" repeated Smythe blankly. "Will Miss Tyler be ready to leave the hospital so soon?"

From his position near Ty's bandaged face, Sam lifted his head, momentarily distracted from his vigil. This was as close as he'd ever heard Michael Smythe come to questioning an order from his employer. Possessing the efficiency of a well-oiled machine, Smythe was also a typical yes man. Sam had never heard him say so much as boo to the billionaire before. Of course, *boo* might not be in Smythe's refined vocabulary. Stannard's personal assistant spoke with a snotty British accent, which was utter bullshit since he'd been born in Indiana, as Sam knew from his files. In Sam's opinion, two years spent at a London secretarial school didn't erase the Hoosier from an Indiana boy. But, hey, he wasn't footing the guy's salary, and Stannard didn't seem to care as long as his personal assistant was effective. And from what Sam could tell, Smythe's phony accent and hoity-toity manners worked wonders. People fell all over themselves, so eager to please, as if they'd been granted an interview with the Prince of Wales.

But the phony accent, combined with Smythe's obsequious attitude, rubbed Sam Brody the wrong way. He was still too much of a New York City cop at heart. It was a constant temptation to grab Smythe by the neck and shake him the way a terrier would a rat. So it was interesting to hear kiss-ass Smythe even hinting that Tyler Stannard might have misspoken.

Stannard glanced at his watch. "My daughter as well. If she's not awake by three, I want you to have a private nursing staff in place, ready to fly back with us. They can monitor her while we're in the air. Tell them we'll arrange immediate transportation for their return once we've landed. No need for them to stay; we can hire some local nurses if my daughter needs it. But I want her out of here. I've got to close that deal on the property in South Carolina soon, or someone else might stumble across it. I don't want Tyler in this place while I'm down south."

"Yes, sir." Smythe's head bobbed up and down as he turned to the phone, punching numbers that would make Stannard's wishes a reality. So much for Smythe's show of backbone, Brody thought acidly.

Tyler Stannard was pacing the floor, refusing to look at the bed in the center of the room. He hated seeing his daughter there, lying pale and lifeless. It brought memories of Catherine rushing back. He'd lost his wife. He was *not* going to lose his daughter. It terrified him how easily she could have died. That damned horse.

"Brody, I need you to go back to the show grounds. Tell Meghan Grimshaw to find a buyer for Charisma. I'm selling the mare."

Sam felt his jaw drop. "Mr. Stannard, Ty loves Charisma. You'll break her heart if you take away her horse."

"I didn't buy the horse to have it kill my daughter. She could have been crippled or killed by that fall."

God, this situation was screwed up beyond belief. Sam racked his brains, trying to find a way to make

Stannard understand how important Charisma was to
Ty. Perhaps if he simply and calmly explained what had
happened. "Mr. Stannard, I know how worried you
must be, seeing Ty hurt like this, but what happened
was a freak accident. The wind was something wicked
out there today. It dislodged the judge's umbrella from
its stand and blew it spinning across the show ground.
Once she comes to, Ty'll know it wasn't the horse's fault.
She's a kid with a lot of grit, Mr. Stannard. I'd be willing
to bet she'll want to be back in the saddle as soon as she
possibly can."

"Which is precisely why you're going to make sure
that horse is sold by tomorrow morning at the latest,"
Stannard interrupted smoothly, his cold glare the only
sign of how furious he was at Sam's show of resistance.
"Tyler's riding career is finished. She'd have had to stop
soon, anyway. I've had Smythe looking into a school in
Switzerland. Its reputation is excellent academically.
Furthermore, it will attend to the social graces she's
going to need as she goes into society. Something I've
begun to notice she's sadly lacking. It's past time Tyler
put away her childish hobbies and acquired a little
sophistication."

So the bastard was going to send his daughter pack-
ing, separating her from the school she'd gone to since
third grade, the one real friend she'd managed to ac-
quire, and dump her in some fancy finishing school in
Europe. To top it off, he was planning to sell the horse
that she'd loved more than anything for the past four
years? Without even giving her a chance to say good-
bye? Just thinking about how it would hurt Ty made
Sam want to break something. Tyler Stannard's face.

Unable to contain himself, Sam blurted out, "Just
what is it you want from the poor kid? Christ, I've seen
children from the projects who have nothing, but at

least their parents give them love. Ty should be so lucky."

Long, slow seconds ticked by as the two men stood on opposite sides of the hospital bed, staring hostilely at each other. "I believe you've overstepped the boundaries of your job description, Brody," Stannard said softly. "You'd do well to remember that I hired you as a bodyguard. I hardly believe that qualifies you to tell me how to raise my daughter. Now, do I need to repeat myself? I want the mare sold by tomorrow."

"Yeah, you can repeat that one till you're blue in the face, Stannard, 'cause you'll have to find someone else to do it. I sure as hell won't. Like you just said, I was hired to protect her. You want to hurt Ty, then do it yourself. I quit."

"You say you wouldn't hurt her, yet here you are walking out on her. A rather glaring contradiction, don't you think?"

Brody's eyes cut like daggers as he looked at his former employer. "Yeah, I'm hurting her, too. But Ty's a smart girl. It won't take her long to figure out who the real son of a bitch is."

Holding his fury in check, Sam Brody reached out his large hand and lightly stroked Ty's bandaged head, bidding her a silent farewell. He only wished he could have done more to help when she needed backup the most, feeling a cold, impotent rage settle over him knowing that he'd failed her. Sam turned and walked out the door, closing the book on this chapter in his life.

A single tear slipped from the corner of Ty's closed eye, leaving a transparent trail against her pale skin.

PART 3

1999

8

Manhattan

Ty's cell phone was pealing a three-note ring from the depths of her gym bag. She ignored it. By the time she'd rooted through the jumble of sweaty workout clothes, the voice mail would have picked up. Whoever or whatever it was could wait until she'd reached her apartment. She glanced at the elevator's other occupant. Balding, in his mid-fifties, several inches shorter than Ty, and a good forty pounds heavier, the elevator man was dressed in the apartment building's navy blue uniform, the jacket decorated with gold-braided epaulettes and brass buttons. At the moment, the man, whose principal job was to press the illuminated numbers on the large gleaming panel, was staring at them as if in rapt fascination, pretending to be oblivious to the persistent rings emanating from the depths of Ty's bag. The obnoxious noise ceased just as the elevator reached sixteen.

"Have a good day, Miss Stannard," the elevator man offered as Ty stepped forward.

"Thank you, John," she replied gravely, even though she and John had enjoyed this exact conversation numerous times today, and stepped into the private foyer that led to her apartment. The elevator door slid silently shut behind her, cutting off the need for further polite conversation. With a sigh of relief, Ty slipped the bag from her shoulder, letting it fall to the marble floor. She picked up the stack of mail piled neatly on top of the small entry table and fished her keys from her suede leather jacket.

The phone was already ringing as she pushed her door open.

"All right already, I'm coming, I'm coming!" she muttered, walking over to the end table by her sofa and picking up the phone. "Hello?"

"Where have you been? I've been calling all over the place!"

"The gym, errands. Hi, Lizzie, what's up?" Ty sank into the plump, cream-colored sofa cushions and kicked off her leather flats. Tucking her legs underneath her, she winced slightly at the unexpected soreness. It occurred to her that she'd been a little too enthusiastic with the weights.

"Oh, nothing, just trying to arrange a wonderful, delightful celebration with the two people I love most in the world, but of course, whenever I try to reach *you*, I might as well be trying to get through to the president. Honestly, Ty, don't you know cell phones were invented for a reason?"

Ty tamped down the guilt that immediately welled up inside her at the memory of the last time Lizzie had been unable to reach Ty. But Ty knew how much Lizzie hated discussing that period in her life. Furthermore, Lizzie'd be appalled if Ty revealed how much guilt she still harbored.

So she kept her voice light, teasing. "Sorry, Liz, I'm not sure I'll ever figure out why these bloody gadgets are so essential to modern man. In fact," she quipped, "I spend hours fantasizing about what I'd do if I ever got my hands around the throat of the so-called genius who invented them! Just the sight of all those people walking down Madison Ave, talking into little plastic rectangles or, worse, looking like badly trained secret service agents, is enough to make me break out in hives."

"Yeah, well, I'm all for fantasizing, but let me tell you, your disdain for modern technology makes you a very difficult person to track down. I've thought of everything—including carrier pigeons. I hate to admit it, but it sure was easier when you had a secretary, like when you worked for Stannard Limited."

"Don't go any further with that thought," Ty warned, massaging the sudden throbbing at her temple. She, too, had topics too painful to discuss. At least half of the messages on her machine, signaled by the illuminated number twelve next to the red light blipping frantically on the console of her phone, were calls from the office of her father's company, demanding her presence. Ty wondered whether Stannard Limited had been forced to hire a new employee whose sole responsibility was to leave these predictable and unchanging messages: "Mr. Stannard is calling to request your presence at his office this afternoon." Wouldn't that be a job from hell?

"That's one of the reasons I almost never pick up," Ty admitted. "The dratted phone rings every other minute. Not even screening the calls helps—I keep losing my place in the accounts and have to start my calculations all over again. It's like one step forward, two steps back getting through these numbers."

Lizzie made a noise of sympathy on the other end. "I can well imagine. I'm just thankful you're dealing with it and not me! Look, you know there's no rush on the

books; we don't have to file anything for months yet."
Lizzie paused for a minute before continuing. "So,
Daddy Stannard's trying to sweet-talk you into a reconciliation?" There was no love lost between Mr. Stannard
and Lizzie.

"He'll get over that particular pipe dream."

"Hmm . . ." Lizzie's reply was noncommittal. She
didn't believe that Tyler Stannard was going to give up
the warped pleasure he got from having Ty around to
manipulate any time soon. He'd enjoyed having his du-
tiful daughter at his beck and call for too long, and he
wasn't the kind who took no for an answer. No, Lizzie
reflected bitterly, he just enjoyed being able to say it to
others.

Ty's voice interrupted her musing. "So, what are we
celebrating?"

"A milestone anniversary, kiddo. Do you realize
today marks exactly eighteen months since the divorce
came through and just shy of a year since you and I
opened the barn? I thought the three of us might go out
to a restaurant after the benefit tonight. Just think of it,
we can spoon mush down Emma's throat while we pour
champagne down ours."

"Sounds utterly irresistible! So I get to see Emma
tonight, too?"

Emma was Lizzie's daughter, Ty's goddaughter, and
in Ty's unbiased opinion probably the cutest two-year-
old ever. A curly-haired strawberry blonde, she was the
spitting image of her mother. Beautiful from the day she
was born, whenever Emma and Lizzie came to the city
for a visit and the two friends took Emma out for a walk,
navigating the dark blue stroller through the busy
streets, little old ladies stopped them to coo and exclaim
over the adorable baby. Fortunately, Emma also had inherited her mother's sunny disposition and, as if know-

ing it would make their day, gurgled happily and energetically into the old ladies' faces. Ty loved her as if she were her own and tried to spend as much time with Lizzie and Emma as she could.

"I reserved a room for Em and a baby-sitter. After the benefit's over, we can pick her up and take her with us. Does Giorgio's sound good to you?"

"My mouth's watering already."

"Well, your appetite might vanish once you get a load of Emma's new favorite food."

Emma had entered the terrible twos with decided tastes. Ty remembered how for an entire month, she'd insisted on eating only green foods, morning, noon, and night.

"So what is it these days?" Ty inquired curiously.

"She's gone orange on me, Ty," Lizzie replied in a piteous tone. "Butternut squash is her top favorite, although I did manage to sneak a few squares of cheddar and cantaloupe into her this morning. You've no idea what a tricky, underhanded mom I've become. I thought green was bad, pureeing broccoli and spinach until I wanted to scream, but this squash stuff is a nightmare! I have to soak her tops for *days*. That, or dye them all orange!"

"Thanks for the warning. I'll make sure I stay out of range. So what time do you want me there tonight?" Ty asked, glancing at her watch. It was just three now.

"Six o'clock. By then, most of the guests will have arrived and you can start working your magic. I need that killer instinct of yours to drum up clients and open checkbooks. If we get a full enrollment for the summer program, we'll be able to offer at least eight scholarships for next winter's program."

"It's at the Waldorf, right?"

"Yes. The organizers wanted it in a convenient location so the out-of-towners wouldn't get lost."

Ty leaned back against the cushions, stretching her long legs out in front of her. She hated social functions. Passionately. "Great. I'll be there with bells on, encouraging one and all to enroll their horse-crazy kids in Cobble Creek's summer horse masters' program."

"Thanks, Ty. But forget the bells. Just wear the Valentino number. The guys'll be too blinded by lust to count how many zeros they're tacking on when they write out their checks. Oh, my God! Look at the time! Gotta run if Emma and I are going to beat the rush-hour traffic. See ya, sweets."

With a small smile at Lizzie's undiminished exuberance, Ty replaced the phone on the cradle. She steadfastly ignored the flashing red light, a reminder of countless messages. Her mind was traveling back, recalling how much Lizzie had been through these past eighteen months, how much Ty wished she'd been a better friend.

Lizzie Osborne Strickland's life had taken a dizzyingly fast downward spiral from the moment her patience snapped, her sense of pride reasserted itself, and she at last filed for divorce from her philandering husband, Michael Strickland, asking also for custody of their baby girl, Emma. Within a mere twenty-four hours after the papers were filed, Michael hired a divorce lawyer widely acknowledged to be the most ruthless in the city. Before Lizzie could catch her breath and her own lawyer knew what had hit them, Strickland emptied Lizzie's and his joint checking account, canceled her credit cards, and pressed charges against Lizzie himself, seeking to have her declared an unfit mother. He even went so far as to claim that she had attacked him in a drunken rage.

Divorce is never pretty, but Lizzie had never dreamed that Michael could sink to this level of viciousness.

He'd seemed like such a great catch.

Lizzie and he met at a party thrown by mutual friends. Lizzie, twenty-three and more dazzling than ever, had graduated from college the spring before. She was living in the city, working for a PR company, and riding competitively on the weekends. One look at Lizzie's gorgeous body and the thick strawberry-blonde mane that fell down to the middle of her back, and Michael, a smooth-talking, ambitious executive at a large telecommunications firm, reacted like every other male who'd ever laid eyes on her. He'd gone straight to the party's host for the name of the babe with the "killer bod" and racked his brains for the best angle to entice her into his bed.

Some men know instinctively how to play to women. Michael Strickland was one of them. He joked, he flattered, he listened to Lizzie's descriptions of her small group of clients and accounts as if they were more than fascinating. He asked her questions, scrupulously careful not to switch the conversation and talk about his job, an instant signal that he considered his own career more important. He hinted broadly that he might be able to line up some new clients for her.

The following day, Lizzie's doorbell rang, and a delivery man presented her with a bouquet consisting of twenty-six tea roses, intermingled with freesia and lilies, the scent of the bouquet as bewitching as it was beautiful to behold. A note scrawled on a thick vellum card accompanied it, inviting her to dinner that evening.

They were an item within days, and two months later their engagement was announced. Lizzie threw herself into wedding plans with her customary enthusiasm, and Michael continued to be the epitome of charm. Ty managed to get together with the fiancés a couple of times, for dinner or drinks, but it was a period during which she was traveling virtually nonstop for her father's real estate company. She'd been too busy and too tired to probe beyond the slick surface of Michael Strickland's character.

And as Lizzie and Ty both now knew, Michael Strickland was a first-class liar and dissembler. Someone as practiced as Strickland was awfully hard to catch.

Both women might have been in the dark about Michael's character for far longer if he, himself, hadn't chosen to reveal his true colors right after the wedding day. In fact, Ty unfortunately got her first glimpse of the real Michael Strickland even sooner, a mere half-hour after the beautifully orchestrated ceremony Lizzie and her mother had organized, with Ty as the maid of honor. Sentimental tears had run down her cheeks as Lizzie, looking achingly beautiful, pledged love and loyalty to the man standing at her side.

Shortly after the ceremony, Ty was in the upstairs guest bathroom, repairing the damage her tears had wreaked on her makeup. Without knocking, without any warning, Michael sauntered into the bathroom, so startling Ty that she almost dropped the wand of mascara she'd been using on her smeared eyelashes.

Embarrassed and surprised by the intrusion, Ty glanced at Michael uneasily, wondering whether he might have been going a little heavy on the champagne. What else could cause him to barge in on her while she was in the bathroom?

He didn't appear to notice her distress. For all the world, he looked perfectly relaxed, his black cutaway emphasizing the muscular build that had made him one of the leading rushers on his college rugby team.

White teeth flashed as he gave her an easy, confident smile. "Ahh, I found you. Lizzie's been wondering where you snuck off to. Told her I'd hunt you down."

If he were drunk, Ty couldn't detect it by his speech or by his eyes. They shone bright and clear in the large bathroom mirror. Catching a glimpse of his own reflection in the mirror, he paused and lifted a hand to his head, smoothing a lock of his gelled short brown hair. Evidently pleased with what he saw, his lips in a cocky grin. Then, as if he abruptly remembered her presence, his gaze abandoned his own image and locked on Ty's. His smile broadened, and Ty was suddenly reminded of a slick used-car salesman.

Quickly, she looked away, thoroughly irritated at his behavior. What was he doing here, in the bathroom with her? Anyone else would have excused himself immediately.

Although she tried to keep her face expressionless, it was difficult to mask the annoyance in her voice. "Please tell Lizzie I'll be finished in a minute, Michael. Don't let me keep you from your guests downstairs."

"No hurry," Michael replied. As if emphasizing his point, he propped a shoulder negligently against the door frame, his broad shoulders almost filling the space. "Everyone's busy guzzling the Osbornes' champagne and gorging on caviar."

This was getting beyond weird, Ty thought, tendrils of fear beginning to unfurl inside her. Well, if he wasn't going to leave, *she* would. Who cared what her makeup looked like, anyway? She closed the small plastic tube of mascara with an impatient flick of her wrist.

Turning to face Michael, she addressed him coolly, distantly, her newfound dislike for him showing. "If you'll excuse me, I'd like to get by," she said pointedly.

He didn't move a muscle, only continued lounging

against the doorjamb. "As I said, there's no hurry. It's a big house, and I found you quickly. No one's going to be missing either of us."

Twin spots of angry color heated her cheeks, in contrast to her voice, which could have given frostbite. "Nevertheless, I think I should go down now."

He ignored her words. "You and Liz are really close, aren't you?" he observed in a musing tone. "Practically sisters . . . what's hers is yours, and vice versa."

The fine hair on the back of Ty's neck prickled in alarm as she realized Michael's eyes had begun traveling up and down the length of her body, lingering far too long on the gentle swell of her breasts.

She had to get out of there. The thought drummed inside her head with an urgent beat.

A distance of about four feet separated them; Ty dreaded the thought of approaching any closer. But the only way to get out of the bathroom was to walk past Lizzie's new husband. Otherwise, she was trapped. The scene was surreal, unthinkable, yet the tension and unease that vibrated within her were all too real. Still, she was damned if she was going to let Michael Strickland sense her fear. Unconsciously, her chin lifted and her eyes hardened until they resembled chips of granite. With nothing but her courage, Ty forced herself to take those steps toward him, fervently praying all the while that he'd move aside and let her pass.

The fear she'd tried to contain exploded inside her as his hand grabbed her arm, his fingers strong, squeezing her tender flesh.

She gave a small cry, no longer able to hide her terror. "What are you doing? Let go of me!"

She struggled, trying to break his grasp on her. Although Ty was tall and fairly strong, her struggle to free herself was laughable. With an appalling ease, Michael

Strickland pulled her closer, her ivory satin bridesmaid's gown brushing against his trousers. A meaty hand clasped both of her wrists, imprisoning her.

"Come on, Ty, don't pretend with me. Everyone says you're still a virgin, but I can tell you're real hungry for it. I knew it the minute I met you."

"Let me go!" Ty repeated desperately. "For God's sake, you're Lizzie's husband. Are you *mad*?"

His other hand began moving over her slender body, fingers crushing the delicate fabric beneath them. He dropped his head, nuzzling the pale, fragrant column of Ty's neck. His hot breath washed over her, filling her with revulsion. Her stomach lurched with panic and fear.

As if from very far away, she heard his voice, though that was all wrong because her flesh was crawling as he pressed closer and closer. "Lizzie's fine," Michael was saying. "The guys are drooling with envy that I grabbed her first, but, hey, variety is the spice of life. No way am I going to miss out on some hot snatch just 'cause I've got a ring on my finger." With that, he rubbed his erection against her thighs, pushing back and forth. Ty cried out, redoubling her efforts to escape his hold.

Michael only yanked her closer, his body suffocating in its nearness. "That's right, come on, baby, gimme some noise."

In horror, Ty felt him grab a handful of her dress and begin working the expanse of fabric up, revealing her slender legs. Panted words accompanied his groans of arousal. "Ty, baby, let me tell you, you are definitely as hot as you are rich." His mouth captured hers in a brutal kiss, his tongue forcing its way deep into her mouth.

Ty never knew whether it was the effect of Michael Strickland's revolting words, the awful destination of his hand, or the obscene presence of his tongue lodged halfway down her throat, gagging her, that saved her. She preferred to think it was the sudden memory of her former bodyguard, Sam Brody's instructions to Ty on how to save herself should she ever be sexually assaulted. "Pee in your pants if you have to, Ty. Puke. Do *anything* you think will repulse the creep enough to make him think twice or give you an opportunity to escape." For whatever reason, and to her later amazement, Ty's body decided to follow Sam's suggestion to the letter. Like a geyser, Ty suddenly reared back and heaved, vomiting her wedding breakfast all over the front of Strickland's pristine black-and-white cutaway.

"Aagh! Goddamn frigid bitch!" Michael screamed in disgust as he leaped back, his own face turning a grayish green as the stench of Ty's vomit assaulted him. Ty would have laughed had she not still been heaving wretchedly, tears streaming down her face.

Tugging furiously at the black satin button, Michael Strickland tore off the jacket, desperate to escape the stinking mess that covered him. Holding it at arm's length, he looked down at Ty with hatred as she huddled miserably in the corner of the bathroom, as far away from him as she could get.

"Listen up, you pathetic cocktease. You blab a word of this to Lizzie, and I'll tell her that you came on to me. She's probably noticed herself how you can't keep your eyes off me. It wouldn't take much to convince her of the truth."

Ty's eyes, glazed with shock, unwillingly locked with his. "She'd never believe that. I'm her best friend."

"God, you are so naive. You bet your puny little ass she would. All I have to do is touch her, and she comes like it's the fucking Fourth of July." Raking her with an insolent gaze, Michael sniggered, his contempt obvious.

"You think your 'friendship' can hold up to what I give her every night? Think again, Ty baby. *And keep your prissy mouth shut.* Or I'll make it so Lizzie never wants to see you again."

Ty hated herself for having been cowed by the likes of him. But Michael's gross self-confidence had shaken her own. She'd been so scared of losing Lizzie's friendship that she'd buried the incident deep within her. And, of course, there'd been the guilt. Could she somehow have unconsciously encouraged Michael's advances? Could her speculative looks really have been so easily misinterpreted?

Certain only that their friendship might be irrevocably damaged if she told Lizzie about what Michael had done, Ty kept the shameful truth bottled up inside.

But all by herself Lizzie soon discovered her new husband's appetite for adulterous affairs. Whispers of his infidelities began buzzing about like flies on roadkill, until soon the majority of Lizzie's friends and acquaintances would look at her with ill-disguised pity before plastering bright, phony smiles on their faces. At first, Lizzie did her best to dismiss the stories. Then she pretended not to notice that her husband came home reeking of another woman's perfume.

Ty felt that there, too, she had failed Lizzie. At a loss about how to approach Lizzie on the subject of her crumbling marriage, she had taken the easy route, letting Lizzie pretend that everything was just dandy. To make matters worse, Ty was often absent, traveling all over the globe for Stannard Limited, locked away in meetings, temporarily stepping into her father's shoes while he recovered from an emergency quadruple-bypass surgery.

Only after the birth of her daughter, Emma, did Lizzie realize she could no longer live with a husband who valued her so little and who made a mockery of their marriage at every opportunity.

It was terrible luck that Lizzie's filing for divorce coincided with a particularly long trip Ty was forced to make. Even though her father had made a complete recovery, he'd insisted on her representing him. As his replacement, Ty'd been obliged to travel to nine different countries, closing deals, inspecting properties, going over the books at the luxury estates her father owned, never coming up for air between whirlwind inspections and negotiating sessions. By the end of that five-week period, Ty had lost close to fifteen pounds she could ill afford to lose and was teetering on the edge of a physical breakdown.

In an effort to escape from her father's constant demands and exaggerated expectations, Ty drove alone from Dublin, where the company jet had dropped her off, to a village on Ireland's west coast. She'd hidden out in a tiny, windswept cottage on the outskirts of Connemara. There was not a phone, fax machine, or computer within reach, and she'd consciously left her cell phone on the plane.

For two wonderful weeks, she tuned out the world, unaware that during all this time, while she'd been traveling and stuck in meetings, Lizzie had been frantically trying to reach her, needing a loan so she could continue paying the lawyers in the custody battle for Emma. To no avail.

Then Lizzie, beyond despair, approached Ty's father. Mr. Stannard not only turned Lizzie down flat but had her escorted out of Stannard Limited's offices and then gave orders to the staff that Ty's whereabouts were not to be divulged. Anyone who disobeyed would be fired.

So, as Ty unwound from the stress of a brutal year of twenty-hour workdays, Lizzie's life was being destroyed. Their savings depleted, Mr. and Mrs. Osborne were unable to continue to offer their daughter financial support. Lizzie was faced with her lawyer withdrawing from her case for nonpayment of his astronomical bills. She was faced with losing her baby girl, Emma.

By the grace of God, Ty returned just in time.

9

The benefit was packed. The glitterati of the New York social scene always responded particularly well to animal causes and this night was no exception. The fund-raiser served as a kickoff for the fall show season and the National Horse Show, traditionally held at Madison Square Garden, little over a month away. Important sponsors and patrons were in full attendance, as well as quite a few professional riders. The cause was a good one: to raise money for nonprofit organizations that helped old, retired horses of every category—pleasure, race, or show. Across the country, a number of horse farms had begun caring for these aged equines, letting them live out their final years in comfort rather than the neglect, abuse, sometimes outright slaughter far too many of them faced once their usefulness was past. Lizzie and Cobble Creek Stables were on the list of patrons for the fund-raiser, having made a sizable donation: an entire year's worth of riding lessons that would be offered in the silent auction, the evening's main event. Already, a large number of people were congregating around the cloth-covered tables where auction items were displayed.

Like many other people involved with horses, Lizzie was more than happy to help this cause. It was heartbreaking to think that a cherished horse or pony that someone sold might one day be led to slaughter. And while it was clear that not everyone could afford to keep horses past their prime, the benefit was a big step toward providing funds for their care and protection.

And from the perspective of Lizzie's fledgling business, getting Cobble Creek's name on people's lips at such an event could only be advantageous. Lizzie had a handful of young riders who had brought their horses to her barn, most of them thanks to Meghan Grimshaw, currently so popular a trainer that she was forced to turn riders away. Determined to build an equally successful riding program, Lizzie, with Ty's help, was planning ahead, trying to round up enough children for a summer camp that would offer three months of intense horsemanship and weekend competitions in the tri-state area shows.

Sometimes together, sometimes separately, Lizzie and Ty worked the crowd, targeting couples, grandparents, any likely-looking candidates, managing with enviable finesse to extol the virtues of the evening's benefit and the cause it served, at the same time putting in a plug for Cobble Creek's young riders' program.

Everywhere they went, heads turned. Beauty and notoriety often have that effect.

Rumors that the stunning, reclusive Ty Stannard, daughter of the billionaire real estate magnate, was present sent whispers abuzzing. Weaving elegantly through the crowd, her silver lamé evening dress catching and reflecting the light that fell from the chandeliers, Ty looked beautifully mysterious, like a silver statue come to life. Her presence endowed the benefit with a special touch of glamour that other guests were eager to believe rubbed off on them, enhancing their own social standing. As Ty passed, backs straightened and smiles brightened.

Of course, the big question on everyone's mind was *What was she doing here?* People in the know immediately spread the word that she must be attending the fundraiser because of Lizzie Osborne—the two had been friends forever.

Heads nodded sagely. Of the two women, Lizzie Osborne was an even juicier topic for discussion than her mysterious, wealthy friend. Even eighteen months later, the weeks of headlines that Lizzie Osborne's deliciously nasty divorce provided for the gossip mill had yet to be eclipsed by a newer, bigger scandal. Each tidbit of speculation about the outcome of the Strickland custody fight had been served up by the *Daily News,* the *Post,* and the *New York Observer.*

All there, in black and white, everyone had read Michael Strickland's shocking accusations concerning his wife, gasping in outrage over their morning lattes. Infidelity, abuse, alcohol . . . When, weeks later, Michael Strickland abruptly recanted and apologized publicly for those accusations—a comeuppance virtually unheard of—overnight Lizzie Osborne was transformed into a symbol of hope for the many women undergoing the emotional torture of a tug of war over a child.

The large, lustrous pearl, suspended from a black silk rope, its upper portion encircled with a tiny ribbon of diamonds, cooled the flesh just below the hollow of her throat. This was the only piece of jewelry she wore, but its elegant simplicity matched the flawless lines of the silver lamé Valentino dress. Nevertheless, Ty thought fleetingly of her heavy antique gold and leather Swiss watch bought years ago in Gstaad, lying on the marble-topped dresser in her bedroom. Even though it was far too clunky and sporty to go with her dress, she wished she were wearing it now. It was too bad that rules of fashion had been drummed into her so ruthlessly and effectively.

How much time before she could escape? It was impossible to trust her own judgment: minutes crawled by like hours under such intense scrutiny and speculation. She'd give anything to be home, curled up on her sofa with a book, a fire burning merrily in her granite fireplace.

The thought of Lizzie and Emma made her shake off her fatigue, the headache that threatened. Ty continued smiling, eyeing faces for potential clients. This was too big an evening for Lizzie and Cobble Creek not to give it one last effort before she called it a night. Her gray eyes traveled over clusters of people, arranged like little islands in the vast expanse of the Waldorf's ballroom.

Ah, there were some likely candidates. Her satin stiletto-heeled pumps played peek-a-boo beneath her gown as Ty glided across the polished wooden floor toward the forty-something couple who appeared to be engaged in a lively conversation with a group of women she recognized as committee members for the National Horse Show. Ty assumed an expression of polite interest. Timing was everything. She'd have to wait for just the right break in the conversation before she could artfully slip in a few glowing remarks about Cobble Creek's riding program.

"Well, I can't say I blame them. You have to wonder what kind of security they have that allows a horse to die in its own stall."

"And what happened, really? How did it die?"

"I heard it choked to death and was lying there for hours before anyone found it."

"Well, that's not what Kiki told me!" a statuesque woman in a copper taffeta gown interrupted. Her voice rang with the harsh boom of authority. "She said Sheppard was higher than a kite that evening, and when he found the horse lying in its stall, it was still alive. Apparently, Sheppard just lost it, went berserk or something. He grabbed a rifle and emptied it into the horse."

There was a collective gasp from the small circle. Filled with self-importance, the lady continued, all eyes on her. "He didn't stop there, either. Afterward, he went and beat up his partner, Jason Belmar, who wound up in the hospital. Someone must have called the cops, because they were crawling all over the place within minutes. That's why Sheppard didn't have time to hide any of the drugs. They found coke and God knows what else in the house. And Fancy Free, one of show jumping's best, shot dead in his stall."

"How ghastly! Well, no wonder he's disappeared from the circuit. And it's true some of his owners have sent their horses to Greg Fawlton's place?"

The taffeta-robed woman nodded vigorously. "Well, of course! Would you leave your million-dollar horse with a man like that? Sheppard's in huge trouble, all right. The police are still going over the place with a fine-tooth comb, and then of course there's Fancy Free's death. Whenever there's anything remotely fishy, insurance companies balk—I hear they're claiming the horse might not have been seriously injured and are demanding an investigation. Even if Steve's eventually cleared of suspicion, it'll take forever before they pay up." Satisfied with that dire prediction, the woman stopped her recital.

"It looks like high-flying Steve Sheppard has had a crash landing," another remarked.

"Fancy Free was such a wonderful jumper! I'd heard they were heavy favorites for the U.S. team next year in Sydney! Surely if Steve could have saved him, he wouldn't have shot his best horse?"

"*Money*, darling." The reply was condescending. "He must have been spending a fortune on his habit. I heard some ugly rumors that Southwind, his stable in the Hamptons, was deep in the red. With this mess, he'll be in even bigger trouble financially. All his clients are leaving. Even the Palmers—who've been with him forever! They had three horses at Southwind and were planning a buying trip for the coming year. Doubtless their new horses would have been trained by Steve, too. That's an awful lot of money he's just lost."

"And the banks are relentless these days. I bet they'll foreclose by the end of the month."

"Well, that farm will be snatched up in a nanosecond. Prime Hamptons property. There aren't many parcels like that left out there, snuggled nice and cozy between ocean and pond."

"It's terrible, terrible, the whole story. To think that someone like that, as talented as Steve Sheppard, would just blow it away."

"Snort it away, you mean."

"You've said barely three words since we sat down, Ty, and you haven't even touched your risotto. Watching Emma eat isn't making you lose your appetite, is it?" There was a smile on Lizzie's lips, but her voice held a note of concern. The evening had been a rousing success, both for the charity and for her riding program at Cobble Creek. It surprised her that Ty was so unnaturally silent and preoccupied.

Ty roused herself from her bleak thoughts. She shrugged her shoulders, making her gown shimmer in the soft candlelight of the restaurant's dining room. "I'm sorry. I'm truly lousy company tonight. It's just that I overheard a conversation at the gala that really threw me. Did you know there were stories circulating about Steve Sheppard?"

"Yes, something about one of his horses dying. It sounded awful. But I didn't really pay attention to it. Since Michael, since our divorce, I've learned that the stories you hear tossed about as gospel truth are usually ninety-nine-percent fiction. Things get mangled and changed, edited and elaborated, until it's like that game of telephone kids play. You know, the original message is 'I think Jimmy's cute,' and it ends up as 'Dolores stole her mother's pantsuit.' "

"Is there any way we can find out for sure?"

Lizzie thought for a minute and then glanced at her watch. "Well, if we leave now, we can reach Vicky before the *Times* goes to bed for the night."

"Vicky?"

"Vicky Grodecki. One of the best female sports writers in the business. She covers figure skating, equestrian events, gymnastics . . . you know, stuff the guys don't want to touch with a ten-foot pole. She'll definitely know anything about Sheppard that's worth knowing— he and Fancy Free were Olympics material. I'd use my cell phone and call from here, but Giorgio would never forgive me," she said, referring to the restaurant's owner. She looked pointedly at Ty's plate. "And you'd better eat some of that risotto. He'll be mortally wounded otherwise, and there'll go our chance at getting our favorite table next time we come."

Ty looked down at her plate of risotto with porcini mushrooms. Her stomach clenched. Then she looked at her goddaughter, who was singing a song about "washing the spider out" as she waved a spoon coated with acorn squash puree. "Emma, sweetie, have you ever tried risotto?" With a bright smile, she scooped up a small amount on the edge of her fork. "Mmm, doesn't this look good!" she exclaimed enthusiastically.

Lizzie laughed. "Go for it, Ty. I'm more than ready for a change of color in Emma's diet."

They were back at Ty's apartment, Emma having fallen asleep on the ride back uptown, her tummy full of squash and risotto. Ty had volunteered to tuck her into the guest-room bed where she and Lizzie would be spending the night, while Lizzie called Vicky Grodecki.

She could still hear Lizzie's voice in the quiet of the apartment as she shut the bedroom door carefully behind her. Not wishing to interrupt, she wandered into the kitchen and flicked on the lights. From the glass-paneled wooden cabinets overhead, Ty took out two cups and saucers and a pair of dessert plates. She filled the copper kettle and turned the gas range on high. The box of loose-leaf chamomile tea and a tin of Florentine cookies were tucked away in the cupboard to the right. Waiting for the kettle to boil, she rinsed a box of fresh strawberries and set them out on a white china plate. In the time it took to arrange everything on a large bamboo tray, a thin cloud of steam rose from the kettle's spout. Ty carried the laden tray into the living room and set it down upon the kaleidoscope-like mosaic surface of the coffee table.

Lizzie was just hanging up.

Silence settled over the room as Ty lifted the teapot's lid. Chamomile blossoms were floating on the surface, their gentle aroma wafting upward. Replacing the china lid, Ty poured the steaming golden liquid into the two china cups. With an expectant glance, she leaned back against the sofa. "Well?"

A sigh escaped Lizzie's lips. For a moment she appeared absorbed in the random patterns her fingers traced against the silk of her pale sea-green evening dress. At last she turned toward Ty, her face uncommonly grim. "It sounds really bad, Ty. Vicky confirmed that Fancy Free's dead, that Steve Sheppard killed him. It's also true that the police were called in and must have found something, because Steve was taken down to the police station—although he was released first thing the next morning."

Ty drew a shaky breath. Somehow she'd refused to consider that the gossip she'd heard earlier at the gala might contain even an ounce of truth. But there it was; Fancy Free was dead. With a concentrated effort, she blocked out the image of that wonderful horse, lying in its stall, shot by its owner. Hands suddenly unsteady, she reached for the cup and saucer, hoping the herbal infusion would settle her nerves. Lifting the delicate china cup to her lips, she took a slow sip.

"And those other rumors, are they true as well?"

"Hard to say. Vicky tried to interview Steve, but he's not talking. Refuses to speak to anyone. His partner, Jason Belmar, was taken to the emergency room but later released. The police hauled him over to the police station, too. Booked him on drug charges. Vicky found out that the only call Jason Belmar made was to his lawyer. The lawyer came and posted bail for him and must have told Belmar to keep his lips buttoned, because he's not talking, either."

"Well, that's probably the smartest thing they can do, given the stories flying around already."

Lizzie nodded, reaching for her cup of tea. "That's what Vicky said. What surprised her is that even the police are playing this close to the chest, which is pretty unusual. She can generally count on someone to toss a juicy morsel of information her way. Her take on it is that the cops want to avoid a drug-related scandal hitting the headlines that might involve very important rich people . . . the owners. Not only would the media and the police risk being nailed with a libel suit, but the golden image of the Hamptons as the carefree playground for big money might get tarnished."

Ty rolled her eyes in disgust. "Right, whatever." She'd seen the rich and famous all over the world at their various "playgrounds." More often than not, it was a pretty sordid sight. "And did she say anything about the financial situation?"

"Unfortunately, yes," Lizzie replied with a glum nod. "It's a mess, and the bankers, unlike everybody else involved, are more than willing to talk about *that*, as you can well imagine. Except for three horses that he owns free and clear, Steve Sheppard's got nothing. His house, his farm, and all the rest are mortgaged and double-mortgaged. His bank balance couldn't buy him a Happy Meal. They're going to foreclose on him by the end of the month—that's just over three weeks from now—and Vicky says that nothing short of a miracle will save Southwind."

Lizzie paused and helped herself to a strawberry from the plate. Leaning back against the plump cushions, she twirled the stem between her fingers, watching the plump fruit dance and spin. Her bright blue gaze held Ty's. "So, you feeling like a miracle worker, Ty?" she asked, her lips parting in a small smile before opening wider to pop the strawberry into her mouth, enjoying the dual sweet sensation of the moment, the ripe sugary taste invading her mouth, the look of embarrassed surprise coloring her friend's pale skin. "Gotcha!" She laughed, reaching for a second strawberry.

Ty conceded the fact with a rueful shake of her head. "I didn't realize I was so transparent."

"Come on, give me a break! How many years have we known each other? I'd have been shocked, desperately worried, even, if you *hadn't* decided to go and save Steve Sheppard in his darkest hour. I know you weren't wearing it tonight," Lizzie commented, nodding at the pearl pendant hanging from Ty's slender neck, "but you still have that medallion he gave you, don't you?"

Ty's blush answered for her.

"Right. Well, then, you haven't forgotten what a decent guy he was to us back then, when we were goofy teenagers, either. Face it, Ty, it's time to strap on those wings of yours and fly to his rescue."

"I don't know, Lizzie. It sounds like such a messy situation. There may not be much I can do."

Waving Ty's doubts away, Lizzie leaned forward, her expression eager. "What are you talking about? Of course you'll be able to help him. Of all the people I can think of, you're the best person, Ty!" She raised her hand when Ty would have interrupted her. "No, I'm serious. Remember, I've seen you in action. You were Emma's and my avenging angel. You came through for me a thousand percent. You got me out of that eternal hell of a divorce proceeding, had that SOB Michael begging for mercy *and* promising he wouldn't contest my custody of Emma. It was truly wonderful watching him eat humble pie and act like he was loving every bite. And when the divorce finally came through, you not only helped me pick up the pieces of my life, you also helped me start a new one."

"Please, Lizzie," Ty protested, "I didn't do anything that you wouldn't have done if our positions had been reversed. After my father behaved the way he did toward you, blowing you off when you came for help . . ."

"Let's not talk about your father," Lizzie interrupted. "These strawberries are too good for me to lose my appetite. The way things worked out, I prefer to believe that everything that happened was for the best. Who knows how long it might have taken you to break free of those manipulative mind games otherwise?"

"Maybe you're right. Twenty-odd years of Father saying 'Jump' and my asking 'How high?' was probably enough."

"That's for sure. It's time to move on, girl, and work wonders for someone else. And a good thing, too, because I'm a little overdue myself. I've got to learn to stand on my own two feet."

A frown crossed Ty's face as she shook her head. "But, Lizzie, there's still tons to do at Cobble Creek. The summer program . . ."

"Will get organized, one way or the other," Lizzie interrupted calmly. "This evening was a huge boost in getting the word out. You know how much I want the barn to be a success. But I'm never going to forget that I already have the most important thing in the world: Emma. Don't worry about Emma and me, or Cobble Creek, Ty. We're going to make it. But now it's Steve Sheppard who needs your help."

"But who's to say he'll want it? You've been my best friend. He's just . . ."

"One of the top riders in America, plus someone for whom you've had a soft spot for . . . jeez, I can't even count the years. But that's beside the point, anyway. What I know is this: my divorce showed me just how quickly things can go down the tube. Steve Sheppard is learning that as we speak. His best horse is dead, his shot at the Olympics has vanished like a puff of smoke, his reputation is tarnished if not ruined, and sure as God made little green apples, his land is going to be grabbed right out from under his feet. And you know as well as I whose hands will be the first grabbing hold of it. If you don't do something to help him, Ty, you're not going to be able to live with yourself," Lizzie predicted darkly.

She was right, Ty conceded with an inward sigh. Lizzie knew her only too well. Ty could never sit back and watch Stannard Limited steal Steve Sheppard's land. She knew the standing order her father had issued to the Eastern Seaboard Resort Communities Division. It had become Stannard Limited's battle cry: Buy every piece of prime land in the Hamptons over ten acres. If its location is even close to the beachfront, be ready to pay more than thirty percent above market price. If the property's auctioned, bid aggressively. Don't let it get away from you. And then develop, develop, develop. There was no way her father's orders would be disregarded, even if she begged the head of the division, who was a friend. He wouldn't risk putting his head on the block. So, unless she stepped in before it came on the market, Southwind wouldn't remain open farmland for very long.

"Hey, what are you doing?" asked Lizzie in surprise as Ty picked up the phone and began punching in numbers.

"If I'm going to keep my father's paws off Southwind, there's no time to lose. I've got to call my lawyer to arrange a meeting, figure out the best way to approach Steve Sheppard. I doubt I can get enough money out of my mother's trust fund, so I'll have to make a list of all my assets, figure out which ones I should sell—I'll need all the cash I can get. The tricky thing will be finding out whether the bank has already worked out a deal with my father's people."

"Can't you call someone at Stannard Limited?"

"They'd never tell me. Wouldn't dare. And it might

tip them off that I'm interested in the property. Believe me, they'd move fast to stop me. No, we have to use the element of surprise."

"How are you going to get the information, then, break into Daddy's office?"

Ty smiled. "Nothing quite so drastic. Remember Sam Brody? He runs a firm now that specializes in corporate security systems. It should take him about five minutes to run through the computer files at Stannard Limited. That'll give me the information I need."

"Isn't that illegal?" Lizzie asked worriedly. She hadn't seen Sam Brody in years. But now that she was an adult, a mother, too, chills of horrified embarrassment raced down her spine when she recalled the shenanigans she'd pulled while Sam Brody worked as Ty's bodyguard.

Ty shrugged. "More like bending the law. Since Sam's firm has ties with the government, he has carte blanche to investigate just about any company he chooses." An enigmatic smile curved her lips. "Something tells me he won't mind gumming up the works for Father, especially if it's to help me out."

10

$\mathcal{H}$e still had time for another drink. In the month since the night of the storm, Steve had poured more alcohol into his system than in all his previous years of casual drinking. It wasn't the quickest way to commit suicide, but efficiency wasn't the goal. He wanted, no, he *needed* to make sure he suffered before he finally died, just as Fancy Free had suffered before Steve put a bullet in him. So he'd drink and torture himself with memories of that night until his body and mind could endure no more.

It took only the minute shift of his head and the slight raising of his index finger to have the bartender, who'd been standing off to the side drying tumblers with a soft white dishtowel, to set aside cloth and glass and reach for the bottle of Jack Daniel's. Wordlessly, he poured a double shot into Steve's empty glass.

Fucking unbelievable, thought Steve with equal parts admiration and disgust. He'd never understood this about bars before, that a person's alcoholic need could be catered to without a single word passing through one's lips. God bless bartenders everywhere. He slapped a crumpled ten-dollar bill on the dark, scarred surface of the bar, idly wondering whether he'd have enough money for the tolls back out to Long Island. Hell, maybe he'd be able to bum a twenty off Tyler Stannard once he signed away his property to the man. His throat clenched spasmodically as the image of his home, his barn, his horses flashed in his mind.

Oh, God, how had his life come to this? Since the moment he'd raced into the pitch-dark confines of his barn, his hair and clothing plastered against his skin from the torrential rain, his heart slamming wildly, Steve had known, from the fear and dread twisting his gut, that he was about to face a living nightmare. The keening scream of a horse in unbearable agony pierced the night, louder even than the thunder rolling all around. He'd been right. His life had become an unending torment of tragedy, betrayal, loss.

Maybe it was time to finish it, finish it for good. He'd just tidy up a few loose ends first. Shifting his lean frame to the left, he shoved his right hand into his sportcoat pocket, rummaging, finding, then drawing out the creased letter from its depths. There, on the head of the stationery, in boldly embossed letters, read a string of WASPy-sounding names, the founding partners of one of New York's most prominent law firms. Representing Tyler Stannard, the lawyers were writing to request Mr. Steve Sheppard's presence at their midtown office at two-thirty P.M. to discuss a business agreement concerning his thirty-eight-acre parcel of land, known as Southwind.

Steve's first reaction had been to rip the letter into confetti, except that his lawyer, Jeff Wallace, received a copy, too, and had telephoned him immediately, urging him to listen to their proposal. If he was extremely lucky, Steve might avoid having to file for bankruptcy. So Steve was here, in this dimly lit bar in Manhattan, because some small part of him still cared enough to want to avoid that final, devastating humiliation. But it was a real small part of himself, Steve acknowledged with a glance at his watch. Twenty-seven past two, and he was about eighteen blocks south of the address on the letterhead. He picked up the glass of bourbon and took a slow sip. Yeah, there was still time for another drink.

The press of the ceiling-to-floor picture window felt cool against her bowed forehead. From the thirty-seventh floor, the people on the street below looked like overfed ants, hurriedly passing one another in muted shades of brown, gray, and black, an occasional red. She wondered whether he was down there somewhere. Perhaps he wouldn't even bother to show.

For the hundredth time she asked herself if this was the best way to approach him. But time was of the essence. Above all, Ty had wanted a meeting arranged as quickly as possible, and the contract ready and waiting Steve Sheppard's signature. Otherwise she'd have no chance against her father's company. Ty's personal lawyer, Douglas Crane, had assured her his firm could provide both. After speaking to Ty on the phone the other night, he'd suggested she come to his office the following morning to discuss the idea further.

"My dear Ty." Douglas Crane had risen from behind his desk to greet her as Crane's secretary ushered her into the spacious corner office. "Can Carol get you anything? An espresso, tea, mineral water perhaps?"

"No thank you, Ms. Grenelli." Ty smiled briefly at the secretary.

"Please hold my calls, Carol."

"Yes, Mr. Crane." The door shut quietly behind her.

"Come and sit down." Douglas Crane gestured to a pair of ornately carved, claw-footed chairs facing his desk, waiting until Ty was seated in one before claiming the second. "You're looking as lovely as ever, Ty," Crane observed with avuncular benevolence.

Ty smiled automatically in acknowledgment. His comment, though more elaborate, was as meaningless as the automatic "Have a nice day" one heard at least thirty times a week. Luckily, the routine pleasantries Ty exchanged with her lawyer would last only about three minutes before Douglas Crane zeroed in on the issue at hand.

"Thank you, Douglas. You're looking well yourself." Nothing less than the truth. For though his hairline had begun an inexorable retreat back along the top of his freckled head, and the bags beneath his shrewd hazel eyes were a bit more pronounced than they'd been the last time Ty had seen him, Douglas Crane had changed remarkably little over the years. In his late fifties, Crane prided himself on the fact that he was as fit as many of his younger associates. Very much like her father in that respect, Ty reflected, immensely grateful not to have to pursue that thought further, as she heard Douglas Crane clear his throat importantly.

"Since our conversation last night, Ty, I've given the matter you spoke of some thought. Let me be blunt." He continued as if his request had been granted. "You mentioned the possibility of retaining a different law firm to handle this arrangement between you and Mr. Sheppard."

"Yes," Ty replied evenly. "That is something I'm considering."

"Well, of course that is your option, Ty." Douglas Crane nodded easily, the bracketing lines around his smile wavering only slightly. "But, being the lawyer who has provided counsel to you for several years now, I must tell you I think it would be a mistake. I have complete confidence that Crane, Adderson and White is more than able to provide everything you need. For instance, Ty, you spoke of the need to proceed in a timely manner?"

"Yes, I'd like to approach Steve Sheppard as soon as possible."

"That being the case, I can arrange to have a preliminary contract drawn up for you by the day after tomorrow. If it meets with your approval, our office will contact Mr. Sheppard and his legal counsel and schedule a meeting between you for the beginning of next week."

"Next week?" That would be quick indeed. Ty imagined the small army of associates that would be involved to pull together a deal this size so quickly.

"Next week," Douglas Crane affirmed. "Were you to approach another firm, however, it very well might take that long just for the paperwork and documents to be gathered together. As Crane, Adderson and White has handled your financial affairs, many of those preliminary—and time-consuming—obstacles will be avoided." He shifted back in his chair with a carefully pleased expression on his face, as though imagining the ghostly presence of partners past and present cheering him on. Douglas Crane hadn't followed in the footsteps of his grandfather, the founding partner of Crane, Adderson and White, for nothing.

Still, Ty had hesitated. "Please don't think I'm unappreciative of the work Crane, Adderson and White has done on my behalf, Douglas. But in addition to the issue of timeliness, I need to count on your firm's complete discretion. You and my father have many dealings. This meeting, the contract . . ."

". . . Are matters of the utmost delicacy and will be kept strictly confidential," Douglas Crane interrupted smoothly, reaching out to pat Ty's slim hand resting on the arm of her chair. "I understand completely. I'll see to it that none of the partners who do work for your father have any involvement in this matter. As for me, Ty, don't you think you can trust me?"

"Yes, of course." She smiled. What else was there to say?

"Good. Excellent. Now, why don't we go over the specifics of what you need? I'll just buzz Carol to bring up the associate who'll be working under me."

And that had been that. Up to this moment, Crane, Adderson and White had performed its services with its signature brand of excellence. Its attorneys had gotten a contract whipped into shape, then sent a letter off to both Steve Sheppard and his lawyer. And now here they all were—all except one key figure. Apparently, Crane, Adderson and White's legal magic only dazzled some.

Still standing at her post by the bank of windows, Ty could hear the impatient murmur of the lawyers, hers and his, mixed in with the slapping sound of papers being shuffled, reshuffled, and replaced once more upon the long black-and-chrome table that dominated the law firm's austere conference room. Presiding in the middle of the table was Douglas Crane, flanked by a young partner and an associate. On the opposite side of the table from Crane, a few seats down, were two somber men she didn't know wearing dark blue suits. These, she'd learned, were the bank's lawyers. Directly facing Crane and all alone was a man in dark beige. She'd noticed him looking increasingly uncomfortable as the minutes ticked by. His identity was only too obvious: Steve Sheppard's lawyer. She presumed he had an office in Southampton, perhaps Riverhead, that he was accustomed to closing simple vacation house sales and pushing building permits through the zoning board. It was probably the first time he had seen the inside of a law firm like this one. Ty felt a pang of sympathy for him.

They'd been waiting for nearly half an hour now. There was a rustle of movement behind her, and from the corner of her eye, she saw Douglas Crane approach. He coughed discreetly and pointed to his watch.

"It's all right, Douglas. Since Mr. Sheppard hasn't called to inform us he isn't coming, we'll simply continue to wait." The tightening of his lips was the only sign of Crane's displeasure before he obediently withdrew to his seat.

The only other person waiting as silently as she was Sam Brody, here at his own request, sitting slightly apart from the lawyers, no doubt watching her as she stood with her back to them all.

A soft but penetrating knock was followed by the low, cultured voice of Douglas Crane's private secretary. "Excuse me, Mr. Crane, Mr. Sheppard has arrived."

"Thank you, Carol. Please show him in."

The sounds behind her altered abruptly, a note of purpose in the chorus of creaking leather as the men shifted in their seats. Now that their period of enforced idleness was at an end, she imagined the lawyers sitting up straighter, adjusting their ties and their shirt cuffs. She knew when she turned around that the expressions of boredom would have vanished, to be replaced with a ponderous solemnity, the equivalent of a poker face that lawyers practiced to perfection.

The swish of the door gliding over the beige wall-to-wall carpet signaled his entrance. Ty remained at the window, staring blindly. So many emotions assailed her at the prospect of meeting Steve Sheppard again, face to face. But two principal ones battled for dominance: anxiety and curiosity. What if Steve Sheppard rejected her offer of help? What if his personality had changed so much in these past ten years that she came to regret the impulse to offer her help? Was she being a total idiot even to try?

And she was curious, too. Curious to discover whether the memory she kept of him remained true. Was he still a man who possessed the power of a golden god, a being who could effortlessly make her heart race and her soul yearn?

Did he even remember her?

11

*O*ver the thinning gray and brown heads of the men, Steve saw the woman. Perhaps his eyes were drawn to her because she was the only person besides him who was standing. Perhaps it was because her back was to him, everyone else in the conference room had their eyes trained on him right now, carefully assessing. But there was something else about her, too. For long seconds, he ignored the others, focusing only on her strangely isolated presence.

Set against the rectangular expanse of the windowpane, she was the centerpiece of a haunting picture. Behind her, overcast sky met the grayish blue, angular lines of the skyscrapers across Park Avenue. Framed by glass, metal, and hazy muted colors, the woman stood, her straight, brown hair pulled back into a simple ponytail, the end of it reaching the small of her back. She was dressed in shades of lavender, a pale knit skirt and a matching top with short sleeves. Her bare arms were pressed up against the windowpane. They were slender and elegant. He couldn't see her face, for her head was bent, staring down at the busy street far below. But somehow Steve just knew. She was going to be beautiful. Really beautiful.

The opportunity to look his fill while her back was turned couldn't be passed up. Not by him. He'd always possessed twenty-twenty vision when it came to appreciating beauty. Silky, ivory-hued stockings caressed unbelievably long legs. Dancer's legs, slim, tightly muscled, and endless. Legs that could make a man forget his name. Her bottom, temptingly rounded, was outlined by the soft knit fabric that tapered at her narrow waist. He thought he would give his soul—he had nothing else to offer these days—for a look at her breasts. If she hadn't succumbed to plastic surgery, they'd be like the rest of her, as delicate as a flower just opening and as breathtaking. At the nape of her neck, where her ponytail didn't obscure it, he noticed a thin silver chain, and on her upraised wrist, a gold watch.

From his vantage point, she looked like a million bucks.

Okay, so that meant she was either Stannard's wife or his mistress, momentarily bored with shopping, deciding it would be more fun to sit in on the meeting and watch her man gobble up the little guy. Whoever, whatever she was, she was way out of his league. Especially these days, Steve concluded bitterly.

There was the muffled sound of chairs being pushed back, and his lawyer, Jeff Wallace, came over to him. "Steve, glad you could join us," Jeff offered by way of greeting, his voice tinged with a hint of reproach. "Let me introduce you to Douglas Crane. Mr. Crane represents Tyler Stannard."

Steve reluctantly suspended his study of the woman standing by the window and grasped the older man's outstretched hand, meeting his gaze unflinchingly. He knew Tyler Stannard's lawyer was taking in his gaunt face, the three-day beard he hadn't bothered to scrape off, his tieless shirt, his tweed jacket reeking of cigarette smoke and booze, the whites of his eyes so bloodshot from alcohol and lack of sleep that his irises, usually an electric blue, appeared almost purple. He held his own gaze steady, his sardonic expression clearly telling the lawyer he didn't give a fuck what anyone thought of him or his appearance. Steve's expression elicited a nervous cough from Jeff Wallace, who then patted him awkwardly on the shoulder.

"Well, Mr. Sheppard, let's get started," said Douglas Crane. "Perhaps you'd like to take the seat next to Mr. Wallace, so that he can answer any questions you have about the contract our firm has drawn up." Steve only shrugged his shoulders and followed Jeff to his place.

As he dropped his rangy body into the chair, a glance at the window told him the woman had moved. Quickly he scanned the room, locating her at the far end of the table, next to a man Steve guessed to be a few years older than himself.

Damn, she was looking down again, her features shielded. All he could see was the top of her finely combed dark hair and the tip of her nose. Not much to go on. She seemed to be reading whatever it was the lawyers were going to use to take his home away from him.

The man next to her, however, was staring right back at Steve, cataloging every detail of his disreputable appearance. Funny, Steve had assumed Tyler Stannard would be a much older man. And he hadn't imagined Stannard would resemble a pro athlete either, but who else could the guy be? All the other stuffed shirts were accounted for. The man's face, too, seemed familiar somehow. Steve was sure he'd seen him before . . . hell, probably in a photograph accompanying an article detailing Stannard's latest real estate deal.

It was clearly a lawyers' show. Douglas Crane was holding forth, leading the small group step by step through the contract. Steve was surprised at how much information they'd obtained on him. It was all there, in black and white; everyone in the room knew down to the last penny just how much money he'd lost through his stupidity. His stomach churned, rage and despair a bitter acid eating away at his insides. He tuned the lawyers' voices out, dividing his attention instead between the gray-skyed window and the dark brown head bowed so assiduously over the many-paged legalese.

The word *partnership* came at him like a cold slap in the face, brutally forcing him to listen to the quietly modulated words. Jesus Christ, partnership? What was going on here?

Abruptly Steve raised his hand, clearing his throat. "Whoa," he commanded, causing everyone in the room to raise their heads. Douglas Crane turned to him, his eyebrows raised questioningly.

"Back up a minute. I need you to repeat what you just said about a partnership. I seem to have missed the beginning of that part."

"Certainly, Mr. Sheppard. It's right here on page sixteen, section four, paragraph three. Mr. Wallace, could you show Mr. Sheppard the relevant passage in his copy?"

A loud, discordant buzzing began in Steve's ears as he read the paragraph Jeff pointed to. The noise only increased as his eyes moved up and down the page, as the intricacies of the deal became clearer and clearer. If his understanding was correct, Tyler Stannard had no intention of buying him out. Instead, Stannard was proposing to enter into a partnership in which he would reinfuse Steve's business with enough money to put him back in operation. In return, Tyler Stannard would have a fifty percent stake in Southwind, as well as in any future profits.

What was going on? Steve asked himself one more time. What would Tyler Stannard want with a partnership in a private riding stable? The man was strictly a land baron, buying, selling, developing. A nifty routine that had made him as rich as Midas. But that was beside the point in any case. There was no way Steve was going to agree to a partnership again. The last one had cost him more than he could bear.

Steve's eyes cut to the man seated at the end of the table. Steve could tell the woman at Tyler Stannard's side was watching him now, but he was no longer even remotely interested in what she looked like.

"Sorry, Mr. Stannard. I don't know what your game is, but no deal. I don't do partnerships anymore." His hands gripped the arms of his chair to push it away. With a quick nod to Jeff, Steve made to leave, missing the subtle exchange of glances that passed between the woman and Douglas Crane.

"Just a moment, Mr. Sheppard," Douglas Crane spoke up. "I'm afraid there's been some confusion. The person in question who is offering a partnership is not Mr. Tyler Stannard but rather his daughter, Miss Tyler Stannard. I doubt very much," he added officiously, "that Stannard Limited would ever consider offering you such a generous proposal."

His daughter? Steve's head swiveled, his eyes pinning the woman seated at the end of the table, at last getting a clear view.

She *was* beautiful, goddamn it.

As beautiful as the rest of her heart-stopping body. The realization only added fuel to the anger deep inside him. Large gray eyes stared back at him from a perfect oval face. High cheekbones and delicately arched brows framed the extraordinary eyes returning his stare calmly, unwaveringly, revealing nothing. Seconds ticked as the two held each other's gaze. If it hadn't been for the slight blush stealing inexorably over her cheeks, he'd never have believed it.

"Tyler Stannard, I presume," he ground out, furious. He didn't like tricks, nor did he enjoy the sensation of being the butt of a joke everyone else was in on. Miss Tyler Stannard had played him for a fool. And he'd had it up to here with rich socialites who got off jerking people around. Propelled by anger, Steve surged out of the chair. Three long strides took him to where she sat at the end of the table. "Get the lawyers out of here, now," he demanded, his lean, six-foot frame towering over her.

Silence, as Tyler Stannard stared up at his angry face, then merely nodded, regal as a queen. The effect had the lawyers, Jeff Wallace, too, standing and wordlessly filing out of the conference room.

"Him, too," Steve growled at the man he'd mistakenly, idiotically assumed was Tyler Stannard.

"No," Tyler Stannard countered. Her chin lifted defiantly as Steve glared down at her. "Sam Brody is my . . . security consultant. He has my utter confidence. Whatever it is you need to say to me, Mr. Sheppard, you can say in front of him." She spoke in a low voice, her accent screaming that here was the best schooling money could buy. In response, Steve's Kentucky twang became thicker, the vowels drawn out, a glaring contrast to the precise rhythm of Tyler Stannard's speech.

"I don't know what the hell kind of game you're playing, *Miss* Stannard. Nor do I take kindly to being duped. You want to discuss anything further with me, then he goes. Now." His head jerked in Sam Brody's direction.

Time seemed suspended as Steve and Ty engaged in a

silent battle of wills. Finally, Ty looked away. "It's all right, Sam."

Slowly, the man called Sam rose to his full height. Reaching it, he topped Steve by at least three inches and probably outweighed Steve's lean equestrian build by thirty pounds. Something about the expression on his face, a menacing look that promised retribution, triggered in Steve an elusive memory. Where was it he'd seen this guy before? Irritated that he couldn't place him, Steve was forced to settle for an answering scowl of his own.

They were alone in the large, deserted conference room, the tension in the air between them palpable.

Ty ignored it. "So, Mr. Sheppard, just what is it about my proposal that infuriates you so? Douglas Crane was quite right when he said that my father's company would never offer you a deal like this. Stannard Limited's tactics are a bit different. They'll simply buy your property as soon as the bank forecloses. You won't receive a cent from them or anyone else. The bank is scheduled to foreclose in ten days' time, isn't it?"

She didn't need to look at Steve to know she was right. Ty had all but memorized the documents Sam had obtained for her and could recite in detail the ins and outs of the mess Steve Sheppard had landed in. Persuading him to accept her help, however, would be an entirely different matter. From the moment he'd entered the conference room, he'd reminded her of a wounded lion, ready to attack anyone who came too close.

"Yeah, that's right. But it will be a cold day in hell before I accept another partner. No way will I let anyone screw me to the wall in the name of partnership, in the name of friendship. My horse died as a result of my gullibility. And if I were ever stupid enough to make the same mistake twice, I certainly wouldn't do business with some rich debutante who probably knows as much about how to run a horse farm as I know how to do petit point."

"I see." Ty paused for several heartbeats before continuing in a casual tone as if they were discussing the weather. "So you're a male chauvinist pig as well as a drunk. By the way, the stench of whiskey is quite overwhelming, though perhaps not to you—I gather you're used to it. Well, Mr. Sheppard, perhaps I'm not as deficient as you assume. For instance, useless, pampered female though I am, I could have told you in ten seconds flat that your bookkeeper was fudging the accounts. How long did it take before *you* caught on?"

Christ. How had she gotten hold of that information? Then Steve remembered good old Sam, her "security consultant." He'd probably tapped into the insurance company's records, which had seized all the computer files detailing the finances at Southwind for its investigation. It was hoping to dig up evidence to prove he'd killed Fancy Free so he could then cash in on his horse's insurance policy. The thought made him sick.

And there sat Tyler Stannard, looking so cool and poised. His fingers itched to shake her, wanting to take his misery out on someone. She seemed the perfect candidate. Maybe if he gave her a taste of the whole sordid story, she'd lose some of that smooth composure. In a fluid movement, he pulled out the chair next to her, dropped down into it, and lifted long legs to prop his booted feet casually on the shiny black surface of the table.

Douglas Crane would have turned apoplectic to see him thus. Ty watched as he fished out a pack of cigarettes from his tweed jacket. An eyebrow shot up, silently questioning.

Ty shook her head. She didn't bother to mention that she very much doubted her lawyers permitted smoking anywhere in the offices of Crane, Adderson and White. Steve Sheppard wouldn't care. She waited as he methodically lit the cigarette and drew a deep lungful of smoke before expelling it slowly. Only then did Sheppard address her question.

"I began to suspect there was something funny going on with the books last spring, but I was busy, finishing up the Sunshine circuit with eight of our horses, ironing out a few glitches with the transportation back north to get everyone back in place for the beginning of the northeastern show calendar. So I left it up to my partner, who'd gone back to Southwind, to straighten out the accounts. Only it turned out that my *trusted partner* was making honey with our bookkeeper, keeping her dazed and happy so she'd cook the books and hide the fact that he was emptying money from the farm's checking account. 'Cause when you're supporting a cocaine habit the size of Jason's, money runs out like sand slipping through open fingers."

She didn't even so much as bat an eyelash, damn her.

"What happened once Jason Belmar knew you were growing suspicious?"

"It was several months before I wised up." The admission left a bitter taste in his mouth, so he took a deep drag of his cigarette. "Jase'd been careful in the beginning, drawing small amounts at a time. Then, later, when his habit was growing really expensive, Jason got Holly, our bookkeeper, to doctor the numbers a bit more, so it'd look as if she'd made a couple of errors, neglected to record deposits, and that was why the figures didn't add up. He sweet-talked Holly into coming to me, all teary, begging me to give her another chance. Holly was a good kid, supporting her retired mother

and father with her salary, and just as snowed by Jase as
I was."

"Had Jason Belmar always had trouble with drugs?"

Steve's lip curled in disdain. "Yeah, sure, of course. I
purposely entered into a partnership with a cokehead.
No, Junior—or are you Stannard the second?" Steve
threw the barbed question out, assured it would find its
mark. "No," he repeated, "it was hanging around with
the likes of *you* that did it to him. Jason was a top-notch
rider when I got to know him in Gothenburg. He'd been
riding for some Swedish owners for about eight years.
We got acquainted, hung around together, talked about
our plans for the future. Turned out he was more than
ready to give up the European circuit and move back to
the States. I'd been thinking more and more about expanding my business at Southwind. So we became partners. Things went well for a time. Then Jase got mixed
up in a crowd that ran pretty wild. Friends of Allegra
Palmer, the daughter of one of my owners. Maybe you
know her, coming from the same circle." His smile was
unpleasant.

That startled her; he could see it in the involuntary
widening of her large gray eyes.

"Uh, yes," Ty murmured, crossing her legs underneath her knit skirt. The ten-year-old memory of Allegra
Palmer plastering herself against Steve's muscular body
flashed in her mind with startling clarity. "I've seen Allegra Palmer here and there. We don't know each other
well, though."

"You're not missing much. But Jase fell for Allegra
pretty hard. She led him on, kept him dangling, and
then dumped him. He was devastated, too stuck on her
to cut his losses and walk away. Afterward, he started
hanging out with her lowlife friends just to be near her.
That was the starting point for Jase's problems. I remem-

ber noticing it in his riding first, little things here and there, a careless mistake in a speed class, a weirdly wrongheaded approach on a course, given the ability or temperament of the horse he was riding. The mistakes began to pile up, one on top of the other. Pretty soon, his horses were getting rattled, losing their confidence. When I talked to him about it, though, Jase claimed it was burnout from the stress of nonstop showing. It happens in our sport, same as in any other, and I guess I simply didn't want to believe it might be anything else. So I suggested he take a bit of time off, work with the younger horses at the farm while I showed his mounts for him and wrapped up the season in Florida."

"How many horses was he riding at the time?"

"Three. I had four of our clients' horses, plus my own, Fancy Free. My other two were sitting out the season, back in Long Island. It stretched me to the max, trying to win with eight horses. I shouldn't have taken on so much, but I didn't want to let our owners down, and Fancy and I were going for Horse of the Year award." Steve paused, and Ty noticed the fine lines around his eyes as his gaze became shadowed. "But sending Jason back to the farm was a mistake. It only let his cocaine habit take over. And I wasn't around to stop it."

"I see," Ty said slowly. "You certainly have a good reason to hesitate at the idea of a partnership . . ."

"Yeah, don't I?" Steve shot back, his tone acid. "That's why your offer will never fly."

"You won't take the chance, even though you're facing bankruptcy? Surely, you realize that your career, your business, will be destroyed. Have you thought about your future?"

Steve remained stubbornly silent, sickened at the thought of his farm gone, his horses sold to cover his debts. "I was thinking I'd open a bar," he joked, hating that he was even having a conversation like this.

She didn't laugh, damn her beautiful eyes, merely continued in that snotty rich girl's voice. "Mr. Sheppard, if you don't consider my offer, you'll have nothing. Not a penny. And you'll never be able to get that parcel of land back. If my father's people buy it, they'll find loopholes to circumvent zoning codes, grease whatever palms need greasing, and turn your open pastures into half a dozen or more 'millionaire's cottages,' complete with swimming pools and tennis courts. And I promise you that the return Stannard Limited will make on its investment will blow your mind. Think about it, Mr. Sheppard. Think about everything you'll lose."

A sudden turn of his head, and Steve Sheppard's gaze hit her with a flash of electric blue. The alcohol he reeked of must be wearing off, because his eyes were much more intense now. Ty's heart took off like a rocket.

"Tell me, Junior, what's in it for you?"

12

*W*hat was in it for her?

Ty'd been dreading the moment when he'd ask that question. Tell him the truth? That in some secret corner of her heart she still cherished her youthful memories, her dreams of him, his existence a golden beacon in the barren landscape of her childhood?

Involuntarily, her fingers moved to the base of her throat and lightly fingered the chain circling her neck. She had only to show him the silver medallion to reveal who she was, to jolt his memory back to that hot summer day ten years ago. A day he'd obviously forgotten but she never had. No, she thought, rejecting the idea. If she told him who she was, he'd have the upper hand and wouldn't hesitate to use her absurdly sentimental attachment to a memory to his own advantage. So, instead, she offered a partial explanation, close enough to the truth to satisfy him.

"I like challenges," she stated simply. "Pulling Southwind Stables from the brink of financial disaster should fit the bill nicely. At the same time, I'll be thwarting my father's all-consuming quest for land and money. He's ruined some marvelous pieces of property in the name of luxury estates. When I was executive vice president at Stannard Limited, I couldn't keep him from pursuing a number of projects that destroyed some truly magnificent open spaces. Now there is one I can stop Stannard Limited from grabbing."

"Pissed at Pop, huh?" Steve observed with the precision of a laser. "Angry enough to blow a cool couple million just to put a cog in Pop's wheel?" He whistled low, in mock admiration. "Of course, that's only for starters. If you've done your homework, Junior, you'll know a horse business that operates at a profit is a rare breed. You know anything about horses, Junior?" Steve inquired casually, picking up the gold pen by her side and setting it awhirl between his long fingers.

"Yes," Ty admitted reluctantly. "I know how to ride, not that I've done very much in the past several years. I haven't had the free time to make that kind of commitment.

"Oh, yes," Steve nodded, delighted that she'd squirmed just a bit, evidence that she was uncomfortable with the direction the conversation was taking. Didn't like personal questions very much, did she? "Let me guess: working too many hours at Daddy's company. The picture's getting clearer here, Junior. You salve your conscience, get back at your Pop, and get the added fun of playing Marie Antoinette."

Ty's eyes flashed at Steve's crack, but refused to rise to the bait. "Horses take time and commitment. I wouldn't buy a horse if I didn't think I could devote enough energy to it."

"First smart thing you've said yet," Steve leveled her with an openly appraising look. "It shows you understand more about horses than a lot of owners I've dealt with."

Which was a strong argument for steering the conversation away from herself, Ty concluded. Otherwise, he might see far too much.

"As I was saying, Mr. Sheppard, Stannard Limited will grab your land without hesitating. I can help, if you'll let me. Please think it over; otherwise, you'll be throwing away your only chance." There, she'd laid her offer on the table; now it was up to him.

The time had come for some serious poker, Steve decided, lighting a second cigarette from the first. He didn't really want it, but that was irrelevant. It bought him time, let him figure out how to play his hand.

And what choice did he have, really? Miss Tyler Stannard was giving him a chance to save his property, his business, his self. But in a fifty-percent partnership. The thought that he'd no longer be head partner, in charge of making the decisions, rankled. Still, he needed the deal. Badly. The sixty-four-thousand-dollar question was, however, How bad did Miss Moneybags here want it?

"Okay, Junior, here's the situation. The longer I think about this offer you've dropped in my lap, the more I get the feeling I need a little extra insurance."

"What do you mean?"

His mouth widened in a warm, easy smile, as tempting as honey dripping from a spoon. Immediately, alarm bells began ringing inside Ty's head. Watch out for a man who can smile like that.

"I'm handing over fifty percent of my business, but what happens when something else comes along that tickles your imagination? For all I know, you may become bound and determined to save manatees down in Florida next week. I've got to have some protection here. Otherwise, what's to stop you from selling your half of the partnership or deciding it's not worth investing any more money into it?"

"I'm hardly about to turn my back on a multi-million-dollar investment or treat it frivolously, Mr. Sheppard."

"Well, now, I don't know that for a fact, do I?" he drawled, all down-home Kentucky charm. Ty wasn't fooled for a minute. "That means you'd better get those lawyers sitting out there, cooling their heels to add a clause or two if you want me to consider this proposal seriously."

"What precisely is it you want added?"

His smile grew wider, causing the little crinkles at the corners of his eyes to deepen. "First, I want a buyout option that allows me to purchase your fifty percent of the partnership as soon as I can pay back what you've invested up to that date."

"And interest?" she fired back, curious to see whether he was bluffing.

He wasn't. "I think eight percent accrued interest would be fair, seeing how you'd be recouping your money." Casually, he crossed one booted leg over the other.

"Any other stipulations?" Ty asked carefully. She didn't trust that easygoing manner for one minute.

"If you happen, for whatever reason, to decide you wish to discontinue our partnership, full ownership of Southwind reverts to me without my paying you a penny. Same goes if you die. No leaving my land to Pop in your will. Oh, and one other thing," Steve smiled as though remembering a detail that had almost slipped his mind. "As stated in the agreement, you'll own a fifty percent stake in my farm. However, I'll be calling the shots. Like I said before, I'm not interested in a rich debutante fooling around with my business. You want to invest your money? Fine. But I run the show."

Ty's temper flared at his words. How dare he presume she had nothing of value to offer besides her money? "Oh, I don't think so, Mr. Sheppard." The dangerous glimmer in her eyes belied the coolness of her tone. "I'm afraid you'll have to resign yourself to a more equitable partnership. There's simply no way I'm going to invest the kind of money we're talking about without ensuring the business is properly managed." She paused to clear her throat delicately, anger still burning inside her. "Much as I hate to point out the obvious, you don't have a very good track record."

For a second, she was convinced it was over, that she'd prodded his wounded pride too sharply. Then his body language changed and, leaning back once more, he gave a careless shrug. "You want to check the books from time to time? I'll send them."

And make sure she never set foot near Southwind. Or stuck her nose into his business. The business *she* was saving.

"That won't be necessary. I'll be staying at Southwind—at least until I'm satisfied things are running smoothly." Anger caused the words to slip out, surprising her and, from the expression on his face, astounding him. The words seemed to hang in the air, while Ty's mind spun uselessly, like a tire on a patch of ice. What had she done? A colossal misstep, that's what. Yet she couldn't retreat—tactically that would be an even greater mistake. "There's plenty of room on your farm; I've seen blueprints. The outbuildings . . ."

"—are all used for storing equipment and machinery," Steve replied, cutting her off.

"And your barn manager, where does he live?"

"About three miles away. He's a local."

Seeing his smile widen with each rebuttal only increased Ty's determination, no matter how ill-conceived the idea. "What about your former partner, Jason Belmar? Where did he sleep?"

"We shared the house," came the reluctant reply. Then abruptly, Steve shifted his weight forward, bringing his face close to hers. His eyes were mesmerizing, a cold hard blue. "Thing is, Junior, Southwind is a *working* farm. Not a resort. Anyone staying at Southwind has to be willing to put in some serious labor. As you yourself admitted earlier, horses require hours of care, involving a hell of a lot more effort than punching numbers into a calculator." Steve paused. A truly beautiful plan was taking shape in his mind.

For the first time since the ear-popping elevator ride up to the lawyers' offices, he was enjoying himself. So Tyler Stannard wanted to move in, take over, dictate to him how to run a horse farm? How long would she last, if she were removed from her pampered, hothouse environment?

In open challenge, his blue eyes skimmed over her, taking in the gentle swell of her breasts. Nope, no boob job there, he reflected, his earlier curiosity satisfied. Women who'd gone under the knife generally wanted a lot more to show for it—too much, in his opinion. But Tyler Stannard's body was a dream come true. And those legs. He frowned, pushing the errant thought away, belatedly conscious of how long his eyes had lingered, cataloging her assets. She was the last woman in the world he should be thinking of in those terms.

As though merely musing aloud, he laid the trap. "It just so happens I'm a little short of able bodies right now. I had to let go of some of my stablehands 'cause I couldn't pay them." His eyes raked her slender form once more, considering. "Admittedly, you're on the scrawny side. Still, you look strong enough." At the sight of him nodding happily, Ty felt a sick kind of foreboding settle over her. "Tell you what, Junior, if you're all fired up about being an active partner and wanting to

keep a close eye on your investment, you better be resigned to ruining that manicure of yours."

Steve Sheppard certainly knew which buttons to
press. Ty ignored the gibe with difficulty. "This is surely
unnecessary. If you sign the contract agreeing to the
partnership, you'll have the sufficient funds to hire these
people back."

"Yeah, and I will . . . eventually. But this way I'll econ-
omize until I've convinced enough clients that I'm not
the demon from hell these weeks of rumors have made
me out to be. So, how about it, Miss Stannard? You up to
the terms, or not?"

The unexpectedness of the situation threw her. Especially as this sort of scenario had been the farthest thing
from her mind when she'd approached him. Coming
into this meeting, Ty had had every intention of being a
ghostly, silent partner—exactly what Steve Sheppard
would have wished for. She'd have supplied the money
and let him run Southwind; the legal business contract
would simply have made everything legitimate. Indeed,
she'd pictured herself fading discreetly into the background once they'd signed the contract, perhaps offering advice—only occasionally, and only when solicited,
of course. That way, she'd have helped save Southwind
but not imposed. But then her bruised ego had caused
her to demand stipulations she'd never intended. And
when Steve Sheppard had fired one right back at her,
he'd shattered that safe, comfortable fantasy to
smithereens.

So here it was. Steve Sheppard had thrown down
the gauntlet. She could back down, let him believe she
was nothing more than frivolous fluff—wealthy but,
beyond that, useless. Or she could shove those preju-
dices down his throat and hope she'd have the pleasure
of watching him choke. But that would entail agreeing

to live in his house and accepting whatever jobs he assigned her.

In spite of herself, in spite of her frustration at being temporarily outmaneuvered, Ty felt a surge of admiration for Steve. He'd walked into this meeting with his life, his career, his finances in shambles, and now here he was, forty minutes later, dictating the terms of their partnership. That took nerve, arrogance, and ruthless calculation. Traits Steve would have honed to a sharp edge from years of professional show jumping. A part of her was secretly glad those qualities hadn't dulled over time. She could understand how he must chafe at the idea of taking on another partner. The conditions he'd laid out gave him a fighting chance, so to speak.

What his terms allowed for was essentially this: Steve Sheppard could break his back trying to repay Ty's investment, or he could try to break *her* and make her forfeit her fifty-percent stake in Southwind. The determined glint in his eyes indicated he'd probably try to work both fronts simultaneously. A truly neat plan, one with short- as well as long-term goals.

Was she up to the challenge?

Ty had never been afraid of hard work. No, it wasn't the prospect of the long, grueling hours involved or the countless jobs he'd undoubtedly throw her way that were making her hesitate. It was Steve Sheppard himself. Ty remembered vividly how infatuated she'd been as a teenager, those wildly handsome blond looks of his captured in countless photographs causing her heart to flutter madly, like the wings of a hummingbird.

Ten years later, the effect he had on Ty was enhanced one hundred percent. Like a potent distillation, his presence made her head swim and her heart pound.

But why? The idealized dream man of her youth had clearly vanished. Here Steve Sheppard was, sprawled casually, contemptuously before her, looking his very worst, about as awful as she could imagine: unshaven, unkempt, eyelids reddened with fatigue and drink, his face set in an expression that conveyed patent dislike.

It didn't matter. Something about him still called out to her.

Ty knew that living in such close quarters with Steve Sheppard would be like playing with fire. Then again, she was twenty-five years old and had been playing it safe for . . . forever. Why not do it? Her apartment already had a contract on it; the sale would close in a matter of weeks. All the money she saved by not renting or buying a smaller place could go directly back into shoring up Southwind financially.

Okay, it made sense economically, if disastrous emotionally and logically. Ty's head lifted at the muffled laughter escaping Steve's lips. The smile on his face wide, entertained by the spectacle of Ty's internal debate.

He was certain she'd fold, Ty thought, feeling her spine stiffen instinctively. No way was she going to be so easily intimidated, so easily bested. Summoning a bland expression, she leaned forward nonchalantly and pressed a round button on the intercom.

"Yes, Ms. Grenelli? This is Ty Stannard. Could you please ask Mr. Douglas and Mr. Wallace to come back in? There are a few details Mr. Sheppard and I would like to insert into the contract."

"As your lawyer, Ty, it's my obligation to point out how disadvantageous these amendments to the contract are. It's a serious mistake to agree to any of these conditions. Steve Sheppard is taking shameless advantage of your compassionate nature. I fear you're going to regret the day you signed your name at the bottom of this contract," Douglas Crane finished heavily.

Ty was glad to note his color had returned to normal. Crane's face had turned an alarming shade of purple as Ty outlined to the lawyers the terms Steve had insisted on. For the following forty-five minutes, Douglas Crane had argued, using his best rhetorical skill, trying to dissuade Ty, to make her see "reason."

Failure didn't sit well with Douglas Crane. It was clear that he was personally affronted by the events of the past hour. Not only did he dislike being on the losing end of a deal, but Ty's apparent naïveté was like a stain of dishonor. Douglas Crane's clients were many things but never saps.

The irony wasn't lost on Ty that Steve, as he was leaving the meeting, virtually echoed Douglas Crane's words, having just signed his name with a flourish next to hers. Only Sheppard hadn't been puffed up with righteous, lawyerly indignation. No, he'd been laughing, a low rumble emanating from his broad chest.

With a careless flick of his wrist, he'd tossed the Mont Blanc fountain pen onto the table, its cylindrical form skittering across the shiny black surface. "Well, Junior. All I can say is that you're going to be mighty sorry you signed on for this pet project. I'll be expecting you at Southwind at the end of the week. Oh, by the way, you got an extra twenty bucks you could spare? And I'd appreciate it if you could deposit a little petty cash into the checking account." He'd grinned in unholy amusement. "A couple thou should do the trick."

Both men, Douglas Crane and Steve Sheppard, were wrong. At least in terms of timing. It wasn't that Ty was *going* to regret her decision to agree to Steve Sheppard's terms. She already did.

What in the world had she gotten herself into?

13

$\mathcal{T}$he place appeared to be deserted. Ty breathed a sigh of relief as she killed the engine of her little silver VW bug, then grabbed her purse and stepped out of the car. Unwilling to announce her arrival, she'd parked the car behind a tall hedgerow in dire need of pruning. Above all, she wanted to postpone the inevitable confrontation with Steve Sheppard for as long as possible. It would give Ty the opportunity to look around Southwind on her own, without Steve Sheppard's undoubtedly hostile presence distracting her.

It was a blustery day. The wind from the ocean was strong, pushing battleship-colored clouds across the sky, whipping strands of Ty's long brown hair across her face. Feeling the autumn chill, she pulled the edges of her black shearling, three-quarter-length jacket more closely about her.

Yet even the grimness of the overcast sky couldn't detract from the beauty of her surroundings. Steve Sheppard's farm, Southwind, was located a few hundred yards off a small, relatively untraveled road, Horsemarket Lane. The slice of land Southwind occupied was

ideal and, best of all, protected, the farm and the immediate area around it having escaped the seemingly relentless development and overbuilding that plagued so
many other areas in the Hamptons. Facing south, Southwind's fields and paddocks ended just shy of the wide,
creamy band of sand that bordered the Atlantic Ocean.
To the west, Ty could see the silvered reflection of one of
the area's many ponds, home to fish, crabs, swans, and
egrets. And adjacent to Steve's property, to the east, Ty
had spotted another farm, from the looks of it a potato
farm, its barns surrounded with acres and acres of
neatly tilled dark brown soil. Ty knew enough about the
history of the South Fork of Long Island to assume the
farm was one of a handful remaining in the area, one
that had been passed down from generation to generation. Since the settlement of the area, Long Island farmers had taken advantage of the favorable soil conditions
to produce renowned and bountiful crops of potatoes.
But, with property values now skyrocketing, an increasing number of these farmers, whose ancestors had
worked the land before them, were finding it far more
profitable to sell out to developers. And who could
blame them when they could make huge sums of
money, far more than they'd ever make growing potatoes, corn, or any other crop the soil could support?

If she discounted the pale yellow corrugated roof of
Steve's indoor riding ring, partially obscured by the main
barn running parallel to it, a glance at the barn and the
outbuildings on Steve's property led Ty to believe that
Southwind, too, must have originally been a potato farm.
Perhaps part of the adjacent property she'd passed,
parceled off during a period of economic hardship. If so,
the split had happened a long while ago, because some en-
terprising individual had planted a continuous, unbroken
line of cheyenne privet along the border of the two prop-

erties, which rose now, a dense, majestic line of green, helping to create a sense of privacy in a landscape where huge skies met flat open land, where each house and building rose up, exposed to all and sundry.

Yes, Ty thought, her father's company would have cut this stunning piece of land like an expensive pie and sold each slice topped with a mini-estate. People would have been lining up to taste Stannard Limited's version of the good life.

Ty's thoughts were interrupted by the distinct sound of crunching gravel. With reluctance, she turned her attention away from the landscape. Steve was seated astride a light bay, walking toward her on a loose rein, the horse's neck bobbing rhythmically from side to side as it made its approach. Its ears were pricked forward, revealing far more enthusiasm than its rider showed. Ty wasn't fool enough to believe it was the smoke curling upward from his cigarette that was causing Steve's narrow-eyed squint.

The slightest tightening of the reins brought his horse to a halt a few yards away from her. A tense silence followed as Steve casually dropped his reins and rested one hand on his thigh, the other cupped around the end of his cigarette. With a final, deep drag, Steve bent over and ground the butt against the heel of his scarred leather workboot. In a gesture that was clearly habitual, he pushed aside the front of his black fleece vest and stuck the tan filter into the left pocket of his denim shirt. The scowl on his face remained. "You came."

It irked her that she didn't rate high enough on Steve's list to warrant a hello, hi, or any other form of civilized greeting. Well, two could play that game.

"Of course. You did specify the end of the week, didn't you?"

Steve ignored the sarcasm underlying her tone.

"Bring your stuff on into the house. I'll be over after I put Gordo away."

So much for any offer of help, but then, what had she expected, the red carpet treatment she'd been shown all her life? She certainly wasn't going to get that from this man, she thought with a flash of wry amusement.

Moreover, it was abundantly clear that Steve wasn't going to spare her another word, another glance. Gathering his reins loosely, Steve now centered his brilliant gaze was on a distant spot between the gelding's ears, over the top of Ty's head. The bay's ears swiveled, listening. Then, as Ty looked on, at first bewildered, then with growing awe, the gelding executed a picture-perfect turn on the haunches. The movement completed, Ty was treated to the view of Steve's broad back, the bay's gleaming hindquarters, and its long, silky black tail swishing back and forth as it confidently carried its rider in the direction of the brown weathered barn.

A heartfelt sigh escaped her lips as she stood, humbled by what she'd just witnessed. She remembered the weeks, the months she'd spent practicing that same basic dressage maneuver, the turn on the haunches, with her horse, Charisma. Of course, she reflected, most riders relied on their reins to hold the horse in check as the pressure from their legs asked it to move only its forelegs in a sideways arc, all the while the horse's hindquarters remaining essentially in place, merely pivoting in a tiny circle until the turn was complete.

But Steve Sheppard wasn't like most riders. She hadn't seen a leg move or a hand squeeze as Steve communicated silently, invisibly, with his horse. And, boy, she'd been watching with eagle-eyed attention the second she realized just what it was he was doing. A magician's touch.

As Ty recalled, he'd always been an especially gifted

athlete. Well, she could rest easy. He was still a phenomenal rider.

In the past, Steve had often pulled off the big, heart-stopping movements during competition that left spectators trembling with excitement and awe. But that was only a fraction of what made Steve such a great rider. It was the subtle things, like the turn on the haunches he'd performed just now, with such uncanny ease, with a naturalness that distinguished his achievements on a horse from those of so many other riders.

Hours, months, years of hard training, combined with a talent blessed by the heavens, enabled him to move in total harmony with his horses. When Steve rode, one couldn't help marveling, How did he do that? Other athletes in other disciplines inspired similar awe in their fans: Michael Jordan, Wayne Gretsky, Joe Montana. Watching them was a privilege one never forgot.

Still, it would have been nice if he'd helped carry in her luggage.

Nothing about the neat exterior of the brown-shingled, saltbox house with its French blue trim and matching wooden door, its mullioned windows and cheerful wooden flower boxes, could have prepared her for the condition of its interior. Stepping through the front door, Ty barely saved herself from falling over a small mountain of muddy paddock boots, field boots, Wellingtons, mismatched sneakers, boot hooks and jacks, and heaven knows what else. Still tottering, she managed to shove aside a dozen or so mismatched articles and deposit the two suitcases she'd brought with her in the small space she'd cleared.

Telling herself that it was the two-hour drive on the Long Island Expressway that had parched her throat rather than the sight of Steve Sheppard looking down at her, so cool and so distant, had Ty wandering toward the back of the house, bypassing the darkly shadowed living room on her right.

One look at the kitchen, however, was all she needed to realize that getting a glass of water in this house would be no mean feat. The stench alone—of rotting garbage laced with the sweeter stink of spoiled milk—was enough to send anyone with half a nostril running. Dishes cluttered the counter like leaning towers of Pisa, needing only a slight shift in the air to topple over. The sink was overflowing, too, with more plates and glasses stacked up to the level of the faucet. It would be impossible to turn on the water without knocking glasses and china over. Ty doubted, too, from the number of filthy glasses littering the counter space, that there was a clean one to be found in any of the wooden cabinets.

Perhaps a bottle of mineral water or a can of soda was hiding in the refrigerator. Trying not to inhale too deeply, Ty walked over and braved a look inside. A wedge of cheddar cheese sporting an impressively thick layer of green mold around its edges. A half-empty package of English muffins that looked as though it had been purchased years ago, the inside of the plastic wrapping moist with condensation. Nearby stood a quart of milk, the triangular spout left open, and four bottles of beer. They looked fine. Ty shook her head and turned on her heel.

He hated to admit it, but she was cooler than ice trickling down the back of your throat on a hot summer's day. Untacking Gordo quickly, Steve had let the gelding out in the upper pasture so that he could roll to his heart's content in his favorite mud spot; he planned to make Ty Stannard groom him later. After that, Steve had hurried over to the house, filled with a devilish curiosity to see her reaction.

Another woman would have taken one look at the pit his house had become and either fainted dead away from shock or else pitched a hissy fit loud enough to be heard all the way to Portugal, then hightailed it from Southwind, never to return.

That's actually what he'd been hoping for. But not her. She'd even made it up the stairs, where he'd found her in Jason's room.

Standing immobile, perhaps petrified with shock.

Only those disturbing gray eyes of hers moving from object to object, cataloging the destruction all around her: the chair smashed in so many bits it could be used for kindling this winter, the coffee table flipped over on its side, magazines and books strewn across the floor, their pages torn and crushed, their spines broken. Not too far away from the wall against which Steve had hurled it was the bright yellow Discman, lying broken in half. Halfway across the room was the CD Jase had been rocking to as he cut his cocaine into five regimental lines, the mirror balanced between his knees. The CD had ricocheted out of the Discman upon impact. Broken candles were all over the place, pools of melted wax stuck to the wide oak planks.

She must have sensed his presence, for she took an involuntary step into the room, distancing herself. The sound of broken glass scraping the floor filled the silence.

"Careful where you step," he said unnecessarily as she froze. "That's seven years' bad luck."

"I doubt that the mirror can get much more broken than it already is." Her voice was strained, raw, the only reaction to the unnerving sight of the destroyed room she wasn't able to hide. "And I thought the kitchen was a nightmare." The joke fell flat, as broken as the rest of the room. "Are you going to tell me what happened here, or shall I leave it to my imagination?"

Steve shrugged. "This was Jase's room; the bed's through those French doors. It's in a bit better shape." Holly had been lying in it, sleeping, dead to the world after a couple hours spent in Jase's arms. The violence of the storm that night hadn't roused her, but the sound of Steve beating the living daylights out of Jase sure had. Poor Holly had cowered in the bed, too terrified to call the cops until the very end, when silence finally descended. Convinced that Jase was dead, Holly managed to overcome her frozen panic long enough for her trembling fingers to punch out 911. Steve supposed he should be glad she had. His horse's death on his conscience was quite enough.

"I found Jase here, making his way through half a gram of coke, his Discman cranked to the max, while outside raged one of the worst electrical storms in decades. Instead of checking on how the horses were doing, he was blowing nose candy."

Ty surveyed the destruction around her, a stark, silent testimony to the violence that had occurred. Although she dreaded asking, she forced the question out. "What really happened that night?"

Steve's eyes became remote as a shadow crossed his face. Shards of glass crunched beneath the soles of his boots as he walked across the room and came to a standstill before the window. The clean, strong lines of his face were in profile to her, his voice low and rough. "It was Jase's night for barn duty. We had a rotation going: Jase; Bubba, my stable manager; and me. It was Jase's turn that night. Bubba was down south, visiting his son, and I, well, I was out . . . on a *date*, of all things." His tone full of self-contempt. "Hadn't been with a woman in months, what with the summer show season and all. When the storm came up, I was in a bar somewhere near Smithtown, sweet-talking a woman named Cynthia into taking me home to her condo. Hoping I might get laid. We only got as far as the parking lot. The rain was coming down in sheets, the sky white with lightning that just kept on and on. I left Cynthia standing in the mud beside her Chevy, knowing in my gut something had happened." His eyes squeezed shut for a moment, as if to block a too vivid memory. "I couldn't get through on my cell phone. Later I found out the electricity had been knocked out on the East End. The phone lines must have been overloaded with people calling. I drove like a maniac through the storm. And when I finally made it back home and opened the car door, I could already hear my horse's screams. They were louder than the thunder and lightning crashing over me." He glanced at her, his face etched in harsh lines. "I've lived around horses all my life, and never have I heard a sound like that before. I made my way to him in the dark. Fancy must have been rearing in fright from the storm. His stall had a haynet in it . . . he was kind of finicky that way," Ty's heart tripped at the fleeting smile of infinite sadness that crossed his face. "He thought eating off the floor beneath his dignity. When I found Fancy, he'd foundered and was lying there on the straw, his coat lathered with sweat, still screaming. His right foreleg was sticking out at a forty-five-degree angle from his shoulder, his hoof twisted around backward in that goddamn fucking haynet."

Steve broke off. Then, drawing a deep, ragged breath, he turned and demanded roughly, "Can you understand the kind of agony Fancy was in? To be lying there with his leg broken that badly, in that many places?" Anguished eyes locked with Ty's.

Ty only nodded, horrified, all too easily picturing the unnatural angle of the horse's broken limb, the mindless struggle of a pain-crazed animal.

At the expression on Ty's face, some of the unbearable tension inside Steve eased. Since the night Fancy died, he'd done little but torture himself with memories. He wasn't looking for sympathy, but knowing that Fancy Free's death affected her so strongly, too, made him feel less intensely alone.

He took a carefully measured breath and continued, his voice somewhat less strained. "The second I saw him there, I knew what I had to do. I ran and grabbed the rifle from the storeroom's cabinet and put a bullet through the best horse I've ever known. I couldn't let him suffer another minute longer; who knows how long he'd already been like that? I don't care what the bloody insurance company says, waiting for a vet would only have prolonged Fancy's agony. And the end, well, it would have been the same."

Abruptly, Steve felt destroyed himself, unable to think of it anymore, the pain of remembering intolerable. He was unaccountably furious, too, for having dropped his guard long enough to allow Ty Stannard to slip past and take a good, long glimpse inside the wasteland of his soul. And what a wasteland it was: horrible, burning, acidic. Most of all, private.

She didn't have the right to trespass on his pain, he thought, all his anger now channeled at his new partner. He didn't need or want her around, prodding festering wounds with her presence, her questions. Best to focus on his righteous resentment, nurse it until it was strong enough to banish any other conflicting emotions—such as that sweet relief from loneliness he'd experienced when he'd seen Ty's expression—and while he was doing that, he'd work on getting her to abandon this harebrained partnership idea.

"By the way, Junior, welcome to Southwind. This, of course, is your room." Although she could probably bunk on the sofa in his office, he wasn't going to let her take the easy route. No, sir. He watched her eyes dart around the shambles of her new room, their panicked path as eloquent as her shocked silence. It had been a really nice setup before, a sitting room and bedroom joined. Wasn't too cozy now, though. Definitely a point scored in his favor, Steve calculated with satisfaction. "You'll find a dustpan hanging in the pantry closet. Might come in handy. Before I forget, you've got kitchen duty tonight." There, that was better. He was clearly on the offensive now. As offensive as could be. Important to keep going. "By the way, that gelding I was riding? He needs to be brushed off later. You do know how to groom a horse, don't you?" She'd be gone in a few hours, Steve thought.

His voice must have travelled light-years to reach her. At last, she gave a distracted nod. "Yes, I know how to groom a horse."

"Good. Gordo's stall door has 'Vanguard,' his show name, on it. Watch your back when you're hooking him up to the cross ties," he warned with a nasty grin. "He bites. If the phone happens to ring while I'm gone, let the machine pick up. These days, it's either some journalist wanting to do an article about my fall from glory or someone I owe money to."

"Where are you going?"

"Out." To get down on his knees and beg Bubba, his former stable manager, to quit the job he'd found at a rival stable and come back to work at Southwind.

But there was no need to share *that* with his new partner.

An unanticipated expense but well worth every penny. Ty capped the pen she'd used to write out two hefty checks and waved a weary good-bye to the group of ladies stacking mops, buckets, dusters into the back of a rusted-out navy-blue station wagon. Last to go in an enormous vacuum cleaner, almost as big as the station wagon's trunk. That was some machine, a vacuum cleaner to end all vacuum cleaners. A large cylindrical shape, faintly reminiscent of R2D2 in *Star Wars*, it required four of the ladies to hoist it off the ground. *Effective* barely described it. Remembering the racket the thing had made, Ty thought it more than capable of sucking up all the sand in the Sahara.

The other check she'd written was already in the beefy hands of a man who'd introduced himself as Red Mundy. Red was the owner of a debris-hauling company Ty had found in the yellow pages, and he had agreed to come directly out to Southwind for an "emergency" removal. He, his son, Stan, and another man named Mack Wyzowski had worked for a solid hour, moving and carrying. Combined, the three men probably weighed close to six hundred pounds, and each time they crossed a threshold, they had to be careful to duck. They'd done a lot of ducking, for Ty had asked them to remove every single item from Jason Belmar's room—even the bed. A mattress company was scheduled to deliver a new one by nine that evening. Nothing would remain to remind Steve, or her, of that gruesome night his horse had died. Having just surveyed the now empty, spotless room, Ty considered the healthy tip she'd added to both checks wholly justified.

The rest of the house was immaculate, too, with the glaring exception of Steve's room, its door shut firmly. It hadn't taken Steve more than a few minutes to figure out what Ty was up to, watching her whip through the yellow pages, then begin telephoning and making arrangements. He'd informed her in no uncertain terms that his bedroom was off limits. "No one sets foot in my room without my permission," he'd snarled, before driving off in a battered pickup to God knows where or for how long. Steve's adamant refusal to have anyone enter his room had come as a surprise, for she assumed it was probably much like the rest of the house: a pigsty. Well, if he preferred to live in squalor, that was his business.

She should be grateful he hadn't objected to the cleaning crew and Red Mundy's debris haulers. Part of her had been prepared for battle, half convinced he'd insist that Ty deal with the mess herself, in the hopes that would be enough to make her run back to New York. Fortunately, he hadn't, for while she was willing to work, there was no way she was going to pretend she was Hercules. Setting this house to right was a challenge as daunting as cleaning out the Augean stables.

Even with the additional hired help, Ty spent hours, first supervising Red and his brawny team and then working alongside the cleaning crew, sorting junk into discard piles, cleaning out the refrigerator, searching for clean linens (by some miracle, there were some), making a list of everything she needed to buy at the store. By the time the hired help had left, Ty felt as if three weeks' worth of housework had been crammed into four hours. But at least the house was livable now.

Walking wearily over to the barn, she told herself that at least this job would be enjoyable. She'd missed being around horses. Not that she'd ever admitted it. After her father had sold Charisma, Ty had withdrawn completely from riding. Some perverse part of her decided that if she couldn't have the horse she'd loved so, she'd give up the sport entirely. A kind of twisted self-punishment that continued for years as Ty denied herself, ruthlessly suppressing the remembered pleasure, the deeply profound happiness she'd always felt around these majestic animals. Not even Lizzie's persistent efforts to get her back in the saddle had succeeded. Now that Ty was here at Southwind, however, she realized that opportunity was staring her in the face.

Vanguard would be her first reintroduction. Then Ty remembered Steve's parting caution about the horse's tendency to chomp. *Oh, joy.*

14

The heavy clouds had darkened considerably when Ty returned from the market she'd passed earlier that morning on her way to Steve's farm; night was falling. The hatchback of her VW bug and the backseat were crammed with grocery bags. Ty felt almost faint with hunger. Thinking back, she realized that the last meal she'd eaten was breakfast, back in the city. Upon arriving at Southwind, she'd been working virtually nonstop. Besides, anything she might have found in Steve's kitchen bore too close a resemblance to a high-school science experiment to be considered edible.

Arms full of brown paper bags, she fumbled with the front door latch, shoving the door open with her shoulder, then kicking it shut so that it closed behind her with a solid thud. A glance into the living room offered a view of Steve stretched out comfortably on the sofa, a long-necked bottle of beer resting on his stomach, his head turned in the direction of the TV, seemingly absorbed in the evening news. He spared her a brief glance before returning his attention to the news program. Ty glared at him, her inspection taking in the dampness of his dark blond hair, the toes of his red socks, propped on the arm of the sofa's faded but impeccably vacuumed upholstery.

At the sight of him lounging there, the grocery bags suddenly gained ten pounds. Her arms ached, and she felt utterly grimy. She hadn't even had the chance to shower off the dried mud that had been caked on Steve's horse which, as she'd brushed and groomed the bay gelding until he shone once more, had resettled over her in a fine, even coat. Ty remembered the involuntary gasp of horror that had escaped her when she'd led Vanguard out of his stall and gotten her first good look at him. Not even women paying hundreds of dollars at luxury spas were ever caked with that much mud!

Her butt was sore, too, from where Vanguard had tried some rudimentary, unanesthetized plastic surgery.

Feeling thoroughly ill used, hungry, and sore, Ty raised her voice loud enough to be heard over the tinny acoustics of the TV and enunciated through gritted teeth, "There are plenty more bags out there. I could use some help." She glared at Steve's red socks, waiting. When only silence greeted her comment, she let out an aggravated "Humph!" and stomped into the kitchen, trying to recall why she was coexisting with a neanderthal.

She was only slightly mollified when she returned and found Steve standing by the front door, bent over, in the midst of shoving his feet into a pair of dusty workboots. Ty's steps slowed to a snail's pace then ground to a halt as she treated herself to the doubly entrancing sight of jeans stretched over tight male buttocks and long, straining thigh muscle.

How was it possible for a man to look this good standing hunched over, balanced on one leg, shoving his feet into a pair of shitkickers? Ty wondered dazedly, feeling a warm, tingling sensation unfurl inside her.

When he straightened, Ty was still glued to the spot like a sex-starved ninny, salivating over his body. Horrified that he might catch her standing there with a besotted expression on her face, Ty quickly brushed past him. Out of self-preservation, she adopted the attitude of her classmates at the Swiss boarding school she'd gone to: nose stuck high in the air as if passing something particularly foul. The pose lasted only as long as it took to escape into the deepening dusk.

Was he doing it on purpose? She'd bet money on it. Tit for tat, she supposed he'd call it. It was unsettling— she'd rather die than admit exciting, too—feeling the weight of his eyes on her as they walked toward the car, her leading the way. Was he looking at her the way she'd been ogling him just seconds before? The idea made her acutely self-conscious, tempting her to stiffen up and check the sway of her hips as she walked toward the car. Cool reason, however, prevailed, and she realized there was no need. It was sheer vanity to suppose he'd care what she did, how she walked.

Perhaps if she'd been anyone else than Ty Stannard, he might be interested in her as a woman. As it was, he'd made it more than obvious that he wanted her around Southwind about as much as she wanted a case of head lice.

For a stuck-up, billionaire heiress, she definitely had a great ass. He'd flicked on the outdoor floodlights. There was just enough light to enjoy the show. She'd ditched the coat she had on earlier, now all she was wearing was a clingy black turtleneck tucked into blue jeans. Both fit her like a glove, emphasizing her narrow waist and long legs. As she walked, her buttocks had just the right amount of lift and fall to keep his eyes riveted. It was easy to imagine wrapping his hands around each cheek, feeling their firm weight against his palms, and drawing her close, real close.

He hoped her car wasn't parked too near, a mile or so down the road would suit him fine. When Steve caught sight of it, however, all thoughts of his partner's tempting butt vanished. Laughter burst forth.

"You've got to be kidding! News flash for you, Junior: Bugs aren't driven by people in your income bracket."

"What do you mean?" she asked. "It's a great car. Plus, it gets twenty-four miles to the gallon."

"Oh, yeah, that's right. All those cute little Toyota Corollas and Honda Civics you see on the roads, they're actually being driven by ultra-chic millionaires tickled pink by the gas mileage they get."

"Of course not. Don't be ridiculous," she snapped defensively. "But that doesn't mean . . ."

"Come on, you can tell me, we're partners, right?" Between sniggers, his voice oozed sympathy. "Pop withheld your allowance this month so you couldn't buy a new Porsche, didn't he? No wonder you're pissed at him!"

When he laughed again, her fingers itched, wanting nothing more than to wrap themselves around his throat. "I suppose it's never occurred to you that when you're the only one laughing, it's a good bet the joke's utterly pathetic." The sarcasm in her tone hiding how much his low opinion stung. Sure, she owned beautiful and expensive things, but she'd never been foolish enough to suppose those things *mattered*, that they defined her worth as a person. And she could easily do without them. After all, they weren't the key to happiness. If Ty had been shallow enough to believe that, she'd never have been able to stand up to her father and walk away from him and her inheritance without a backward glance.

But Steve Sheppard didn't know that, and worse, he certainly didn't *see* that. When he looked at her, all he saw was dollar signs. It was no doubt easier to assume that Ty was nauseatingly materialistic, something out of *Lifestyles of the Rich and Famous*. Well, if he wanted an image that reflected his narrow preconceptions, she could give him one in spades, damn him.

"I didn't realize cars interested you. A shame, I did have a Rolls-Royce Silver Cloud. Of course, it was just for the city." Her lofty tone implied that no one in his right mind would be caught dead in anything else. "Lovely car, as was my Lotus."

"So? You trying to blend in with the natives here? Should have bought a truck, Junior, an American truck, preferably with a hundred thousand miles on its odometer."

"I have no interest in pretending to be something I'm not," Ty retorted scathingly. "No, I sold both those cars last week."

"Let me guess." His teeth flashed in the darkness. "The garage payments were getting too steep."

The words were there, on the tip of her tongue, ready to reply that she didn't really need a chauffeur-driven Rolls out here—even though this was the Hamptons— and that the Lotus was only fun when you could put the pedal to the metal and make it fly, but she held them back, abandoning the disgustingly wealthy routine. She'd forgotten how quickly it grew tiresome. "Actually," she replied coolly, "I thought we might need the money."

His laugh was rich and deep. It occurred to her that

if he'd only stop directing it *at* her, she'd love the sound of it.

"Sure thing, Junior. And if I buy that one, no doubt you have a bridge somewhere near Brooklyn to sell me, too. Go on, give it your best shot," he encouraged, a smile lingering. He hadn't had this much fun in months.

"In case you didn't know, we're going to need as much ready cash as possible to reinvigorate this business. There are a lot of immediate expenditures facing us. Creditors. Major purchases. Employee payrolls." She ticked off the items one by one, as a teacher would with a student who'd bombed a pop quiz. "And unless they're antiques, even luxury cars depreciate in value. Naturally, they were the first things I sold." Ty explained calmly. "The same, however, can't be said for my Fifth Avenue apartment, but I was able to triple my initial investment on the sale. The market has been absolutely wild lately, don't you think?"

Steve didn't get a chance to reply, for she'd already turned and yanked open the back door, grabbing a hold of two more bulging grocery bags. "Anyway, I love my new bug. Who could possibly resist a car that has a built-in flower vase in its dashboard?" Gracing him with an "I don't really give a damn what you think of me anyway" smile, she left him standing there in the dark.

What in hell was that all about? Steve asked himself as he stared blankly at the ridiculously cute little car. The interior light of the VW shone brightly, providing the only illumination. One minute Ty Stannard had been doing a passable imitation of the Duchess of Windsor, the next she was lecturing him as if she intended to take over Alan Greenspan's job at the Federal Reserve. What was all this babble about ready cash? As the daughter of

a billionaire, didn't that make her at the very least a mul-
timillionaire? Why in blazes should someone as rich as
she go and sell off her fancy cars, her apartment on Fifth
Avenue, trade it all for a VW, and start lecturing him on
fiscal responsibility?

It was absurd. She doubtless had millions—and millions to spare—even if this gamble with Southwind
ended up a financial fiasco.

And what was he doing, believing anything she said,
anyway? Most likely, it was nothing but a play for sympathy. She was merely concocting some sob story so that
he'd back off and forget about regaining control of the
farm. The truth of the matter was, she was his adversary
in what had been the equivalent of a hostile business
takeover. With instincts no doubt learned at her daddy's
knee, she'd figured out a stratagem to lure Steve into a
partnership he didn't want and now she had a fifty percent share in his dream.

Even if some part, some tiny part of her cock-and-
bull story were true, why should he care? It had nothing
to do with him if she wanted to sell everything she
owned. No doubt a lot of rich people were nutcases.

Yet an unexpected stab of guilt pierced him when he
saw, to the right of the steering wheel, a slim black
flower holder with a jaunty daisy nestled inside nodding back at him.

And walking back toward the house, he found it impossible to chase away the memory of Ty Stannard's
subtly erotic beauty from his mind.

Or to check his growing need to experience the thrill
of her body pressed close against his own.

The tempting aroma of garlic and onions sauteing
filled the kitchen as he carried in the last two bags and
deposited them on the gleaming butcher-block counter.

It was great to see the house clean again. The place was spic and span. She'd even thought of flowers, he noted, eyeing the vase of orange and yellow mums on the windowsill.

He'd been intending to tackle the mess himself, but that was before he'd been cornered into this partnership. Afterward, he'd come back to the farm, and the overwhelming filth, the destruction of Jase's room, had taken on a new light. They could work to his advantage, be a definite plus. And so he let the dirt and disorder accumulate, avoiding the stench by spending as much time outside as possible. It seemed a small price to pay, as he'd half convinced himself it would do the trick and that Ty would wimp out immediately.

But no. She'd set the house to rights with the efficiency of a five-star general coordinating battle troops for a full-scale attack. Clearly, for "General" Tyler, failure was not an option. If she expected him to acknowledge this first success, she was sadly underestimating him.

But now she was cooking dinner.

Steve tried not to breathe, afraid he'd pass out from sheer olfactory pleasure. It had been almost a month since he'd eaten anything that involved more effort than opening a can of tuna or smearing peanut butter on bread. The bulk of his diet had been liquid, the main ingredients hops and malt. From the corner of his eye, he saw two thick steaks and a small mountain of sliced vegetables. Feeling his knees go weak, his stomach betrayed him, too, growling loudly enough to be heard over the sizzle and pop of rapidly cooking onions.

Worriedly, he glanced at her. Fortunately, she appeared not to have heard his stomach welcoming the prospect of a decent meal. She was standing over the stove, a long wooden spoon in her hand, gently stirring the onions. On the back burner, a heavy enamel pot was sitting over a high flame. Its lid rattled musically as jets of steam shot upward. He watched her grab a dishtowel, shift the lid to the side, and poke at the pot's contents with a fork.

"What are you cooking?" he asked casually, as if he weren't willing to sell his mother for a bite of home-cooked food.

"Steak, stir-fried vegetables, boiled potatoes. If you're interested in eating, you can set the table. There's some salad in one of those bags that needs washing, too. Dinner should be ready in about twenty minutes."

As she didn't seem to be pouting or holding a grudge against him after their conversation by the car, the least he could do was to eat her food.

Awkwardly, they worked around each other, both doing their best to pretend the other didn't exist. It was about as successful as putting out a forest fire with a water gun. Steve making the uncomfortable and unpleasant discovery that if he ventured anywhere too near his new partner, his system went haywire, his heart pounding as if he'd scaled Mount Everest. Unfortunately, because of the kitchen's design, the cabinets holding dishes and utensils were clustered on either side of the stove. It had never been a problem before, but then he'd never had a woman who looked as good as Ty Stannard in his kitchen before, either. That being the case, whenever Steve reached for a dish or some cutlery and found himself mere inches away, all the oxygen whooshed right out of his brain, rendering him so witless, so stupid, he kept forgetting what he was doing. Again and again he'd come back to the same drawer, the same cabinet.

With each return trip, he found his body drifting

closer, crowding her, until the rivets on his jeans were brushing up against her hip, and his eyes were straying, taking in the curves of her body, the delicate lines of her face. For the first time, he noticed the faint scar at the edge of her eyebrow. It did nothing to mar her beauty, only made it so she wasn't perfect. It was sexy as hell. Far too much about Ty Stannard was sexy as hell.

For what had to be the umpteenth time, he yanked open the cabinet to the right of her head. If she'd only turn this way, they'd fit together like two pieces of a jigsaw puzzle. And wouldn't that be nice. *Nice: frigging understatement of the year.*

"Excuse me, but what *are* you doing?" Her face was flushed, her smoky gray eyes round with confusion. And, he prayed, awareness.

"Salad bowl," he mumbled in reply, so far gone he could have been speaking in Chinese. He inhaled deeply, trying to pull more air into his lungs and clear his head. Lord, she smelled good, all lemony and sweet, even better than the dinner cooking behind her.

He thought about what it would be like to kiss her. It wasn't the first time the thought had crossed his mind. He'd been entertaining the idea with disturbing frequency since laying eyes on her at that meeting with the lawyers. Like a fine wine, the fantasy of kissing Ty Stannard got better, developing body, complexity, nuance, each time he indulged in it. Right now, what he wanted to do was to take her in his arms and let his body have what it craved: her soft curves pressed tight against him. His lips would explore the slender column of her throat, where the warmth of her skin mixed with the subtle scent of lemon, spices, and flowers. A slow, sensuous journey would lead him to her mouth, that mouth that he'd been looking at far too often. With a

gentle caress, his tongue would greet those rosy pink
lips, and they'd part for him, her soft moan of surrender
inviting him in.

Steve's head dipped toward Ty's.

The shrill buzz of the stove's timer rang loudly behind them, making Steve stumble quickly backward,
nearly landing flat on his ass. He stared at her, appalled at what he'd almost done. If possible, Ty's eyes
had grown even wider than before, her breathing
shallow. But that was nothing compared to him. He
felt as if his skin had shrunk two sizes. Probably
caused by the killer erection that was about to bust
the zipper on his jeans. Please, God, don't let her look
down.

Feeling like a horny creep in his own damned
kitchen, he grabbed the salad bowl and slammed the
cabinet door with enough force to rattle all the dishes inside. Ty gaped at him, her mouth a perfect *Oh*. She
clearly thought he'd gone mad, which he had.

As he was trying to gather enough brain cells together to formulate a satisfyingly cutting remark, the
two-note chime of the front doorbell rang, saving him.
Steve rushed to answer it, escaping from the kitchen,
getting the hell away from the woman who was turning
practically every aspect of his life inside out.

By the time the delivery men hauled Ty's new queen-
size bed up the stairs, Steve had recovered his scrambled
wits enough to go back on the attack. He didn't want her
thinking that almost-kiss by the stove meant he was attracted to her or anything.

"Shoot, Junior," he drawled as he shut the door behind the departing deliverymen, "when I saw you
threw out Jase's bed, I was convinced that was your
subtle way of letting me know you wanted to share
mine."

"Don't be absurd," Ty shot back angrily, her face pale.

"Just as well. You're not really my type." With that, he grabbed a jacket from the hook on the wall, shrugging into it as he said, "Can't stay for dinner after all. Forgot I had a meeting with a friend. Sweet dreams, partner."

15

*N*estled in a corner of the Four Seasons grill room was a table set and permanently reserved for Tyler Stannard, *Mr.* Tyler Stannard. Its location was ideal, away from prying eyes and eavesdroppers yet close enough to the oversized tinted window that it was bathed in the soft golden light that streamed in during the day.

Sitting across the rectangular table from Douglas Crane, Tyler Stannard monitored the subtle but telling signs of the lawyer's discomfort. His guest's roast quail, surrounded by colorful wilted greens and nutted wild rice, sat untouched, the roll of french bread crumbled into tiny, unappetizing bits, equally neglected. The glass of red Bordeaux quickly drained for the third time.

"I can't help but feel deeply disappointed by the recent turn of events. I keep wondering why it was left to my company to contact you, Douglas. Surely, after having directed business your way for so many years, I could have expected Crane, Adderson and White to mention that my daughter intended to enter into a business partnership without my having to go fishing for the information." Like a telephoto lens, Stannard zoomed in on the involuntary tic that made Douglas Crane's left eye quiver unpleasantly.

"Mr. Stannard, please understand, the swiftness of your daughter's decision took us all, my associates and me, very much by surprise." The lawyer hemmed, his throat working nervously. "I had anticipated that there would be at least a week's worth of negotiating before anything was signed. With that in mind, the wisest course was to wait until the details became concrete. When your daughter informed me of her decision to sign the contract at once, I assure you I made every attempt to dissuade her." Douglas Crane reached for his wineglass once again and drank thirstily. "What she did was pure folly," he finished, not bothering to disguise the scorn in his voice.

"That shows how little you understand my daughter, your client," Tyler Stannard replied coldly. "It was a serious error to underestimate her. Had the situation been carefully analyzed, you'd have realized what she already had, that the timing of the deal was crucial. If Stannard Limited had been alerted soon enough, we could have trumped her offer and still walked away with a more than comfortable profit margin. Now, not only have we lost that property, but my daughter is involved in a contractual arrangement that is unsuitable and unacceptable." At the last, Tyler Stannard's voice rose dramatically, as if someone had jerked the volume knob, a loss of control so rare that Douglas Crane involuntarily glanced left and right at other grazing billionaires and power brokers, acutely aware that conversation had abruptly died around their table.

"Mr. Stannard," Douglas Crane offered hurriedly, "my partners and I did everything we could to . . ."

"Yes, yes, I know," Stannard interrupted with a wave

of his hand. His voice had returned to normal. "You weren't about to risk losing my daughter as a client."

"Crane, Adderson and White prides itself on providing expert legal advice . . ."

"Indeed." Stannard inclined his silver head in agreement. "It does. Only consider the damage your firm will suffer when I drop a few hints about my dissatisfaction with the firm's recent performance. It's astonishing how many connections to people and companies we have in common, isn't it?" Tyler Stannard reflected, sounding far more friendly, even congenial. Over the years, he'd refined threat and intimidation to a subtle art. The smile on his face alone was enough to cause Douglas Crane's palms to sweat. "Just so there won't be any further regrettable misunderstandings, let me outline what I expect, Douglas," Stannard continued smoothly, confident of who held the power and control here, knowing the prestigious law firm would scramble to grant his every wish. "I want copies of the contract, the financial statements from the banks and the mortgage companies. I want all the details regarding my daughter's trust fund from her mother, how she financed the deal between her and this Steve Sheppard down to the last penny, how much money she has left to spend. *I want everything.* Have it delivered to my office this afternoon by four. And by tomorrow morning, I expect to find a memorandum waiting for me, from you, explaining exactly how you're going to blast that contract to smithereens."

"But, Mr. Stannard . . ."

"There are no buts. My daughter has recently become . . . misguided, influenced by the wrong people."

Unbidden, Lizzie Osborne Strickland's name flashed before him, accompanied by the specter of her pale face, her eyes staring at him, uncomprehendingly at first, dulled with hurt and despair, then filling with bitterness as understanding finally dawned. That meeting still clear and fresh in his mind, as though it occurred only yesterday rather than close to two years ago.

"I don't make personal loans, Mrs. Strickland, especially when it's obvious they don't stand a chance of being repaid—this one certainly won't be, given the size of your debts. My advice to you is to rethink this idea and try for a reconciliation with your husband. Although, after your disgustingly public display of naïveté, I can't imagine that he'd want you, even if you were to crawl on your hands and knees."

Good, Stannard remembered thinking, watching Lizzie Osborne Strickland recoil at his words. The few previous occasions when he'd had to tolerate her company, Tyler Stannard had never detected any particular sign of intelligence in the young woman, but this time, she seemed to have grasped the essential message quite quickly. She wouldn't be grubbing a nickel from him.

And then he'd gone in for the kill. "By the way, Mrs. Strickland, don't be so foolish as to suppose my daughter will lend you that large a sum, either. It would be useless to run to her with your unsavory marital problems. You see, I control most of her funds. I believe my secretary can show you to the elevators. Have a pleasant day, Mrs. Strickland."

Thinking back, Tyler Stannard acknowledged that refusing his daughter's friend had been a gross mistake. Perhaps his biggest blunder. If he'd simply paid the lawyers' fees, he'd have been in a position to determine the future of Lizzie and Ty's friendship.

Or, rather, lack of it.

It would have been the perfect way to rid his daughter of Lizzie's undesirable presence for good. Instead, he'd erroneously assumed that not only could he thwart her but that Tyler wouldn't be taken in by the woman's self-induced and wholly deserved plight.

He'd been too sure of his daughter. And of the reach of his influence over her, especially in the months following his open-heart surgery. Once the initial gravity of his physical condition had passed, Stannard had recognized that his illness could be exploited to his advantage and bring his daughter into line. For directly after finishing college, there'd been a disturbing phase when Tyler had displayed increasing and unmistakable signs of restlessness. Rebelliousness. The quadruple bypass on his heart had stamped that out most satisfactorily. Without voicing a murmur of dissent, she'd assumed responsibility for the company while he recuperated from the operation at home in Greenwich. Her seeming acquiescence had lulled him into assuming she'd bend to his will indefinitely.

But no. Upon discovering his refusal to help Lizzie, Tyler had turned her back on him, her own father. Her parting words still rang loudly, echoing inside his head: "I'll never forgive you for this, for the way you hurt my friend. How could you deny, then humiliate someone so important to me?"

"Lizzie Osborne has never been good enough for you. Her recent vulgar and exhibitionist behavior is precisely the sort she revels in. Moreover, she's perfectly willing to drag others down into the mud alongside her. You, for instance. This misplaced pity on your part is making you forget who you are, Tyler. Who you are as my daughter and as heir to the company, to the fortune I've put in trust for you."

"None of which means anything to me. Lizzie, however, is my oldest friend and one of the finest human beings I've ever met. I'm going to do everything I can to help her."

"Your reaction disappoints me. Deeply. These last few months led me to believe that you were beginning to understand your role, the importance of your future."

Ty's head had reared back as if he'd struck her. "You can't honestly think that all the work I've done for you, for the company, has been because of my exalted name, my supposed position in the world, or the promise of the fortune you never fail to dangle before my eyes like some scrap of meat for a hungry dog."

"Don't be ridiculous. This tendency of yours for cheap melodrama is unbecoming . . ."

"You just don't get it, do you, Father? You know, when you were in the hospital being operated on, you might have inquired about the latest advances in genetic engineering. Because it's pretty clear you don't need or want a daughter. You want a clone. But don't worry, Father, someone with your money should certainly be able to purchase that."

With her bitter words still ringing in the air she'd left, sending in her letter of resignation to the Manhattan office the very next day, accompanied by another letter, addressed to him personally, informing him that she was retransferring to him all her shares in Stannard Limited and that any money from the trust fund he'd established for her would be refused. His daughter, in effect, had cut herself off from him completely.

Rejecting all further contact with him, Tyler had used a portion of the trust fund established by her deceased mother to bail Lizzie Strickland out of trouble. Then she'd gone on to help finance a riding stable for the new divorcée.

And now this: his daughter entering into a partnership with a down-on-his-luck, two-bit horseman. The situation was intolerable. "It's imperative this contract between Tyler and this man, Steve Sheppard, be broken," he informed the lawyer, rising from the table as he spoke, forcing the other man to do the same. "I won't keep you any longer, Douglas, as I'm sure you want to get back to the office immediately. I look forward to hearing from you."

His hands twitching, Douglas Crane cast a glance at his untouched plate. Humiliation burned inside him. He, Douglas Crane, was being treated like little more than a lackey. However, threats by Tyler Stannard were never idle. The man was too rich, too powerful to ignore. With the loss of a few key clients that Stannard was able to influence, the law firm could say good-bye to revenues of fifteen, perhaps twenty million that year. And then, when Stannard's brand of poison spread?

Tyler Stannard had them stuck between a rock and a hard place. What Stannard proposed was highly unethical, borderline illegal—at the very least, the firm would be breaking confidentiality—but if they didn't dance to his tune, he and his fellow partners would go without the healthy roster of clients and equally healthy income they had come to expect as their due.

Tyler Stannard watched as, dismissed, Douglas Crane left the understated luxury of the Four Seasons grill room. He was satisfied the lawyer's memorandum would provide him with excellent advice on how to break up the partnership his daughter had entered into. Then, it would be only a matter of time before she returned to her proper place in the empire he'd built.

16

*W*here and when did this man ever sleep?

It was as if she'd stumbled into some Gothic novel, Steve Sheppard doing an excellent imitation of a tortured soul. Perhaps a haunted one, too. The past three nights had convinced her of that, one after the other following the same disturbing routine.

She'd be lying in her bed, tossing and turning, unused to her new surroundings and far too anxious about the tangled mess she'd landed in to do more than drift off for a few minutes at a time. For the remainder of the night, as the moon followed its path across the sky, Ty stared sightlessly at the ceiling, glancing occasionally at the bedside clock, frustrated thoughts of Steve racing through her sleepless mind.

The man was an enigma, one minute distant and sarcastic, the next piercing her with such heat in his crystal-blue eyes that she was briefly tempted to believe he found her attractive. But before she could decide for sure, he'd have switched back to the coolly remote figure of before.

Was this Jekyll-and-Hyde routine part of a plan to

make her feel so totally off-kilter she would give up and sign over her half of the partnership? Answers eluded her, leaving her to toss and turn some more.

But then, at roughly two A.M. each night, she'd hear the light tread of his footsteps pass her door, followed by the creaky groan of the wooden stairs yielding under his weight, and finally the muffled thud of the front door being shut.

All hope of a good night's rest shattered, she'd listen in vain for his return.

In the morning, no matter how early she arose, there he'd be, sitting at the kitchen table, a cup of coffee at his elbow, horse journals, horse show entry forms, and auction notices spread out before him, a pen stuck behind his ear and a yellow legal pad filled with his bold scrawl. Not that he ever showed her what he'd written. As the days passed, it was becoming abundantly clear that other than writing out and signing checks to pay off his debts, she wasn't going to be trusted with a single important detail of his business. *Their* business, but Mr. Sheppard seemed to determined to ignore that particular clause of the contract.

Well, tonight she'd had enough of the mystery surrounding his nocturnal peregrinations. She'd had enough of a lot of things around here. Ty grabbed a matching sweatshirt and pants and pulled them over the silk teddy she'd worn to bed. After shoving her feet into a pair of sneakers, she was out, standing in front of Steve's bedroom door, and, before giving herself time to reconsider, was rapping hard against the wooden panel. The sound echoed loudly in the quiet house.

No response, so she knocked again, just to be absolutely certain his footsteps in the hallway minutes ago hadn't been a dream. Nothing but deafening silence the second time, too. Cautiously, she turned the doorknob and stepped inside.

It took her breath away. First the initial shock, swiftly followed by the burst of anger. She didn't know how long she stood there, looking around in disbelief at Steve Sheppard's room. "The sneaky rat!" She exhaled, primed for a major reckoning with her partner.

Half expecting to find him in the barn, she went there first. A couple of lights, casting a soft yellow glow, illuminated the perfectly swept aisles, the deep roominess of the box stalls.

Ty moved quietly down the center aisle, aware of the muted, muffled sound of horses breathing. The three sleepy equines that remained at Southwind didn't even bother raising their heads to see who was trespassing upon their rest. She walked past them, past too many empty box stalls, and out through the slight gap left in the sliding carriage doors at the far end.

The glowing tip of his cigarette served as a miniature flare in a night where everything else was obscure. Recalling a technique described by an author she loved to read on business trips, Ty squeezed her eyes shut for several seconds, impressed by how much more her eyes could make out in the inky darkness when she reopened them.

He was off to the side, sitting by the wooden fence that enclosed one of the nearer pastures. His back was bowed, his head bent.

Her sneakers crushed the roughly mown field, made crisp with cold night air, giving him ample time to hear her approach. It wasn't until she was a few feet away that she understood where they were, why he was sitting there. Her brief flash of temper at his duplicity faded away.

"Mind if I join you?" Her voice sounded hushed,

softer than the night sounds that surrounded them or the rumble of the ocean off in the distance.

"Go ahead. It's a free country." His voice was quiet, too, nevertheless, she detected the fatigue and resignation underlying it.

Ty sank down to the ground near him, and there they sat, the long, black, rectangular expanse of freshly dug earth before them. Sudden hot tears pricked at the corners of her eyes as she stared at the uneven clumps of dirt. Her heart ached for him, for the depth of his loss.

She cleared her throat, searching for something to say. "I should tell you, the game is up. I went into your room a few minutes ago."

"So you've discovered my dirty secret." He didn't sound terribly surprised by her admission, or as if he even cared.

"*Dirty* isn't quite the adjective I'd use," she replied, remembering the understated simplicity of the bedroom's furnishings. The king-size bed, the row of bookshelves lining the opposite wall, the dark brown velvet sofa, brightened invitingly with colorful, plump cushions, the standing lamps placed at each end. The room was a haven, tastefully decorated with a keen, masculine sense of style. And not a single smelly sock in sight.

"Okay, I confess, I like things just as neat and orderly as you. Guilty as charged."

Her long hair brushed her shoulders as she shook her head in self-disgust. "Stupid of me to fall for it. I should have guessed it was a put-on the moment I figured out why you keep shoving all your filters in your front pocket. You can't stand for even a cigarette butt to fall on the ground and mess up Southwind," she accused gently.

"The filters on butts don't decompose."

"No, they don't, but that doesn't seem to bother any other smokers I've run into. Just to satisfy my curiosity, could you tell me how long you planned to let the rest of the house fall into unspeakable rot?" Ty inquired, her voice mild. "How long were you going to keep up the pretense?"

She felt the air stir as his broad shoulders lifted in a careless shrug. "Who knows? It was a reasonable bet, thinking you'd clear out when you saw the state of the place. Wouldn't you have been tempted to play it the same way?"

"Maybe, but it was still a low-down rotten trick, and now that I do know, I'd appreciate it if you used the dishwasher." She hoped she sounded properly chastising but doubted she was succeeding—on reflection, her profound relief at discovering that she wasn't sharing a house with the world's biggest slob outweighed her annoyance at having been taken for a ride.

The image of his neatly ordered room flashed in her mind once again. "Did you study history in school?" The question was casual, as if she weren't deeply curious to know more about this frustrating and complex man. The titles of the books lining his shelves had been a surprising revelation. But at least now she knew why he'd made that crack about Ty thinking she was Marie Antoinette. She wondered how many people were aware of this side of him.

"You mean college? Didn't have time for it. I've been riding full-time since I finished high school. But there's a lot of free hours to read when you're on the road, stuck in airports, soaking horses' legs, sitting around during rain delays, that sort of thing. You can only shoot the shit with friends for so long, and, anyway, I've always liked books."

"And the photographs? Are they yours, too?"

The tip of his cigarette burned brighter for a second or two.

"Took a real good look, didn't you, Junior?" The tone was slightly mocking. "Check my sock drawer, too?"

When she didn't reply, Steve let out a heavy sigh. "Okay, yeah. My parents bought me a camera when I first went overseas. I got to know Europe pretty well, traveling from country to country, following the show circuit there. Photography's been a great way to record all the places I've been."

"They're very good." An understatement. The quality of the work she'd seen far surpassed the typical holiday snapshot. "Am I right in thinking the large one over your bed was shot near Zurich?" It was a stunning picture, taken at dawn, the morning sun mixing with the mist and mountain peaks.

"That's a couple years old, from when I competed at the Zurich International. Fancy Free won the Grand Prix for me there." Steve paused, staring blindly at the thick clumps of dirt in front of him, while memories of that summer swept over him. Fancy had been in tip-top shape, full of his signature razzle-dazzle. The crowd had gone wild, cheering madly as Steve and Fancy Free turned in perfect round after perfect round. Fancy had loved all the attention, knowing it was his due. God, he missed his horse so damn much.

Ty's voice broke into his thoughts. "I remember the beauty of those mountains, the peaks especially. The notion of time vanishes completely up there, perched on top of the world. There's no past or future, it's just you and clouds and air."

"Sounds as if you know the area well. Winter skiing?" he drawled.

"I was at a school in Switzerland, in Gstaad, for four years."

"Oh. Did you like it?"

"No." Her response was flat, unequivocal.

Steve was beginning to expect the unexpected from her. For the past three days, he'd watched her—surreptitiously, of course. Three days of observation to realize just how different a woman she was. Definitely not the spoiled, flighty type. No, she was a class act, unflappable and efficient. With no fuss or muss, Ty got things done. He'd dumped some shit jobs on her, too, both yesterday and today, waiting to see what she'd do—everything from paying the mountain of overdue bills that covered his office desk, to telephoning the insurance company and badgering them for information on the status of his claim, to cleaning out and organizing the tack room. He'd even given her water buckets to scrub. She'd tackled each without a murmur of complaint.

It annoyed the hell out of him that he was beginning to like her.

That she was way too bloody desirable for his peace of mind wasn't helping a whole lot, either. Especially when he could tell that most of the time, she wasn't even trying to turn him on. Like now. Simply sitting next to him, warm, quiet, talking to him as if she were trying to understand, as if it *mattered*.

He wanted to touch her. Badly. The thought hadn't ceased drumming inside his brain. He ached to wrap his arm around her shoulders, pull her close, and breathe in the intoxicating scent of lemon on warm skin that was her. As if of its own accord, his hand rose. Then stopped and dropped. Because doing what he wanted, holding her, kissing her, would be too fucking stupid for words, and his stupid quota was already maxed out.

Christ, what was it they'd been talking about?

Oh, yeah. School. He wondered why a girl like her hadn't enjoyed being at one of those swank Swiss schools, the kind of school that has no need to advertise, its clientele assured: children of royal families, of oil magnates, of the ultra-rich. Her kind. "So what was wrong with the place?" he asked at last, picking up the thread of the conversation.

"I don't think any one particular thing stands out in my memory. It was just the school's overall atmosphere. I didn't like being in a place where the teachers judged the students and the students judged each other solely in terms of their parents' bank accounts."

"Bet that's true in a lot of rich kids' schools."

"Yes, probably." She fell frustratingly silent.

"So, what'd they teach you there?" he found himself asking, just to hear her voice.

Her soft laughter had a musical quality. "Oh, everything. That is, everything they considered essential to producing picture-perfect representatives of the upper class. Lots of economics, languages, history, math. Of course, we girls were given extracurricular classes in ballet, table setting, flower arrangement, and comportment."

"Comportment?"

"You know, walking, standing, turning, descending stairs, getting in and out of a low-slung sports car dressed in a brand new pair of Manolo Blahniks. All these skills were considered absolutely essential." Humor still laced her voice.

"What the hell are Manolo Blahniks?"

"An eastern European torture device designed especially for women."

"Come again?"

"Shoes," she explained patiently. "Very high heels."

"Jesus." He exhaled. "I thought you were talking about chastity belts." The corner of his mouth tilted, pleased that he'd made her laugh. "How'd you do?"

"At school? Oh, I was raised from birth to be an over-achiever. Anything less than perfection is unacceptable to my father. I can run in my Manolos if I have to, though that wasn't actually required. Running was frowned upon."

Silence descended once again as Steve tried to imagine that kind of an upbringing. Then Ty spoke. "I was wondering whether I could ask you something."

"Depends what it is."

"Would you mind telling me what your plans are? As your partner, I think I have a right to know. You can't seriously intend to rebuild your business by having me scrub water buckets and groom your horses. Though I'm sure it probably hasn't occurred to you, it's possible I can help."

The momentary sense camaraderie between them vanished into the frigid night. Steve's back stiffened. "Don't sweat it, Junior. The only help I need from you is the green kind. Matter of fact, I've been devoting most of my waking hours to mapping out how I'm going to spend all that 'ready cash' you've been stockpiling. That is, when I'm not thinking I should have my head examined," Steve finished softly, bitterly under his breath.

She caught it. She didn't miss much.

"Oh, please." Her own voice was now heavy with sarcasm. "Whatever for?"

"Who wouldn't in my shoes? First of all, I must have been frigging nuts to enter into this partnership with you . . ." *Especially because I'm wasting way too much time thinking about how badly I want to jump your bones. When instead I should be figuring out how to get you to sign over your half of the partnership.*

"Not everyone would immediately conclude that was a sure-fire sign of insanity," she retorted drily. "And second?"

"And second, for missing a horse so goddamn much that every night, I'm either sitting in his empty stall or out here by his grave, looking for answers in the dark." The despair was as raw and ugly as the large rectangle of torn earth before them.

A sense of helplessness gripped her as she sat, not knowing what to say, her mind awhirl. There was so much anger and pain inside him. More than anything, Ty wished she could reach out and touch him but didn't dare. She was sure he'd only rebuff her, thereby making the situation between them even more awkward and uncomfortable.

"Everybody deals with grief in their own way," she observed at last, speaking quietly. "I don't think there are any special rules written down outlining appropriate behavior when you've lost something or someone you love."

"And you're clearly an expert." He fired back, eager to lash out, letting the words hang there, a razor sharp barrier between them.

Ty thought of the mother she'd never had, the woman who'd died giving birth to her. She thought of her horse, Charisma, vetted, sold, and delivered to new owners without her even able to say good-bye. Thought of the hurt of being packed off to a finishing school, thousands of miles away from home, from everything familiar. "No, I'm not an expert," she agreed, suppressing the slight tremor that threatened her voice. She wasn't entirely successful but prayed he wouldn't notice. Ty refused to lose her composure in front of someone who thought so little of her, who wanted nothing to do with her. Then, in a tone layered with the impeccable politeness drilled thoroughly into the students at Ty's Swiss alma mater, she spoke. "Excuse me, won't you? I find I'm suddenly tired." She rose swiftly, gracefully to her feet, her retreating figure quickly enveloped in the cold, black night.

From Tyler Stannard's penthouse office in the towering steel-and-glass skyscraper built and owned by Stannard Limited, breathtaking bird's-eye views spanned all of Manhattan. On a clear day, such as this, Stannard could see as far south as the Statue of Liberty. The sweeping vista, like so many other things he possessed—from the butter-soft matching black leather sofas and armchairs hand-stitched in Italy to the large eight-by-ten-foot electronic panel that, at the push of a button, descended silently from the ceiling—underscored the impression that Tyler Stannard was a man who had the world at his fingertips.

Clients appreciated this. Delighted to receive an invitation to view videotaped presentations of Stannard Limited's newest development or luxury resort, they would sit, their bodies curled into the supple leather cushions, sipping vintage Dom Perignon from fluted glasses. Those who expressed appropriate interest would be flown to the chosen site in one of Stannard Limited's jets.

This morning, however, Tyler Stannard wasn't remotely interested in the view from his fortieth-floor windows or in any other aspect of his penthouse office. His eyes were trained on the papers spread before him, covering the sleekly modern desk carved from Brazilian wood which he'd commissioned from that country's top designer.

In an effort to make amends for his blunder of the past week, Douglas Crane had performed his task with admirable efficiency. Stannard's eyes skimmed the row of numbers from his daughter's financial reports, registering the funds she'd raised by selling her apartment.

Evidence of yet another bold move. Wise to sell now rather than wait until a later date when she needed the money. With the real estate market as volatile as it was and the viability of so many internet companies in doubt, it was better to rake in the profits than be stuck in a market gone bust.

She'd also anticipated that he'd block her trust or at least attempt to. In his brief, Douglas Crane had outlined that tactic as having limited potential for success but an option which Tyler Stannard could eventually pursue. Ty's trust had been established by her grandparents, for the benefit of her mother. After her death, Ty became the sole beneficiary. The trust was managed by a bank in Delaware, one of a handful of financial institutions accustomed to serving very rich families that had remained independent. The bank officer looking after the trust was an elderly gentleman from the old school. In Crane's opinion, it was unlikely Stannard would convince him that Ty's recent actions were in any way inconsistent with the provisions of the trust.

He'd try anyway. He pressed the intercom button. "Smythe, please call Bill Whiting at First Delaware. Set up an appointment for this week, next at the latest. I'll go to Wilmington if that's what he wants."

"Yes, Mr. Stannard," came the immediate, expected reply.

Stannard returned to the documents before him once more. He'd been studying them almost continuously since yesterday afternoon when they'd been delivered, wanting to distill his own impressions of the situation before reading Douglas Crane's memorandum, which he'd done earlier this morning. Unfortunately, his conclusions and Crane's were, for all intents and purposes, identical: his daughter had taken every precaution. The contract between her and Sheppard, while unorthodox, was squeaky clean. No lawyer was going to be able to convince a judge otherwise. Her finances were in order; she had enough disposable income to cover immediate expenditures if she wasn't too extravagant. And if Steve Sheppard's business picked up, bringing in paying clients, she might not have to rely on her trust fund for quite some time—a second argument against using the trust fund as the primary focus of attack.

If a weak link in this scenario existed, it had nothing to do with his daughter. But Steve Sheppard might well prove more vulnerable. Douglas Crane had faithfully described Sheppard's initial reaction to Ty's proposal. Clearly, Sheppard was bitterly opposed to the idea of entering into a new partnership and arrogant enough to demand the conditions inserted into the contract in the hopes of regaining full control of his business.

Stannard assumed his daughter wouldn't walk away from the partnership, however hard Sheppard pushed her. She hated failure as much as her father. So that left the option of offering Sheppard the money required to buy his daughter out. Yes, that would work. But, as both he and Douglas Crane had concluded, it was going to have to be a waiting game, with Stannard circling high overhead, waiting for the perfect moment to swoop down. First, Ty had to spend enough of her own money setting Southwind to rights that she'd be unable to match the amount her father offered Sheppard. It was a given that the sum would have to be colossal. Then that would be the end of the game.

Let's see, it was October now; he'd wait until December to make his move. Tyler would be back in her rightful place at Stannard Limited in time for the new millennium.

Stannard stood up and walked to the glass wall fac-

ing east, into the morning sun. In his mind's eye, he
could see all the way to the tip of Long Island. Yes, he reflected, satisfied with the plan, Steve Sheppard was undoubtedly the weak link. It would take a substantial
sum, even for a man of his wealth. But it would be
money well spent.

17

$\mathcal{T}$he remainder of the night passed much as its beginning had, with too little sleep and far too much anguished tossing and pillow punching. With the first feeble chirping of birds, though, Ty opened her gritty eyes, resolved to continue her effort to win Steve Sheppard's confidence. Unfortunately, this renewed determination did nothing to erase the violet circles shadowing her eyes.

Before even throwing off the covers to roll out of bed, the first thing Ty did was grab her cell phone and make two calls. First, she left a message on Lizzie's machine, asking her to fax or e-mail the client list they'd composed for Cobble Creek and add to it any other wealthy horse people Lizzie knew of. Anyone who competed or who liked to spend money lavishly and conspicuously. Before saying good-bye to Lizzie's machine, she also remembered to ask for Vicky Grodecki's number at the *Times* and her private number, too. Next, she called Sam's office, knowing they'd connect her to him immediately.

"Sam, it's Ty."

"At last. I was getting ready to call out the National Guard."

"Things have been a little busy around here."

"Sheppard running you around in circles? Figures."

"I never kidded myself that this was going to be easy, Sam. And," she added dryly, "I'm sure if I had, you'd have taken the time to open my eyes."

She heard Sam Brody's deep chuckle on the other end.

"Any word on the big bad wolf?" Ty asked, coming to the point of her call.

"Yeah, unfortunately. I was planning on calling you today about it. I asked a friend of mine, a private detective I've known since way back when I was on the force, to put a tail on Douglas Crane. Guess who he had lunch with the day before yesterday at the Four Seasons, and you get to go to the head of the class."

"Sam, I've never been anywhere else," Ty replied gently, smiling as Sam's laugh came over the line once more.

"Sorry, Ty, I forgot: a mind like a steel trap. It's only that soft heart of yours that gets you into trouble. Why don't you just forget this entire . . ."

"Sam . . ." Ty interrupted warningly.

"Right, okay. Save Sheppard's sorry hide if you want. Where were we?"

"I believe we were discussing Douglas Crane's lunch partner."

"Well, after your lawyer—you might want to think about hiring a new one, by the way—left the Four Seasons, he went back to his office at Crane, Adderson and White and stayed there until ten P.M."

"That's not terribly exciting, Sam. Sounds just like what any dedicated lawyer would do."

"Not terribly exciting at all," Sam agreed equably.

"Not unless you start considering why a *senior* partner would be staying that late at night, working on something that could probably be handled by a junior associate. Or whether whatever Douglas Crane was up to had anything to do with the two hand deliveries to Stannard Limited from Crane, Adderson and White that afternoon and yesterday morning."

Ty was silent for a few seconds, her eyes shut. *Damn.* "You've got a point there."

"Want some advice?"

"Please," Ty answered with a sigh, dragging her free hand through her sleep-tangled hair. Her head had begun to pound. They beat to the sound of Douglas Crane's voice asking whether she doubted his trustworthiness. *Idiot.*

"Get going. Don't wait for your father to come out with the heavy guns. With or without Sheppard's help, you've got to start drumming up clients."

"Actually, Sam, you'll be pleased to know I figured that out all by myself at about four o'clock this morning. I just left a message with Lizzie."

"The dynamic duo." Sam groaned, recalling the countless escapades the two girls had dreamt up. "Sheppard's not going to stand a chance if Lizzie gets into the act, too. How's she doing, by the way?"

"Great. Happier than I've seen her in years. Cobble Creek is getting more and more riders, and Emma is the sweetest kid you've ever seen. She looks exactly like Lizzie. Of course, Lizzie's as beautiful as ever. She was cutting quite a swath through the men at the benefit we attended the other night . . . Sam?" Ty broke off, alarmed. "You okay?"

"Fine, fine . . . swallowed my coffee the wrong way." He coughed again, loudly. "Listen, Ty, I've got to go, but I'm going to pull up your financial files, check them over. They'll give us a clearer picture of what your father is planning. I'll get back to you as fast as I can."

"Thanks, Sam, I appreciate it."

"Any time, kiddo, any time."

Ty replayed the conversation she'd had with Sam as she showered, drowning out her howls of frustration under a torrent of hot water. By the time she was rummaging through her closet for some dark clothing, stuff that could withstand serious abuse, she'd vented most of her anger at her lawyer's perfidy. After all, it had been a calculated risk using Douglas Crane, and who could argue that another lawyer would have been able to withstand the enormous pressure her father could exert any better than Crane? The important thing was that she and Steve had a contract, signed and witnessed. Now it was a matter of getting Southwind up and running.

Choosing a pair of dark brown jeans and a dark gray cardigan that she buttoned over a white cotton camisole, Ty brushed her hair back, twisting it into a bun at the nape of her neck, quickly averting her gaze from the reflected image of a grim, too thin, pale face, eyes smudged by dark violet shadows. Nothing like a couple of days in the country to put a rosy glow in your cheeks, she thought sourly. And how was it that she had been cursed with a face that showed every sign of stress and magnified it one hundred percent, she wondered, jabbing hairpins into the back of her skull with masochistic viciousness.

She caught Steve at the breakfast table, secretly pleased to find he looked almost as haggard as she. When he didn't deign to look up from his newspaper, Ty's temples began to pound anew. This, she truly did not need. *Here we go again, round six*, she thought cynically.

"I need to borrow your truck."

Her voice was level, but the flash of silver in her eyes warned him she was half expecting him to refuse.

And if he did, what would she do?

The tension in her body was unmistakable. When combined with that dangerous glint in her eye, it was fairly obvious she would just as soon wring his neck, grab the keys from him, and burn rubber down the length of the driveway. Oh, yes, Ty Stannard's temper was definitely doing a serious burn.

He figured she was still pissed from last night. He pretended to read on, ignoring her, knowing he was fanning the flames. Did she even realize how much passion was there, waiting to explode? It turned him on like hell. If Steve thought he could trust his own reactions, he'd have pushed her over the edge, just for the pleasure of watching all those emotions inside her erupt. But he couldn't.

Ty Stannard was driving him as nuts as he was her. But, Steve conceded, probably not in quite the same way. He seriously doubted his partner had spent the night trying, unsuccessfully, to block out erotic images of the two of them naked, entwined, their bodies moving against each other, slick with desire.

The muscles of Steve's jaw clenched as he felt the rest of him harden in response to the image he'd conjured. *Shit, not again.* He had to get her out of here before she caught on to the fact that he was sitting at the kitchen table with a hard-on bigger than the Montauk lighthouse.

So give her the keys to the bloody truck, already! Wordlessly, he let go of the newspaper with one hand to dig out the keys from his front jeans pocket, then hesitated. Christ, his hand wasn't going to fit.

Those intense gray eyes stared, waiting.

He shifted underneath the table, bringing his hips farther beneath the overhang, out of sight. Awkwardly, he pried the keys loose and tossed them across the table. And found himself asking, "What's the matter? Your bug break down?"

"I need something with an open cargo space. I'll be back later," Ty replied, her voice clipped, wrapping her fingers around the bunch of keys. When Steve Sheppard started telling her *his* plans, then she'd start sharing her own, reveling in the childishness of her attitude.

"Better be. I need you to clean out the van and make a checklist of all the supplies we need to replace. New York's coming up, in case you'd forgotten."

In case she'd forgotten! She had to grind her teeth to keep from shouting at him. She'd have to be a total idiot not to be acutely aware of how big a show this was for him.

The National Horse Show, held at Madison Square Garden, was the grand finale in the Northeast, before the horse show circuit moved south and the Florida season commenced. For decades, New York area horse people had flocked to the weeklong show, and, instead of bickering, she and Steve should be planning how they were going to attract new clients for Southwind. Ty wasn't certain Steve was aware of how numerous the rumors circulating were. Or how damaging. He needed more than a good ride to convince owners to entrust him with their expensive horses.

For reasons she refused to examine too closely, Ty was determined to help Steve. Ty even thought she had some pretty good ideas that she was eager to set in motion, but he was making it so damned difficult. The temptation to give in to her mounting frustration was almost irresistible: to jump up and down, scream the roof off, her mouth frothing rabidly, until at last Steve shut his own clever, snide one and listened to her.

Doubtless giving him the shock of his life.

The mental image had her grinning, cheering her up enough that she gave his keys a jaunty toss in the air. Without sparing another word for her irascible partner, she headed outside. Breakfast and restorative coffee could come later, much later. Because this had to be done first.

The tantalizing glimmer of an idea had come last night as she lay in bed, Steve still out there in the dark night, alone with his harrowing memories. That unsettling knowledge had been the source, for one thing was now perfectly obvious to Ty. Before Steve could get back on track with his business, he had to get over the loss of his beloved horse.

A daunting task, helping someone mired in grief. But Ty refused to be stymied. That's why she was going to carry out any project that stood half a chance of succeeding. If this failed, well, then Steve would doubtless continue being his stubborn and bull-headed self. Eventually, given enough time, he'd realize that she, too, was as hard-headed and persistent as they came. The trouble was, since speaking with Sam, Ty didn't know whether they had that much time to spare.

When Steve worked with horses, he was able to block out the rest of the world including all the worries and doubts that currently hung over him like an ominous black cloud. Of course, the irony was that these days, he had only three horses to work with. The amount of time he was able to banish his troubles was far too brief. There was Vanguard, known around the barn as Gordo, who was his top horse right now. Keeping Gordo company in the spacious, modern, and depressingly empty barn were Macintosh, a big happy tank of a horse whose hooves were practically the size of dinner plates, and a young mare called Cantata, bright and quick but green as grass.

Steve's mare, Cantata, was still in Preliminary Jumper classes, learning the ropes. So far, she'd handled herself well. She was a nice mover and possessed a good and willing heart but was nowhere near ready to face the tougher courses and higher fences of the Open Jumper division. Steve wasn't even bothering to bring her to the Garden for the National Horse Show; she wasn't up to that level of competition, and he wasn't going to risk frying his mare's brains because he didn't have a full stable. So that left Gordo and Macintosh, both horses who'd give it their all, but Steve wasn't feeling too optimistic about their chances. Winning the Grand Prix, the Puissance class, or the Speed class with either one of them would be about as easy as walking on water. Nevertheless, he was going to do his damnedest.

With Fancy Free's death, Steve had not only lost a horse he loved, he'd lost the finest equine partner he'd ever had. Finding a replacement for Fancy any time soon, or having someone step forward and offer him a mount of Fancy's caliber, were both fantastic dreams that couldn't be expected to materialize.

Although the Olympic trials for the USET weren't scheduled until early summer, Steve felt he'd pretty much lost that opportunity, too. But in the end, if anyone were to ask, Steve wouldn't hesitate to reply that the loss of Fancy Free hurt far more than forfeiting a shot at the Olympics.

It was time to begin the slow, arduous crawl back from the hell pit in which he'd landed. Riding well was the straightest path out of it and the only way he knew to persuade clients to come back to Southwind. If that didn't happen soon, all the money Ty Stannard had invested in Southwind would go right down the drain.

Thinking of Ty brought a scowl to Steve's face as he stood next to Gordo, fastening his horse's throat latch, then checking that the running martingale was properly adjusted. Bending down, he tugged rubber bell boots over the gelding's front hooves, then crab-walked back toward the horse's hindquarters, buckling on the gelding's leather ankle boots. Gordo had a tendency to "grab" himself when he jumped, his hind hooves banging into his forelegs. To prevent injury, Steve always rode him with boots on his fore and hind legs.

What was it about her?

He was thirty-four years old. His relationships with women had always been uniformly relaxed and mutually appreciative. He liked women, and women liked him. Period. In the past, though, he'd kept relationships casual, never letting anyone too close emotionally.

His career always came first. And after witnessing time and again how spoiled creatures like Allegra Palmer destroyed men with stunningly casual ease, Steve had given wealthy women an especially wide berth.

But for some inexplicable reason, Ty Stannard was turning him inside out. It wasn't because she was damnably lovely but because she actually seemed to care. That was what got to him. And it elicited a bizarre and unwelcome reaction. Every time he spent more than five minutes with her, anger started simmering inside him, he, who normally was the epitome of Southern, laid-back casual—at least when he wasn't competing in a jumping class. Part of him wanted badly to trust her, but the other part knew he'd be three kinds of a fool if he did. Frankly, it scared him how much he needed to believe in her. But then the anger would win out, triggering the resentment within. Christ, thought Steve bitterly, he was a bloody mess inside.

Gathering Gordo's reins in his gloved hand, Steve led him down the broad, clean-swept center aisle of the barn and then left, where the indoor ring was connected to the barn by a short corridor. He stared straight ahead, refusing to count the number of vacant stalls they passed.

This was the last jumping day he planned for his two geldings. After this morning's workout, his horses wouldn't see another fence until they entered the arena at Madison Square Garden. Then their legs would be fresh, and, with any luck, so would their eagerness to win. The remaining days before the National Horse Show would be reserved for flat work, concentrating on drills that called for shortening or lengthening strides and for keeping them rounded and collected.

Getting a horse listening and balanced on the flat was of supreme importance in show jumping. If your horse left the ground uncollected, chances were that, at the very least, a rail was going to get knocked down. Once that happened, it was a real slippery slope; the horse might get rattled, lose its concentration—if only for a millisecond, but a millisecond was all it took—and then *wham!* there went another rail, perhaps a refusal, and more penalty points tacked onto your ride.

The day before, he'd raked the surface of the indoor ring and positioned the jumps the way he wanted them for today's workout. He'd only set up five: a triple combination, then a brush jump on the diagonal line to a vertical set on another curve eight strides away. He'd made the mini course challenging enough for the two geldings given their different temperaments and abilities. Of the two, Gordo was the more experienced. A thoroughbred, he was a fast and aggressive jumper, which was great when chasing seconds in a speed class. But Gordo's hot temperament meant that unless Steve kept him well in hand, the gelding's preferred MO was to charge full steam ahead and attack fences from impossible distances. The triple combination was precisely the sort of element in a jump course where Gordo lost it. If the takeoff distance on the first fence was too long, that left him scrambling and flat in his approach for the next two. Most of the time, Gordo and Steve got lucky. But Steve couldn't rely on luck this time around.

Macintosh was the flip side. A big, seventeen-hand chestnut Hanoverian, he was the equivalent of a Sherman tank compared to Gordo's Maserati-like feel. Solid as a rock, powerful enough to get lift-off over higher fences and wider spreads without even having to think twice about it, Macintosh was a solid ride, careful to a fault. And therein lay the problem. Getting Macintosh to crank up the speed was like waiting for the bank to clear a check, an exercise in frustration. Steve had learned to rely instead on the horse's natural balance and awesome power. Often, they could successfully eliminate strides in a distance, or pull off radically angled approaches to a fence, anything that might shave off seconds and compensate for the gelding's lack of overdrive.

If there was a positive side to the nightmare of the past six weeks, it was that Steve's horses were totally rested and refreshed. He'd scratched their recent shows, he himself too stressed and battered emotionally to ride in competition the way his horses deserved.

Steve was pleased with the results of the self-imposed break. Although Gordo was full of spit and vinegar, the concentrated flat work and gymnastic exercises they'd been doing for the past month were paying off. Steve'd been able to keep Gordo rounded, jumping off his haunches through the triple combination.

Steve was cooling Gordo down, walking him slowly

on a long rein, patting the bay's sweat-darkened coat that was slowly drying as Steve allowed himself the pleasure of a cigarette. Through the open double doors at the end of the ring, he heard the rumble of his truck's engine. It was coming closer, the rattle of metal louder as the truck bumped its way over the field.

What in hell is she doing now? he asked himself, straining to catch sight of the battered pickup. The sound of the engine died abruptly, indicating that she'd parked somewhere in the pasture, frustratingly, however, outside the window's periphery. That nixed his chances of spying on her from a safe distance. He'd have to go check out what his partner was up to once Gordo was cool to the touch.

18

Ty grabbed the wheelbarrow's handles and set off, back toward the truck, the long-handled shovel banging against the rim as she pushed. The nursery had sold her the tallest pair of apple trees they had in stock. It was a good thing she'd had the foresight to ask the men loading the trees to place them at the very rear of the truck. As it was, she was covered with dirt from shoving the burlap-encased root balls the mere inches it took to bring the trees to the edge of the truck's tailgate.

Okay. This is it, Ty thought, pushing the wheelbarrow as close to the back of the truck as she could manage. There was a wisp of hair stuck fast against the end of her nose which she blew at, lower lip thrust outward. Then, when the strands didn't budge, absently swiped at them with the back of her hand, while staring fixedly at the truck's cargo, contemplating her next move.

Should she stand on the ground and try to pull the trees down into the wheelbarrow, or hop back on the truck, sit down on its bed, and give the ball a solid shove with her boots? She'd go with option number one; the second was too chancy. She might push too hard and knock the tree sideways, perhaps damaging the trunk as well as the root ball in the process.

Double-checking that the tree was in position, she scooted around the wheelbarrow, reached out, and wrapped her arms around the wide dirt- and burlap-covered ball. She gave a hard tug, pushing backward with her legs, feeling her arms strain with effort.

"Want to tell me why you're hugging trees in the middle of the day, in the middle of my field?"

Ty pulled again, ignoring him, the words they'd exchanged last night still stinging. He wasn't worth wasting her breath, especially since she was panting already, and the dratted thing hadn't budged an inch. She gritted her teeth, yanked harder, this time throwing her back into the effort. She pulled until her muscles screamed. Nothing. *Bloody hell.*

"Here, move out of the way. You're going to hurt yourself," Steve said, suddenly beside her. "I'll get the thing down."

"It needs to go into the wheelbarrow."

"I figured that. All right, you ready? Guide it into the barrow as I lower it."

"Okay," Ty replied, too grateful to argue. She was coming to the conclusion that Steve Sheppard possessed a real gift for making her feel like an emotional yo-yo. She assumed he was fully aware of his ability.

They stood on opposite sides of the wheelbarrow. Steve positioned his feet beneath the overhanging steel panel of the truck's gate, then leaned forward to grab hold of the root ball. As he wrapped his upper body around the base of the sapling, whipcord-lean muscles flexed beneath soft flannel. Ty's mouth went dry as with a single, fluid movement, Steve hauled back, bringing the root ball toward him, pebbles and dirt scraping roughly against the metal bed. For a second the burlap-covered ball hung suspended over the wheelbarrow, Ty quickly thrust her arms out, grabbing hold.

"Okay, I've got it. You can lower it now." Ty said breathlessly, disturbingly aware of his body close to hers.

A minute later, Steve was following her with the wheelbarrow as she led him over to the grave. When she came to a stop at one end of the freshly overturned earth and turned to him, he raised a dark blond brow in silent inquiry. Nervously, she cleared her throat, abruptly uncertain whether perhaps she'd gone too far, whether she'd trespassed unforgivably.

"They're apple trees," she explained, stammering a little. "According to the man at the nursery, there hasn't been a hard frost yet, so the trees can be safely planted. If Mother Nature cooperates, they might even bloom next spring. I thought . . ."

"Fancy loved apples," Steve interrupted quietly. "They were his favorite treat. What was your idea, a tree on either end?"

She nodded, then surreptitiously studied his face as he stepped back and looked at the scene before him, as though imagining the two trees framing the spot where his horse lay. Ty's breath hitched as she caught the small smile that lifted the corners of Steve's mouth.

"Yeah, Fancy will like lying in the shade of apple trees," Steve pronounced, grabbing the shovel from the barrow and walking over to where she stood. "You want me to start digging, or should we go and get the other tree first?"

"Let's get the other one and position them the way you like. Afterward, I can run back to the shed and grab a second shovel. The digging'll go quicker that way."

"Right. Let's do it." Steve thrust the shovel into the soft ground, hefted the tree from the depths of the wheelbarrow, and lowered it gently next to where Ty stood. She was glad his concentration was elsewhere. It was hard to remain unaffected by such a casual display of strength.

Without a hitch, the two of them repeated the same procedure for the second tree. As soon as it was aligned, Ty sprinted back to the shed for another shovel.

Steve paused in his own digging to watch Ty racing back to the grave, metal shovel swinging by her side. She was flushed and dirty, her gray eyes shining as they met his fleetingly. Without fanfare, Ty immediately set to work, propping her booted foot against the lip of the shovel and pushing down hard, then bending knees and back to scoop out the rich, brown soil. Steve's heart performed a strange acrobatic leap, as if suddenly set free, seeing her there, looking so lovely, dirty streaks and all. There she was, his wealthy million-billionairess, digging in the dirt because that might make him feel better. The notion boggled his mind, completely outside his realm of expectations. Just knowing that she'd spent time thinking up the idea, out of concern for his dead horse, out of concern for *him*, stunned him. That she was out here, doing this grubby work, hauling trees, digging in the dirt, was no less than astonishing.

He hadn't anticipated such simple yet exquisite kindness from her.

Resting his forearms against the top of the shovel's handle, he regarded her curiously. "You know, you could have hired one of the men at the nursery to give you a hand. That's how these landscape companies make their fortune out here."

Ty nodded, continuing the rhythm of thrusting the shovel into the ground and upending dirt. "Well, I did have to ask them for instructions. I've never planted a tree before," she confessed with a quick, shy smile. "But it didn't seem that difficult when they explained how to do it. Besides, if they'd done the work, it wouldn't have been the same, would it?" Ty asked, knowing the answer in her own heart. "But I'm glad you came around to lend a hand," she confessed a little breathlessly, working the shovel around a particularly cumbersome clump. "The digging's bound to go a lot faster. And those trees must have grown during the ride over. They're a lot heavier than they were supposed to be!"

Steve chuckled, a sound that had Ty's heart drumming with happiness. Then the two of them resumed digging in earnest—and for the first time since Ty's arrival at Southwind, working side by side in companionable silence.

"They look wonderful," Ty pronounced, filled with quiet satisfaction at the sight of the two small trees neatly planted, bracketing Fancy Free's grave.

"Yeah, they do," Steve agreed. "Thank you, Ty."

At his quietly spoken words, bittersweet emotion flooded her. This was definitely a day for firsts: here he was, finally treating her like something other than the enemy.

And he'd said her name, rather than some clever nickname he'd invented. She drew in a shaky breath, telling herself not to read too much into this apparent transformation.

"There were some nice wooden benches on sale at the nursery. I thought maybe . . ."

"Yeah, that'd be good." He nodded. "The ground's getting damn cold, even without a frost." When he grinned, Steve's blue eyes crinkled. Lord, he was attractive, disarmingly so. This new, easygoing version of Steve Sheppard was making her positively lightheaded.

The feeling only intensified when he reached out and retrieved the shovel from her hand, his fingers casually brushing her own.

As from a distance, Ty heard him ask, "What do you think of alfalfa and timothy?"

Thoroughly flustered by the fact that even the slightest contact of his skin against hers set her pulse racing and her body trembling, Steve's question left Ty completely at a loss. "I beg your pardon?"

"For the ground," he explained. "How about sowing some sweet hay so it grows over the grave?"

"Oh, of course. I can already picture it in the summertime. It'll be a lovely spot."

"Thanks to you." Their eyes met and held. Then, with an abrupt sigh, Steve raked a hand roughly through his closely cropped hair. "Look, I'd like to apologize. I've been acting like an ass."

He paused, giving her the chance to flay him alive, yet a quick glance at Ty's face told him she wasn't going to take it. Still, he knew he had to apologize. "I assume from your silence that's your polite way of agreeing with me," he observed wryly, startling a laugh from her.

"Hmm, I guess you could say that," she said.

"Look, I don't want you as a partner—we both know that. But I've said some things that were out of line, like that crack last night I made about you not understanding anything about losing something you love. I've been feeling really bad about that. It was uncalled for, and I'm sorry. I don't know anything about you . . ." As he spoke, Steve glanced over at Ty to gauge the effect of his words, breaking off abruptly, concern etching his brow. "Hey, you're trembling." He stepped closer, taking in her pale face and shadowed eyes.

"It's nothing," Ty mumbled, refusing to look at him, suddenly feeling too close to the edge emotionally to withstand his scrutiny. It must be the stress, the nerves, the fatigue. "I'm just cold all of a sudden."

The force was magnetic, drawing him to her, thoughts careening inside his head, blaring commands for his body to follow. *Touch her. Hold her. Kiss her.*

His movements were slow, unhurried, but thrillingly certain nonetheless. And so right. Fiery excitement coursed through his veins as he grasped her delicate shoulders and brought their bodies into perfect, sweet alignment. Steve's head dipped, his chiseled profile a baby's breath away from her own. Blue and gray eyes met. Intense longing mixed with apprehension were mirrored in them both. For Steve, the desire he'd felt building inside him these past days won out, conquering all.

"I'd really like to kiss you," he whispered, and took her faint indrawn breath for a yes. Firm lips descended, brushing a gossamer kiss against her softly parted ones. Withdrawing only to return, their lips met in a second, clinging caress, and Steve felt a jolt of recognition race through him.

The taste of Ty was unlike anything he'd ever experienced. He needed more.

A heart-stopping smile spread across his face as he took in the helpless trembling of her lips, her shoulders. She was shaking like a leaf. Steve leaned into her, the warmth from his body enveloping her. "Still cold?" he asked in a husky voice. "Let's see whether together we can't warm you up."

This time his lips swooped down to claim. And Ty never even considered resisting. A golden, honeyed languor seemed to fill her. Her senses caressed and heightened, she gave herself over to the wonder of Steve's embrace.

It was nothing like her dreams of him—those youthful, romantic fantasies, so pale and tepid. How could she have imagined the wild, blasting heat of him? How his touch would have her melting? How she'd lose herself in his passion-fired eyes, in his drugging kisses, in his hands learning the curves of her flushed body? And the brilliant sparks, dazzlingly radiant, the colors of fireworks on a sultry summer's night that he ignited inside her? No, she could never have imagined something like this.

Ty swayed closer, loving the hard, dangerous heat of him, the way he responded immediately, arms tightening, bands of warm steel, mouth fusing against hers, stoking her need until it became a wildfire, searing them both.

Never could Ty have imagined such glorious passion. Nor could she ever have imagined that they would be interrupted at a time like this.

By a man, leaning against the pasture's wooden fence, yelling Steve's name, making the two of them jump the proverbial mile apart—as if, instead of heated flesh, they had grasped live wires. After the sweet inferno of Steve's embrace, the air around Ty seemed arctic, slicing through flesh right to the bone. Too shaken by the intensity of their kiss and her response, it took her several seconds before she realized that one of the reasons she felt the cold so acutely was that Steve had made quick work of the buttons on her sweater. She was standing in a pasture, her sweater hanging from her elbows.

Cheeks flaming, Ty tucked her chin, her fingers fumbling with the bone buttons on her cardigan, her eyes darting nervously between her fingers' clumsy effort and the stranger who approached, eating up the distance from the barn to the grave with a long-legged stride.

Panicked at the thought that he'd be upon them with her sweater half undone, Ty gave a strangled sound of distress. Then Steve was there, standing before her, screening the man's approach.

"Here, let me help," he offered, covering her hands with his own. She could hear the smile in his voice. As if of their own volition, Ty's hands dropped away, and her eyes lifted, locking with his. Calmly, deftly, Steve restored the sweater to rights.

"You're awfully good at this." A touch resentful that he appeared so unaffected by their kiss, so unfazed by the fact someone was practically upon them. Though, of course, it wasn't *he* who was half undressed.

"You should be grateful I inherited my pop's hands. Best hands in the country," Steve boasted with a grin that would have caused an eighty-year-old granny to blush. Ty was no less unaffected.

"It's too bad Bubba couldn't have timed his visit a little better," Steve murmured as his mouth dropped to nuzzle the soft, subtly perfumed flesh just below her ear. "Things were just getting interesting." He moved his lips down, pressing against the thin silver chain around her neck, enjoying the contrasting textures of metal and warm skin, wanting nothing more than to resume his previous exploration. Undo all those buttons, one by one, slip his hands beneath that provocative camisole Ty was wearing, and treat himself to what he'd find underneath. Breasts gently rounded. And braless. Just thinking about it nearly destroying him.

When he heard Bubba call out, "Yo, Shepp, you still running a horse farm?" far too near to where he and Ty were standing, Steve groaned softly, forced to settle for one last chaste kiss on Ty's brow. Reluctantly, he stepped back, creating a respectable, wholly unwelcome, distance between Ty and himself.

"Bubba, great to see you." *Only wish you could have shown up an hour later.*

"Shepp, looking good, man." A huge grin split his dark complexion, and his eyes moved back and forth between Steve and Ty. Steve couldn't blame Bubba for being curious. He and Steve went way back, and Steve previously had always been the soul of discretion when it came to women.

"You weren't BS-ing me, were you, Shepp, when you said my old job was waiting?"

"Hell, no, Bubba. Damn, I'm glad you decided to come back!" Steve extended his hand and shook the other man's heartily, his left one clasping Bubba's muscular shoulder. Steve turned to Ty. A flush still colored her cheeks, and her eyes were so large, Steve could discern the fine black ring at the edge of her irises, encircling paler, light-flecked gray, reminding him of a storm-tossed ocean at dusk. Turbulent and wild. The traces of passion lingering on Ty's face made a vivid contrast to the sweater once more demurely buttoned, hiding skin he knew was smooth as silk. Steve fought the impulse to get rid of Bubba fast and drag Ty off somewhere they could be blessedly alone once more.

No, he decided regretfully, this thing between them would have to wait. Bubba was key, absolutely essential to Southwind's smooth operation. There were few men Steve trusted as he did Bubba around his horses. He was the best.

"Ty, meet Bubba Rollins, my newly rehired stable manager. Took a thirty-percent raise, six games of pool, and an unlimited supply of Rolling Rock during the negotiations to get him to come back to Southwind. I even sweetened the deal a bit and let him win the last two games," Steve said, grinning at Bubba's immediate and noisy protest. "Bubba, this is Ty Stannard. My new part-ner, your new boss."

Ty's hand disappeared into the huge grip of the man standing before her. His size dwarfed her, too, easily topping six foot four. Bubba's head was shaved, reveal-ing a dark, shiny dome, emphasizing the strong bone structure of his face. A small gold hoop pierced his right ear. A black denim jacket covered his wide shoulders; underneath that a dark green hooded sweatshirt. Blue jeans and big (Ty would guess size fourteen), well-worn workboots accompanied the attire.

Ty's eyes lifted to find his had been inspecting her equally closely. Her shoulder blades snapped back as she met Bubba's gaze, painfully aware of how she must look: covered from head to toe in a thick layer of dirt, hair falling in straggly strands about her face. Unlike Bubba Rollins, not terribly impressive.

"I'm pleased to meet you, Mr. Rollins."

"Bubba," he corrected her with an easy smile. "We don't stand on formality here, do we, Shepp?" He hadn't missed the deep blush coloring her high cheekbones nor her swollen lips, stained a darker rose. Yes sir, Ty Stan-nard had just been well and truly kissed. And from the glaze of shock darkening those gray eyes, Bubba guessed it wasn't something that happened frequently.

Had to be a story behind that one, he thought. She was too fine-looking a woman not to have men buzzing about her, bees on honeysuckle.

"So, Shepp; so, Ty," Bubba added deliberately, wait-ing the space of several heartbeats for her to protest, waiting to see if she was one of those stuck-up ones, an-other Allegra Palmer perhaps. Pleased when Ty didn't object to a black man from the wrong side of the tracks calling her by her first name.

That was ten points in her favor right there.

They didn't need the likes of Allegra Palmer around here anymore. She'd always thought a mite too much of herself, insisting Bubba address her as "Ms. Palmer" when everyone else at Southwind was on a first-name basis. What a spoiled thirty-year-old brat she'd been.

In Bubba's opinion, the only good thing that had come out of the tragedy of Fancy Free's death was that Allegra Palmer and her family had left the barn, her parents too blind, too hypocritical, to admit that Allegra's antics, her messing around with Jason Belmar, had been one of the key factors that caused the whole stinking mess.

"Well, now, you two planning on getting this stable up and running so I got more to do than twiddle my thumbs?"

"Yeah, we're working on it," Steve replied, not needing to look over at Ty to know her expression would be one of comical disbelief.

Okay, so they hadn't exactly been working on it *together*, but that could change. Steve was willing to admit that his belligerent attitude of the past few days was as clever, and useful, as shooting himself in the foot. Ty was too strong a woman to be put off either by hostility or by hard work. And he'd begun to like her too damn much to continue being the jerk of the millennium.

If he wanted to regain control of Southwind, he'd have to come up with a better game plan. Right now, however, they might as well see just what they could accomplish working together instead of against each other. Steve steadfastly ignored how much the white-hot passion with which Ty had responded to his kisses influenced this sudden change of heart.

Well, wasn't this an interesting piece of news? So now she and Steve were a team, working together. Of course, had that truly been the case, then she undoubtedly would have been aware of Steve's decision to rehire Bubba Rollins—not that Ty didn't approve wholeheartedly. Southwind needed a stable manager, as well as at least a half dozen grooms, to ensure smooth operation once the barn was again filled to capacity. Wealthy owners expected nothing less than the best for their horses: pristine grounds, immaculate stalls, gleaming tack, horses cared for like pampered royalty. For Southwind to offer that kind of deluxe environment, capable and responsible manpower was required. If Bubba Rollins represented the first step, then great.

But to believe Steve's smooth talk, that he might truly be prepared to work productively with Ty, well, she'd reserve judgment on that. She needed further proof of just how much Steve was willing to share with her.

Sharing. She would *not* think about the kiss. Not now. Its intensity had rocked Ty profoundly. In its wake, she was left unsettled and confused. Not knowing how to act, how to think, not fully comfortable with or even trusting Steve's abrupt change of attitude.

She needed to get away, regroup and regain her sense of balance, her sense of self. "I'm sure you and Bubba need time to discuss 'our' plans," Ty offered, stressing the last. Steve wasn't going to get the satisfaction of thinking his kisses had turned her head to total mush—though they had.

She bent down, intending to grab the handles of the wheelbarrow, but Steve intercepted her. "Here, I'll get that," he said, gently but firmly moving her aside. "You've got a real thing about shouldering responsibilities, don't you? Bubba, you'll have to watch her on that."

"That'll be a nice change," Bubba replied as the three of them began walking toward the barn.

"By the way, Bubba, we got a saddle around here that could fit Ty?"

"A saddle for me?" Ty's voice squeaked in surprise.

"Yeah. I was thinking you could warm up Macintosh for me while I ride Cantata. I'm running late, what with one thing and another, and I've got an appointment with the insurance agent this afternoon."

"But I couldn't possibly . . ."

"Sure you could. You told me you've ridden before."

"Yes, but . . ."

"Did you show?" Steve asked, not giving her a chance to finish.

"Yes, I was competing in Junior Jumper before I gave up riding. But that doesn't mean . . ."

"Means you can't be too awful, or else you'd have quit the sport much sooner. You get to that level, and you've got to be pretty good. Too easy to wind up with a broken neck otherwise. Nothing to worry about, anyway. Macintosh is super-forgiving, and I'll be keeping a real close eye on you." He gave a quick grin as though that was all the reassurance she needed, but when he turned to ask Bubba a question, he missed Ty's finger involuntarily tracing the scar on the side of her eyebrow. "So, Bubba, you think you can find one?"

"Yup." Bubba nodded. "I seem to remember one left here a while back." Man, did he remember. Damned hard to forget the temper tantrum Allegra Palmer threw the day after she left her three-thousand-dollar Hermès saddle out in the pouring rain and was told in no uncertain terms by Steve that she'd have to re-oil it herself; Bubba had better things to do with his time than salvage equipment ruined through gross negligence. The noise that woman had made! The way Allegra had practically screamed the barn down, you'd have thought Steve was forcing her to clean every scrap of leather at Southwind. Bubba was certain Allegra's saddle was still in some corner of the tack room, still sporting discoloring water stains. For when Steve hadn't relented, Allegra had simply driven into the city and purchased a brand new Hermès at Miller's. All so she wouldn't have to spend an hour or so oiling her own saddle.

Terrific, Ty thought, when Bubba nodded his head and said he'd get right on it. A cold knot of anxiety settled like a weight in the pit of her stomach at the prospect of getting back on a horse for the first time in eight years, her every move—correct that, her every blunder—noted by Steve's expert eye. Kind of like playing a round of golf with Tiger Woods. Or stepping out on the dance floor with Gene Kelly. She could refuse, but mulish stubbornness kept her quiet.

So much for having a chance to regroup, to recover her emotional equilibrium after the tumult of Steve's kisses.

19

At least she'd gotten to run back to the house, change into her breeches, grab a cinnamon raisin bagel, and guzzle down a cup of lukewarm coffee before facing the music—Macintosh, that is. Steve had hustled her off to the house, saying that he and Bubba would get the horses ready while she changed.

Breathe! Ty commanded herself repeatedly, whenever she felt close to hyperventilating. True, Macintosh wasn't some old hack that would plod around a ring in a semicomatose state, indifferent to the rider on its back. But she'd ridden before, owned a horse for years. For Pete's sake, she'd even shown in hunter, equitation, and junior jumper classes. Surely she'd be able to pull this off and ride adequately enough not to make a complete fool of herself.

Sure, a nasty voice inside her head sneered back, *but it would be a whole lot easier to impress Steve with your riding skills if you hadn't been so darned stubborn these past eight years.*

Well, she'd heard that riding after a long break was basically just like the old adage about getting back on a bicycle: one never forgot.

Oh, of course, that persistent voice mocked. *A bike and a thousand pounds of horse with a mind of its own? Sure thing, the similarities are endless!*

Forgetting to breathe again, Ty choked on a mouthful of bagel, feeling it scrape its way down her throat, all the while praying that Macintosh was indeed as forgiving as Steve promised.

"So Shepp, you going to fill me in on my new boss? Like where you found her?" Bubba had rooted around the tack room and finally unearthed Allegra Palmer's old saddle. He'd propped it up on the lower half of a stall door and was carefully rubbing conditioner into the abused leather. This was the best he could do right now. Later on, he'd oil the entire saddle thoroughly, coaxing the leather back to life. Next to him, Macintosh was hooked to the cross ties, standing patiently while Steve went over the horse's shiny chestnut coat with a bristle brush.

"I didn't. She found me. Ty's father is this big real estate guy. Ever heard of Stannard Limited? Yeah, just about everyone has. Anyway, she came to me with this idea of helping me get Southwind back in business if I agreed to a partnership. She was convinced her father was about to buy up the property and develop it."

"Develop it? Turn Southwind into lots of rich city creeps' houses? I like this woman already."

"Yeah, it would have killed me, too, Bubba." Steve bent over and ran his hand down Mac's foreleg and fished a hoof pick from the back of his pocket. Two careful strokes along the frog of the hoof, and it was clean.

"Bubba, we need to get the farrier out here before New York. I hate the footing at the Garden."

"Will do," Bubba answered. Then, refusing to abandon their previous topic of conversation, he asked in a bland voice, "So, was that why you were acting so *grateful* to her out in the pasture?"

Steve shot him a dirty look before ducking underneath Macintosh's neck to pick out the second hoof. "Hell, no. Nothing to do with it. She'd gone and picked up two apple trees at a nursery this morning. Wanted to plant them for Fancy."

"Nice idea." Bubba paused, his sponge suspended over the saddle's pommel, thinking it over. "Real nice."

"Yeah. Kind of floored me, to tell you the truth. Then one thing led to another . . ."

"Uh-huh." Bubba's voice rumbled. "Well, that explains it, then."

"What explains what?" Steve asked, positioning the chestnut's rear leg against the top of his thigh.

"Why you can't keep your eyes off her. Never seen that look in your eye around a woman before."

"What the hell are you talking about? I don't look at her in any particular way at all. And you've been here how long, half an hour? Kind of jumping to conclusions, aren't you?"

"Don't think so, boss man. You and I go back close to eleven years. You're looking at her, all right, real special-like. Surprises the heck out of me. I swear, I thought you only looked at TBs that way."

"Thoroughbreds?" Steve clarified dryly. Finished with Macintosh's hooves, Steve grabbed the bridle hanging on a nearby hook and walked over to the cross ties. Unsnapping them, he slipped the reins over Mac's head, and unbuckled the horse's leather halter.

Bubba came up beside him, placed a snow-white saddle pad on Macintosh's withers, then lightly deposited the Hermès saddle on top of it. The leather conditioner he'd used had already soaked into the fine grain of the saddle, like rain in the desert.

"Yeah, thoroughbreds, TBs," he repeated, picking up the thread of their conversation. Reaching underneath Macintosh's belly, he grabbed the girth that Steve normally used on the gelding and slipped it through the looped end of the martingale before fastening it. Macintosh gave a quick toss of his huge head at the sensation of the girth tightening around him.

"And what have thoroughbreds got to do with it?" Steve asked, despite the fact that he wasn't sure he really wanted to hear Bubba's answer.

"See, that's what makes it interesting.'Cause it means you're definitely broadening your horizons, Shepp. This is the first time I've ever seen you salivating over a TFB. In case you don't know it, that stands for 'trust fund baby.'"

A sudden, dangerous blue, Steve's eyes narrowed. "You're not suggesting I'm after her money, are you, Bubba?" he asked softly, holding the other man's gaze.

"Hell, no." Bubba shook his head calmly, unperturbed. "'Course not. If you'd been interested in rich chicks, you could have had your pick long before now. Allegra was ready to hop in the sack with you any day, any time, all you had to do was say the word. Her family could have kept you in million-dollar horses for the rest of your life. This Ty Stannard must have something extra special—other than looks and money," Bubba mused. His mouth widened in a crafty smile. "You figured out what it is yet?"

"No," Steve replied testily, thoroughly annoyed by the whole conversation. Bubba was a tough man to shut up when he felt like talking. "But I promise I'll let you know the second I figure it out." His sarcastic tone was lost on his barn manager.

"Now there's a promise I'll hold you to." Bubba laughed, adding an "Oh" as he caught sight of long legs encased in black breeches approaching them. "Here comes that ultra-fine specimen now."

Since Bubba was standing near them in the center of the indoor ring, a broad smile of amusement lingering on his face, Steve did his best not to look at how nicely Ty filled out a pair of breeches, only enough to affirm that she had great lines. Even he didn't kid himself that he was talking bloodlines.

Everything became that much harder when Steve went to give her a leg up. True, Ty probably could have managed to haul herself up into the saddle by dropping the length of the stirrups, but Macintosh was a big horse. And Steve's fingers itched at the chance to touch her again, however briefly.

"On the count of three," Steve instructed, grasping Ty's booted leg in his cupped palms, trying not to breathe too deeply. He was worried he might do something really stupid if he caught a whiff of Ty's perfume, Bubba only ten feet away notwithstanding.

Ty turned, nodding wordlessly, and Steve saw her eyes, positively enormous with nerves.

"Hey, don't worry," Steve said softly, sympathetically. "Riding Macintosh is easier than sitting back in a big, old, comfy recliner and watching the afternoon game on TV. Just make sure you don't fall asleep. Okay, ready? One, two, three."

At three, Ty pushed off from the ground with her right leg, hands gripping the saddle's pommel and cantle, pulling herself upward—though she hardly needed to, Steve's strength easily propelling her into the saddle.

She settled herself, her thighs automatically adjusting themselves to Macintosh's breadth. It felt a little like straddling a barrel. Immediately, she gathered her reins, holding them loosely while Steve checked her stirrups.

"Let's drop them two holes. Your legs are longer than Allegra's. But first, swing your leg forward so I can tighten your girth. Mac always blows himself up." Steve moved over to Ty's left, intending to lift the saddle flap.

"I can do it," Ty said. Already some of her initial nervousness was wearing off, replaced by rising excitement. She wanted to get going, to see whether riding at twenty-five matched the sweetness of her memories. "This was Allegra Palmer's saddle?" she asked, tugging Macintosh's girth a notch tighter.

"Yeah, she abandoned it after leaving it out in the rain one night. You mind using her cast off?"

"Why should I? The saddle fits fine, although it's a little more padded than I'm used to. But that might be a good thing, considering how long it's been."

"Uh, exactly how long ago was it since you rode?" Steve asked, lowering Ty's right stirrup as she worked on the left.

"Eight years," Ty admitted, shamefaced. "Are you sure you trust me on Macintosh's back?" she asked, ready to jump off despite her growing enthusiasm if Steve hesitated.

"Eight years," Steve repeated, shaking his head. "Hell of a long time to be away from the saddle. Difficult to imagine. Let's see what your body remembers after this many years. Just take it nice and easy. Why don't you walk Mac on the rail for a while, give yourself the chance to get the feel back." Steve turned, addressing his stable manager. "Bubba, d'you mind tacking Cantata for me and bringing her out?"

"No sweat, Shepp," Bubba replied easily, already heading toward the paneled gate. "Good luck, Ty," he called out with a grin. "Don't go landing on your butt, now."

"Thanks, Bubba. I'll try my best to avoid it."

Steve let Ty walk around the perimeter of the indoor ring for the next several minutes in peace. She was sitting all neat and tidy, perhaps a mite too stiff. As if she were entering her first equitation class. He needed to give her something to think about; maybe that would loosen her up a bit.

"All right, Ty, here's the deal: Mac's got a real soft mouth. You only need to keep a light contact; he doesn't respond well to grabby or jerky hands, so loosen your reins just a fraction. That's it. While you're working him on the flat, you want to maintain an unbroken line extending from your elbow to the bit. Good, keep contact with his mouth, but don't fuss."

Steve gave her a minute to absorb his instructions, drawing a cigarette from his vest pocket and lighting up. Exhaling a stream of smoke, he continued. "Now, let's move on to your legs. You look real pretty up there and all. But there's no way you're going to be able to keep Mac rounded and beneath you once his attention wanders if you're perched too far forward of the vertical. He's a good horse, not a robot. You need to sit up straighter and *down* into your saddle. Don't be afraid to use your butt, even if you do land on it," Steve advised, pleased when he startled a laugh out of her. She was beginning to relax.

"That's better. Bring your leg back a hair more. Right, just like that, so you've got him listening. How's he feel?"

"Lovely. Big, far bigger than my mare was. Then again, maybe I've just forgotten the sensation of being on a horse's back."

"Doubt it," Steve replied with a laugh. "Even I feel like I'm climbing onto a huge tractor or a World War II tank when I switch from another horse to Macintosh. But he's as steady as they come. Solid as the Rock of

Gibraltar. All right, let's see you move him into a trot now. Remember: light hands, strong, centered lower body."

And so it went, Steve offering minute corrections, explaining Macintosh's temperament and habits and how best to work with them. Ty quickly slipped into her own habit of total concentration, speaking little, making adjustments with her body as Steve indicated.

It was only when Steve instructed her to smile that Ty realized she'd been frowning, deep in concentration, trying to make her body relearn movements once ingrained. "Sorry," she called out, just as Bubba led Cantata into the ring.

"Nothing to apologize for. Ah, Bubba, here you are. I was worried Cantata might be giving you trouble or that perhaps you'd gotten lost on the way to the tack room," Steve joked, guessing that Bubba had purposely lingered over grooming the mare to give Ty extra time with Steve coaching her from the ground. "Ty looks good, doesn't she, Bubba?"

"Not half bad," Bubba agreed, handing over the mare's reins to Steve. Steve and Bubba's eyes met and Steve mouthed the word *thanks*.

Ty couldn't suppress the wide smile that spread over her face when she heard their comments. Lord, it was great to be back in the saddle again. And these two men had just earned her undying loyalty for not making her feel like a total bumbling clod. Macintosh was wonderful, too: smooth, powerful, and so exquisitely trained that he responded to the lightest of aids. His trot skimmed over the ground, legs flexing and extending with an airy precision. His canter was unbelievable, too, like sitting on an enormous, puffy cloud as it drifted over the summer sky. Ty had felt as if she could canter forever on his back—that is, until she started noticing the twinge of pain in her ankles. The unnatural and, more pertinently, unaccustomed angle they were forced into from dropping her heels deep in the stirrups had caused them to stiffen (though *freeze* might be the better term). A fine trembling had started in her inner thighs from gripping the saddle, and her lower back was aching as though someone had taken a baseball bat to it.

"Hey, Ty," Steve called, interrupting her mental checklist of aches and pains. "Why don't you bring Mac into the center of the ring? You can hop off, and I'll switch saddles."

With equal parts relief and regret, Ty walked the big chestnut over to where Steve, Bubba, and Cantata were grouped. She closed her hands, bringing Macintosh to a halt in front of Steve.

"He's a great horse." Ty leaned forward to rub the gelding on his slightly sweaty neck. The color of his sleek coat had deepened slightly, now a rich, dark copper, and she smiled as Macintosh dropped his head to rub the cheek strap of his bridle against the inside of his foreleg. Her own horse, Charisma, had often done the exact same thing when the workout was finished, as if saying that the bridle she tolerated was all very well and good, but enough was enough.

How she'd missed all this, Ty realized with a start: the intense physical rush that came from being involved with these beautiful animals.

With a final pat to Macintosh's muscled shoulder, Ty straightened and dropped her stirrups. Tight lips masked a grimace as a dull pain wrapped itself around and seemingly through her ankle bones, like a snake twisting its way through the limbs of a tree. In an effort to block out the pain, she focused all her energy on lifting her right leg over the saddle.

Oh, God, this is awful, Ty whimpered silently, her

thigh muscles screaming their protest. "Steve, thank you for letting me ride him. He's so smooth." Ty felt she did a pretty decent job of enunciating through gritted teeth. By keeping her molars clamped tight enough, she sounded almost normal. Moreover, she couldn't start howling.

"Yeah," Steve replied, holding Macintosh's reins while Ty lowered herself to the ground. "He would have made an excellent dressage prospect. Thing is, he can jump just about anything you put before him. He's got great scope. Fearless, too. Macintosh's only weakness lies in being a one-speed wonder—getting him past that easy, rocking chair canter of his is like waiting for molasses to drip in January."

Ty felt somewhat like molasses herself. She'd slipped down from the saddle, tentatively planting her feet on the ground. Her bones seemed to have disappeared, replaced by a toxic slime oozing through her system. She'd read articles in which athletic coaches explained how lactic acid was produced by the muscles during exercise. Well, if one of those coaches were to run some super-sophisticated biochemical test on Ty right now, she'd no doubt qualify as a hazardous waste site.

She stood gripping the sides of the saddle for a few seconds, hoping it would be enough time for her legs to lose their jelly-like state, praying that neither Steve nor Bubba would notice the pathetic and oh-so-humbling shape she was in. She worked out! She wasn't some couch potato who deserved this kind of muscular pain!

Unfortunately, her attempt at disguising her current state of agony succeeded only too well. Steve's next words sent Ty's mind reeling, her system into deep shock. "What do you think about warming up Cantata for me?"

"But, but . . ." Ty stammered, unable to form a coherent thought, let alone a sentence.

"You did a real nice job on Mac. Cantata's a little heavier on the bit, and her gait is a lot more forward; you won't need to use much leg on her. Actually, she gets a little goosey if you do. In that respect, she'll be a real holiday after riding Mac."

Could she have formed the words, she was sure she would have protested, demurred, asked for a rain check, figured out some way to get out of this, but her mind was obviously functioning at reduced capacity. Too many things were going on. Here Steve was, still being nice, no, downright kind to her, allowing her the privilege of riding, not one, but two of his horses. It was thrilling. It was scary. She didn't know what to think.

Not that it mattered, for Steve's next words tipped the scales completely. "This could work out to be a big bonus, Ty, your being a decent rider and all. It means that once we get more horses, I can rely on you to be warming up one while I'm coaching or when we're at a show and I've got more than one horse entered in a class. You're only going to improve with a bit more practice."

Ty shot him a suspicious glance, half convinced that this was an elaborate put-on, skeptical that he was truly thinking in terms of their working as a team, that there might be a future for them as partners, but Steve was busy pulling off his own saddle from Cantata. In a stupefied daze, Ty found herself lifting the saddle flap and releasing the buckles on Macintosh's girth.

You'd definitely call Cantata a different ride from Macintosh, thought Ty. Newly added to the list of aches and pains were her shoulders, biceps, and triceps, those areas rebelling from Cantata's being a much hotter and more forward horse than the warmblooded Macintosh. Ty also now possessed an exact definition for the term *goosey*. That's what happened to an excitable thorough-bred's hindquarters when you made the mistake of sitting a little too forward in your seat and allowing your legs to slip behind you. It had taken three laps around the ring before Cantata quieted down once more. Ty hadn't made that mistake again. One goosey session was enough to last her shoulders for the foreseeable future, thank you very much.

Ty might as well be ruthlessly honest with herself. She could think of only one point on her body that wasn't feeling sore and abused: the tip of her nose.

She was in truly pathetic shape, but she was also feeling gloriously happy. Alive. Cantata had been an exhilarating challenge from the first nudge of Ty's heels. Adrenaline had rushed through her as she focused on collecting the young, headstrong mare, keeping her controlled and nicely rounded in her gaits.

But even more thrilling had been the opportunity to share the ring with Steve and watch him work. During the moments when she'd been walking Cantata on a loose rein, allowing the mare to stretch her long, graceful neck and the muscles of her back, she'd been able to observe Steve cantering Macintosh over the jumps he'd set up.

When you loved a sport, an activity, an art form, and had the rare chance to watch a true master at it, the experience was profound, inspirational. For Ty, it was that and more. During the years when she'd avidly scoured the sports programs on cable TV, or attended shows where Steve was competing, the stage where he'd ridden had been the show ring. There, it was all the glorious brilliance of the competitive moment—but brief, like a comet shooting across the night sky. Today, she saw a whole other aspect, no less moving, no less brilliant, and, now that she was older and more mature, ultimately far more satisfying.

It was the work. The intensive training. Again and again, Ty saw Steve take Macintosh through careful, precise movements, broken down to their most basic elements. Then she watched how he gradually, patiently rebuilt them, adding and expanding until they became a flow of twists, turns, flying changes, and jumps.

It made her appreciate anew just what it took, what it meant when the moment arrived for horse and rider to canter through the show ring's in-gate, primed to negotiate a jump course of enormous technically and physically demanding fences. That afternoon, Ty glimpsed a small part of the effort and preparation that served as the foundation for the grand, fluid, and, above all, harmonious style with which Steve Sheppard rode his horses. Ty wouldn't have missed the chance to watch for the world.

A short time later, Steve left Ty and Bubba, ran to his truck, steering it carefully over the bumpy pasture, where Ty had parked it, then roared down the driveway, already late for his appointment with the representative from the insurance company at their local offices in Riverhead.

Steve's opinion of insurance agents, never very high in the first place, had sunk to an all-time low following Fancy Free's death. They'd been stalling for way too long now, giving him the run-around, demanding an autopsy, documents, second and third opinions from veterinarians—demanding every imaginable thing under the sun before agreeing to review the claim, let alone cough up the money they owed him.

He'd provided everything they asked for. He still

couldn't bear to think of the autopsy report; knowing he'd been right to put Fancy out of his pain was cold and measly comfort indeed. But at least it meant that Steve had been vindicated in the eyes of the insurance agency. An awful, tragic accident but one the company was obliged to cover financially.

And, by God, they were going to hand over his money.

"Why don't you let me take the saddle off Cantata for you? I need to give it another oiling, anyway. The leather's in pretty sad shape," Bubba suggested as Ty and he led Cantata and Macintosh into the barn.

"Oh, I can do that, Bubba."

Bubba eyed her speculatively. Steve was right; this was a woman who'd drive herself into the ground rather than give up. Ty had been moving more and more stiffly with each passing second, though she'd held up real well in the saddle, an impressive feat for someone who hadn't ridden in eight years. He hadn't even seen her start to wince and shorten her stride until Steve took off for his meeting.

Didn't want Steve to know how bad she was hurting. Stubborn, Ty was. Well, Steve and she should get along dandy, then. Steve, too, was as stubborn as a mule. Now he'd have two hardheads to look after, Bubba reflected wryly.

If she just kept moving, her legs might not buckle on her, and she wouldn't land in a heap in front of Bubba's oversized workboots. And anyway, she wanted to help put the horses away. Ty wasn't sure she had the courage to face the flight of stairs up to her bedroom.

They hooked Cantata and Macintosh to nearby cross ties, the horses facing each other, then proceeded to untack and rub the horses down.

"Bubba, tell me about yourself. Where did you and Steve meet?"

"Out here. I was between jobs when Shepp bought this place. I heard he was looking for help, so I showed up one day. Shepp took me on, taught me everything I know. Which was considerable—didn't know squat about horses."

"Had you wanted to work with them?" Ty asked curiously.

"Hell, no." Bubba patted Macintosh's neck affectionately. "I just wanted work. Damned hard to find if you're a black man who only made it through high school. By the time I met Shepp, I had a wife and two kids to support. We'd been squeaking by—I'd been doing carpentry for some local contractors, lawn mowing, working as a grocery clerk—but none of the jobs ever lasted. I'd have tried fishing, too, except I get seasick. Feel queasy even *looking* at the ocean when the surf's up."

"Dramamine?" Ty asked, gingerly picking up a soft brush and going over the mare with long, even strokes.

"Knocks me out. Can't take the stuff. The big problem around here is, most jobs are either seasonal or don't pay diddly if you haven't got a college diploma. Shepp was one of the few year-rounders willing to hire me. A damned good man," Bubba pronounced as he settled a dark blue plaid horse blanket over Macintosh's gleaming body. "Coming to Southwind was the best move I ever made."

"And how old are your kids?" She was nearly panting with the effort of lifting the blanket over the mare. Bubba came to her rescue.

"Fifteen and nineteen."

"But"—Ty looked at him in astonishment—"you can't be more than . . ."

"Thirty-six." He waited, a small smile hovering on his lips as understanding dawned.

It didn't take more than a second or two. Ty had always been good at numbers. "I'm sorry, Bubba," she offered quietly. "I hope I haven't offended you."

"Naw, I'm pretty damn lucky." Bubba patted the mare and grabbed the wooden carryall next to Macintosh's stall. He knelt down by Macintosh's right foreleg, and his long, nimble fingers proceeded to wrap it with a navy-blue bandage. "Got a fine woman and two great kids. Glo—my wife—and I got married as soon as I landed my first job. She's working, too, now that the kids are older. We've got a daughter, Serena, in tenth grade. Looks just like her mother did at her age—that's why I've put double bolts on our front door," Bubba added with a quick grin. "Fortunately for Glo and me, Serena don't know boys exist. Her head's all filled with computers. Bought one for Christmas last year." The pride in his voice was clear. "And my boy, Will, he's just starting his first year at college. Vanderbilt, full scholarship."

The expression on Bubba's face had Ty smiling warmly in return. "That's fantastic. Congratulations. You and your wife must be very pleased."

"We are. Owe a lot to Shepp there, too, of course. He got Will hooked on those history books he's always reading. Now my kid wants to get a degree in political science. And he let Will hang here at Southwind, learn about the horses. Will's been helping out, mucking out stalls, riding, and what not, since he was thirteen."

"Vanderbilt's in Tennessee, isn't it? That's a long way from the East End of Long Island."

"Glo, Serena, and I went to visit him this fall. Weekend of the accident." With a somber expression, Bubba unsnapped Macintosh from the cross ties and led the horse to his roomy box stall where the gelding made a beeline to his feed bucket, rooting around for the apple treat he knew he'd find there. Ty watched the smile that crossed Bubba's face as they listened to the methodical chomp of the horse's teeth. A smile that grew wider as Bubba waited patiently for Macintosh to come back and stick his head over the stall's half-door. Whether he claimed to or not, Bubba Rollins' love for the horses in his care was there for anyone to see.

With a final pat on the gelding's fiery red coat, Bubba walked over to Ty and Cantata. "You know how to wrap a horse's leg?"

"Yes."

"Cantata wears wraps to bed, too. Here, you take the right side, I'll do left." For a few minutes, they worked over the mare in silence, fingers moving quickly, competently. With the second quilted wrap and bandage in his large hand, Bubba's voice was quiet, a soft rumble. "I should have known not to trust Jase with the horses, he'd been acting weird lately, you know, unpredictable. Can't believe I didn't guess he was messing with drugs."

"It's not always easy to tell."

"Yeah, Jase always used to get pumped up, real excited during competition. I suppose snorting coke was the same. I guess if he'd been doing heroin, it would have been easier to catch," Bubba reflected bitterly. "The judge in charge of his case ordered Jase to a detox clinic down in Maryland, where his folks come from. Good for Jase he's out of the area, 'cause I could kill him for what he did to Fred."

"Fred?"

"What I liked to call Fancy. You know, like Fred Astaire, the dancer. That was my nickname for him. Damn, that was a fine horse. I suppose you know how hard this mess has been on Steve. I didn't want to leave him or Southwind, but . . ."

"But now you're back, and Steve is obviously thrilled, and I'm very happy, too," Ty said firmly, if not unsympathetically. "What we need now is to get this farm filled with beautiful horses again, don't you think?"

"Yeah. But it's not going to be easy." Bubba's tone was glum.

"No, it's not," Ty agreed. "Steve and I will need your help. So, what I'd like you to do, Bubba, after we feed the horses, is to make up a list of anything that needs to be repaired or purchased here. This place has to be in A-1 condition."

"Already is." Bubba bristled. "Shepp don't cut corners when it comes to the care of his horses."

"Of course not," Ty replied. "But you've been gone for at least a few weeks now. Go over everything with an eagle eye. If there's anything missing or broken, make a note of it. Same goes for the lounge and the viewing area. That definitely looked a little worse for wear," Ty said, referring to the room located at the end of the indoor ring, where owners and riders could sit during the winter months or on rainy days and observe the horses being exercised in the indoor ring.

"What you got in mind? Personalized cappuccino makers, foot warmers, that sort of thing?" Bubba asked, his disdain for the idea obvious.

"Hardly seems Steve's style, does it, setting up a mini Starbucks in the lounge?" Seeing Ty's small smile, Bubba slowly relaxed.

"No," she continued, "but I'll probably order a new sofa and some lounge chairs. And we should put up photographs of Steve riding. There must be some around here."

"There's a bunch crammed into the top drawer of Shepp's desk in the office."

"I'll get some wooden frames to hang them. Southwind's facilities need to look as appealing for humans as for the horses, Bubba. It's tacky, I know, but we have to go the extra mile here. Word has to spread that Southwind is back in operation and running better than ever."

"Not sure a new sofa's going to cut it, Ty," Bubba said, shaking his head.

"No, but we have to cover all the angles. I'm planning on having some journalists come out as soon as possible. More than likely, because of Steve's reputation and the fact that this is the Hamptons, they'll be accompanied by a photographer. Southwind needs to look perfect. Can you make that happen?"

"I'll get right on it." Then, with a gleam in his eye Ty was beginning to recognize, he added, "But if you're all fired up about everything around here needing to be in tip-top shape, then you'd better go on back to the house now and take a real long, hot bath. Those muscles of yours get any stiffer, you're going to start looking like the tin man from *The Wizard of Oz*."

"But the apple trees. They need watering . . ."

"After I've watered these guys, I'll drag the hose out there," Bubba replied patiently. "Go on, get going." He made a shooing gesture with his hands.

Ty slowly straightened to her feet, amazed that she couldn't hear her bones creaking. "Well, if you're sure . . ."

"Lady, if I can't handle this, you'd better fire me right away. Moving the way you are, I can probably finish all the chores I got left in the same amount of time it would take you to haul the water hose out to the pasture. Oh, that reminds me. You might want to take some of this with you." Bubba bent down and retrieved a dark brown bottle from the carryall. "Here." He held it out to Ty.

"What is it?" Ty asked suspiciously. The label was worn, showing only the picture of a horse's leg on it.

"Absorbine. Smells like you-know-what, but it works wonders after a hard workout. Our horses swear by it," he vowed with a small grin.

Ty uncapped the bottle and sniffed tentatively. Bubba gave a rich laugh at her expression. "Like I said, it stinks to high heaven, but if it's good enough for Shepp's horses when they're ouchy, it should do the trick for you. Just work it into the muscles that hurt."

"Bubba, you don't have enough Absorbine in this bottle to use on all the places that hurt!"

"Don't worry about that, boss. I got a couple gallons of the stuff back in the storeroom. And I'd say you're gonna need it."

"It shows that bad, huh?" Ty asked, chagrined.

"Don't think Steve caught on, if that's what you're worried about. Go ahead, try it. Otherwise, you won't even be able to crawl out of bed tomorrow."

"That's not what concerns me right now. I just want to be able to crawl *into* bed!"

20

$\mathscr{S}$teve caught himself whistling as he stepped out of the shower the following morning. *Whistling!* Momentarily stunned, he stopped, then, with a grin, started up again.

Yes, things were definitely looking up. The insurance agent he'd met yesterday afternoon had been different from the previous morons he'd dealt with. Thank God. A woman, she'd ridden competitively herself—dressage—so she counted as a definite horse lover. Nancy Bayard assured Steve that he'd be receiving full reimbursement for the loss of Fancy Free. He could expect the company's check within two weeks; she'd already processed all the relevant papers. Steve, who'd driven over there, ready to throttle someone if he was once more given the run-around, almost fell to his knees in gratitude.

Two weeks. The National Horse Show would be over by then. He could take a few days off, go south, and do some horse buying. Bubba was back. He'd look after Southwind while Steve was out of town. And Steve was ninety-nine percent sure that Carlos and Enrique, two brothers from the Dominican Republic who'd worked as grooms for him, would be returning to their old jobs. They'd been enthusiastic when Steve had dropped by their modest ranch house the other day. He'd chosen Carlos and Enrique to approach first; they'd always gotten along well with Bubba, sticking around after work was over to go up against Bubba and Steve in a game of hoops. So that made three people he could rely on to keep Southwind running smoothly while he was away. Hell, if he timed the visit down to Kentucky right, he might even be able to ask Will Rollins to ride the horses over Thanksgiving break. The kid knew Southwind's horses almost as well as Steve did.

Of course, Ty could ride the horses, too, at the very least make sure they were exercised lightly during his absence. It had been something of a shock—a pleasant one but a shock nonetheless—to discover how well she rode. Clearly, she'd benefited from some first-rate instruction. That aspect was hardly newsworthy; her pop would have wanted only the best for his daughter. What was striking, however, was her natural ability. Within minutes of settling herself across Macintosh's broad back, she'd intuitively made small corrections to her lower leg, her upper body—adjustments far more subtle than the sort he'd suggested—that had the gelding moving fluidly, responding to Ty's presence in the saddle.

Lots of riders were reactive, not listening to the horse until something was wrong or until their trainer spoke up, pointing out the problem and offering a solution. In other words, through lack of experience or lack of natural ability, these riders waited until there was already a problem with their horse's gait, their horse's approach to a jump. Steve realized at once that Ty possessed the instincts and sensitivity to understand that riding was a continuous and special kind of dialogue, mental as well as physical, carried on between horse and rider. In order to bring out the finest in a horse, a rider had to anticipate—not fuss—employ skill and a deeper kind of knowledge of what made the horse tick. It was the difference between riding and being taken for a ride.

After watching Ty first on Macintosh, then on Cantata, there was no doubt in Steve's mind. Ty could be a damned fine rider if she chose.

But leaving Ty here in charge of Cantata, Gordo, and Macintosh's workouts while he was down in Kentucky didn't appeal to Steve at all.

Because he wanted her with him.

The notion struck him, as startling as the renewed sense of happiness he was experiencing. He wanted to take her south, introduce her to his folks, show her the place where he'd grown up.

Yesterday evening, he'd come home to Southwind and found the exterior light shining brightly over the front door. In the kitchen, the light there illuminated its spotless condition. Those two lights were the only signs that his return was anticipated. A weird emptiness had washed over him at the quiet stillness of the house until Steve saw, anchored by the brown ceramic bowl supporting a colorful pyramid of fruit, the white rectangle of stationery: *Turning in early. Food in refrigerator. Ty.*

Her neatly penned note, all of two sentences, buoyed his spirit. Why, he couldn't articulate precisely. He tried to tell himself he'd been disappointed at not being able to share the good news about the insurance company finally coughing up his money. Ty was his business partner, after all. But that explanation didn't hold water. She wasn't there, so why was he feeling better just because she'd left a note? What Steve was reluctant to admit was that he'd wanted, needed evidence that Ty was thinking about him. That she was thinking about him perhaps as frequently as his thoughts turned to her.

With a sudden hunger, born of the lateness of the hour and Ty's reference to food, Steve had opened the refrigerator door and was soon busy rummaging through its contents, depositing items on the butcher-block counter. Within minutes, he'd fixed himself a plate, piled high with slices of cold roast chicken and a beet, endive, and walnut salad Ty had prepared, with a huge chunk of extra sharp cheddar cheese and a couple of thick slices of freshly baked bread. Taking a bite out of his wedge of cheese, he kicked the refrigerator door shut behind him. Then, grabbing the overladen plate and hooking his finger around his bottle of beer, Steve wandered into the living room.

Life certainly had improved since Ty had moved in, he thought, sinking down onto the faded blue sofa. Hard not to like a woman who knew how to stock a refrigerator. Thing was, he acknowledged with a small smile, swallowing a long sip of cold beer and resting his head against the sofa's soft cushions, there was something about her. Hell, he'd probably like her even if she insisted on filling the cupboards and refrigerator with unsalted rice cakes, iceberg lettuce, and Diet Coke.

After polishing off three-quarters of the chicken, the entire salad, and almost half of the bread and cheese while CNN filled him in on what was happening in the world, Steve, feeling full of good will, had cleaned the kitchen, wiping down the counters, folding the dish-towel neatly, grinning as he recalled how Ty had oh-so-politely requested that he make an effort to put the dishes away in the dishwashing machine.

With the kitchen as pristine as he'd found it, Steve had returned to the living room, tired but not yet ready to go upstairs to bed, choosing instead to stare blankly at the screen while his thumb surfed the channels. An old Hollywood movie caught his attention, and he watched it for a time, the plot and characters coming back to him bit by bit.

He remembered wishing she were with him then. He was feeling real good, mellow with decent food and that second beer he was slowly nursing. He'd have liked to sit on the sofa with her, close enough that while they were watching the movie together, his arm could rest along the back of the sofa, his fingers lightly tracing the curve of her shoulder. He'd have turned to her to say something about one of the actors, and his eyes would have fixed instead on the delicate shell of her ear, the creaminess of her skin, the way her eyelashes, so thick and long, curled, a dark mink shade to their very tips. His eyes would travel the clean lines of her profile, that sexy little scar at the edge of her eyebrow. Inside Steve the memory of the kiss they'd shared would repeat, fresh as the first time. How she'd tasted, how he'd brought her to that flash point of burning heat and desperate, mind-blowing need. How he could do that to her again. And give her more. How he could take her to the very beyond.

He'd gone to bed hard, aching, and alone.

This morning, he'd awakened that way, too. But at least he'd slept, Steve acknowledged, vigorously toweling himself off, the ice-cold shower having restored some of his self-control. And while he had been waiting for sleep to claim him, his thoughts had been, for the first time in weeks, centered on a beautiful woman. That was progress.

Steve didn't bother glancing out the window. It was too early to tell what the day would be like. But he remembered the weather forecaster last night had called for cool temperatures so he pulled on a sweater over his jeans and T-shirt. The sweater, heather blue, was a favorite—thick, soft, and reversible, too, the other side a light green. His parents had picked it up for Steve during a trip they'd taken to Scotland and Ireland. It had become so worn over the years that even the chamois elbow patches his mother had diligently sewn were beginning to fray.

He would brew some coffee, make a mug for her, rap on her door, and give her the news about the money, Steve decided, skipping every other step as he descended the stairs. Flicking on the radio, he padded around the kitchen barefoot, despite the fact that the ceramic-tiled floor was bone-chilling cold at this hour. The sensation helped wake him up. Spooning coffee into the machine, he dusted off his hands on jeans the same hue as his sweater and equally worn.

Steve ascended the stairs as rapidly as he'd come down them, the steaming coffee held before him. In Paris one year, when he'd been competing at the Grand Prix held there, he'd been fortunate to witness the bizarre spectacle of café waiters in a race. They had streaked down the boulevard, arms outstretched before them, balancing a tray piled high, laden with cups and saucers. He felt a little like that now, only not quite as successful, hot liquid sloshing uncomfortably over the mug's brim and onto the back of his hand.

After a loud and enthusiastic knock on her bedroom door, Steve freely interpreted the muffled reply he heard as an invitation to enter.

Damned lucky he didn't lose it right there and tip the hot coffee all over himself. She was down on the floor, wearing teeny-tiny lycra bike shorts, a pink ribbed tank top, and nothing else. That he could have handled, although his heart rate would have taken at least an hour to return to normal. No, it was what she was *doing* on the floor that had his tongue hanging out like a desert lizard's catching a drop of rain, his eyes popping with sudden, uncontrollable lust.

Christ, not even his little sister's Barbie dolls could have done *that*, was all his sizzled brain could come up with.

Ty's legs were extended perpendicular to her body, her torso flat on the bare wooden floor in front of her. Feet arched, toes pointed, her nails were painted a delectable pinky coral. It looked as if she were capable of staying in that position for the foreseeable future. Steve swallowed and took a deep breath, trying to think about something other than all the interesting things one could do with a body that flexible.

Then he noticed the smell. "Whew, Jesus! What did that cleaning crew use in here?"

Slowly, she shifted her arms, bending them until she was propped on her elbows, her body now raised at a slight angle. Her legs remained stationary. Steve heard her voice come from somewhere beneath her shoulder.

"It's not the room," she corrected, "it's me . . . Absorbine." Her head shifted as she lowered her torso back down to the ground, groaning slightly as she did.

Ty was far too sore to feel even remotely self-conscious. She was trying to stretch her inner thighs in a Russian split. It had taken fifteen minutes to ease herself into this position, a feat usually accomplished quite naturally. Now that she'd worked her way down to the ground, she wasn't about to move. Anyway, she was decently covered, and she'd bet her father's annual income she didn't have a thing Steve hadn't seen before.

"You okay?" he asked.

"Do I look okay?" Her tone was acidic. She flexed her feet, groaning once again.

Yes, indeed. More than okay, but obviously they were coming at the issue from different points of view. Now that Ty had explained the source of the odor, Steve could identify it. While admittedly strong and astringent, for some reason Absorbine had never seemed quite so overwhelming before. Must be the superior ventilation in the barn, he thought, his eyes beginning to water. "You sure you didn't go a little heavy on the Absorbine? It's pretty strong stuff."

"I only used the one bottle. Bubba assured me he has plenty more. Maybe if I rub a gallon or so into my calves and thighs, I'll begin to feel marginally better."

He looked at her legs and found himself volunteering.

"No thanks," Ty replied dryly. "But if you'd be willing to walk on my back, I'd be eternally grateful."

An outrageous suggestion, but she really hurt. Badly. Otherwise, never in a million years would she have made such a request. Muscles Ty had never bothered to worry about were so incredibly tight that she wanted to bawl like a baby at the pain, at the gross injustice of her body betraying her this way.

"My walking on your back would make you feel better?" he asked incredulously. "I weigh a hundred and sixty-eight."

"Oh, yes." Ty's head rubbed up and down against the bare wooden floor. "A bit heavier than Lars, but that's okay. Go ahead," she encouraged. "I won't break. Though I doubt I'd even notice if I did," she added as an afterthought.

"You, uh, want me to step on you while you're like that?" Steve inquired, trying to keep his voice casual, approaching her carefully, his eyes glued to the one-hundred-eighty-degree line her legs formed from her hip sockets. While he was learning to expect the unexpected, this was pushing the envelope on weird, wild, and never to be believed. Ty had seemed like a pretty straitlaced woman up to now.

"Oh, right. Wait a sec." Like the arms of a corkscrew, her legs slowly came together. Steve watched, mesmerized, his mouth dry.

As though stepping into dangerous waters, Steve lifted his foot hesitantly, not knowing what to expect as he lowered it onto Ty's slender back. He stared fixedly at the little pink lines of her ribbed tank top, holding his breath in suspense. When she didn't scream out, he placed a little more weight on her.

"Go on, you've put, what, half your foot on me?"

"I'm going to crush you," Steve warned, swallowing a huge lump lodged in his throat. It settled in his belly, spreading, one part anxiety mixed with nine parts lust.

"No way. Just don't step on my spine, 'kay? Mmm, that's right. Lord, that feels good." Ty exhaled in dazed contentment as her body was gently compressed between Steve's weight and the wooden floor boards.

Man, Steve thought, standing with both feet firmly placed on the small of Ty's back, absorbing her little mews of contentment, his confidence growing apace. Last night's fantasy of making out with Ty on the sofa was downright tame compared to this—not that he wasn't a hundred percent sure he could kick up the level of erotic exotica if need be.

Ty's body felt incredible beneath him.

Steve would never have guessed the soles of his feet could be this sensitive. The texture of her tank top, the way it slid over smooth, resilient flesh, muscles, and bones . . . each minute detail registered, becoming part of him.

Wiping sweat from his palms against the faded fabric of his jeans, Steve extended his arms for balance and took a small step up the length of her back. Her soft groan had sweat popping out all over again. "So, you generally into kinky stuff? Whips, bondage, warm honey? And who's Lars?"

"No, this is as kinky as I get." She gave a muffled laugh that sounded awfully close to a purr, Steve noted, his body temperature rising a couple notches more. "But I do usually pay Lars to do . . ." She pronounced a japanese term that Steve thought sounded awfully like *sushi*. "Perhaps that qualifies as kinky, now that you mention it. Lars is fabulous. A Swedish demigod with an adoring clientele, every single one of them begging to lie down and be used like rugs. The names of the people that man has walked on would astound you."

An image blossomed in Steve's mind of a pasty-faced creep, who probably had weekly sessions reserved for him at the local tanning salon, stomping on Ty. Didn't she know she could get diseases that way, athlete's foot at the very least?

Ty's voice cut into his thoughts. "By the way, for your information, this is the *only* time I'm going to let you walk all over me." He'd been doing a close approximation, anyway, since the very first day at the lawyers' office, Ty reflected, remembering his attitude toward her. "This is an *emergency* situation. Don't read more into it than that."

So Ty considered this a one-shot deal, did she? That she could use him and then throw him over for some plantar-wart-ridden moron named Lars? Time to show his partner just what he was capable of. What she was up against. "Oh, yeah? You sure about that?" His voice was mild, disinterested even, as slowly, deliberately, Steve curled each of his toes into her, pressing down firmly. Exultant when he felt her response, her muscles and bones melting beneath his soles. From her lips an involuntary moan of helpless pleasure.

A broad grin split Steve's face. Sure as the sun rose in the east, he was gonna get—and in the very near future, too—another chance to walk all over Miss Ty Stannard.

Minutes slipped by as Steve continued his sensual path up and down Ty's back. He was gearing up to suggest a full body massage at no extra charge when the doorbell rang, surprising him enough to jump lightly off her back, the floor a decidedly second-rate surface now.

Steve watched Ty roll gingerly to her side. Distracted, the doorbell relegated to some distant region of his brain, his eyes roamed over the length of her body, admiring the yards of silken flesh her shorts and tank top revealed. Yes, he decided, Ty could definitely benefit from a deep tissue massage.

Dear Lord, her abused muscles were still aching. While her inner thighs were doing somewhat better after stretching them out in the split, her hamstring muscles felt like old rubber bands, ready to snap. Preoccupied, Ty stared balefully at her legs, racking her brains for a stretch that might relax them, only little by little becoming aware of Steve's heated gaze. When her eyes encountered his, a brilliant, blazing blue, bright with arousal, Ty's heart thudded madly against her ribs.

The room, quiet except for the sound of Ty and Steve's breathing, was once more disturbed by the insistent chime of the doorbell. This time the ring was even longer, a finger driving its way into the wall

"Uh, hadn't you better answer the door?" Ty asked, her gaze trapped in his.

And leave? Like hell. "Whoever it is will go away."

But whoever it was didn't. A third, then a fourth ring came in quick, impatient succession, and Ty rose stiffly to her feet, the spell broken. She raised an eyebrow at him.

"All right, all right, I'm going," Steve grumbled. Side-stepping the mug of coffee he'd placed on the floor, he reached down to pick it up. "I brought you some coffee. Probably stone cold by now." Poor kid, Steve thought, with a mixture of sympathy and amusement as Ty walked toward him with overly careful, too-precise steps. She was moving the way a quarterback did after being sacked, unsure she could trust her legs to support her. "Guess this means you don't want to go for a bare-back gallop on the beach with me."

"Very funny. Ha ha." Ty cast him a withering glare, not amused in the least. "Go see who's at the door. I'll be down in a minute."

"You might want to open some windows before you leave. Aerate the place. You're probably killing brain cells by the millions."

At least I have them to kill, she nearly retorted, but didn't, remembering the incredible way Steve could use his feet. "Go away," said Ty, in her severest tone, taking baby steps toward her closet.

Only the presence of a truly gorgeous woman could temporarily dispel from Steve's mind the image of Ty's body one short flight of stairs above and all the things he planned to do with it.

Only a truly gorgeous woman, with Titian-red hair, cornflower-blue eyes, and mouth stretched wide in a thousand-watt smile, saying, "Surprise!" prevented Steve from immediately slamming the door in her face and running back up the stairs to Ty's room so that he could begin working on fantasies one through a thousand.

He paused, allowing himself the pleasure of a good second look. A woman this beautiful didn't darken a man's doorway every morning—or any other time of

the day, for that matter. A rare gift should be appreciated, he said to himself, as a smile of masculine approval
lit his tanned face, set his blue eyes twinkling. As far as
Steve was concerned, one couldn't ask for a finer start to
the day than he'd had so far.

"Sweetheart," Steve drawled, "as surprises go, this is
one of the nicest I've ever had the pleasure of receiving.
Do I know you?" Not that he really cared. He was quite
willing to play host to this woman, acquaintance or not.
Her face, though, seemed familiar. Maybe they'd met in
a bar or a restaurant in town.

Her laugh was as delightful as the rest of her. "Actually, I'm here for Ty. I'm a friend of hers, Lizzie Osborne." The vision extended her right hand.

Steve shook it, replying, "Steve Sheppard." At the
mention of Ty, however, a peculiar thing happened to
him. Somehow, the sheer man-oh-man of this woman's
presence paled.

"Oh, I know who *you* are, Steve," Lizzie replied
cheerfully. A terrific voice, he couldn't help noting, the
kind that made you want to smile. Still, he preferred
Ty's, sometimes clipped and snooty, other times soft and
achingly vulnerable.

"Is Ty around?"

"Upstairs. Should be down in a minute. Would you
like to come in?" Steve stepped back from his position
by the doorjamb.

Lizzie glanced behind her. "My daughter's asleep in
the car. We set out early to avoid the traffic around New
York. I'll try to get her out of the car seat without waking
her."

"Need a hand?" Steve asked, following her out to a
dark blue Volvo station wagon.

"More like moral support." Lizzie flashed a grin over
her shoulder. "Ordinarily, Emma's a sweetie, but she

gets real cranky if she's awakened from a nap. If you could just grab the bag from the backseat, that'd be great."

Lizzie opened the back door quietly and bent over the form of a toddler strapped in the car seat. Steve caught sight of strawberry-blond hair curling wildly, cheeks flushed with sleep. Carefully, Lizzie unbuckled the center strap and began to lift her daughter, handling her as delicately as if she were a Fabergé egg.

A wasted effort. Whether Lizzie's daughter sensed the slight shift in her body as she was lifted or felt the cool of the morning on her rosy cheeks was anybody's guess. Whatever the reason, by the time they reached the front door, Emma had worked herself into a full-blown snit and was busy communicating her displeasure to anyone within a mile of the house.

Lizzie's soft crooning of "Emma, hon, guess where we are? We're at *Ty's* house, just like I told you," along with the kisses she was planting on Emma's tearstained face, had little effect. They entered the house with Emma still going full force.

It was a sign of just how thrilled Ty and Lizzie were to see each other that their cries of "Hello," "Surprise," "I can't believe this—what are you doing here?"' were audible over the din Emma was making.

When Ty said, "Here, let me take Emma; maybe that will distract her," Steve sent a quick prayer heavenward. His eardrums were starting to ring.

But the noise became even shriller as soon as Lizzie got within range of Ty. "My God, what's happened to you? Those circles under your eyes, you look like death warmed over . . . and that *smell!* What is it?"

Ty, too chagrined to explain, began lurching toward Lizzie and Emma with all the grace of someone just recovering from two busted legs. At that point, Lizzie's horror underwent a swift transformation. Eyes flashing, she whirled, snarling, "What have you done to her? She's crippled!"

His head snapped back as Lizzie advanced menacingly. And he'd been dumb enough to categorize Ty's friend as an easygoing party girl? The woman was out for blood. "If you've hurt Ty," the virago continued, coming far too close for comfort, "I'll make you rue the day you were born, you . . ."

Hands up, Steve took a hasty step backward. "Whoa, hold on there, all I did was walk on Ty's back, and she *asked* me to . . ."

Ty spoke up. Loudly. Drowning out Steve's reply and Emma's continued squawks. "I'm okay, really, Lizzie. Lizzie," she repeated even more loudly, finally getting her friend's attention. "*I'm okay*. Just a little stiff. I went riding yesterday."

Fortunately for Steve, Ty's words registered. As the words sank in, Lizzie's reaction was comical. Jaw slack with astonishment, a huge grin began spreading over her face. Then, with an ecstatic "Yes!" Lizzie pumped her closed fist in the air, boots stomping as she ran in place, Emma bouncing in her arms.

Victory dance complete, she pounced, planting a loud kiss on Steve's cheek. "You, Steve Sheppard, are a good man," Lizzie exclaimed, beaming approval. "An *excellent* man. Thank you! Thank you! Thank you! Emma, honey, give Steve a big kiss. He got Ty back on a horse again!"

Emma seemed to share her mother's quicksilver temperament. No longer put out now that the adults were providing such noisy entertainment with which to distract her, Emma happily stretched out chubby arms. A split second later, Steve received another, much wetter buss on the cheek. Then the toddler, leaning dramatically away from her mother's body, was immediately transferred to Ty's impatient embrace.

Steve watched Ty hug Emma fiercely, the little girl's arms wrapped about her neck. An odd sort of contentment filled him as Ty stood there, her dark, sleek head close to Emma's, whispering about how big she'd gotten in the past two weeks, while Emma jabbered on in a high-pitched voice about ponies, toys, books, Mommy, and food.

The mention of food was enough to send the small party ambling into the kitchen. Steve poured coffee, Ty sat at the kitchen table with Emma on her lap, Lizzie hunted through the refrigerator for juice for Emma, also pulling out eggs, butter, bread, and maple syrup. Everyone tried to talk at once.

"The reason we're here, waking you up at the crack of dawn, Ty, is that my fax machine went down yesterday. Darned thing went on strike. But as it happened, I was heading out this way in any case. I'm checking out some ponies this morning for the parents of one of my riders." She mentioned the name of a stable in Amagansett, located about nine miles east of Steve's place in Bridgehampton. "If I find one that's suitable and in my price range—a big if—I'm hoping to buy a school pony, too. Naturally, I came up with the brilliant idea that we'd drop by, hand over the client list and Vicky's number, look at some ponies, and satisfy my insatiable curiosity about how you're doing." Lizzie grinned. "In other words, I'm breaking your cardinal rule and mixing business with pleasure."

"That right, Ty, you don't believe in mixing business with pleasure?" Steve asked, a wicked smile playing over his lips. He was standing near the kitchen sink, a hip cocked negligently against the butcher-block counter, hands wrapped around a mug of coffee.

He was too handsome by half. "I've always been told that it's an invitation to disaster to mix the two," Ty replied, pleased that her voice sounded so steady.

Steve merely smiled, saying nothing. But she could feel his eyes on her mouth, instantly conjuring the incredible sensation of what it had been like to feel his lips moving over hers. Hurriedly she looked away, but then made the foolish mistake of glancing down at his bare feet.

Embarrassment swept through her. Now that the moment had passed, she couldn't believe she'd been so, well, so *brazen* as to ask Steve to walk on her back. Then she thought of how Steve's weight bore down upon her, the force easing all the knots inside her, making her loose with pleasure. Such incredible pleasure. And she didn't mix business with pleasure? Hah! What a total hypocrite she was. She knew it, and so, obviously, did Steve.

Hastily, Ty redirected her thoughts. "It's really great to see you and Emma."

Lizzie handed Ty a cup of juice for Emma, which the two-year-old tried to grab with both hands. "Ditto for us, Ty. We're also pleased to make Steve's acquaintance," she added archly. She hadn't missed the look Ty and Steve had exchanged. Or that it positively sizzled. Lizzie was thrilled; this had been a long time coming. "You've got a truly beautiful place here, Steve."

"Thanks. I like it. Landscape's real different from where I grew up in Kentucky, but few places can match the sky and light that you find in eastern Long Island," Steve replied easily, not for a single moment forgetting this woman's fierce protectiveness toward Ty. He'd give a good deal to know why Lizzie Osborne felt it necessary to protect her friend. And something about the whole scene in the entryway teased his memory. Similar to the way the name of a long-ago classmate hovers but remains frustratingly elusive.

It occurred to Steve that if he could get Lizzie Osborne alone, he might unearth some very useful information about his partner. Like what made her tick. Like why some things about her seemed strangely familiar.

"So you're in the horse business, too?"

"More like the pony business," Lizzie corrected with a grin. "Mainly pony hunters and children's hunters for my older kids. Of course, that may change as my clients grow up. You know, get rid of their braces." She wondered when Steve Sheppard was going to remember exactly who Ty was. It was tempting to jolt his memory a bit, but Ty had already shot her a stern look, giving a quick shake to her head. Lizzie regretfully abandoned the idea, saying instead, "I've got a small stable, Cobble Creek, located outside Bedford. The drive's close enough that I get kids from the city as well as local riders."

Steve drained his coffee and placed it on the counter beside his hip. "Well, I'm sure the two of you have a lot to talk about." A man with two sisters, he knew what to expect when women got together with friends. "I've got to head over to the barn and feed the horses. Bubba'll be coming by later."

"Why don't we get breakfast ready while you're gone?" Lizzie offered. "Then you and Ty can tell me about your plans for Southwind when you get back."

"Holy heavenly host, Ty, he's gorgeous! Way better than when we were kids, if you ask me. Tougher. It's horribly unfair the way men improve with age." She gave a dramatic sigh as she placed a bowl of dry Cheerios in front of Emma. "Here, Em, munch on these. How about we make some french toast? We skipped breakfast."

While Emma happily grabbed oat rings by the fistful

and dry Cheerios scattered over the round wooden table, Ty came over to stand by Lizzie. Lizzie hid a smile at how carefully her friend was moving, asking instead, "How's it going between you?"

"Educational. It was pretty naive of me to think that just because I wanted to help Steve out of this situation, that would make everything easy." She sighed. "He's a complex man."

"Yeah, but if he weren't complex, you wouldn't be interested, and you know it, Ty." Lizzie paused, expertly cracking an egg with one hand against the rim of a mixing bowl. "Just for the record, what did those guys you'd bring along as dates talk about that had your eyes glazing over a mere thirty seconds later?"

Ty laughed, raising her hands in surrender. "Touché! Okay, I admit it. I have a major problem with men who never deviate from their two favorite topics of conversation: how much money they made this week, and how much money they're planning to make *next* week."

"Ugh! Totally brain-dead!" Lizzie exclaimed in disgust. "No wonder you never wanted to sleep with any of them! But I bet Steve's not like that," she speculated with a small smile.

"No," Ty agreed ruefully. "He's arrogant, obnoxious, bullheaded, and a general pain in the neck. He can be downright devious, too," thinking of how he'd purposely encouraged her belief that he enjoyed living in a moldy, dust-filled ruin of a house. But then, with customary honesty, she found herself adding, "He's also smart and funny and cares about people." Ty briefly explained Steve's relationship with Bubba Rollins. "And lastly, he's devoted to his horses. Fancy Free's death really shook him."

Lizzie nodded sympathetically, beating the eggs with quick flicks of her wrist. "In short, he's perfect for you."

Ty opened her mouth to object, then thought better of it, knowing she couldn't fool her best friend. "Yes," she agreed, "I'm afraid so."

"Well, buck up, kiddo. I caught the way he was looking at you, and I think he's more than ready to mix a little pleasure with this particular business."

"Already has," Ty mumbled, a rush of heat spreading through her.

"I heard that, and you'd better tell all, or I won't let you have a slice." As if to make good her threat, Lizzie cut off a thick chunk of butter and dropped it in the frying pan. Sizzling, it melted quickly. "Okay, ready for the first one. We'll see how many we need to make. Start talking, kid."

The scent of cooking batter soon filled the kitchen, its aroma mouthwatering. "All right," Ty grumbled reluctantly. "He kissed me yesterday."

"Good girl." Lizzie nodded encouragingly as she lowered another egg-coated slice into the pan. "And?"

"And . . . oh, God, it's so confusing, Lizzie . . . he kisses like he means it, but I've been thinking about it a lot—the kiss, that is—and I've come to the conclusion he was just doing it out of gratitude, thanking me for having planted these trees."

"You think he was kissing you out of gratitude?" Lizzie's voice was incredulous.

Ty shrugged. "Sure. He's a really physical person—Lizzie, he can do things with his hands," Ty said, a delicious shiver racing down her spine at the memory of Steve's caresses. "And he's already mentioned he hasn't had sex in a while." Ty could so easily picture the woman, Cynthia, whom Steve had been trying to hustle into his bed, that Ty was confident she'd be able to pick her out of a lineup. She'd be blond, pert, buxom. Really *cute*. All the things Ty wasn't. "So I think Steve was probably feeling . . ."

"Horny," Lizzie supplied dryly. "Ty, I'm truly disappointed in you. Have you taken a look in the mirror lately? You don't honestly believe a guy like Steve's only willing to kiss you, a beautiful woman, out of *gratitude* or because you're convenient and he hasn't had sex recently? You've got to be kidding!"

"Of course not," Ty protested uncomfortably. She wasn't used to talking like this, even with Lizzie. It was during moments such as these when she envied Lizzie her supreme confidence in dealing with the opposite sex. For Ty, too many years had passed during which she'd been subjected to the attentions of men who either fawned over her or paraded around like preening peacocks, neither reaction having a thing to do with Ty the person but rather with the neon-lit dollar signs that floated around the Stannard name, attracting men, making them behave like complete morons. Steve wasn't like them, Ty knew, but that didn't mean she believed he was truly attracted to her, either.

"Look, Ty," Lizzie said with some exasperation, reading the bleak look on her friend's face, "let's stick to cold, hard evidence here. Just the facts, ma'am. You've already admitted he kissed you like he meant it . . . well, what happened next? Remember, we're talking french toast here."

"Nothing, really. Bubba came by, and that was the end of that, which was probably a good thing . . ." Ty's voice trailed off.

Lizzie said warningly, "Ty . . ."

"All right. Steve already had my sweater off without my even knowing it. Then, this morning . . ."

"Yes?" Lizzie prompted. "This morning . . ."

"Well, I asked him to walk on my back." Ty ducked her head.

"Oh, my. That is extremely . . . intimate."

"I *know*. I can't believe I asked him. I was probably a little out of my mind. You wouldn't believe the pain I was in when I rolled out of bed. Lizzie, I rode two of Steve's horses yesterday," Ty informed her eagerly. "They were unbelievable! Riding's definitely got me hooked once more—even if I never walk properly again. It serves me right for being such an overachiever and kidding myself that I could ride two horses in one day."

"Serves you right for being so darned obstinate that not even *I* could convince you to get back in the saddle all these years," Lizzie added.

"Thanks for reminding me."

"That's what friends are for. Look, Ty, I'm ready to rhumba on the roof, I'm so thrilled you're riding again, but we can talk about *that* later. Let's get back to the principal topic here. You were really, really stiff, and you asked Steve to walk on your back?"

"Yes." Ty pressed her lips tight together. "Ow!" she exclaimed as Lizzie poked her in the ribs with her elbow.

"And," Lizzie supplied.

"And . . . God, Lizzie, it was amazing! It felt a little uncomfortable, you know, because of how sore my muscles were, but it was also really erotic. Within two minutes, my brain was mush. And then, oh, Lizzie, he did this thing with his toes, just below my shoulder blades. He moved them. Individually. Slowly."

"Wow!" Lizzie replied, deeply impressed.

"Yes. Definitely wow!"

Silence descended as Lizzie absorbed the implications of Ty's description. "So, good hands, excellent feet," she murmured with the beginnings of a smile. "Ty, honey, you are in luck. I think it's safe to assume we're talking about a man who knows how to use his digits."

A few minutes later, Steve returned to the kitchen to discover Ty and Lizzie, their arms wrapped about each other's shaking shoulders, their bodies convulsed with laughter. Meanwhile, Emma, not wanting to be left out of the fun, was circling around the pair, flinging Cheerios confetti as she ran.

Welcome to bedlam, he thought, suppressing a grin as he sat down before a platter piled high with steaming stacks of french toast.

21

"*H*ere's the list we wrote up last year." Lizzie withdrew a stapled sheaf of papers from a slim leather attaché case sandwiched between picture books and boldly colored plastic toys in Emma's canvas tote bag. She passed it to Ty.

"What's that?" Steve asked, shoving his plate toward the center of the round table. The four of them had made quick work of their breakfast, Emma eating a healthy portion of the french toast, too. "It's a good color for her," Lizzie had offered cryptically.

Pointing her perfect chin toward the sheets of paper in Ty's hand, Lizzie explained, "It's a list Ty and I made of everyone we knew, or had connections with, who had even the remotest interest in the horse world. We used it to set up a network for Cobble Creek—but that was a very specific selection—parents, grandparents with kids of the appropriate age."

"I'd like to go through it again," said Ty, "This time with an eye to adults who ride, own, or might want to form a syndicate with like-minded people and purchase some beautiful, talented, and expensive horses."

"Oh, before I forget, Ty, Vicky's number is on the pink stick-em, upper left-hand corner."

"Thanks."

"Mind if I look at this list of yours?" Steve shifted in his chair, closer to Ty.

"Of course not," Ty replied, trying not to be distracted by the nearness of him. "I'm hoping you'll add names, too. Once we've decided who we should approach first, I'll start telephoning and drafting a letter to send out. That is, after I've reached Vicky."

"Vicky, who's Vicky?" Steve asked, with a flick of his index finger against the small pink rectangle of paper. His eyes were scanning the list of names and addresses, neatly printed on the first page.

"Vicky Grodecki of the *Times.*" Seeing Steve's eyebrows shoot upward, Ty elaborated. "With the National coming up, I think we can get her to do an interview of you, perhaps come out with a photographer and take some pictures. I'm also going to call the editors at *Practical Horseman.* They often do long features with nice spreads."

Steve didn't comment. His eyes were moving slowly down the list of names. Then, "You two been digging through the social register here?"

"Actually, no. Most of these people are business types, captains of industry. They've made their fortunes and are ready to spend."

"Great. Type A personalities who are going to tell me they know how to train their horses. All they really need is a heavier bit, spurs, crop, perhaps a baseball bat to whack the horses between the ears, 'cause everyone knows horses are dumber than shit and these 'captains of industry,' why, they've made reams of money, so they must be real smart and . . ."

Ty held up her hand. "Okay, all right. Got the message. We'll only focus on serious horse people who'd be interested in riding with you, or want to form a syndicate."

"Which adds up to a big zero," Steve replied coolly. "You're forgetting a horse was killed in my stable. You think anyone with half a brain is going to trust me any time soon?"

Lizzie cleared her throat gently. "Steve, you've got to put that behind you. Tragedies happen. You know that. Horses out grazing in a pasture one beautiful summer day. Soon after, they're brought back to their stalls and are running a fever. Their breathing becomes increasingly labored. Before too long, they're dead because of one puny mosquito bite. How many horses died last summer because of the West Nile virus?"

"That's different," Steve said, his brows drawing together in a forbidding line.

"Is it? I can easily imagine the bitter self-recrimination of the people responsible for the care of those horses. How they must have come up with dozens of scenarios where they prevented their deaths. Just like you and Fancy Free." Lizzie eyed him steadily before continuing, "Steve, you're a great horseman. People know that and are going to trust you."

"That's true, Steve," Ty observed, tracing her finger along the folded edge of her napkin. "If there's anything they might still condemn you for, it's for having lost your money."

"No way, that's ridiculous." Steve shook his head, unwilling to believe that Fancy Free's death and not catching Jason Belmar with his hand in the till could even begin to compare.

"I'm serious," Ty insisted. "Bad business practice. Losing piles of money is for many people a far bigger no-no. That's why when Vicky Grodecki comes to interview you, you'll have to make sure you mention *repeatedly* that I'm your new partner and that I'm investing heavily in Southwind."

"Won't be necessary, as you'll be right by my side, like jam on a biscuit. You didn't actually think I'd go solo into this interview?" Steve's mouth quirked in amusement. "Sorry, partner, no dice. It's going to be a whole lot more convincing if the genuine article is sitting right next to me."

"But no one's interested in me . . ."

"Oh, no, of course not." Steve scoffed. "The readers aren't going to be dying of curiosity to find out why the daughter of billionaire real estate tycoon Tyler Stannard is going into the horse business? Hell, most people will be far more interested in *you* than in anything I have to say."

Ty was opening her mouth to argue when Lizzie spoke. "Steve's got you there, Ty. For any interview to make the kind of splash you want, you've got to jump right in there with him."

At Ty's moue of distaste, Steve laughed. "Welcome to the club, Ty." Nice to know he wasn't the only one who didn't want his life picked apart by the press. "Maybe this idea of yours isn't so harebrained after all. I think I might enjoy our chat with this Vicky Grodecki, all the fascinating stuff I'll learn." His laughter redoubled when Ty turned to him and deliberately stuck out her tongue.

Yes, thought Steve, he might very well pick up a few interesting details about Ty when they sat down for a cozy session with Vicky Grodecki. But Steve still considered Lizzie his best source of information. The women were obviously close, a friendship Steve sensed ran deep and true. That's why when he heard Ty decline Lizzie's invitation to go to the stable in Amagansett, citing the need to go through the client list, sort out promising candidates, and make some telephone calls, Steve volunteered to go in Ty's place.

"You'd be willing to come with me?" Lizzie asked, looking startled but pleased. "These are ponies, remember."

Steve shrugged. "Damien's stable has got nice horse-flesh, period. Who knows, might find something I want for myself."

"And you don't mind holding Emma while I try out the larger ponies? I'd kind of thought Ty would be able to come with me . . ."

"Why don't you leave Emma with me?" Ty suggested. "We haven't had any time together."

"But your work . . ."

"I can get most of my things done while she's playing. Then while I'm waiting for people to return telephone calls, I can play, too."

"That'd be great. She'll probably go down for a nap soon, anyway, we woke up so early this morning," Lizzie said enthusiastically. "I hope this doesn't inconvenience you, Steve."

"No, no. It's always fun to check out other stables. Besides," Steve added with a grin that charmed effortlessly. "It'll be a pleasure to become acquainted with such a close friend of Ty's."

Lizzie bounded up from the table saying she'd be back in a second and that they could take her car—she needed to fill the tank for the return trip—but Ty's face was all too easy to read.

That's right, Ty, he acknowledged silently as their eyes held, hers openly suspicious, his innocent as a choir-boy's. *Lizzie and I will have lots to talk about.*

They left Ty and Emma immersed in washing the dishes. Emma was standing on a stepladder next to Ty, her arms plunged deep into warm, soapy water, which slopped over onto the wooden counter as she enthusiastically scrubbed plates and mugs before presenting them for Ty's inspection.

Steve drove, knowing far better than Lizzie which roads would avoid the double nuisance of having to pass through the center of Bridgehampton and having to drive for long stretches on Route 27, a road that, even off-season, Steve detested. He took his time, tooling down the twisting roads at a sedate pace, happy to have Lizzie Osborne's undivided attention.

"You and Ty go back a ways," he observed casually.

"Third grade," Lizzie responded readily. "Mrs. Ottom. Rhymes with rock bottom." Her lips curled in a smile. "Ty was new that year. We had the misfortune of being stuck in a class packed with the cattiest little girls in all of New York City. They never gave Ty a chance."

"What do you mean by that?"

"Come on, I'm sure you can imagine how hard it is for people to deal with the kind of money Ty's father has. Those girls were as horrid as they could be. But their loss was my gain, because Ty and I ended up being best buddies, and a better friend I've never known. She's Emma's godmother, you know." Lizzie paused, her head turned slightly toward the car window, as though she were admiring the dense stands of scrub oak the car passed. "I might not even have Emma if it weren't for Ty."

Steve glanced over, bewildered. What was she talking about?

There. She'd said it, a subject she hated discussing to the very marrow of her bones. But Lizzie had the impression that Steve had no idea what kind of person Ty really was—just how special a human being he was involved with.

"I married a man who cheated on me from the word go. Though Michael probably jumped the gun on that, too." Her voice was flat, without inflection. In hindsight, Lizzie was convinced that Michael was never capable of being faithful. She was also fairly certain that Michael had been sick enough to hit on Ty, too. Ty must have had something to threaten him with, something deeply humiliating if ever revealed publicly in order to have Michael drop the custody suit so quickly. Something that would derail Michael's ambition for a future in politics. But Lizzie would go to her grave before ever voicing any of her suspicions. She just thanked God that Michael was history. Whatever disgusting moves he'd put on Ty could remain there, too.

"For a long time, I was heavily in denial about our marriage. The stories we tell ourselves!" Lizzie laughed softly. "It wasn't until I became pregnant with Emma that I realized I had to get out."

Behind the steering wheel, Steve shifted uncomfortably. This wasn't exactly what he'd had in mind when he envisioned how he might pump Lizzie for information. "Divorce sucks," he said, wishing he could offer more than a dumb-ass platitude.

"Yeah, especially when all its nastiness is highlighted in local papers." Lizzie's lips thinned in a small smile as Steve's eyebrows shot upward. "You read the gossip columns?"

Steve shook his head. "Don't have time for that sort of crap."

"Now I know why I instinctively liked you. My divorce was the equivalent of a five-course meal for most of New York for several months. The details were delicious. The papers, and their readers, too, apparently, couldn't get enough. They wanted dessert, too. The icing on their cake was when word leaked out that

Michael had put a stop on our joint checking account. Everybody oohed and aahed, my so-called friends shook their heads, but not one of them ever considered lending a hand."

Again, Lizzie broke off to stare out the window as if the present scenery of dried and withered cornfields were a marvel. From the corner of his eye, Steve saw Lizzie rub her brow wearily, but her voice, when she continued, remained even.

"Within an alarmingly short period of time, all my money, as well as my parents' savings, had been eaten up by the lawyers."

"The fees those guys charge are unbelievable."

"You can say that again. But the point of this story is that Ty bailed me out. Actually, she did more—somehow, she managed to twist Michael's arm to drop the custody battle. Then she paid all those terrifyingly huge fees I owed the lawyers. I don't know what I would have done without her. I was close to losing it—a total basket case, convinced Michael would win, that Emma would be taken from me. I was so wrecked emotionally and psychologically, I kidded myself into thinking that Ty's father might help me out."

"Wait a second." Steve shook his head, trying to keep the story straight in his mind. "You went to Ty's father for help?"

"Yeah, but sanity returned pretty damned quickly. It only took Stannard's incomparable manner of saying, 'Sorry, no dice, bimbo.' After turning me down flat, he warned me not to breathe a word of my problems to Ty, then had me physically escorted off the premises."

Steve frowned. "But he must have known you and Ty were close, right?"

"Yeah, but a bigger son of a bitch you will *never* meet. How Ty survived growing up alone in that house with him I'll never know . . ." Sam Brody's name was on the tip of her tongue, but then Lizzie remembered she wasn't supposed to jog Steve's memory. She bit back the words, saying instead, "I guess that's why underneath it all, she's a hell of a lot tougher than he could ever be. I think . . ."

Lizzie would have continued, but Steve interrupted, zeroing in on a detail Lizzie had thrown out so casually. "What do you mean, alone? Are Ty's parents divorced?"

Lizzie looked over at him strangely, then with dawning comprehension. "Good God, she hasn't said a word, has she? Well, that's Ty for you. She'd rather walk over burning coals than reveal any of the sadness in her life. I think she's afraid someone will accuse her of doing the 'poor little rich girl' routine or something like that. No, her parents aren't divorced. Ty's mother died giving birth to her. She doesn't have any family except for her father—I'd say that's worse than having none at all."

Steve closed his eyes for a second, then massaged his temple with his left hand, letting his right hand do the steering. Jesus, what a fucking idiot he was. Self-disgust flooded him as he recalled his snide comment about how he doubted little Miss Stannard knew a bloody thing about loss. At that moment he'd have loved nothing more than to jump out of his skin so he could give himself a few hundred swift kicks in the ass.

"Go on, tell me what happened next," he instructed, not at all certain he wanted to hear any more.

"Well, one of my many failings is that I rarely listen to anyone's advice, above all never from men who think they can threaten and intimidate me. *That* lesson I learned from Michael, my ex. Soon after the fiasco with Ty's father, Ty returned from overseas where she'd been working for her father's company. I told her everything: the endless court battles, the lawyers' fees, my parents' and my money drained to the last penny, my pathetic attempt to beg a loan from her father. What happened next still keeps me awake at night, wondering whether I should have had my lips surgically sealed. Then I think of Emma, and selfish though it is, I can't help but feel better."

"What'd she do when she heard?" asked Steve, though he was beginning to suspect he knew it all already, because in his heart he knew exactly the kind of person Ty was.

"She disinherited herself. Well, that might not be the exact term for it—I'm not sure that actually can be done legally. But what Ty did was just as effective: she told her father to f--- off. Ty turned in her resignation letter the next day, quitting her position at Stannard Limited. She also informed the old man that she'd reject any money from the company or from him, and that included this huge—and I mean *huge*—trust fund Stannard had created for her. She walked away from it all—money, power, prestige—for me and Emma."

It was a good thing Edgemere Farm didn't have any jumper prospects lounging around in its warm, roomy box stalls. As it was, Steve almost missed the turn-off for Damien Schoenberg's place. He wouldn't have been able to concentrate worth a damn if a horse had been trotted out for him to look over.

He simply couldn't get Ty out of his mind.

He was trying to sort it all out. When he was a kid, Steve's family had often spent winter evenings working on enormous jigsaw puzzles, puzzles so large they covered the bridge table the Sheppards set up in a corner of the living room, not too far from the fireplace. As the family became increasingly adept, they graduated to more abstract puzzles, ones with fewer details and more subtle shifts of color. Steve remembered how he'd loved taking a piece in his hand, holding it in his palm, and rotating it slowly, his eyes glancing now and again at the piece's curves and scalloped edges. He'd contemplate the gaps that remained, areas emphasized by the dark wood veneer of the bridge table, knowing that with patience and perseverance, he had all that was necessary to complete the image before him.

That's probably why he was standing in the center of Damien's outdoor ring, feeling increasingly dazed and disoriented as the pieces of the puzzle that was Ty Stannard began to fit. Certain key elements were still missing from the picture, but the details beginning to emerge left him stunned.

For some inexplicable reason, he'd gotten extraordinarily lucky.

Into his life had walked a beautiful, intelligent woman who possessed such an extraordinary degree of spirit, of compassion, that it left him feeling humbled.

He truly admired Ty for what she'd done for Lizzie; in this life, it was all too easy to be a fair-weather friend. And it took incredible guts to stand up to one's family. Especially if it meant turning one's back on the only relation one had left in the world. The decision must have torn Ty apart. But what Steve couldn't fully grasp was why she had bothered to do so much for *him*. A stranger. What had he done to deserve her generosity, her care? That part of the puzzle remained unsolved.

Since they'd arrived at Edgemere, Steve had simply been going through the motions, observing with a distracted eye as a roly-poly pony, practically as wide as it was tall, called Wisp—a grave misnomer if ever there was one—was led into the ring for Lizzie to try. And try Lizzie did. Not even a good five minutes of squeezing and clucking could persuade the pony to move out of a lumbering walk. Damien had hastily signaled one of the grooms hanging around the exercise ring to run back to the barn for a crop.

Steve glanced at his watch. Lizzie was making a valiant effort with Wisp, but he doubted it was worth the trouble. In addition to having a distinct aversion to any gait faster than a walk, the pony also possessed the disconcerting habit of abruptly dodging into the center of the ring and yanking up any blades of grass it happened upon. If she'd wished, Lizzie certainly could have gotten the pony's attention pretty quickly. But she was purposely trying to mimic the moves of an inexperienced rider. It would be the kids who climbed onto the back of this obstinate fatso who'd have to deal with him, not her.

Wisp perked up a bit when a crop was finally placed in Lizzie's right hand. As the pony moved reluctantly into a trot and then a canter, Steve, in a habit formed years ago on the track, glanced down at his watch again and timed how long it took Wisp to complete a lap of the ring. As he expected: he'd seen turtles move faster than this pony.

He pulled a cigarette from the pack nestled in his front pocket and lit it, wondering how much longer Lizzie would take to decide. If she intended to use Wisp as a school pony or as a beginner's mount, anyone on this pony's back would need far stronger leg muscles than most young kids were equipped with to get Wisp's attention and keep him focused. Unless, of course, Lizzie planned to have them swatting the pony every other minute with a crop which, in Steve's opinion, was a lousy way to teach beginners. Advanced riders would be ready for something a tad more responsive.

Lizzie must have drawn pretty much the same conclusion, because a minute later she brought Wisp into the center of the ring and hopped off. She gave the pony an affectionate pat on the shoulder, then turned to Damien. "He's a nice pony, Damien, real solid. But I think I'd like to try out the other ones you mentioned on the phone. See whether they're more what I had in mind."

Steve coughed into his fist, hiding a smile. Lizzie Osborne knew the horse trade business. If presented with a clunker, be polite, never tell the owner your real opinion, but make certain he gets the message you're nobody's fool. Then maybe he won't waste your time on the next go-round.

The next two ponies Lizzie rode were in an entirely different category from Wisp. Lizzie tried a cute-as-a-button Dartmoor pony named Fly, whose coat, a glossy bay, was set off by four white stockings and a white star between its eyes. Fly moved nicely, too, approaching the couple of cross bars Lizzie took him over with ears pricked forward, alert and confident. Because of her size, Lizzie didn't attempt taking him over any larger fences, but Steve could tell she was pleased with Fly's attitude.

The second pony was larger, a Welsh mix and considerably bigger than the Dartmoor. Sassafras was snow white and had a bit of mischief in his eye, the kind of impish spunk that made ponies a whole different story from horses. But Sassafras moved over the flat like a pro and had his flying changes at the canter down cold. Lizzie was able to try him over a few larger fences, too. He cleared them with a good six inches of air. Of the two ponies, Steve himself preferred Sassafras. He was a pony a kid could grow on, physically as well as developmentally, one that would keep a young rider thinking. The smaller pony, Fly, was a little too "made" for Steve's taste, a pushbutton pony. Where was the fun in riding a pony that could go and win a blue ribbon all by itself? On the other hand, he didn't know what Lizzie's clients were like, and he wouldn't dream of telling her how to do her job—she seemed more than competent. That was what Steve had told Damien Schoenberg when the trainer expressed surprise—pleasant surprise—at Steve's unexpected presence at Edgemere. No, he was just along for the ride, keeping a friend of a friend company.

Lizzie brought Sassafras to where Damien and Steve stood and dismounted. "I like Fly and Sassafras a lot, Damien," she said, slipping the reins over Sassafras's neck and stroking the pony's velvety gray muzzle. The pony's lips curled and flapped beneath Lizzie's fingers.

"Both of them are great ponies. Nice manners. Sound, too. And they've both shown in A-rated shows. Fly's often champion or reserve champion by the end of the day," Damien stated proudly, confirming Steve's opinion of the little bay.

Lizzie handed Damien the reins, and the three of them began walking toward the parking area near one of the other exercise rings, this one filled with students trotting in single file. Damien motioned to a teenage girl standing by the railing who immediately came over and relieved Damien of Sassafras, leading the white pony back to the barn.

"What I'd like to do, Damien, is call my clients and find out when we can bring their daughter out to try Sassafras and Fly. Would it be convenient if I called you later today or perhaps this evening?"

"Of course." Damien nodded agreeably as the three of them came to a standstill in front of Lizzie's car. "I'm usually up until eleven. I'll look forward to hearing from you." He turned to Steve and extended his hand. "Steve, it was good to see you. You going to the National this year?" he inquired a shade too heartily. Like many in Steve's circle of professional riders and trainers, Damien had fumbled awkwardly during the first few minutes of their conversation, unable to express how saddened he was by the recent tragedy at Southwind.

Steve shook Damien's extended hand. "Yeah, I'm bringing Gordo and Macintosh. It won't be the same without Fancy," he admitted, "but Gordo and Mac have been going great lately."

"Well, best of luck."

"Thanks. I'll see you around, Damien, and if you hear of any jumper prospects, give me a buzz."

22

$\mathcal{D}$ishes washed, dried, put away, Emma chattering continuously throughout, Bubba come and gone, with a chuck to Emma's dimpled chin and a list for Ty of items she might consider purchasing: new jumps and jump wings (although she'd have to consult Steve to find out which kind he wanted), an indoor horse shower and dryer Bubba wanted to install at the far end of the barn, sofa, armchairs, and coffee table for the lounge, and videotaping equipment. At the bottom of the list, Bubba had written in block letters: MORE STAFF, CUS-TOMIZED BASEBALL HATS, AND ALL-WEATHER GEAR.

Ty grinned when she read these last items. It seemed Bubba was getting into the spirit of the endeavor. Well, if Southwind's manager wanted additional help and fancy logo baseball hats, that's what he'd get. Ty only wished Steve would prove equally enthusiastic.

Emma loved to draw, which was fortunate. It allowed Ty to begin telephoning, drafting letters, and tracking down Vicky Grodecki as well as other editors at various horse journals. She was sure at least one of them would be interested in doing a piece on Steve and Southwind. As Emma sat on the floor, filling page after page with colorful slashes, dots, and cyclone-like spirals, Ty jotted down notes, dialed numbers, and mulled over what she considered her greatest challenge. In essence, it was a marketing problem. What sort of lure could they use to entice people to Southwind so that they could see firsthand what a beautiful farm this was, what great facilities Southwind boasted, and, most important, what an outstanding trainer Steve was? Printed articles and photographs, the kind of publicity magazines and papers provided, weren't enough. They needed more, something special.

Ty sat in the armchair, mulling over possibilities, discarding one after another, staring down at Emma's strawberry-blond ringlets, noting absently how the red highlights in the two-year-old's hair reminded her of the golden strands in Cantata's mane. She paused, inspiration a tingling electricity flowing through her veins. That was it!

Steve had been terrific coaching her on Macintosh and Cantata. Imagine the number of people who would give their eyeteeth for that kind of personalized instruction from someone like Steve. If she could get Steve to offer a weekend clinic where riders could board their horses at Southwind, during which they'd receive three days of lessons and coaching, working on the flat as well as over fences, horse people would be scrambling to sign up.

The idea of a clinic had a second advantage, too, Ty realized, becoming increasingly excited. Not only would people be beating down Southwind's gates for a chance to rub shoulders with a rider as great as Steve Sheppard, but once they saw how fantastic a coach he was, they'd want to stay on permanently. But that wasn't all, she thought, a smile growing on her face. Steve could use the clinic as a kind of admissions test: only riders with whom Steve felt he could really work would be invited to board their horses at Southwind, to train and show with Steve. An effective way to weed out potential headaches like Allegra Palmer. And by now, Ty understood Steve well enough to realize he'd be much more cooperative if given control over the decision process. With a triumphant grin, Ty tossed her pen into the air and sprang if not nimbly, then enthusiastically, from the chair.

"Emma, love, I've got it! This is cause for celebration! What do you say we go get you a big cup of milk?"

"Orange juice!" Emma countered.

Ty considered. It wasn't milk, but at least it was good for her young goddaughter. "Okay, orange juice it is, and I'll make a huge cup of coffee. Black, with loads of sugar, 'cause I deserve it!"

Scooping Emma into her arms, they left artwork, displaying Emma's talent with colors, scattered over the living room floor and went off in search of vitamin C and caffeine.

The slow, steady drip of the coffeemaker had finished, its glass pot filled with dark brew, the aroma of which wafted through the warm kitchen. Emma was busy guzzling orange juice from the spout of her plastic cup, her legs scissoring back and forth against the smooth wood of the kitchen chair, and Ty's mind was busy working out details. There were twenty box stalls in Southwind's barn, three of them occupied. That left room to accommodate seventeen horses. Good. Too big a clinic, and the riders wouldn't receive the kind of personalized attention from Steve that would make an event like this special, alluring.

Ty had just lifted the coffeepot to help herself when

the front doorbell rang. Probably Bubba with more items for his wish list, thought Ty with a smile.

"Hey, Em, let's go open the door. Yes, you can bring your juice. Coming," Ty called, raising her voice in the hopes it might carry sufficiently. She bent slightly and hefted Emma onto her left hip, keeping a wary eye on the juice cup, which was listing rather alarmingly toward the front of Ty's button-down shirt. "On second thought, let's leave the juice."

The front door opened to reveal, not Bubba Rollins, but Sam Brody. "Sam!" she cried in surprise. "What are you doing here?"

" 'Morning, Ty." Sam grinned, his eyes meeting hers briefly, before settling on the cherubic face of Emma. Ty caught a flicker of emotion in Sam's tawny eyes as he gazed at the toddler, who, in turn, was staring back at him with open curiosity.

"Come on in, Sam." Ty stepped back, her free hand ushering him inside. "Emma and I were just making coffee. Emma, honey, this is Sam, an old friend of your mommy's and mine."

Sam appeared astonished when Emma immediately stretched out her arms upward and diagonally, their goal the corded column of Sam's neck. Recovering himself, Sam quickly grasped Emma.

Well, isn't this interesting? thought Ty, amused, watching the pair now that she and Sam had finished performing the exchange of Emma's outstretched body. Emma was running her palms up and down Sam's bristled jaw, the golden-brown stubble apparently fascinating to the toddler. Even more interesting was her ex-bodyguard's reaction. For a second, while Emma's tiny hands went about their sensory exploration, Sam had stood, apparently frozen in shock. Then suddenly, with a grin that brought to mind a Barbary pirate, Sam had ducked his head, planting his mouth against the side of Emma's neck and had blown an outrageously loud strawberry against the toddler's soft skin.

Emma had shrieked in delight, her hands fisting into Sam's short dark hair. Pumping her sturdy little body up and down in his arms, Emma demanded, "Again, again!"

Four wet strawberries later, the three of them were seated around the kitchen table, Emma bouncing happily on Sam's knees, Sam seemingly totally at ease in his role as Emma's newest plaything.

Ty placed a cup of coffee before him. "Congratulations, Sam," she laughed, "Emma's taken a shine to you."

"Great kid. Obviously has excellent taste in men. I take it Lizzie's somewhere nearby, too?" His voice was casual.

Ty nodded. "She and Emma arrived earlier this morning. Lizzie's looking at some ponies out in Amagansett. I imagine she'll be back soon. So what brings you out here? Getting visits from my two closest friends on the very same day is nothing short of amazing. Wonderful but amazing."

"No, we didn't plan it," Sam said with a smile. "Pure coincidence. It's been years since I've seen or talked to Lizzie." His left hand ruffled Emma's curls, as cautiously Sam brought the coffee cup to his lips, avoiding Emma's squirming body.

Ty was right, Sam acknowledged. Emma did resemble her mother. Sam could picture Emma in fifteen years' time, effortlessly dazzling the entire male population, and a fiercely intense need to protect filled him. Similar to the one he'd experienced when he'd received a matted photograph in the mail, announcing Emma's birth. The picture had shown a tiny baby, wrapped in a light pink blanket, sleeping peacefully. What had held

Sam spellbound, as he battled emotions, was the image of Lizzie.

Lizzie, all grown up, that incredible reddish-gold hair cascading down her shoulders, its ends brushing Emma's blanket. She'd been smiling, but her smile hadn't quite erased the sadness shadowing her eyes. Eyes Sam remembered as always being so full of life, mischief, and joy.

Emma bounced, hard, bringing Sam abruptly back to the present. *Forget it, Brody,* he said to himself. *It ain't going to happen. Never in a million years.* "She probably doesn't even remember me." he added, not realizing he'd said the last aloud.

"Oh, I can assure you Lizzie remembers you, all right. It's not as though you're an easy man to forget. Are you going to tell me why you're here, or am I supposed to guess?"

"If you did, you'd only get it half right. That means I'd better tell you—wouldn't want your grade average to drop," Sam teased, grinning at Ty's narrowed glance. "Main reason I'm here is as a favor to another friend of mine. He's got a great-aunt living alone out here, in Georgica. Ninety-something and still going strong. But Alex worries she's too isolated living with no relatives nearby. He asked me to install a security system in her home, one that's hooked up to the police as well as to his office in Manhattan. But the only way he could persuade her to allow me to set it up was if I agreed to give her private lessons on this computer he bought for her. Mrs. Miller wants to visit museum Web sites, download information, go into chat rooms, all that jazz, but she keeps getting lost in the Web. Spent yesterday afternoon and evening with her. An insatiable woman, Mrs. Miller," Sam finished, his grin even broader.

"You do that sort of thing?" Ty would have thought

this kind of work would be peanuts to him. Sam's company, Securetech, in addition to having a contract with the government, was also consulted by some of the country's biggest corporations.

"As a favor to Alex Miller, yeah." Miller had been one of Securetech's principal and earliest investors. A financial wizard, he had a nose for sniffing out young, developing companies. Alex Miller's interest had given Sam's fledgling business a crucial boost during those tumultuous early months. Now Securetech set the standard by which other companies in the security field measured themselves.

That Ty didn't recognize Alex's name didn't surprise him. Unlike her father, Alex Miller preferred to work behind the scenes. His name rarely hit the headlines, making the influence he wielded all the more impressive.

"I've also got some information for you about your father," Sam continued, getting back to the reason for his unexpected presence. "As I thought, someone's accessed every bit of financial information available about you. I followed the cookie trail, and it went back to Crane, Adderson and White. Your father wouldn't want it to lead back to his own company. Time to figure out when he's going to strike and what tactic he'll choose." Sam would have said more, but Emma abruptly surged to a stand, weaving as she tried to balance on his muscular thighs, effectively bringing Sam and Ty's discussion to an end.

Sam's hands automatically spanned Emma's waist, supporting her, her eyes now almost on level with his. Cornflower blue met amber gold as child and man solemnly took each other's measure.

"Hey, squirt."

"Hey, Sam," Emma's high-pitched voice returned. "Emma needs to go potty."

Sam's mouth quirked. "Awfully glad you decided to share this with me. You want Ty to take you?"

"No, you!" Emma bounced on his legs for emphasis. Sam glanced over at Ty, who shrugged and smiled. "Use the one next to my bedroom. It's upstairs, take a right, second door on your left." Sam nodded, rising, Emma perched on one forearm.

"Okay, off we go. Want me to carry you, Emma?"

"No, I wanna walk!" Emma declared, sliding down Sam's rock-solid body fireman fashion. It was a long trip. Then tugging Sam's fingers, she led the way out of the kitchen.

Alone, Ty took a deep, steadying breath. Sam's news concerning her father was the figurative equivalent of the antidote being almost as poisonous as the venom itself. She shouldn't be surprised. After all, her father had been trying to control her life for as long as she could remember. That she was twenty-five years old would hardly be reason to stop. What caught Ty unawares was the pain and how it sank its barbs into her heart. She'd truly, foolishly, believed herself past the point of caring what her father did.

When the front door opened, voices in the entry signaling the return of Steve and Lizzie, a new concern superseded all others, her father's machinations included. Sam, Lizzie, and she. In the same place. With Steve. Oh, please, God, not today!

Ty shot up from her chair by the kitchen table. "Hi," she called out, a minor feat, considering that panicky foreboding leached her mouth dry, making her tongue seem two sizes too big.

"Hi." Lizzie breezed in, shucking her jacket, Steve following close behind. "Where's Em?" Lizzie inquired, looking around.

"Um, upstairs." Ty motioned vaguely with her hand.

"Conked out, huh?" Lizzie nodded sagely. "All this excitement must have got to her. Emma's such a great napper," she said, pride lacing her voice. "Steve, do you mind if I use the phone?"

"Go ahead, there's one by the sofa in the living room," he replied, all the while looking at Ty.

"Thanks. I'm going to try and reach Catherine's parents, see when they can arrange to come out and try out the ponies at Damien's. They're going to flip over the little Dartmoor pony I rode, Fly, though I'll do my best to have them think in the long term, in which case Sassafras is the better choice. Mmm, is that coffee I smell? Save me a cup, would you? This shouldn't take long."

Before Ty could stop her, before she could figure out how to inform Lizzie that Emma was most definitely *not* napping. That Sam was there. Sam, whom Lizzie hadn't seen in years . . . Sam, who right now was upstairs earning his stripes as Emma's new best friend. Lizzie was gone, leaving Ty and Steve.

She gulped. "Hi, how'd it go?"

"Fine. I like your friend. You okay? You seem a mite shaky." Actually, she looked terrific, if a trifle pale. She'd changed into an azure blue shirt, the vee offering a tantalizing glimpse of skin he'd been thinking about far too often. Her blue jeans were ancient, decades older-looking than she, white with age, frayed at the hems, and tight enough for him to have his fingers itching. Yeah, she looked great. Casually devastating.

Steve hadn't been alone with Ty since this morning, since the mind-blowing-back-walking session, and as much as he truly did like Lizzie, he wanted her gone. He hungered for a chance to taste Ty's lips again, to explore that silky-smooth flesh with his hands. To possess. But it wasn't about to happen with her best friend in the next room and a two-year-old asleep upstairs.

"Uh, what are you doing?" Ty squeaked, her voice no

longer hers to control. His hand was around her arm, just above her elbow.

"Taking you into the kitchen so we can have a cup of coffee together. Like I said, you look a little shaky." *Liar, you'd use any excuse to touch her.*

"Don't you need to go ride or something?" Anything to get him out of here.

"Farrier's working on Gordo. Mac's up next. They need new shoes before the Garden. I've got enough time for a coffee break."

"Oh." Damn. There went her hope of avoiding a meeting between Steve and Sam. Perhaps Steve wouldn't remember, anyway. It was probably sheer conceit to assume that just because *she* could remember every second of their long-ago encounter, Steve would.

"You take it black, right? Sugar?"

"Yes, please." Lord, she must be truly smitten. No other reason for the secret thrill she experienced hearing he knew how she liked her coffee.

Steve carried the mugs toward the table. He had such beautiful hands. Strong and square, they were testimony to years of hard work. Blunt-tipped nails at the end of long, elegant fingers. Clever hands, Ty remembered.

"So, what've you been up to?" Steve asked, pulling out the chair next to her. "How'd the morning go? Make any headway on the list?"

Ty nodded. "And Bubba came by with a wish list."

"Yeah. Mentioned it when I saw him in the barn. Told me if I had one of those shower and heater jobs, it wouldn't take him an hour and a half to groom Gordo every time he decided to take a mud bath."

"What about the other items on the list?" Ty asked, wanting to be sure he agreed before she started placing orders.

"Some of my old stablehands will be returning by the

end of the week. I'd already talked to them. We can hire more as the barn fills up. The rest is cosmetic, right? I'll leave that up to you," Steve finished with an enigmatic smile.

And what precisely did he mean by that?

That she had good taste or, rather, that he still wasn't going to let her make any decisions of real importance? Ty thought of her idea for the clinic. That certainly didn't fall under the category of cosmetic. Well, no time like the present to clarify the situation.

"I also came up with another idea for Southwind."

Steve took a slow sip of coffee, his blue eyes watching Ty steadily over the brim, all too conscious of the number of times he'd brushed her off in the past few days. His pop would have blistered his ears if he'd witnessed Steve's recent behavior. And pop would have been right. "Go ahead, I'm listening."

Ty blinked in surprise. "Right. I was trying to come up with something different to build up Southwind's clientele. It occurred to me that we need to give them a sampling, whet their appetite."

"And how do you plan to do that?"

"A clinic."

"A clinic?"

"Yes." Ty nodded eagerly. "Just one weekend, so it doesn't interfere with your show calendar. We could schedule it for some time in December. That'll give us enough time to get the word out, get everything prepared. We'd offer three days of riding: instruction over the flat, over fences, videotaped with your comments dubbed in a voice-over so that the riders could refer back to problems you pointed out. The horses could all be boarded here, giving the owners an opportunity to see what a beautiful place this is."

He was silent. Silent long enough that Ty had to fight

the urge to fidget. Then, "A busy mind you have, Ty. It'd be interesting to clock. My guess is it's been racing at about seven thousand rpm."

"And you prefer your women dumb and blond?" Dear Lord, why had that slipped out? She must have awakened this morning with a mental image of Steve's date, Cynthia, emblazoned on her brain.

Steve grinned. "Not particularly. These days, frighteningly intelligent brunettes seem awfully appealing." His grin widened when Ty's eyes darted away to peer into the bottom of her cup, as though fascinated by the dregs. "And you think a clinic would attract riders who want to train with me?"

His words had Ty's gray eyes meeting his, comfortable once more, now that they'd left the subject of Steve's taste in women. "Of course," she said with a nod. "I'm willing to bet money on it."

"That so? How much?"

With what could only be described as a cocky smile, Ty named a sum that had Steve shaking his head in laughter. "Sorry, no can do. Even though I'd love to take you up on it, I never bet more than I can afford to lose."

Ty extended her slim hand across the table. "A gentleman's bet, then. But you're still going to lose," she promised, clasping Steve's warm hand firmly. "Remember, I've got firsthand experience. I'm the one who got a private lesson from you."

Did she have any idea how willing he'd be to give her private lessons in any number of subjects? He'd be a real diligent and thorough teacher, no area left uncovered, no subject he wasn't willing to explore in depth. He wondered what it would take to convince her.

"Before you go any further with this clinic idea, you'd better make sure Bubba's agreeable. This bird ain't gonna fly otherwise," he cautioned. "It'll require a lot of extra work." Extra work for Bubba. And for himself, too. That was why it surprised Steve to realize how good, how right, it felt to have Ty sitting there, a huge, happy smile on her face, her eyes shining bright, a kid at Christmas.

"I'll go talk to him right now," she was saying, already rising from her chair. She couldn't believe it! Steve was willing to do it, hold a clinic. If her sore muscles had permitted, she would have performed a tap dance on the table. "Maybe if I offer to groom Gordo for him, he'll be so grateful he'll say yes. Then I can flesh out the details, advertising and the like, while you're riding."

"Speaking of which, can I interest you in hopping on Mac's back again today?"

Those incredible eyes of hers grew round as saucers. "You're joking, right?"

"Nope," Steve replied calmly, shaking his head. "Best thing for you. 'Course, riding bareback on the beach might be a little much." His strong white teeth flashed in a smile at Ty's loud and decidedly inelegant snort. "Seriously, I guarantee you'll feel loads better if you ride Mac for a while—think of it as the hair of the dog that bit you. But if your muscles are still ouchy . . ." The timbre of his voice dropped, reaching out to her like a caress. "I'll be more than happy to walk on you again." *For starters*, he added silently.

"Sounds like a win-win situation, Ty," Lizzie said with a broad smile, unabashedly eavesdropping as she entered the kitchen and made a beeline for the coffee pot. "Go for it."

"What do you say, Ty? Yes?" Steve's voice husky and low.

Ty stilled as his question echoed inside her. What could she say but yes?

She was in love with him. A basic, fundamental, and terrifying truth. A fact she'd been refusing to acknowledge, perhaps not even recognizing it. Since, in all probability, she had loved Steve from the moment she laid eyes on him.

It was useless to pretend love had blossomed only yesterday, or the day before, or even at the meeting with the lawyers. Some bizarre, incomprehensible twist of fate decreed that at the impossibly tender age of fourteen, Ty Stannard would have a golden kernel planted deep in her heart by none other than Steve Sheppard. Unacknowledged, untended, her love for Steve had been growing inside her these past ten years, its roots now deep and strong.

Helplessly, Ty looked across the table. Steve was waiting, balancing the wooden ladderback chair on two legs. His tanned fingers wrapped around an apple he was absently polishing against his sweater, the sweater's hue making Steve's eyes as brilliant and compelling as a sun-kissed ocean.

He smiled. And her heart did a little flip. How could a moment be so casual on one level and yet so perilous?

She opened her mouth to speak. But then the fearsome wonder of this discovery, the complexity of emotions it engendered, seemed so overwhelming that when her mouth parted, with the word *yes* right there on the tip of her tongue, only needing her voice give it life, Ty hesitated. In that split second, Ty saw the danger that lay before her: her yearning heart might reveal far too much in that simple *yes.* And all that Steve would learn from it. And reject.

That moment's hesitation cost her.

In the game of "If only . . . ," Ty supposed that if only she'd had the courage to say yes directly, braving what-

ever sudden insight flashed in those perceptive blue
eyes, if only she'd said yes, then she and Steve would
have already been out the door, heading toward the
barn, neatly skirting the disastrous quicksand of discovery Ty had feared.

But no. Into the kitchen walked Sam Brody, a vi-
brantly happy Emma perched high on his broad shoulders. A volubly happy Emma, too. The toddler launched
into giggles of pure ecstasy when Sam was forced to
duck in order to avoid cracking Emma's curly head
against the lintel. At the sound, three pairs of eyes—two
shocked, one resigned—swiveled and locked on Ty's ex-
bodyguard and her goddaughter.

For several seconds, which to Ty stretched into hours,
one could have heard a pin drop. Then, as had happened ten years ago on a swelteringly hot summer day,
all hell broke loose. A quieter hell yet unmistakable
nonetheless.

A gifted director would have made good use of it, the
sheer awfulness of the situation, zooming in on Steve
and Lizzie's expressions, capturing the emotions that
raced over them, delighting the audience.

Lizzie standing, stunned and dismayed to find her
baby girl getting a taste of the high life on the shoulders
of a dangerous-looking, roughhewn man.

Sam staring back at her, his lips a straight line. A man
who'd always excelled at masking his own emotions,
whose golden eyes missed very little. Not Lizzie's
shock, as it segued into fear, anger, then something else,
as Lizzie finally recognized exactly who it was supporting her child.

Sam Brody, looking nothing like Lizzie's memories of
him. So solid, yet leaner too, his powerful muscles well
defined beneath the light knit shirt he wore, a mountain
on which her daughter Emma presided as queen.

How in God's name could he be so young? was the errant and wholly unwelcome thought that crossed Lizzie's mind. She scowled in irritation. And, for perhaps the first time in her life, found that the use of her tongue had deserted her. Her feet, too, oddly frozen.

The same, however, could not be said for Steve.

Click, click, click. The tumblers slid into place, the lock on that ten-year-old memory finally releasing. Now that last, tantalizing piece of the puzzle stared back at him, the picture complete.

Oh, yes, Steve was remembering everything. And feeling a hundred times a fool for not having recognized Ty Stannard before. A fool these three people just loved to ridicule.

For the second time in the space of twenty minutes, Steve gripped Ty's elbow. Now, however, it was more like a steel manacle closing around a prisoner.

"Excuse us, won't you?" Steve snarled, raking both Sam and Lizzie with a contemptuous glance before dragging an unwilling Ty out the front door.

She tried digging the heels of her paddock boots into the ground, but Steve was walking too fast for her to find purchase. "Where are we going?" she demanded, jerking her arm in the slim hope that it might free her from his hold.

He ignored her efforts as he would a dust mote. "Somewhere far enough away so that I can throttle you in peace." He didn't want those "good friends" of hers running to her rescue. Steve's stride ate up the ground, taking them past the barn, past the pasture where Fancy Free's grave was located, to the far outdoor ring. He came to an abrupt halt near a jump, a rustic wooden gate, painted white with two tall yew bushes planted on either side. "Okay, this is good enough," he said, jerking her around to face him. They stared at each other, eyes clashing. Steve took a step back, and Ty's chin lifted in defiance as his gaze raked up and down her body.

He let out a mirthless laugh. "All grown up now, are we?" His Kentucky drawl cut like a whip. "You must've been having yourself a real good laugh, what with my being too dumb to recognize you." With lips curled in an insolent smile, his eyes took in her breasts, the gentle curve of her hips, and he laughed again. The sound had Ty flinching. " 'Course, you have changed a great deal. My compliments, Junior." He sketched a mocking salute.

The temper Ty had been valiantly holding in check these past days erupted. She stepped forward, her fists clenched at her sides. "Listen, you overgrown creep. So you didn't remember me. So what? Was I supposed to go running up and ask for your autograph again? Bat my eyelashes and remind you of how we met long ago?" Her voice took on a simpering note. "Oh, Mr. Sheppard, I've always been such a fan of yours. Do you remember Lake Placid, 1989, when I . . ."

"Cut the bullshit, Junior. You know exactly what I'm really talking about. I'd begun to think you were different. But no. When you get right down to it, you're the same as those other spoiled, wealthy women after all. You get off playing games with people."

"That's not true! I've done everything I can to help you out of a stinking mess!"

"Oh, you've done more than that. Don't tell me you need your memory refreshed? No worry, mine's back in working order. Let's see. This makes the *second* time that you've intentionally misled me. I don't work real well with partners who are liars. I should know, having had one before."

"Oh, that's rich, Steve, coming from you. Well, I'll tell you what *I* don't like in a partner. I don't like partners

who are overbearing, stubborn, manipulative clods.
Since coming to Southwind, you've been doing your utmost to see how far you could push me. Hoping I'd
break and give up. I've been working my butt off to help
you save this farm."

"Lying your butt off, you mean."

God, how she wanted to sock him. "Bull. You know
damn well you'd never have agreed to make a deal with
me if you hadn't believed I was my father. Want to know
why, Sheppard? I'll tell you. Because you're prejudiced.
Not every rich woman is like Allegra Palmer and her
friends. And so what if I didn't tell you that I was some
girl you met ten years ago? Big deal. You call that dis-
honesty? I call it survival."

"What in hell are you talking about?"

"You want honesty, Steve? Why don't *you* show some
for a change? Answer me this: How would you have
treated me if you'd known I'd offered to save your sorry
self because one day, long ago, when I was a gawky, infatuated fourteen-year-old, you were kind to me for
about fifteen minutes. The first person who'd ever been
kind without expecting something in return." Her gray
eyes sliced through him. "Go ahead, Steve, tell me honestly . . ."

His eyes narrowed.

A cynical smile lifted her lips. "As I thought. Don't
bother, Steve, I know exactly what you'd have done.
You'd have milked a teenage crush for all it was worth.
Because basically, the man you were ten years ago has
vanished," Ty accused, knowing she'd struck her mark
at his slight recoil. "You'd have turned on that devastating Southern charm, a sure bet it would make me so
moonstruck I'd gladly sign over my half of the partnership." The memory of his heated kisses invaded, rekindling her outrage. "You were starting down that path,

anyway—" Ty broke off abruptly, biting her lip, wishing it were her tongue. Perhaps he wouldn't catch what she'd been referring to.

Steve moved with startling speed. One hand again imprisoning Ty's wrist, the other cupping her chin. Forcing her to look at him. Self-righteous anger coursed through his veins, camouflaging another emotion, one he didn't want to acknowledge right then. But then he looked at her, really looked at her, at the haunted expression in those lovely gray eyes. And was lost. The hand gripping her wrist gentled. His other opened, the work-roughened pads of his fingers tracing the ridge of her jaw, down the slender column of her neck.

She trembled. In agonizingly slow motion, Steve's fingers slipped around the delicate silver chain encircling Ty's neck and lifted it, drawing the necklace between them.

His breath suspended, the metal dragged gently between his fingers, inch by inch. And then, there it was, cradled in his broad palm. Steve's thumb brushed the raised image of the galloping horse. The medallion was still warm from where it had rested in the fragrant valley between Ty's breasts.

It was difficult to reconcile the memory of that plain, awkward girl with the lovely, sophisticated woman standing before him now.

"How about this for honesty, Ty?" he said quietly. "I didn't have to remember who you were to know that I wanted you. I wanted you from the moment I saw you at the lawyers' meeting. And every aching hour since then." The lightest of tugs had her body swaying closer, temptingly closer. His lips descended, hovering, his breath fanning lips that trembled uncontrollably. "I didn't have to recognize that adorably shy teenager," he continued huskily, "to know I was falling hard for the maddeningly beautiful and intelligent woman she's become."

Desperate, feverishly hungry lips met, crushing, devouring. Hands clutched, molding, bruising in their need to feel, to have. On and on, it seemed as if they might never stop. And when Steve finally, reluctantly drew his lips away from hers, they remained standing, foreheads touching, lungs heaving from lack of air. Giddy from it, from happiness.

The smile Steve gave Ty erased years from his face as he pressed curved lips against her smooth brow. His hands found hers, lacing their fingers together, bringing their entwined hands to his lips. "You're so lovely," the words interspersed between teasing nibbles, her knuckles apparently delectable.

"You're not so bad yourself," Ty teased, smiling with joy. As though unable to resist the temptation of her smile, Steve plundered them anew, awe and fierce arousal flooding him when her lips parted eagerly beneath him, welcoming him.

"Where are we going?" Ty asked breathlessly, when at last Steve lifted his head. He was tugging her hand, pulling her along, that happy, boyish grin lighting his face.

"We're going for that ride. Come on, I want to show you one of my favorite spots."

23

Lizzie was still scowling.

"Mommy, Mommy, look at me!" Emma chirped, her palms plastered against Sam's jaw, her legs scissoring his neck. "I'm on Sam!"

"So I noticed, sweetie," Lizzie replied dryly, her face clearing as she gazed up at her daughter. "Maybe you want to get down now?"

"No, no! Sam's my new pony, Mommy." The words rushed together as one. "Look how I'm riding!" Emma cried, bouncing up and down to prove it.

The scowl was back in place as Lizzie glared at Sam.

"Hello, Lizzie, long time no see."

"Hello, Sam." She didn't bother to hide the irritation lacing her voice.

A thick brown eyebrow cocked questioningly. "What's with the hostility, Lizzie? Thought you'd be happier to see an old friend."

That was precisely the problem—in a nutshell. Sam Brody was at least fifteen years younger than Lizzie's memory would have led her to expect. How could he stand there, so virile, so confident . . . so *young*? Ignoring his question, Lizzie said, "I'd appreciate it if you released my daughter."

"Emma seems pretty happy where she is. You've got a great kid, Lizzie."

"I know. Her only fault is that she's too trusting."

"Too trusting? Oh, I get it. She hasn't recognized me as the big, bad wolf I really am."

"That's right. Come on down now, Emma."

Emma started to protest, but Sam smoothly cut in. "Hey, Emma, how many somersaults will it take before you're on the ground again?" A gleeful "one" had her twirling above Sam's head, bright red Keds skimming his golden brown hair; "two" was on level with his forehead; and so it went, until they reached "five," and Emma was once more standing on her own two feet. Emma beamed; her mother glared. Sam gave them both an amused smile and went to pour himself a cup of coffee.

"I think you've had enough excitement for one morning, young lady," Lizzie informed her daughter. "Quiet time beckons."

"Ty's room is to your right, first door on the left."

"Thanks. Come on, Emma, say bye-bye to Sam."

"Emma can say good-bye later. I'm not planning on heading back to the city until after I talk more with Ty. From the look in his eye, I'd say Steve Sheppard has a full hour's worth of yelling to get out of his system."

"Highly unlikely," Lizzie replied, only too happy to contradict Sam. "This whole identity issue is just a minor setback. You probably didn't catch the way he looks at her. Sheppard's more than half in love with Ty," Lizzie finished confidently. She affected a big yawn. "Well, I'm feeling rather tired myself. More than likely, I'll fall asleep next to Emma."

Sam shook his head gravely. "Shame on you, Lizzie.

You never used to run chicken. What's the matter? Afraid I'll bite?"

"Of course not," Lizzie snarled, flashing her own white teeth. Unfortunately, however, no comeback sprang to mind sufficiently cutting to put Sam Brody in his place. She'd walk on rusty nails rather than admit that seeing him again after all these years was even remotely disturbing, unnerving. It was nothing more than surprise that had her heart beating so. Surprise that Sam looked so very different.

Her memory must have short-circuited, leaving her disoriented, rattled. Which in turn explained her body's bizarre reaction. No way was this anything close to attraction. Especially as Lizzie hadn't experienced even a smidgen of arousal for a man in more than two years. It was merely an elevated state of agitation—brought on by believing Emma asleep upstairs, only to find her riding Sam's really strong shoulders—Sam, who had no business being here. That would leave any woman, any mother rattled. Yes, that was it.

Satisfied with her explanation, Lizzie lifted Emma into her arms and swept out of the room without a backward glance, hoping Sam Brody would get the message loud and clear. She couldn't care less about his comings or goings.

It was only when she got to the stairs that her steps slowed, her shoulders slumped. But what if lust had indeed had the perversity to strike her? Unexpected, unwanted. Hitting her while she'd stood gaping at Sam, the way lightning might split a lonely tree, setting it ablaze.

It would be horrendously unfair. She now considered herself thoroughly immune to men. Meaningless flirtations were one thing, perfectly acceptable, something society expected. But Lizzie never went beyond flirting anymore. The men who foolhardily tried to pursue her found themselves running up against a formidable wall, topped with broken glass and barbed wire.

Not that Sam Brody would be remotely interested enough to discover that wall for himself, let alone scale it. But if he were so inclined, then he'd suffer the same fate as the others. Reaching the top step, Lizzie paused for a moment on the landing and glanced down, as if able to see right into the kitchen below.

She vowed that Sam Brody would never suspect he had the power to make her burn.

Lizzie Osborne had scampered through her youth, a fuzzy marmalade kitten, insatiably curious, naively reckless, utterly irresistible. As Sam sat thinking of the woman upstairs, he realized that the little kitten had grown claws. He wondered how much of that adorable fuzzball still existed.

The adult Lizzie reminded Sam far more of a feral cat, ready and willing to maul, especially if someone she loved was threatened. But then, just as Sam had been adjusting to this new, updated version of Lizzie, she'd changed before his eyes.

A hell of a transformation, to go from lynx to porcupine in the blink of an eye. Good thing she'd been nervous, otherwise that random barrage of quills she'd shot might have found their mark.

For some reason, Sam clearly threatened her. He'd spent too many years as a cop and then as a bodyguard not to be able to recognize fear when he saw it.

Why should she fear him? Certainly it wasn't because of his former profession. When he'd been working as Ty's bodyguard, Lizzie had never been fazed by his presence or unnerved that his duties included the potential for violence. In any case, his former profession was moot. Sam's life was different now, no longer that of a man ready for violence and death up close.

So, if Lizzie didn't fear Sam because he'd been a New York City cop, that meant he must threaten her as a man. Sam's head dropped as he let out a string of vicious curses, the words extra shocking in the quiet, light-filled kitchen. At that moment, Sam would have given anything to find Lizzie's ex and treat him to a going over he'd never forget.

Fucking bastard to have hurt Lizzie, to have dimmed that special spark in her eyes.

"Whew, that was some seriously bad-ass cursing. You'd make a sailor blush," Lizzie said, sauntering casually back into the kitchen as if she'd fully intended to return the whole time.

Emma had fallen asleep mere seconds after Lizzie had laid her down in the middle of Ty's double bed. Watching her daughter's face as she slept, Lizzie had consciously dawdled, hoping if she tarried long enough, fate would remove Sam Brody from the scene. Eventually, however, Lizzie forced herself back downstairs, determined to prove herself aloof to any base sexual attraction.

If Sam was surprised at her reappearance, he didn't show it. "Welcome back, Lizzie. It was getting lonely down here. Sheppard must still be venting steam."

Lizzie glanced at her watch, stunned at how much time had passed. "I hope Ty's all right. He can't really be that mad. Maybe I should go out and see."

"Now it's my turn to disagree," Sam said easily, amused when Lizzie's eyes narrowed. "Our barging in would be like adding fat to the fire. Besides, Ty's a big girl. I'm sure she can handle whatever Sheppard throws at her. Take a seat, and tell me what you're doing these days. Fill in the gaps for me."

She didn't have much choice. Sam could be right about provoking Steve even more if she butted in on him and Ty. Anyway, Lizzie was still waiting for her telephone call to be returned, and she didn't want to wander too far. And if she fled back upstairs, Sam would have proof positive she was running away from him.

She plopped down in the chair with all the grace of a sack of potatoes. If she'd been in the habit of picking her nose, she would have. Anything to erase that speculative gleam in Sam's brown eyes. Had they always been so golden glittery, like topaz stones?

"Sure, let's chat. What do you want to know, Sam? Emma's a darling, but you don't need me to tell you that. She's the light of my life. My business is growing. I've got new riders and more boarders this year. Things have been going well enough that I've been able to hire an additional instructor, as well as a barn manager who lives in one of the outbuildings I converted. That's been a huge load off my mind; it's allowed me to be able to make trips like this for clients and not worry about who's in charge of the barn or who's taking over my lessons. Let's see, what else?" Lizzie shrugged and pasted a vacuous smile on her face. "Life's great. That about sums it up."

A neatly whitewashed version of her life, Sam concluded. No mention of the anger, loneliness, and bitterness she'd undoubtedly felt when her marriage ended. No mention of how wearing it must be to raise a child by herself—no matter how cute Emma was. "And how about you personally, Lizzie? How are you doing now that you're all grown up?"

"Oh, I'm fine," Lizzie said breezily. "The days seem to fly by, what with work and taking care of Emma."

"What do you do for fun up in Bedford?"

"Fun?" Lizzie repeated cautiously, as if it were a dangerous word.

"Yeah, fun. Movies, dancing, romantic dinners . . ."

Lizzie laughed. "Don't really have time for that, Sam. I'm a working woman."

"A shame. There something the matter with the male population in Bedford that some guy hasn't come and swept you off your feet?"

Alarm bells were clanging loudly inside her head as her anger hit the danger zone. Where did Sam get off, thinking he had the right to give her the third-degree treatment? Who did he think he was, her older brother? Well, he could think again. He wanted to pry into her private life? She'd give him an earful.

"Oh, don't worry about me, Sam," Lizzie reassured, saccharine sweet. "There are plenty of guys to choose from in Bedford if I'm ever inclined. But you know, since I found Bob,"—her breasts rose and fell in a happy sigh—"He's really spoiled me for anyone else."

The words left him reeling, a swift punch in the gut. This guy Bob must have made the moves on Lizzie awfully quick. She'd only been divorced, what, a year and a half? "Bob, huh? He lives near you?"

"Mmm, yes. As a matter of fact, Bob lives with me. I can't bear being too far away."

Jesus, Ty hadn't mentioned anything about Lizzie shacking up with anyone. Was it her stable manager, perhaps the instructor? The pain in his gut grew, Sam recognizing it for what it was: jealousy eating him alive. "Tell me more about this guy. Sounds like a real catch." The words were out, in spite of himself, and it took all of Sam's control to keep his voice casually indifferent. Control that nearly snapped when he realized she was laughing.

These many months, Sam had purposely kept his distance, wanting to give Lizzie time to heal, to get over the pain of Michael Strickland. She seemed fine now, though. Tears were falling from the corners of her eyes, her body rocking helplessly on the wooden chair, while he sat immobilized, consumed with frustrated jealousy, 'cause some SOB had once again beaten him out of the chance to woo Lizzie Osborne.

Minutes elapsed before Lizzie even attempted to rein in her mirth. "I'm sorry, please forgive me, Sam," she gasped, shoulders shaking, the back of her hand wiping tears from her cheeks. "I have a little confession. But to you, Sam, seeing how we go way back, I'm sure I can tell the truth." As though imparting a state secret, Lizzie leaned forward across the table, her face charmingly open, earnest, her spiked lashes framing wide blue eyes. An alluring, husky note enriched her voice. "You see, I, uh, paid for Bob . . ." If possible, her eyes widened some more. Shimmering with moisture, they floated before him. Pressing fingers against trembling lips, Lizzie waited for Sam's reaction.

Her words clanged inside Sam's head. Lizzie buying a man? What had she gotten mixed up in?

He swallowed. Hard. Wanting to be sure his voice came out carefully neutral. "You bought a man, Lizzie? Are we talking solicitation here?"

"Oh, no!" Lizzie shook her head, the action doing little to relieve Sam's sense of unease. "I guess I'm having trouble explaining. Bob stands for B . . . O . . . B . . . ." Lizzie articulated the letters slowly. "My battery-operated boyfriend. But, considering what he does for me"—Lizzie let a dreamy look come over her face, her lids growing heavy, half-closed shutters on a hot summer's day—"I simply had to give him a name. It's so much more . . . intimate."

God, she was having a blast, Lizzie thought. A few

more minutes, and the high and mighty Sam Brody would really be cut down to size. As though her neck muscles had grown weak from remembered pleasure, she let her head fall back, taking the opportunity to sneak a quick peek at Sam's face.

The man had a face carved from granite, and his eyes were trained on her. With a hundred percent intensity. Good. Time to crank up the heat. A breathy sigh tumbled from her lips. "Oh, he's just wonderful, Sam. Big. Powerful. So deeply satisfying. But can you guess what the very best part about him is, besides the fact that he can go on, and on, and on? It's that when I'm done, all I have to do is give a little click, and he goes back in his drawer." At the snap of her fingers, Lizzie's eyes flew open, cold and hard.

Seconds ticked while Lizzie and Sam stared silently at each other, neither giving an inch, the tension between them growing, crackling. "So you see, Sam," Lizzie observed with a smile that no one would ever mistake for friendly, "Bob does an excellent job of providing me with the only interesting thing I've ever found in a man. Until they make men equipped with an on/off switch, he's perfect."

Damn it all to hell, seethed Lizzie. How could Sam sit there, that cool smile playing over his face, as though she'd just shared a really good off-color joke? By all rights, he should be totally cowed, his masculine vanity trampled, lying on the ground next to his crushed ego. She'd reeled him in expertly, her timing and delivery flawless. Any other man would be fire-engine red with outraged bluster, all the while looking for a corner where he could slink off to lick his wounds. Most of the men she'd encountered wouldn't hesitate to reduce a woman to a mere sex object, but they were damned uncomfortable when the tables were turned.

Above all, Sam Brody should not be looking pleased as punch. And relaxed. It was insulting. Why wasn't he running upstairs to dive into a cold shower? That had been a truly hot performance she'd just given. She wished he'd cut that out, too, this thing he did, rubbing his thumb and index finger along the line of his stubbled jaw. Lizzie tried not to notice how broad the pads of his fingers were, tried not to imagine how it would feel to run her own fingers against that chiseled face.

Jumpin' Jehosaphat, Lizzie was one fine woman. He'd have kissed her right there and then, till they were both lying across the kitchen table, if he weren't dead certain she'd try to pop him but good. A hell of a show she'd put on. A rare treat. Might have worked on somebody who didn't understand Lizzie's character quite as well as Sam.

No matter how cold her eyes could grow, how lethally her words could slice, Lizzie was a sensualist through and through. A woman to be touched, tasted, and teased all over, and for whom being able to reciprocate in kind for her lover would only heighten her own pleasure. A woman like Lizzie cried out for candles, whispered words, and rose petals crushed against her skin. In short, fantasies and top-of-the-line vibrators just weren't gonna do it for her. Sam was more than willing to put his theory to the test.

Lizzie's fingers were drumming impatiently on the tabletop, her mulish expression indicating she considered the show was over already. Nope, not by a long shot. Now it was his turn.

"Tell you what, Lizzie," Sam began, the beginnings of a grin lifting the corners of his mouth. "Why don't the three of us get together, you, me, and this 'Bob'. Try us both on for size, so you can make an informed choice."

What a pig, Lizzie fumed. She *knew* it. As soon as Sam hadn't assumed that pathetically wounded, simultaneously hostile look she'd been aiming for, she'd guessed this would be the tack he'd take: Me macho lover, you one lucky gal.

As though considering Sam's words, she hesitated, her fingers tracing patterns against the table. "I'm sorry, Sam," she replied with a sad but resolute shake of her head. "It's kind of you to offer, but you're far too good and old a friend. I couldn't bear the responsibility of knowing how you'd feel afterward." She raised a slim hand, stopping him before he could speak. Delicately, she cleared her throat. "You're aware, naturally, of the medical reports documenting this kind of thing."

"And what kind of thing would this be, Lizzie? What reports exactly?" Sam rocked back in his chair, ready for the second act, knowing he was going to enjoy himself immensely.

Her brow furrowed. "Oh, you must have seen them. There've been so many of them recently. Clinical studies, I mean. Showing the psychological devastation that occurs when men have their sexual prowess put to the test and are found . . . lacking. Apparently, when one's inadequacies, one's intimate *failures*, heretofore suppressed, buried deep, deep in the psyche, are suddenly exposed, it completely destroys one's self-confidence. There are cases where the ability to perform is permanently impaired."

He leaned forward, a warm, indulgent smile on his face. Long and tapered, his index finger traced the back of her hand, skimming over veins, circling knuckles. "Why don't you let me worry about that?"

Lizzie fought the urge to snatch her hand away, and resolutely ignored the fact that her insides were melting.

"Oh, Sam, I couldn't," she breathed, praying he would read the unevenness of her voice as heartfelt concern. "Because, you see . . . with, oh, how can I put it gently? I really don't want to add to your worries. With *older* men—men *your* age? Well, suffice it to say, Sam, that not even a truckload of Viagra would help."

24

Life was strange. Ty's world had been transformed with the swiftness of a scenery change in a Broadway play. All it had taken was Steve's whispered confession followed by a storm of passionate kisses to release this keen, piercing joy inside her, chasing away doubts and fears.

The impromptu ride they'd shared was wonderful. Ty on Macintosh, Steve astride Gordo, side by side they'd ridden over Southwind's pastures, then Steve had led her to where seagrass-covered dunes overlooked the Atlantic. As the horses stood with nostrils flared and lifted to the sea breeze, Steve and Ty absorbed the beauty of the scene before them. Wild and empty, the beach on this crisp autumn morning was deserted, a private paradise.

Carefully, they'd picked their way down the narrow path to the broad band of sand bordering the ocean. Abreast of each other once more, they'd trotted, then cantered, Macintosh's gait even more like a rocking horse's with the deep sand as footing, making it easy for Ty to follow the powerful horse's rhythm. Her first time ever riding on a beach, it had been nothing less than magical. The feel of the sea-dampened wind whistling past her face. The endless horizon, where morning clouds gave way, revealing a sky of bright brilliant blue, its color weightlessly suspended over the deeper gray of the Atlantic. The accompanying roar of waves rushing to meet sand.

That's what Ty's world was like right now. A dazzling spectrum of colors and boundless opportunities. An enormous, engulfing symphony. This new world created solely because she loved and was loved in return.

Which is why she was momentarily taken aback when she reentered the house, feeling so changed, a different person from the one she'd been an hour ago, only to discover Sam and Lizzie still in the kitchen. It was as though here, inside the walls of this house, time had stopped.

Well, no, Ty amended, at least one thing was different. Sam was laughing his head off, great deep bellows of laughter, and Lizzie was looking uncharacteristically put out. Wait, that was too mild a description. Spitting mad.

"Hi, what's up?" She couldn't help the smile stretching from ear to ear. She was too happy.

Lizzie didn't appear to notice. She was already bounding up from her chair, casting a withering glance Sam's way. "Nothing at all. I think I hear Emma, though. I'll let you and Sam talk. I know he needs to leave really soon."

"What's the matter with Lizzie?" Ty asked, perplexed, watching her friend tear out of the kitchen.

"Nothing at all," Sam mimicked Lizzie's reply. Whatever he'd found so amusing continued to hold him in its grip. Recovering finally, "How'd Sheppard take the news? From the blush on your cheeks, I'd guess not too badly."

"He was very . . . understanding."

"I bet." Sam replied dryly. "Good luck, kiddo. You'll have your work cut out for you."

"Thanks, Sam. But I really think we're going to make it." She blushed. "Um, I mean, get Southwind back in the black, find some good horses for Steve."

"If anyone can do it, it's you, Ty. But, much as I hate to burst that bubble of happiness you're floating on, I suggest you run through the statements I brought with me. They're copies of everything you gave to Crane, Adderson and White, lists of assets and all the financial transactions prior to bailing Sheppard out. I'm willing to bet Emma's weight in gold your father has these on his desk right now. Maybe you'd like to review them, crunch the numbers, tell me what you think."

As Sam went and fetched his briefcase from the entry hall, Ty's eyes closed wearily. No, she did not want to think about this right now. But when a pile of papers was pushed wordlessly in front of her, her eyes opened, bleak resignation in them.

When Steve came into the kitchen a few minutes later, Ty was sitting at the table, so thoroughly absorbed in her study that she didn't even notice him. Sam merely glanced up, then nodded silently, pointedly at Ty. Easing quietly into the chair next to her, Steve eyed the papers before her, curious. Like an oversized game of tarot, they were lined up in a row, Ty reading one, replacing it, sometimes switching its order.

Christ, what she'd told him was true, every word. Steve studying one itemized page, then another. She'd sold all that stuff to raise extra cash: the apartment, the cars, expensive antiques. Another page showed proceeds spent already, paying off mortgage bills and bank loans, taxes. He'd need a calculator to tally it all up.

Ty's voice drew Steve's attention away from the papers. "He'll do everything he can to put a lock on the trust fund. Perhaps he'll succeed this time, arguing that I'm developing a pattern of irresponsible and reckless behavior. If he can convince the trust's overseer that there's misuse of the funds, we'll last six months. A year if we bring in enough horses. It's the obvious choice." Her voice was emotionless, the words sufficient to cast a pall.

By 'he,' Ty obviously meant her father. Steve couldn't imagine a parent who'd do that to his child, remembering the unconditional love and support he'd always received from his own family. Why would Ty's father try to thwart her business plans for Southwind? Was this some sort of twisted retribution for having snatched coveted property from under his nose? Or something else entirely?

"I didn't get a chance to mention it, Ty, but the insurance company is going to pay full coverage for Fancy's death. The check should be coming soon."

Ty gave Steve a distracted smile. "That's good. If my father succeeds in bringing this to court, and the judge decides I'm violating the terms of the trust, we may need it."

"Who's the overseer?" Sam asked.

"Bill Whiting, in Delaware. I guess I should call him right now."

The telephone gave its own shrill ring at that moment. Hurried footsteps thudded down the stairs. "I've got it," Lizzie called out, a red-cheeked Emma in her arms. "It's probably the Hineses. Trudy said Ralph would call back about now."

Her conversation was quick, she was back in five

minutes. "Great news," she announced happily. "The Hineses are free today. They're going to drive out, be here by this afternoon. I managed to reach Damien, too. He's expecting us at his place at four-thirty, meaning Emma and I can head home this evening. Hey, what's all this?" she asked, frowning, belatedly noticing the papers arranged systematically.

"Just junk," Ty replied, rising. "I'd better go deal with it, though, if you're through with the phone. I'll give Vicky Grodecki another try while I'm at it."

"Well, one out of two isn't so bad," Ty said, half an hour later. "Mr. Whiting had already left for lunch. His secretary told me he had meetings scheduled for the rest of the day but that he'd be sure to call tomorrow. I did manage to catch Vicky Grodecki, however. She jumped at the idea of doing a profile of you, Steve. She'd like to come out and do the interview the day after tomorrow, if that's convenient."

"Sounds fine." Steve nodded, wishing they were alone. A strained expression lingered on Ty's face, but Steve couldn't do much about it with a house full of people. Couldn't do what he wanted, which was pretty basic, really: pull her into his arms and kiss her until she no longer knew her own name, much less her father's. "I thought I'd go over that list Lizzie brought. See what names I can add."

The past half-hour, while Ty had been on the phone, the place had been a circus. Emma climbing all over Sam Brody as if he'd suddenly transformed into a human jungle gym. Lizzie trying to coax the toddler away— doing her damnedest, at the same time, to pretend Sam didn't exist in the first place. An impossible goal: Sam wasn't a man easily ignored. But Lizzie was bound and determined. She'd chatted Steve up as though she thought he was the cleverest thing since the microchip. And hadn't graced Brody with a single word.

Something had Lizzie Osborne wound tighter than a top. She relaxed a bit when Ty finally rejoined them.

"Hey, Ty, Emma and I are starving. How's this for a great idea? Why don't we treat you to the works at the Candy Kitchen?" It'll be a girls' lunch," she stressed, in case Sam and Steve were too dumb to get the point.

Lizzie had them out of the kitchen in less than thirty seconds, practically shoving Ty out the door and calling out a cheerful "See you later" to Steve.

She might have gotten away with ignoring Sam altogether if it weren't for Emma. Emma went dashing back to wrap her arms around Sam's trousers. Picking her up, Sam received a wet kiss on the cheek for his efforts before Lizzie managed to distract her daughter once more with the promise of a grilled cheese.

" 'Bye, Sam," Lizzie said coolly. "What with our living in the country and all, I doubt we'll be seeing you again . . ."

"Oh, I may make it up to Bedford in the near future. Just to satisfy my curiosity."

Steve saw something dangerous flash in Lizzie's eyes.

"Well, busy as I am, it's highly unlikely I'll be able to fit you in . . . my schedule. You can always call and leave a message, though. Come on, Ty. Let's take my car so we don't have to move the car seat."

The silence was incredible following their departure. Both men sat, slightly shell-shocked. "She always like that?"

"Yeah. Classic Lizzie. A fire storm. Knowing the public hell her slimebag of a husband put her through made me a little worried that some of that, uh, wild spirit of hers might have been destroyed."

Alive and well, if Steve was any judge. "Looks like she gave you the brush-off big-time, though," he observed, not exactly teary-eyed to see Ty's ex-bodyguard brought so low.

"Yeah," Sam replied, seeming unconcerned. "She's been brushing me off for the past hour. The woman's got some of the most imaginative put-downs I've ever heard. Good thing my feelings don't bruise easily, otherwise, I might start to think she doesn't like me."

"No, she clearly finds you irresistible." Steve walked to the refrigerator. "You hungry?"

"Yeah. What you got?"

"You sure you want to order a sundae on top of everything else, Lizzie?" Ty looked at her friend with deep concern.

"Ty, believe me on this: there are times in a woman's life when excessive calorie bingeing is an absolute must." Especially if you're twisted in lust over some hunk warrior who has the nerve to pop back in your life just when you've successfully convinced yourself you will never want another man. Especially if the guy's all wrong for you. That's when you go for the extra fudge topping.

The waitress delivered Lizzie's mountain of ice cream and fudge and a smaller orange sherbet for Emma to the booth where the three of them sat. Both mother and daughter dug in with relish. The Candy Kitchen was a favorite lunch spot for the Hamptons' summer crowd. The ice cream homemade, and delicious. Today, however, the restaurant was virtually empty, it being midweek in October. Only a few locals were perched atop the blue vinyl stools, elbows propped on the white formica counter, reading their newspapers, eating club sandwiches or burgers, drinking bottomless cups of the Candy Kitchen's house brew.

Ty didn't bother playing the game of who's who people usually engaged in when at the Candy Kitchen or any of Bridgehampton's other restaurants. She was watching Lizzie in stunned amazement. Never had she seen her friend go at food this voraciously before—not even when they'd been gluttonous teenagers.

And Lizzie was behaving peculiarly in other respects, too.

It took a while to figure it out, at least six vicious spoonfuls later. But a pattern was definitely emerging. Ty began noticing that for every time Emma mentioned Sam's name, Lizzie would scoop up about two tablespoons' worth of ice cream and shove it into her mouth.

"How was it, seeing Sam after so long?" Ty asked, testing her theory. Yes, indeed, there went the long-handled spoon, plunging in, gobs of chocolate sauce and ice cream surfacing, following a direct route to Lizzie's mouth. "You get a chance to catch up on your lives and everything? It's been years since you saw him last, right?"

Lizzie clutched her empty spoon in a death grip. "Yeah, years," she muttered, eyeing the sundae balefully. Then, with a loud sigh of defeat, she stabbed her spoon into the middle of a mound of mint chocolate chip. "If I eat any more, I'm going to be sicker than a dog," she admitted. Her usual peaches and cream complexion was already an alarming shade of green in Ty's opinion, but she let it pass. As kids, Lizzie had always been able to eat her under the table.

"Okay, Ty. This is really bugging me, so you've got to tell me. Just how is it that Sam doesn't look a day above forty?"

"Must be well preserved, I guess," Ty said, biting the inside of her cheek. "Because we celebrated his fortieth birthday a couple of months ago."

"Good God! He's only forty? Really?" Lizzie choked out, as surprised as if Ty had said eighty-five instead. "No way!" she challenged, incredulous.

"Uh-huh." Ty nodded. "Late July. Sam took me out to dinner, then we went dancing at Nell's. One of my better dates, I assure you. The other women at Nell's must have thought so, too. All those come-hither wiggles of their hips . . ."

Lizzie wasn't interested in their night at Nell's. "But how could he be so young?"

"Well, he'd only been with the NYPD for a few years when Father hired him away. He doesn't talk about it much to me, but I do know that while he was on the force, he received promotion after promotion in Vice. A real hot shot. Father wouldn't have hired him otherwise."

"But he always seemed kind of old and serious, you know? And fat," Lizzie protested, a little desperately.

"Fat?" Ty repeated blankly. "Oh, I know. You're thinking of the jacket. Sam always wore a sport coat to conceal his shoulder holster. And back in those days, men's jackets had that boxy look, didn't they? I guess that might have made him look bulkier. No," Ty continued, shaking her head, "I don't think there's any fat on him. Afraid it's pretty much solid muscle."

"So you mean to tell me he always looked like this, only younger?"

"Um, pretty much," Ty replied, deadpan.

Lizzie rubbed her hands over her face. "Oh, my God. Where was I, on Mars?"

Ty laughed. "No, Lizzie, not exactly. You were, however, way too busy checking out our little corner of the earth to pay much attention to my bodyguard. Let's see, there was Connor Ferle, Mitch Robertson, Eddy Wills . . . who else am I forgetting? Not that it matters, anyway. Even if you had noticed that Sam is a . . ."

What word could describe her friend and former body-guard?

"Hunk," Lizzie supplied dryly.

"Indeed. Even if you had noticed, you don't really think Sam is the kind of man who'd take advantage of teenage hormones? Remember, you were barely sixteen when he quit working for my father. Of course, you're both grown-ups now, aren't you?"

"Not going to work," Lizzie replied glumly, taking up her spoon once again. "I'm off men."

"Right."

"Mind if I take a look at your barn?" Sam inquired. He and Steve had ransacked the refrigerator of its last edible crumb, creating mammoth sandwiches for themselves that they washed down with yet another fresh pot of coffee.

"Sure, be my guest. I need to ride my last horse of the day, I'll give you a personal tour. You interested in horses?"

"Only insofar as helping Ty's new business venture pisses the hell out of Tyler Stannard. For that pleasure, I might be willing to invest deeply. Come to think of it, I've never owned an animal before."

"Hey, don't let me hold you back. Especially if you've got money to burn." He opened the door for Sam, and the two men began walking toward the barn. "I gather Stannard is a real number. How'd you get involved with him in the first place?"

"I was working Vice."

"New York City?"

"Yeah. One day, Captain calls me in, says some rich fat cat wants us to do a background check on a nanny he wants to hire for his only daughter. A basic courtesy job. One the Captain's happy to perform, given the size of the guy's wallet and the healthy donation he's willing to make to the precinct. Turns out, though, that this prospective nanny's second cousin happens to be linked to one of the major crime families operating out of Sicily. The same family thought to have orchestrated the kidnapping of a wealthy Italian businessman's child."

"Not a good thing to have on one's résumé, I guess."

"No shit," Sam agreed. "Anyway, there'd been a wave of kidnappings, mainly in Europe, but here, too. Freaked a lot of people, Stannard included. He took the Patty Hearst kidnapping real personally. Anyway, to make a long story short, Stannard hired me away from the force. Wasn't hard to do. I'd been on the force three years, and frankly, I'd seen enough to last me a century. Crack cocaine flooding the streets of New York, hopped-up dealers gunning each other down, innocent bystanders, too. Pregnant kids prostituting themselves for a two-dollar hit. Police shootings soaring. When Stannard made the offer, I figured I'd work for him, agree to guard his kid for a year, tops, then use the money to start my own business. Only a year turned into eight."

"Money must have been pretty good," Steve said with a sideways glance.

"Didn't have fuck to do with it," Sam replied flatly. "I stayed for Ty. There was something about her. Such a scrawny kid, but with these huge, sad, grown-up eyes. I couldn't resist, didn't matter that her father was a total asshole, at least until the day I quit."

The words were out before Steve could stop them. "You got a thing for her?"

Sam laughed, a rich, full laugh. He thought of the folder bulging with clippings of Steve that Ty had kept hidden in one of her drawers. "Ty? I love her. But she's like a kid sister—only closer." Sam slowed to a halt, a few yards from the barn's double doors. "Too bad, though, 'cause there aren't many people like her. You let her down, Sheppard, and I'll come after you."

The two men assessed each other silently. "Fair warning," Steve replied at last. "You want to see the home of that future horse of yours, Brody?"

"Yeah, don't mind if I do."

Lizzie was on her knees, hugging the toilet, retching miserably, too weak to stand any longer. She'd made it through the meeting at Damien Schoenberg's stable by sheer willpower, speaking little and only through gritted teeth. The half an inch of foundation covering her moldy green pallor kept the Hineses from noticing anything too terribly amiss. Damien probably thought this was her tough horsewoman persona, that she was ready to bargain till midnight if necessary. The Hineses had come away with a terrific pony at a great price. And Lizzie had snatched up Sassafras. Even in her wretched state, Lizzie had known better than to pass up such an opportunity.

It had hit her full force on the way back to Steve's. Suddenly too dizzy with nausea to steer, she'd had to pull the Volvo over, her clammy forehead resting against the wheel, praying it would subside. To Lizzie, those miles back to Steve's place took an eternity.

Safely back at Southwind, Lizzie gave up the battle with her body.

Hand clamped over her mouth, eyes glazed and panicky, she'd raced past the living room where Ty and Emma were curled up on the sofa, reading one of Emma's favorite picture books. Her feet pounded loudly on the stairs, the sound bringing Sam to the bottom landing. His cell phone, the tinny voice of his personal assistant, temporarily forgotten.

And here she was, forty-five minutes later, still heaving up her guts. The faint creak of the door, accompanied by the subtle shift of air signaled the presence of someone entering the bathroom, but Lizzie was beyond caring. From behind her huddled form came the sound of running water, then of something passing through it, interrupting its flow. Abruptly, Lizzie gagged, her stomach muscles contracting violently once again, though she'd long passed the point where even a single greasy french fry remained in her system. Weakly, she sat back on her haunches. And felt the cool press of a moistened washcloth against her clammy forehead. She made out the outline of a large masculine hand.

Her eyelids fluttered shut. "Go away," she moaned, attempting to turn her head away.

Sam's hand merely followed her. "Shush. Here, take this pill, but don't drink too much water. It'll only start you up again."

Lizzie's eyes opened just enough to see the fat pink tablet lying in the palm of Sam's hand. "I can't swallow anything. Go away and let me die in peace."

"Nope. Come on, Lizzie, this is going to make you feel much better. Good enough so you can yell at me all you want."

"That a promise?"

"Cross my heart."

Weakly, her fingers closed around the pill, pushing it into her mouth. The rim of a water glass hovered, and she tilted head to drink from it. Sam allowed her one sip. In tired anticipation, her eyes closed, waiting for the next bout to hit.

Next to her, she felt Sam's body shift. What felt like a knee brushed her shoulder. He was sitting on the rim of the bathtub. Leaning toward her, he began moving the washcloth around her face, its cooling dampness refreshing, heavenly.

Lizzie frowned, her face scrunching against the cloth. "What are you doing here?" The question came out muffled. Batting the cloth away, she repeated it.

Sam's quiet laughter mixed with the sound of running water. "Ty wanted to come," he said, once more bathing her features with the freshly dampened cloth. "But I insisted. I told her, quite convincingly, too, I'm the only one who could get you so annoyed you'd forget about puking. How am I doing, by the way?"

"You get an A plus for effort. You're free to leave now." She really did not want to be sick in front of him.

"Don't worry, you can thank me later."

"You, Sam, are a man doomed to disappointment."

"This is idiotic. I do not need a chauffeur, caretaker, baby-sitter, hand holder, or whatever cockamamie title Sam wants to give himself. I am perfectly capable of driving back to Cobble Creek tonight without *him!*" After all, it was Sam who'd gotten her into this mess in the first place. If she hadn't been doing her best to bury her lustful feelings under a mountain of fat, grease, and sugar, she also wouldn't have been wrapped around the base of the toilet, wondering whether she'd live to see another day.

Lord, she hadn't eaten stuff quite so lethal since before Emma was born. These days, she was strictly a steamed-vegetables-over-brown-rice sort of gal. If she really wanted to go wild, maybe a sprinkle of sesame seeds or a dash of soy sauce. Sometimes, all she ate were Emma's colored leftovers. Since motherhood, her system's tolerance for high-calorie junk was practically nil. She'd known it, yet had shoved all that food into her body on top of a gargantuan breakfast of french toast. Her folly was wholly deserved, but that didn't mean Lizzie had to admit to it, did it?

Ty scooted by Lizzie, busy fixing weak mint tea and dry toast. Although Lizzie's rioting stomach seemed to have settled, she looked wrung out from the ordeal. Ty wished she'd stop balking. "Be reasonable, Lizzie. You've been sick for the past hour. You're pale as a ghost, and you've got a three-hour drive in front of you. If you really need to be back by tomorrow and can't spend the night here, then you should at least take Sam up on his offer. He can drive you in your car and pick up his own next weekend. He's coming back for another computer session with Mrs. Miller, anyway."

So much for counting on Ty to support her, Lizzie thought petulantly. They were all ganging up on her, even Emma, whose immediate acceptance of Sam felt alarmingly close to betrayal. And Steve, who'd only known her for a few hours. The look he'd given her was downright disapproving after Lizzie had curtly declined Sam's offer to drive her back to Bedford.

Didn't they understand? She needed to remain independent. And giving even an inch to Sam Brody would mean his taking the proverbial mile. A mile that covered a whole lot of ground Lizzie wasn't willing to relinquish.

She hated the varying degrees of censure in their expressions. As though she were some naughty, spoiled, irresponsible child.

Wasn't that ironic! She was the only one among them who had a child, who had the care and responsibility of a daughter twenty-four hours a day, seven days a week . . . Her shoulders slumped in sudden defeat.

Of course, she was going to let Sam drive them back. Never would she risk an automobile accident with Emma in the backseat just because she stupidly refused to admit how woozy and exhausted she felt.

Walking over to where Sam sat with Emma, quietly

reading Emma's favorite book about a mouse named Maisy, Lizzie spoke, her tone subdued, "I'll go take Emma to the potty one more time. Come on, Em," and lifted her daughter out of Sam's lap. "We can leave whenever you're ready."

Their eyes met, then Lizzie looked hurriedly away, disliking the understanding she'd glimpsed in Sam's.

25

The house emptied of Lizzie, Sam, and Emma, kisses, hugs, last-minute instructions, and waves of good-bye exchanged, Ty knew a sudden nervousness, a sudden longing to escape, to be safely ensconced in the backseat next to Emma, the easy acceptance of old friends soothing and effortless. She could flee from this man standing by her side and all he represented.

Her voice came out a nervous croak. "I, uh, think I'll take a bath." She was staring fixedly into the distance, as if even now she could make out the long-gone Volvo.

"I've finished with that list. Added a few names. If you like, we can go over it before dinner and hash out the details for the clinic."

"All right." Dinner. Alone with him. No wall of angry silence separating them. Ty's palms felt clammy. This time, the urge to run irresistible. "I'd better go."

His beautiful partner was a bundle of nerves and doing her damnedest not to show it. Steve knew her well enough now to read the distress signals. Her eyes had grown bigger and bigger as Sam maneuvered the car, one hand on the wheel, the other waving a casual farewell out the rolled-down window. Steve had caught her surreptitiously wiping her palms against the seam of her faded jeans, the slight stammer in her speech when she addressed him. And if by chance he'd been too dense to decipher those clues, Ty had lit up the stairs as though her tail was on fire, practically tripping over herself in her hurry to get away from him.

He couldn't blame her; he was nervous, too.

With anticipation.

It was thrumming through his system, making his skin itch, his heart ricochet against his ribcage. The kind of adrenaline rush he usually experienced before his number was called in a speed class. He was pumped, no doubt about it.

But for the first time in his life, Steve was going to err on the side of caution. If he came on to Ty like gangbusters right now, she was going to spook. Better to let the passion build slowly between them, so she'd be with him every step of the way.

How did a woman dress when she suspected, feared, and fervently hoped there was a ninety-nine-point-nine-percent chance she'd be making love in a few short hours?

Ty could ace a number of quizzes on the proper attire for all sorts of social functions—everything from corporate business meetings, to state dinners, to charity balls, to evenings at the opera followed by midnight champagne and oysters at a four-star restaurant. But what did one wear to a simple dinner, tête-à-tête, in a farmhouse on eastern Long Island?

Did she go for the vamp look? Something so blatant it screamed, like a car alarm at three A.M., "Take me, I'm yours"? Hugely embarrassing if it turned out she'd misread the signs and, besides, not her style, anyway.

But she definitely wanted an outfit that would pack a wallop, some sensual *vavooom*. Something that would have Steve willing to walk through fire just to touch her. There was the rub: she was going for *subtle vavooom*, much harder to achieve than in-your-face *vavooom*.

She turned the spigot, adding hot water to the tub. The frothy layer of fragrant bubbles had begun to thin somewhat while Ty lay back against the porcelain rim, mentally reviewing the contents of her closet.

Why hadn't the proper outfit for a situation like this been addressed at her boarding school in Switzerland? An utter waste of four years. If things hadn't been quite so crazy this afternoon, Ty could have hauled Lizzie in front of her closet and pleaded with her to pick out some ensembles—just in case—but that was hardly fair to someone who'd been bent over a toilet for a gut-wrenching hour. Besides, it was up to Ty to figure it out.

Groaning loudly, Ty sank under the warm water, completely submerging herself. Feeling the soothing warmth around her, she briefly entertained the notion of simply staying put, lulled by a warm, watery bed. In all likelihood, she was getting bent out of shape over nothing. Steve hadn't actually made any overt sign that he intended or even wanted to make love to her tonight.

Confusion and the need to breathe had her breaking the surface with an annoyed sputter. This was nuts, embarrassing, pointless, and ridiculous. Either they were going to make love or they weren't, Ty so thoroughly flustered that the glaring obviousness of this particular insight wasn't immediately clear. Her thoughts continued rattling about, like useless foreign coins stored in a tin box.

Toweling herself off, Ty adopted the following mantra: the bath had left her squeaky clean, she smelled nice, she wasn't about to dig yesterday's jeans from the bottom of her hamper. That would have to suffice in terms of her ability to excite and seduce.

Almost an hour later, however, Ty's room resembled ground zero for a natural disaster—correction: this mess was clearly woman-made. Heaps, piles, and trails consisting of bold splashes of color and texture marked the room, dizzying the eye. A Jackson Pollock of fabric and accessories.

Yet, so far, Ty was only satisfied with her choice of bra and panties. Silk and lace from Italy, they were the color of a rich claret and as heady to the senses. Wearing them made Ty feel like sin incarnate. Definitely the desired effect, but at that point, Ty stalled, filled with indecision, looking around her, hoping for inspiration that had little to do with the divine and everything to do with the flesh.

She heard the sound of her door opening and managed to grab the bath towel from her bed and shield herself with it.

"Sorry," Steve said, not sounding sorry in the least to find her standing there, the towel scant protection. A smile played over his handsome features. "I knocked, not too loudly, I admit. Thought you might have fallen asleep." Then, somehow, he was already close to her, inches away, and Ty hadn't moved, a startled deer caught in the mesmerizing blue of his eyes.

"You getting rid of all your worldly possessions here, Ty?" His voice was husky, sending shivers along her bare skin.

"Oh," she started. "You mean this." With one arm holding the towel firmly in place, her other arced over jumbled clothes. "Well, I . . ." Ty swallowed, her thoughts scrambled, as mixed up as the egg batter Lizzie beat this morning. To such a degree that what was uppermost in her mind was a bubbling sense of relief, euphoria that she no longer had to figure out what to wear. From there, the simple truth tumbled out readily. "I was having trouble deciding what to wear."

His gaze released her momentarily, casually inspecting the mayhem of Ty's bedroom. Damn, had she been spending all this time figuring out what clothes could possibly enhance her beauty? For him?

While during those long, excruciating minutes he'd been going slightly mad with impatience just to *see* her. He'd busted three Ticonderoga pencils, snapped them into little pieces, waiting for her to show, watching the hands of the kitchen clock move with agonizing slowness.

His lips quirked at the absurdity of the situation. "Got a little secret for you, sweetheart. You could be dressed in sackcloth and baling twine, and you'd turn me on." His smile, warm and intimate, spread, setting sparks off inside her as his eyes roamed over the large fluffy towel hiding her, the thin maroon straps hinting at what lay underneath. "This works, too."

Ty watched, transfixed as the gentlest of tugs from Steve's finger around the edge of the towel had it slipping, then tumbling to the floor, as if of its own accord.

"This works even better," Steve observed in a hushed voice, more a reverential whisper. With trembling hand and breath suspended, Steve touched her. She stood in silent offering, her eyelids suddenly heavy, languorous, as his body met hers. His fingers spread, slowly tracing the gentle slope of her breasts above the scalloped edge of lace.

She was devastating. Never had he known a woman's beauty to affect him this way, to humble and arouse him until he had no thoughts but of her. The lines of her body were as smooth, as elegantly sinuous, as a marble statue. But where marble remained cool and unyielding, Steve's fingers reveled in Ty's supple resiliency, the pulsing heat of her skin. Craving more, lips joined hands, searching out the wild hammering at the base of her throat, the scented hollow between her breasts, that sweet haven where his medallion had nestled for so long. Beneath his mouth's explorations and his hands caresses, Ty's nipples peaked, straining beneath deep red silk and lace for his touch. Urgency drummed madly with the need to see, to taste. In their haste, his fingers, usually so clever, fumbled with the front clasp, then stilled at Ty's moan. Her head was thrown back, exposing the length of her neck, her hair a dark mantle framing her ivory shoulders. She was a vision, a glorious pagan vision.

Her moan ended in a soft gasp of surprise, for Steve's hands had swiftly changed their course, wrapping about her legs, her back, lifting her effortlessly until she was cradled against his chest. His mouth covered hers, their tongues dueled in a searing kiss.

"My room," he murmured, raining kisses over her brows, the tip of her nose, his feet already heading toward their destination. He cast a final, amused glance at her room, adding, "I'm not sure I can wait long enough to find your bed."

"Yours is bigger, anyway. I think we'll need it," Ty observed, surprising them both.

Against her shoulders, his chest rumbled. "That's my Ty, always thinking." Her face warming unmistakably, Ty ducked her head. Only to find herself thoroughly distracted by the corded column of tanned skin.

The feel of Ty nuzzling the base of his throat had Steve's arms tightening involuntarily, and his steps quickening.

She was undressing him with exquisite slowness, as though he were every present rolled into one, indulging herself, pausing to nibble at his heated flesh, looking long and hard, touching, tasting again, as each golden inch was revealed to her. By the time Ty removed Steve's shirt, he was shaking, bright flags of color staining his cheeks, his eyes glittering in the subdued light of the bedside lamp.

"You're so beautiful," Ty breathed, her hands gliding over the sculpted contours of his chest. Beneath her palms, Steve's lungs were working like bellows, drawing in deep draughts of air. She smiled at the novel sensation, amazed she affected him so. The power she wielded was heady. Testing it, her fingers spread, lightly tracing the ridges that delineated his ribcage, thrilled when he shivered, started, and dragged more air into his lungs.

"Ty, I'm dying here." Though his voice was raw with need, Steve made no move to stop her exploration.

Ty laughed softly. "Oh, no," she contradicted happily. "You seem very much alive to me." Her gray eyes watched as the tip of her nail followed the beguiling path of dark blond hair leading from his stomach to where it disappeared behind the top metal button of his jeans.

With the same agonizing deliberation, Ty's fingers set about a new task, freeing one flat metal button at a time, pausing now and again to brush against the rigid proof of his arousal straining against the denim.

When her fingers reached for the last button, Steve's hands grabbed her wrists, stopping her. "Ty, look at me." The harsh, barely controlled timbre of his voice causing liquid heat to pool in Ty's center. His face, too, thrillingly different now, stark with passion. "I need to know," he commanded softly, his eyes searching hers. "Have you done this before? It's a question of pace here, sweetheart. If this is your first time, I don't want to rush you. Problem is, you've got me real close to the edge."

A quick shake of her head. "No, never," Ty whispered. She searched his face for a sign of disappointment, relief flooding her as his lips sought hers in a kiss more eloquent than words.

She was his. Only his. A fierce possessiveness had swept through Steve at Ty's whispered admission. His heart pounded with the knowledge. "I wouldn't have thought it possible. A beautiful woman like you," he murmured, his lips freeing hers with a smile.

"Well, it wasn't as if I actually planned to be a twenty-five-year-old virgin or anything," Ty replied, discomfited. "A long time ago, in Switzerland, I came awfully close. But then I realized I was about to do something for all the wrong reasons, the principal motive being revenge. It seemed pretty ridiculous to have sex with someone just to spite my father." She ducked her head. "Fortunately, the boy I was with was quite understanding. Since then, though, I haven't been involved with anyone I care enough about to trust."

"And you trust me?" His hands were framing her face, lifting it so that he could look deeply into her eyes, captivating in the half-light.

"Yes," she said simply, loving the feel of his hands against her skin. Loving him. With a wistful smile, she continued, "I obviously can't pretend any vast sexual experience. On the other hand, it seems as though since about a week ago, I've been thinking about it a lot, how wonderful it'd be to have you touch me like this." At that her body swayed closer, her lips parting in a sigh of pleasure as his arms enveloped, his hands welcomed her, proving her words. Her eyes drifted shut, lost in sensation.

His lips brushed butterfly kisses over her closed lids. "This could be pure coincidence, but I've been thinking pretty much the same thing. Seems to me it's time to put thoughts into actions."

"Oh, yes," was all Ty managed before Steve captured her mouth, his tongue now mating feverishly with hers, setting off fine tremors within her. Ty's arms lifted, encircling his neck, pressing urgently, wantonly against him.

He urged her even closer, inviting her to feel the bold heat of his erection. He heard her breath catch as his hands, after beguiling her with lazy caresses, reached their destination. A practiced flick of his fingers had Ty's bra falling away.

It was beyond exquisite, the feel of his strong hands covering her, replacing the silken barrier, the feel of her aching nipples pressed against his palms. Ty arched closer, her breath shuddering, mixing with Steve's as hands and mouth claimed her.

With heated whispers and broken moans, Ty and Steve fell as one onto the enormous bed, rolling, limbs entangled, locked, and gloriously naked. Delirious with pleasure, Ty's senses were overwhelmed. By Steve's mouth, his hands, the feel of his hard body moving over her, by the needy, heated words whispered in her ear.

Blindly, Ty reached for him, guiding him to her, whimpering in frustration when he resisted, pulling back to sit on his heels, depriving her of his glorious weight. An inarticulate cry escaped her lips, her eyes pleaded, and her arms reached to draw him back down.

With a fiercely gentle smile, Steve's hand smoothed her brow, his, too, damp with sweat. "Shh, easy, love. Just a sec, I promise. You need protection." He leaned over and pulled the nightstand drawer open, retrieving the small foil packet. The smile turned roguish, quickening her breath. "Would you like . . ."

"Oh, yes, please." She sat up beneath him, an eager student.

Steve grinned. Always polite, his Ty. The grin vanished, as he sucked in his breath, nearly undone. Polite and wonderfully imaginative, too. Her hands were carefully smoothing the condom over his shaft. Task complete, they were in no way finished with him. Sweat beaded his forehead as she handled him boldly, exquisitely.

Submitting for as long as he could, Steve shoved her gently back down onto the mattress. "My turn now." A wicked promise. Moving down her body, his tongue and teeth sampled, tasted, blazing a fiery trail along the silky-smooth length of her, until at last he reached the apex of her thighs, the dark nest of curls. A feathery touch, and his fingers came away wet with her slick heat. He murmured his approval, but knew he wanted more for her. He wanted to give her everything. One finger sliding, then two, her broken cries at the feel of him inside her the sweetest sound. Almost there. They slid upwards, stretching gently, pushing, as his mouth descended, finding her.

Ty's scream of pleasure filled the room, her climax breaking, ripping through her. Hips lurching off the bed, Steve's mouth and fingers following, absorbing her violent tremors. Then, as her body began to settle, he was over her, knees spreading hers wide. Feeling his fingers withdraw, Ty half sobbed, half whimpered, her body instinctively following.

God, she was tight. "Ty, look at me." Their eyes locked at the roughly whispered command, as Steve positioned himself and pushed inexorably into her slick heat.

She was panting beneath him, eyes as huge as a gray dawn, lips swollen from his kisses, so beautiful he thought his heart would never be the same. "Kiss me, Ty." As he captured her mouth, his hips flexed, thrusting deep past the barrier, imbedding himself. That decisive movement sending her beyond words, beyond thoughts, beyond anything she'd ever known before.

She was draped over him, one knee bent across his leanly muscled thighs, her breasts pressed against him, watching with rapt fascination the meandering pattern her index finger traced across his chest, around the flat circle of his nipples, and down the taut line of his stomach. Steve's own hand was moving, too, stroking the length of her back, the gentle slope of her buttocks, back up her spine. His heart thudded steady and strong in his chest, at last having resumed its normal rhythm.

A smile had been growing on her face with each kiss and every languorous lathing of her tongue over Steve's cooling flesh. At last a giggle escaped, quickly muffled by another kiss.

"You're, of course, going to tell me what's got you so happy. Besides the obvious, though any and all compliments would be much appreciated."

"You, Steve, are the very last person to require ego stroking," Ty replied, lifting her head to brush his lips with hers, the smile in her eyes, too. "But here goes. I was just thinking that this was most definitely worth waiting for." Her voice became low with emotion. "And that I'd have been willing to wait a lifetime if it meant I could be with you, like this, even once."

"Thank you, Ty." Hands no longer directionless reached, pulling her under him in a single fluid motion, then lifted to cradle her face. Lips melded, sharing honeyed happiness. "Thank you," Steve murmured huskily again, "for coming into my life."

PART 4

26

"*Y*ou certain you can handle a stick shift? It's not like your Bug, you know."

Steve was fingering the collar of her shearling coat. She shivered in helpless response, her body now so sensitized to his touch that even the light caress across that area, where her hair was drawn back and held in place with a thick barrette, had Ty trembling, desire stirring deep within her. A desire that seemed infinite, never-ending. Ty remembered how easily Steve had summoned it only a short time ago. Rousing her from sleep into the heated bliss of his lovemaking. Her body felt it still. Tingled and ached ever so sweetly.

Lips pursed, she rolled her eyes, pretending to be insulted. "Yes, I can handle a stick shift." If they'd had more time, she'd have saucily suggested taking him back inside where she could prove it. But that would have to wait for New York. "I promise I won't grind the Jaguar's gears even once."

Steve's expression was skeptical; she could see it even in the darkness of this cold November morning. "Really, Steve," Ty insisted, "I have driven some nice cars before."

And Ty was looking forward to getting behind the wheel of something a little more muscular than the Volkswagen. The Jaguar was beautiful, she could see why Steve fussed over it. Ty hadn't even been aware that Steve owned any vehicle other than his beat-up truck, until he'd backed the Jag out with a full-throttled roar from the garage the day before. A gold XKE convertible, its license plate sporting "FF1."

"Palm Beach Grand Prix. The Jaguar Classic," Steve had offered in explanation as she'd stood, openly admiring its sleek lines. "Fancy Free blew away the competition. We also won a Volvo that year, but I sold it. That was the Year of the Car for us."

Understanding that ninety percent of what made the car so important to Steve was its tie to Fancy Free had her rising on her toes and placing a trail of light kisses along his stubbled jaw. "Steve, I promise I'll take excellent care of it."

His hands stroked, drawing her closer. "All right." Then, as if he couldn't help himself, he added, "Because, you know, Bubba can drive . . ."

"No." Ty shook her head, her ponytail brushing his knuckles. "Bubba should ride in the van. He's much more use to you there than I could ever be. I'll drive behind. *Carefully.*"

"Okay," Steve agreed reluctantly. "Now, when we get to the Garden, you peel off and take the car to the hotel's garage. Bubba, Enrique, and I will deal with Gordo and Mac. You remember which side-street entrance to use at the Garden to reach the stalls? You've got your visitor's pass?"

Ty nodded. "In my purse." Steve wasn't leaving a single detail to chance. She stifled a yawn, feeling her eyes grow heavy. It was barely quarter to four in the morning, and his hands were doing such wonderful things to the back of her neck. If she'd been a cat, she'd have arched her back and purred her contentment.

But Steve was still talking. "After we've rendezvoused at the Garden, you and I can go back to the hotel. Gotta make sure you get some rest. Big night tonight." Warm breath fanned her face, his mouth descending, his arms enfolding her, and he was tasting her as though they had all the time in the world, as though the van's engine wasn't running and the horses weren't bandaged, waiting to be loaded, equipment checked . . . everything ready for the four A. M. scheduled departure.

God, he felt wonderful, she thought, kissing him back. So right, hard and warm against her. His hands had slipped inside her coat, bringing their bodies into achingly perfect alignment.

She heard a low growl of hunger when Ty tugged on his lower lip, biting down gently. A week and a half had passed, days filled with work—riding, telephoning, organizing what seemed like a myriad of different details—followed by nights cocooned in the strength of his arms, a place where she was made to feel beautiful, cherished, desired.

Just a week and a half, and Ty had an even greater respect for Steve's abilities. He was smart, funny, charming, imaginative, and tireless.

"Yo, lovebirds, you two mind unlocking lips for a moment so we can load these horses? Or maybe you don't want to go the Big Bad Apple and win glory and prize money?" Bubba was standing framed in the light of the barn's open doors. From the sound of his voice, Ty guessed he was smiling. He'd been giving them grief whenever the opportunity presented itself, and, as Steve and Ty seemed unable to refrain from touching each other, Bubba's opportunities were many and varied.

Bubba was making the most of it, enjoying himself immensely.

"Just coming, Bubba. Want to make sure Ty knows the routine."

Ty and Steve ignored his loud snort.

"Hey, Bubba," Ty called, hoping to distract him. "Mind if I borrow your cap? I want to drive with the top down."

Both Bubba and Steve replied identically: "No way!"

"I'm not letting you borrow this," Bubba returned indignantly. "What's to stop it from flying off in the middle of the LIE?" The custom-designed baseball caps for Southwind were a source of great pride for Bubba. Using the computer he'd purchased for the family, his daughter, Serena, had leaped at Ty's request to create a logo for the farm. After playing around with different ideas, Serena had come up with four designs she considered worthy. The vote had been unanimously in favor of two silver horses racing against a navy blue field, "Southwind" embroidered in flowing cursive underneath. Ty had placed a rush order with a company that could deliver everything—baseball hats, rain gear, warmup jackets—in a week's time. Bubba, Enrique, and Carlos had matching jackets and caps. Nothing like team identity, Ty thought with a smile.

"Jesus, Ty, you don't really think you're going to drive my car with the top down on the Long Island Expressway?" Steve, too, sounded genuinely appalled. "Those commuters are half asleep, Ty. They catch a glimpse of you, there'll be a ten-car pile-up, guaranteed."

She punched his shoulder lightly. "Cut it out. It'll be lovely, all that wind blowing, the sun rising behind me."

"Yeah, lovely. Another time, Ty. We can ride with the top down all the way to Kentucky if you want. Trust me on this, I know what I'm talking about, and I don't want to be worried about what accidents you and that flashy car of mine are causing."

"Please, Steve." Ty smiled up at him and let her body melt against his.

"Aw, Christ," His hands gripped her, pressing urgently. "You're playing dirty, kid."

What a wonderful thing to be able to do, to tease and tempt.

How thrilling to discover she could distract him with just a smile, a whispered plea. And to know it was okay—that he could do the same to her. The knowledge of shared power, the wondrous intimacy of it, filled her with dizzy euphoria.

He cupped her bottom, his erection evident in spite of the layers of clothing separating them. "I should have waked you up even earlier. Maybe we should go upstairs, make sure you've brought everything you need."

A soft moan tumbled from her lips. It was no use pretending she wasn't aroused; he knew her too well. Knew that all he'd have to do was take her by the hand, lead her through the cold, predawn darkness and up to his room, and she'd be his.

"What time is it, anyway?" Steve asked, his mouth open against her throat.

"Quarter of four," she breathed, wishing it were hours earlier.

"Shit! We've got to get on the road." He kissed her hard. "To be continued at the hotel, babe. Promise me you'll drive carefully. And no eye contact with sex-deprived executives."

Macintosh and Vanguard, both veterans of the show circuit, boarded the van with total aplomb, utterly relaxed, their ears pricked forward. Their hooves thudded

against the thick black rubber-padded ramp, as Steve
and Bubba led them up into the van's interior, then
backed them into the wooden partitions. They stood
calmly, their sleek bodies covered in plaid Baker blankets, legs wrapped with thick bandages. Steve and
Bubba snapped ties to either side of their halters, the
leather obscured by the fuzzy fleece to keep the horses'
fine coats from rubbing. They were ready for the trip to
begin.

The mini convoy rolled out the driveway and
through the still-sleeping town of Bridgehampton a hair
past four A.M. Steve was determined to avoid New York
congestion, unwilling to have the horses endure the
stop-and-go of snarled streets and traffic lights. As one
might assume, trailer trucks were a disaster when navigating through the canyonlike streets of New York City.
Horse vans were no different. By timing their arrival in
the city for six-thirty at the latest, Steve was hoping to
beat the added insanity of the peak rush hour.

Ty had diligently tailed Southwind's dark blue horse
van from the minute they pulled out onto Horsemarket
Lane. The drive had been uneventful, no lust-struck executives careening into the median. When they reached
Times Square, however, Ty was suddenly immensely
grateful that they were only bringing two horses to the
National. The large, boxy shape of the four-horse van
was quite big enough (they were using extra space provided by the four-horse van to store hay and feed, as
well as all the equipment for the horses). Ty would have
had palpitations following Steve's larger, eight-horse
van, watching him negotiate turns, terrified that disaster
might strike, in the form of a speeding taxi skidding out
of control, broadsiding the van, or a car cutting in front
of Steve and forcing him to slam on the brakes.

Craning her neck to see around the horse van so she

could check the passing street numbers, Ty breathed a sigh of relief when Madison Square Garden finally appeared on her right. Out the driver's-side window, Steve gave a jaunty wave of reassurance, his signal that she could head back uptown.

Ty checked her watch. Six forty-five. Excellent time. Now to drop the car off at the Plaza, where Ty had reserved a suite. Of course, the hotel wouldn't have their suite ready this early in the morning, but that was okay. Ty would be able to leave the luggage and ask the concierge to have their bags unpacked, so Ty's evening gown and Steve's dinner jacket wouldn't be hopelessly wrinkled.

The patron and exhibitor party for the National, a function Steve rarely bothered to attend, was this evening. But this year was exceptional; Ty and Steve's presence essential. It would be their first public event as partners, a perfect opportunity to woo prospective owners and clients, and their best hope to turn the tide of ugly gossip and rumors surrounding Steve and Southwind.

In addition, Vicky Grodecki would be there. Vicky had driven out to Southwind the previous week to conduct her interview. When they'd finished, Vicky had mentioned that the *Times* would be doing a big feature on the National Horse Show—its history, and its role in the coming millennium as the city's premier horse show. Having dropped that useful tidbit, Vicky had casually suggested that they might consider attending the patron and exhibitor party, especially since Vicky's interview with Steve and Ty would already be out, guaranteeing that their names would be on the lips of every horse person in the region. Vicky would be able to do a follow-up on Steve and Ty, have the photographer snap a few pictures of them. It could only help Southwind.

Steve had won Vicky over completely, Ty thought with a smile. He'd been an interviewer's dream: patient, articulate, funny, and heartbreakingly candid. The Steve Sheppard of that afternoon made excellent copy, and the *Times* reporter couldn't help but appreciate it. When Vicky arrived, Steve and Ty walked her around Southwind, the photographer accompanying them.

Later, back in the farmhouse, Steve had answered Vicky's questions about Fancy Free's death, about ending his partnership with Jason Belmar, and beginning a new one with Ty Stannard. "We're starting from fresh, Vicky," Steve had explained. "Ty and I will be making a buying trip next month, looking for some young prospects. We've already had a few people express interest in having us buy horses for them. I'm really excited about that. Every day that I walk into the barn, I miss Fancy. He was one of the best. But it's time to move on and open ourselves to new possibilities. I've always loved working with young horses, so this is a great chance to start with a fresh crop of youngsters. Vanguard and Macintosh, two of my more experienced horses, are coming along well. My mare, Cantata, is showing real potential. All of us are eager to start the winter season."

"Ty mentioned that you'll be offering a clinic here at Southwind. When will that be?" Vicky Grodecki asked, pen poised to catch Steve's answer.

"That's right, we've scheduled it for mid-December, before the Florida season begins. The clinic is intended for riders interested in showing in amateur owner and jumper classes. I'll be concentrating a lot on flat work and gymnastic exercises. It should be fun. The facilities here at Southwind are perfect for this sort of small, intensive clinic. We'll be videotaping each session so the riders can review my comments, not be forced to remember everything I've said—it's hard to take notes when you're on horseback," Steve finished, smiling, with a pointed glance at Vicky's notebook filled with hurried scrawl.

"And how can people register for your clinic?"

"We've posted a Web site that gives all the relevant information. The clinic will be limited to fifteen, so I can really focus on the individual horse and rider."

"And is it true Southwind will be open to owners who want to show their own mounts?"

"Yes."

"Miss Stannard? How do you see your role at Southwind?" Vicky asked, changing tack abruptly. "While you've been involved in equine charities, this partnership with Steve represents a new venue for you, doesn't it? Quite a departure from real estate development."

Before Ty could formulate a response, Steve interjected smoothly, "Not really, Vicky. While the heart and soul of Southwind may be centered around horses and driving cross country from show to show in a horse van, it's a business nonetheless." Flashing a smile and private wink at Ty, he added, "Since Ty and I go way back, I was absolutely delighted when she approached me with the idea of forming a partnership."

"Yes," Ty agreed calmly enough, though her cheeks burned at Steve's casual stretching of the truth. "You see, my business experience frees Steve to concentrate on what he does best. In addition, we've got a terrific stable manager and staff working with us."

"So you see yourself as the financial and business end of this venture?"

"Certainly. Everyone has their area of expertise here."

"And Ty, after a hiatus of several years, has also begun riding again," Steve added. "I'm hoping that by next spring, she'll be leading my amateur riders. As a matter of fact, Ty is exactly the kind of amateur rider we hope to attract to Southwind. Riders who are serious about learning and improving and who enjoy the added challenge of showing, too."

Ty had tried not to look too startled by this surprising bit of information Steve tossed out so casually. She compete again? But when Vicky Grodecki apparently took the idea at face value, Ty didn't attempt to disabuse her.

It was only later, after Vicky had exhausted all her topics for Steve's interview and left with photographer in tow, that Ty confronted Steve, asking him what in the world he'd been thinking of when he'd made that particular comment.

They were riding in the large field closest to the ocean. Using its ample size to best advantage, Steve had installed some of the bigger, more technically demanding jumps that riders encountered in Grand Prix courses. Southwind's course boasted such elements as a water jump, a bank jump, a wall, and a wide brush jump. Interspersed among these obstacles, all essentially immovable, were other fences, gaudy sunrise panels, triple bars, wide and high. Jumps that often caused horses to hesitate.

Steve had been working with Cantata over a number of the fences while Ty exercised Macintosh on the flat. Unlike Mac and Gordo, the mare wouldn't be competing until they went south to Florida for the winter season. Keeping her comfortable with these trickier obstacles was essential for the young horse.

As Steve and Ty cooled down Cantata and Macintosh, letting the steaming horses meander in a relaxed, loose walk, Ty found herself thinking back to Steve's interview with Vicky Grodecki. "I can't believe Vicky fell for some of the malarkey you fed her!"

Steve pulled the cigarette from his mouth, exhaling as he spoke. "What do you mean? Nearly everything I said, if not the gospel truth, was close enough."

"What about that hogwash about my showing?" Ty persisted, shaking her head, "What made you think of that?"

"Come on, Ty, you know as well as I that when people read these articles, they want a story that's going to grab them. We gave them a good one. A hint of romance, a man redeemed, a woman following her passion. Anyway, who's to say your competing again is malarkey?" Steve replied. Perhaps she was unaware of how totally at ease she was on his horses. "In the space of one short week, you're already a hundred percent improved. That's damned impressive, considering how good you were the first day you rode Macintosh and Cantata. You're a terrific rider. Moreover, you're a natural-born competitor; not in the sense that you want to go out and beat the pants off the guy next to you, but you're a perfectionist. And competing in a show would allow all that hard work and training to crystalize into one perfect round. Wouldn't you like to see how far you can take your riding?"

It amazed her that he'd figured out that particular facet of her personality in such a short time, understanding that for someone like her, competition wouldn't be against others but against herself. "I do occasionally wonder if I could be as good a rider as I was. Or if I could possibly even improve beyond that level," she admitted. "But I hadn't really considered it seriously."

"Why not?"

"Well, watching you, Steve, can be somewhat daunting. And I guess I didn't think my skills were sharp enough after such a long break."

"More than sharp enough. Not that I'm suggesting

you turn pro. You'd have to be nuts to want to do that, you can take my word for it. But, to tell you the truth, I had another reason for telling Vicky Grodecki you're planning to show again. I thought we might send a message loud and clear to Daddy dearest."

Ty looked at Steve, startled. "And why would we want to do that? As far as I'm concerned, the less contact, the less I have to think about my father, the better."

"Yeah, but while you're working your butt off to get a business running again, your father's out there, lurking in the shadows, looking for a way to sabotage your efforts any way he can."

"He'll have found a pretty darn effective way if he manages to block my trust fund," Ty remarked flatly.

Steve grunted in disgust. "The overseer said it would take months to settle if it went to court, right? Something tells me, though, that your father would much prefer to go in for the quick kill."

"How charmingly put." Ty replied with a strained smile. "But accurate, nevertheless. Go on. I can see you've been thinking about this."

"Probably because I've developed a real dislike for your father recently. Which is strange. I'm normally a pretty easygoing kind of guy," Steve drawled, making Ty laugh. His hand reached out, stroking the soft skin along her cheek. God, he loved touching her. Indulged himself whenever opportunity presented itself for a stolen touch, a brush of skin, a quick, heated kiss. Steve wished that they weren't riding right now, that he could pull her into his arms and kiss away the hurt caused by her father. "Do you remember when you told me the story of how your father sold your mare, deciding that your days on horseback were finished? Well, I'm betting it'll piss him off royally when he learns you're riding again, even thinking of entering competitions. Suppose we succeed in angering him enough? He's going to see red, wouldn't you agree?"

"Actually, my father's more the type to see iceberg white," Ty corrected. "But yes, he has very specific ideas of what his twenty-five-year-old daughter should and should not be doing."

"And showing would definitely be on his no-no list," Steve said with a grin. "Smart, rich, successful heiresses should be doing more serious, more important things than climbing into a saddle and taking a horse over a bunch of brightly painted fences. Have I got it right?"

"To a tee," she said, smiling at Steve's all too accurate analysis. "The only thing that worries me is not whether my father will react but *how.*"

"Ty, Sweetheart, it's a given that he's going to attack. If we piss him off really badly, he may act prematurely. You must be sick and tired of these behind-the-scenes skirmishes, and I sure as hell hate the look that fills your eyes every time you relearn what an SOB he is. Let's get him out in the open and have our final battle."

"And as an avid student of history, you're assuming that my father is Napolean reincarnated."

"Maybe a little taller, if it's true you and he look alike," Steve conceded. "But yeah, let's get him out of your life. He can go develop a luxury retreat on Elba."

Recalling their conversation, Ty feared Steve was being overly optimistic about their chances against her father should it come to an open confrontation. Her father possessed such a ruthless, maniacally blinkered view of life, it enabled him to crush opponents with terrifying ease. But as she turned the Jaguar east on Fifty-ninth Street, doing her utmost to avoid potholes, Ty resolutely pushed the gnawing worry to the back of her mind. She had several hours until she was to meet Steve at the Garden.

Enough time for a complete overhaul at her favorite salon. She knew Steve was going to dazzle the crowd at the Garden. Well, that meant that tonight, at the party, it would be her turn.

"Bubba, where in hell is the cell phone?"

"Front pocket of your jacket. No, that's your cigarettes, try the other one. There you go. Who you calling, your broker?" Bubba was leaning casually against the row of makeshift stalls set up in the lower level of Madison Square Garden. All around, horses were being groomed, saddled, watered, fed. A controlled kind of pandemonium reigned. Steve was oblivious to the noise, the bustle around him, the constant activity such an integral part of life on the road, something he took for granted.

"No, I'm trying to reach Ty," Steve distractedly informed him. He was staring at the phone, a frown marring his face. "I want to tell her not to bother to come down, that I'll meet her back at the hotel. She'd offered to lend a hand warming up Mac, but some of the horses I've seen are totally wacko. Explain to me, Bubba, how it is I always forget how bloody small the warmup area is here. I've been in garages that are bigger."

"I believe that memory lapse of yours has something to do with the fact that you won your very first Grand Prix here. And 'cause you've got a sentimental streak a mile wide."

"Yeah, well, I don't want Ty blaming herself if she can't get out of the way of some crazed one-ton, four-legged bomber. No place to maneuver, let alone ride."

Bubba watched his employer glaring fiercely at the cell phone in his hand, as though it were some evil token. "You know her number, Shepp?"

"Yeah," Steve nodded absently. "But damn it all, I've forgotten the code to unlock this thing."

Bubba held out his hand with a long-suffering sigh. "Here, give it over. You and Ty are perfect for each other, you know that? Both of you cell phone challenged." Expertly, he punched in numbers, then asked Steve for Ty's. Now it was Steve's turn to assume a pained expression as he was forced to wait while Bubba chatted with Ty for several minutes, describing in typical, colorful detail everything from how the unloading had gone to what the other horses stabled next to Mac and Gordo looked like. Finally, Steve tapped Bubba's heavily muscled shoulder and with an exasperated whisper of "Do you mind?" relieved his stable manager of the phone.

"Ty? Hey, babe. How's everything?"

Bubba observed Steve listen, ask questions, and murmur a few responses of his own, a smile playing over his face. He was no longer surprised by the expression Steve wore whenever Ty was near. It amused him, though, that Shepp's face got that dreamy look on his face just by hearing Ty's voice over a staticky connection.

Steve was a goner, all right. Deeply and irresistibly in love. It seemed, too, that Bubba's first impression of Ty had been right on the mark. She wasn't some superficial socialite looking for easy amusement. Ty was in just as deep as Steve. Bubba, Carlos, and Enrique already had a friendly wager going about the precise date when wedding bells would begin ringing. Of course, they hadn't breathed a word of *that* to the boss man. Even with Bubba's constant ribbing, Steve and Ty were doing their best to be discreet—and failing miserably. Bubba remembered how the two of them had been passionately embracing earlier that morning. It had made him want to find Gloria, fast.

Thinking of his wife, Bubba nudged Steve. "She called Carlos yet, made sure everything's fine at Southwind?"

Steve nodded, giving him the thumbs-up sign. Carlos was staying at Southwind, taking care of the place and Cantata until Bubba and Enrique got back with Mac and Gordo. Then, while Shepp and Ty were down in Kentucky, visiting his folks and scouting for horses, Bubba, Gloria, and Serena were going to stay at the farm. His son, Will, would be joining them, exercising the horses while Shepp was gone.

It'd be great having Will back for a visit, no matter how short. Maybe he could persuade Will, now that he was a mature college man and no longer necessarily viewed his younger sister as a whiny crybaby, to take Serena out to the movies so Bubba and Glo could have a little time to themselves . . .

Steve clicked off the phone, looking pleased. "Everything's fine. She called Carlos. Cantata's out in the pasture; he's going to longe her this afternoon. The new jumps we ordered for the indoor ring should be delivered tomorrow. He's going to set them up over the weekend."

"Ty mind about the change of plans?"

"No, she's got stuff she wants to do in the city. Said she wanted to go visit Sam Brody—remember the guy I introduced you to the other day, Ty's ex-bodyguard?

"Big guy who wants you to buy a horse for him?"

"That's the one. Well, apparently something's up between him and Ty's best friend, Lizzie. She's been trying to get the story out of them all week."

Bubba shook his head. "Female curiosity."

"Don't let Ty hear you say that," Steve advised with a grin. "She's not big on stereotypes. To tell you the truth, I'm a little curious myself. They'd be one interesting couple if they actually got together. Lizzie Osborne seems like a woman who'd give Brody a run for his money."

"Speaking of couples, you going to go out and get that lovely partner of yours a token of your esteem? A trinket, a negligee, something that will show her how much you care?"

Steve looked horrified at the suggestion. "Christ! You think I ought to? Ty seems so self-sufficient, you know? Like she doesn't need anything. What could I possibly get her?"

"Haven't a clue, Shepp," Bubba replied cheerfully, not in the least dismayed by Steve's chagrin. "But I do know that women set a pretty big store by whether a man goes to the trouble of showing in a real *materialistic* way that he's been thinking about her. Myself, I'd go for something beautiful, 'cause it suits her."

"Thanks a bunch, Bubba. And here I thought I only had building up a new clientele and winning a Grand Prix to worry about."

"Anytime, Shepp, anytime."

27

$\mathcal{I}$t was almost six when Steve arrived at the Plaza. He'd had to spot Enrique and Bubba for an hour while they went off in search of an early dinner; a flip of the coin decreed it would be Chinese. For the duration of the horse show, Bubba and Enrique were sleeping on fold-out cots in the spare stall Steve had reserved adjacent to Gordo's. In case of an emergency, it was essential someone be on the premises. By keeping each other company, not only was boredom alleviated, but it also meant that either Bubba or Enrique could take a quick break or make a run to the local deli for a sorely needed bag of chips or soda.

Steve felt distinctly out of place dressed in filthy blue jeans and equally dusty paddock boots when he crossed the mirrored and columned lobby of the Plaza. If anyone else was wearing blue jeans around here, they were the kind of jeans one's personal maid diligently pressed and starched, hanging them neatly in a closet, and that were purchased for three to four times what Steve paid for his Levi's. Boots worn in a place this swank would be hand-stitched alligator, ostrich, or rattlesnake, with nary a scuff mark on them. Steve was half expecting the man behind the reception desk to call security and have him discreetly escorted off the premises. Thus, it came as a huge shock to have the man address him before Steve even opened his mouth.

"Mr. Sheppard, good evening. We've been expecting you. May I be the first to welcome you to the Plaza and to wish you the best of luck this week."

"Good evening, and thank you," Steve replied, if possible even more startled. Man, there must be hundreds of people passing through here every hour, and this guy recognized *him?* It boggled his mind. Leading him to wonder, too, what else this man knew about him—his shirt size, for instance, or how he liked his eggs cooked. "I was wondering if you could tell me my room number. I forgot to ask Miss Stannard."

"Suite 1600." The man was already turning toward the dark-wooden cubbyholes at his back and extracting a slim white envelope. "Inside you'll find your electronic key, Mr. Sheppard. The elevators are just to your right. Your bags were seen to earlier, might there be anything else we can get for you? Champagne, perhaps?"

Yup, the guy probably did know his shirt size, what kind of toothpaste Steve used, too. He couldn't wait to tell Bubba about this. "A bottle of champagne would be great. Could you send it up as soon as possible, please?"

"Of course, Mr. Sheppard, I'll see to it right away."

He followed the sound of running water through the open bathroom door. She was in her element, surrounded by marble tiles of a light cream streaked with veins of darker brown. Thick, white, fluffy towels were piled high on the shelf above her. Suspended from polished steel hooks, two matching white terrycloth bathrobes were reflected in the opposite mirror. The bathroom was like the rest of the suite: a testimony to understated opulence, each detail heightening one's sense of comfort and luxury.

Ty's body was hidden by mountains of bubbles, only her creamy shoulders and the graceful line of her neck visible. That, added to the wide smile of pleasure she gave him as he walked into the bathroom, made his heart kick in, its tempo running amok.

"Hi. This is some place you got us, partner," Steve said. Perched diagonally on the rim of the tub, Steve reached out his hand, skimmed it lightly over her damp skin with casual possessiveness, letting it dip beneath bubbly water to graze her breasts, resurfacing slowly once more.

"So you like it?" Her voice catchy, as inviting as the rest of her.

"Well, it ain't Motel Six, but I guess I'll survive." If the bubbles would thin out, then he might see the rest of her, naked and wet.

"It's a bit much, I know, but the location is convenient, and there's something about this place . . ." Ty bit her lip, only partially stifling the moan of pleasure as Steve's fingers again dipped beneath the water, drawing lazy circles around her nipples.

"Sorry, I didn't catch what you were saying." Steve grinned, his hand moving even more boldly. "Mind repeating that?"

She gave him a look that promised retribution. "I was saying that something about staying at the Plaza makes me feel like Eloise. Tempted to do really naughty things." Then, with a sphinxlike smile, Ty lifted her leg, bringing her pointed foot up so that it nestled in Steve's lap.

It took all his skill, balance, and formidable control not to tumble into the tub right then and there. The witch, he thought happily. Where had she learned this kind of magic? The wet heat of her foot pressing against his erection, driving all rational thought from his mind.

"When's the party?" he managed to ask as his hands tugged at the buttons on his shirt, his jacket already in a heap by the tub.

"Seven. But the best people are always late," Ty added happily, her toes curling into him, testing.

"Thank goodness for that." His torso was bare now, and he lifted her foot, dragging it up the hard blocks of his stomach, past the smooth contours of his chest, and up to his ravenous mouth. "So, this place makes you feel naughty?" Steve asked between prolonged nibbles and tastings of her damp pink toes. "That's certainly a four-star recommendation in my book." This time Ty's moan filled the steam-clouded bathroom. With the greatest reluctance he lowered Ty's foot so he could unfasten his jeans, shedding them and his boots with truly impressive speed. As he stepped into the tub, she rose to meet him, meringue-shaped masses of bubbles clinging to her.

Urgently, Steve pulled Ty to him, needing her so much. "Time to get naughty."

If tardiness went hand-in-hand with that enviable aura of exclusivity and chic, nobody rivaled Ty and Steve at the patron and exhibitor party for the National Horse Show that evening. They couldn't have timed it better, actually. More than an hour late—from romping in the bathtub, sharing deliciously chilled champagne, and Ty needing time to repair her makeup and hair— their arrival was marked with the kind of excitement that was usually accompanied by a drum roll building to a dramatic crescendo. Cocktails were still being served; events such as that evening's often dragged on interminably, and the people clustered in small groups were growing bored, their cocktail chitchat all used up, their eyes scanning the room restlessly, looking for a new source of interest, something to perk up their flagging attention.

Then, suddenly, there was one.

Ty Stannard had arrived, looking so beautiful that people simply stared, arrested. She was dressed in a shimmering midnight-blue tulle-over-silk evening gown, the weightless tulle floating ethereally about her tall, slender body. Her shoulders were bare, skin flatteringly revealed. The color of creamy ivory, smooth and glowing with health, it called out to be touched. Her hair, artlessly styled into a high, twisted chignon, accentuated the delicate lines of her face, the clear gray of her eyes shone with energy and happiness.

Standing beside her, Steve Sheppard looked as natural in his severely cut dinner jacket as he did in the breeches, blue jeans, or worn leather chaps that most who knew Steve saw him habitually wearing. He possessed the kind of athletic build and classically structured face that made him look good in anything he wore, but this evening the women in the enormous ballroom who got close enough to him and Ty let out an involuntary sigh, wishing they could look like Ty Stannard. And wishing, too, that they could have a man like Steve Sheppard at their side. Especially once they recognized the special smile hovering on both Ty and Steve's faces.

Steve and Ty paused on the threshold of the ballroom's entrance, Steve having just handed Ty's full-length velvet cape to the coatroom attendant. "Now I understand why you sent me downstairs to ask for the Jaguar," Steve was whispering out of the corner of his mouth, his voice pitched for her ears alone. "It's gonna be real hard to think about anything but getting you out of that frothy number."

"This is not frothy," Ty whispered back, her smile lifting a notch. "This is evening business attire. Formal, not frothy. Remember, we've got work to do tonight."

"I haven't forgotten. Business before pleasure. But the way you look right now, it's impossible to resist contemplating how I'd like to mix the two. Or we could ditch this right now. Just say the word, Ty." His knuckles brushed the almost transparent tulle.

"The word is *work*," Ty said firmly, pressing her lips together. She loved his banter, how he made her feel desirable with such effortlessness. "Time to get to it, Steve. We've got everyone's attention. You remember the people you're going to concentrate on?"

"Yes, ma'am. And if I have any questions, I'll come pick that awesome brain of yours," Steve drawled, a bit peeved by Ty's ability to focus on the decidedly less than thrilling task of spending the remainder of the evening talking up Southwind, when all *he* wanted to do was head straight back to the Plaza and have that thoroughly likable gentleman behind the reception desk send up another bottle of champagne to their suite. The pleasures to be found at the Plaza were definitely growing on him.

It hadn't been too terrible, Steve was forced to acknowledge two hours later. Luck had been on their side tonight. The first sign had been the major flub up in the kitchen that had delayed the dinner. While harried waiters carried out additional trays piled with canapés and hors d'oeuvres to appease the hungry crowd, setting them down on the long, rectangular banquet tables at the far end of the ballroom, Steve and Ty used the extra time to mingle with potential clients and patrons for

Southwind. Working separately, they went about their business. They chatted, horse talk cleverly mixed with nuggets of tantalizing information about Southwind—its facilities, the clinic Steve was holding, Steve's winter show schedule, what stables he was planning on visiting for his buying trip, hinting that Europe, too, might be included later next spring. Ty and Steve had coached each other carefully.

In the beginning, Steve was frankly astonished by the powerful aura Ty's name carried. He hadn't really believed Ty when she'd insisted it would make a difference if people knew she was backing him financially.

It was his first real glimpse of the power of big, big money. Throughout the evening, Steve was asked repeatedly to confirm the rumor floating about that Ty was Steve's new business partner. Upon hearing his response, people became downright energized, looking at him with bright, eager expressions, firing off questions, saying they'd always intended to check out his place in Bridgehampton, that they'd be getting in touch with him directly after the National. After a few rounds, Steve learned just how long it was necessary to stay after detecting that sudden spark in the listeners' eyes. He'd excuse himself, saying he hoped he'd be hearing from them in the near future, and move on, ready to tackle the next group.

Yes, Steve thought happily. The evening, thanks to Ty, was going really well, his sense of optimism increasing with each contact he made. Even if only some of the people they talked to tonight came through, he and Ty might very well manage to get Southwind solidly in the black.

A couple times Steve came real close to bungling it. But there, too, people had been unbelievably indulgent. It happened while he and Ty were still working the cocktail crowd. In the midst of a conversation, Steve caught sight of Ty across the room. That was all it took. His eyes upon her, and he was lost to the world, coming back only after receiving a discreet but nonetheless firm nudge to the ribs, and a prompting cough that pierced his desire-fogged brain. A second sign that luck was on their side this evening, for each time Steve suffered one of these spells, conscious only of his desire for Ty, he was in a group of men. The shared grins of understanding, the nudges, the hearty slaps on the back that followed, made for a true male-bonding experience.

Ty and he were placed at different tables. Naturally, Steve's initial instinct was to try to switch cards with someone so that he could be near her. But, as it happened, Vicky Grodecki was seated next to him, and Steve was forced to shelve that particular idea. Ty would have given him hell if he'd ditched the *Times* reporter. Anyway, he liked Vicky. She knew her stuff and didn't pepper him with idiotic comments the way many of her colleagues tended. They spent forty animated minutes talking about great riders and horses, about America's chances in the upcoming Olympics. Steve realized that there were definitely worse people he could be stuck with while trying to chew his way through overcooked beef and undercooked vegetables.

But by the time the dessert of soggy angelfood cake appeared in front of everyone's place, Steve felt he'd earned all the brownie points he needed for the coming week.

Throughout this evening, he and Ty had talked the talk. Now it would be up to him to walk the walk.

He had to go out there tomorrow and all of the upcoming week and ride at the top of his form. And if it so happened that Macintosh and Gordo weren't up to snuff, then Steve would have to use all his talent and skill to overcome that.

A few notes were launched into the air as the hired band found its way into a Gershwin tune. All around Steve, people were happily abandoning their desserts in favor of the dance floor, the women's long dresses swishing against the polished wood. A sense of fierce anticipation surged inside him as he realized the business portion of the evening was over. A lot of time left for pleasuring Ty. Steve got up and made his way over to her table, where a strange man was speaking to her, leaning close, the sleeve of his evening jacket touching her forearm.

Steve decided on the spot that if the guy thought he was going to do business with Southwind, he could think again. This was as close as he'd ever get to Ty.

"Excuse me." Steve could afford to be polite. Ty was his.

Ty stood, forcing the man to do so, too. "Steve," Ty said simply. Not needing to say more.

Steve's smile spread, warming, in direct contrast to the other man's increasingly hostile gaze.

"I thought you might like a dance before we leave," Steve suggested, holding out his hand.

"That would be lovely," Ty murmured, linking her arm with his, then turning to her dinner companion. "It was good to catch up with you, Edward. Best of luck with those stock options."

Edward didn't get a chance to reply, for Steve was already escorting Ty to the dance floor. "Want to tell me why I feel like I've got a knife sticking out between my shoulder blades?" Steve asked, easing her into his arms.

He moved easily over the floor, his steps graceful, as graceful as everything else he did. What a relief not to be subjected to some clunky, heavy-footed box-step. Ty loved dancing, but these days men seemed to believe it was perfectly acceptable to dance with a total lack of imagination and coordination. She'd seen people in checkout lines who moved with more vitality and awareness than some of her recent dance partners.

"So, who was that guy? He hasn't stopped staring at us, by the way."

"Probably not. My father tried to set me up with Edward a few years ago. Edward's everything he's looking for in a husband for me. Rich, ambitious, excellent family."

Steve's arms tightened fractionally, relaxing only when he felt her sink into him without hesitation. "Did you hit it off with this Edward?" His eyes watched hers carefully.

Ty laughed softly, shaking her head. "Not exactly. He's simply one in a string of phenomenally boring men my father tried to foist on me. Though Edward certainly gets excited talking about mergers and acquisitions."

Steve brushed a whisper of a kiss against her hair, inhaling the subtle trace of her perfume. "You know, I've been wondering about that. Mergers. How is it you're not already married, with a passel of kids and three Ferraris in the garage? I'm assuming getting you hitched to the right man would have been high on your father's to-do list."

Before Ty could respond, Steve saw an opening and took it, twirling her about in a perfectly executed turn. Ty gave him a smile of pure delight, and his left hand dropped, enjoying the sensation of her moving through layers of tulle and silk.

"Oh, Father had plans for several key mergers, as you call them. But I put a stop to it. One of my better moments, actually. Inspired."

"Don't keep me in suspense, sweetheart." He was coming to love the light of mischief that entered those gray eyes.

"I informed him that if he kept shoving eligible men at me, I'd hold a press conference and announce that I was a lesbian. His face has only turned that particular shade of purple a couple of times that I know of."

Steve gave a shout of laughter, Ty's softer one joining in. Heads turned momentarily, then, recognizing the source, knowing smiles broke out, followed by hand-covered whispers, hiding excited titters. Still laughing, Steve pulled Ty into a whirling spin, the lights above them blurring into gold-yellow streaks.

As his feet slowed, Steve whispered in her ear, "You're incredible, you know that?" Angling his head, his lips played sweetly over hers. "Brilliant." From the corner of his eye, Steve saw Edward staring at them, his expression downright nasty, then Vicky Grodecki, saying something to her staff photographer. They, too, were watching Ty and Steve on the dance floor. "Feel like giving your father a new angle to worry about?"

"Would this be part of your plan to turn him into an enraged maniac?"

"Could be. If not, we can always use it as a Christmas card." Steve locked his gaze with that of the photographer and inclined his head toward Ty. He seemed to divine Steve's intent at once. Lifting his zoom lens, he caught Steve bending Ty over his arm, his lips capturing hers in a searing kiss.

By the time the kiss ended, it wasn't only the photographer who'd caught it. Around the dance floor, several people burst into spontaneous applause.

"You're the hit of the evening, Ty." The Gershwin tune had ended, but Ty and Steve continued dancing, Steve unwilling to let her go. The new song was slower; Steve held her close, their thighs brushing. She fit beautifully against him, her high heels bringing her even with his height. His body acknowledged the perfect fit, hardening, wanting an even tighter fit. *Soon,* he promised himself. *After this last dance.*

"Do you always create this kind of excitement, this kind of energy, just by walking into a shindig like this?" he murmured, curious.

Ty was silent for a moment, then lifted shadow darkened eyes to his. "Yes." It was naked honesty in her voice, not vanity. "This is what I was born to do, Steve. What all my father's careful grooming was intended for. People are attracted to the image of someone like me, not caring whether there's anything of substance beneath it. It's just the money," Ty explained softly. "But I've learned how to use all this to some advantage. Like tonight, for instance, helping Southwind. That's made this evening less difficult to bear than it might have been." Her voice dropped, so he had to strain to hear it. "Without you, this would have been my world: an endless succession of people fawning over my father's money. Take me away, Steve. Please."

Wordlessly, his hand found hers, and he led her away from the glittering ballroom and softly flattering lights.

The drive back, nestled in the supple leather seats of the Jaguar, did much to buoy Ty's spirits. They rode with the top down, the night air cold, the lights of the city all around them. Steve had been forced to release Ty's hand in order to shift the gears and steer, but Ty needed to touch him the way she needed air to breathe. As Steve drove, her fingers traveled up and down the solid length of his thigh muscles. Neither spoke, the sexual hunger growing between them, its presence as palpable as the cold air on their skin.

Steve was proud of the fact that he kept his hands to himself through the endless lobby, up the interminably long elevator ride, and all the way to the door of their suite. But the effort took its toll. A fine trembling made it next to impossible to insert the electronic key into the scanner. Next to him, Ty whimpered softly as the lock resisted his efforts, an insistent red light blipping back at them.

"Steve . . ." There was desperation in her voice. He looked at her, taking in the flush of her features, the out-of-focus gleam in her eyes, the moist, parted lips. Cursing fluently, he shoved the card down hard, almost breaking the door off its hinges when at last the small green light appeared.

Desperation didn't lessen, but it changed like quick-silver.

Steve's hands moved over Ty deliberately, possessively, tugging the concealed zipper down her back by the tiniest of fractions, then pausing to touch, to kiss, to worship each area revealed for him alone.

Where he was slow, Ty's hands traveled like lightning, divesting him of his jacket, sending studs flying through the air, their landing muffled in the thick beige carpet. And when her hands at last smoothed over him, he burned for her.

Released, the tulle gown slipped down soundlessly, becoming a fabulous textured wall of cloth around her legs. Steve helped her cross the barrier, his heart pounding as he drank in the sight of her. A strapless bra and panties of black silk, thigh-high silk stockings, three-inch stiletto heels.

He might never breathe normally again. A choked laugh escaped him. "Jesus, the gown was distracting enough. If I'd known what you had on *underneath* that sea of froth, I'd have been a drooling idiot. Thank you for saving me from certain embarrassment."

"You're welcome, I thought you might prefer to be surprised."

"I could die a happy man from a surprise like this," his tender but delightfully wicked smile causing Ty's heart to trip.

Steve took a step backwards so he could see all of her, every wonderful, mind-blowing inch of her. A vision he would never forget. "Those shoes, were they designed by that guy, what's-his-name, you were talking to me about?"

It took a moment to recall the conversation they'd shared that night by Fancy's grave. It seemed eons ago.

"Yes, these are Manolo Blahniks," she said, extending a leg encased in sheer silk. She pointed her foot so Steve could better examine the wildly patterned brocaded shoes perched atop impossibly high heels. "Do you like them?"

"I think the man is definitely onto something: shoes as torture devices." His eyes traveled up the length of her. "I know, they're killing me." Backing up, he lowered himself into a rust-colored velvet armchair, his eyes never leaving the vision before him.

"Walk this way," he commanded softly, settling into the chair with studied casualness, as though his heart wasn't about to bust through his rib cage. "Yeah, that's right, nice and slow."

A smile curved Ty's lips as she did Steve's bidding. The comportment teachers at her boarding school would be aghast, horrified, if they learned to what use Ty Stannard was putting her very best walk right now. *And to what effect,* she thought happily. With every step, molten heat pooled inside her, her body tightening around it, readying for the explosion about to rock her. Its source the fire blazing in Steve's eyes.

She stopped. Her whole being fixed on him, on the heavy rise and fall of his naked chest, on the black waistband temptingly half unbuttoned. Her hands lifted, undoing the clasp between her breasts. The bra fell to the floor behind her. Her hands skimmed down to the edge of her high-cut panties.

"No." His voice a dark rumble, harsh and wildly erotic. "Not yet. I need a closer look first. Come here. That's right," he encouraged approvingly as Ty did his bidding.

Their knees were brushing now. Steve reached out, molding his hands around the backs of Ty's thighs, touching silk and warm flesh, supporting legs suddenly unsteady. Lazily his fingers toyed with tops of her stockings, following the elastic border around, back and forth. Above him, he heard her breath shudder.

He splayed his fingers, exerting the slightest of pressure. "A little wider, love."

The whispered heat of his words against the flat of her tummy set off exquisite shocks through her. Yet it was only the beginning. Hands, mouth, tongue joined, moved over Ty in a sensuous meandering, dipping into the hollows of her hips, her navel. Moving, always moving, until they reached hot flesh hidden by sweetly dampened silk. Once there, beginning again. With a keening cry, Ty's head fell back, her eyes shut, submitting to Steve's distinctive brand of torture.

28

"*Ex*cuse me, but you're Steve Sheppard, aren't you?"

Steve turned his head in the direction of the voice, interrupting his thoughts of handing Macintosh to Enrique so he could steal outside and smoke a cigarette in peace. The woman astride the massive dark bay who'd ridden up beside had him changing his mind about how much he really needed that smoke. She must have just entered the exercise ring; otherwise, he'd have noticed her. At the very least her horse.

"Yeah." He nodded, his eyes moving appreciatively over the woman's mount, simultaneously checking her out, too. Pretty impressive package the two of them made. "And you are?"

"I'm Cassie Miller."

"Miller, sounds familiar . . ."

"A name more common than Jones," Cassie Miller replied with a quick smile. "I . . ."

"No, wait," Steve interrupted, holding up a hand. "Give me a sec. My memory's been real shaky recently," he said ruefully. "But Miller, Miller . . . Cassie Miller . . ." He snapped his fingers, his face clearing. "Yeah, I remember you. You were the kid who stole the show at the Classic this summer. Unbelievable performance."

Cassie Miller blushed becomingly. "Thanks. It came as quite a shock, winning an event that big. Orion was everything I hoped he'd be—and more—that day."

"Sure was. You beat out me and Fancy, and I'd had my eye on that prize money for the whole month of August."

"Um, actually, that's why I approached you. We heard about Fancy Free's death down at our farm in Virginia, and I just wanted to tell you how sorry I am. He was a great horse. Always worth rooting for."

Steve smiled, touched by the sincerity in her voice and the fact that she'd cared enough to approach him. "Thanks. So, this is Orion. I didn't see him up close that Sunday. Probably too busy sulking." He gave a low whistle. "Nice-looking animal." Not bothering to hide the envy in his voice.

"Yeah, he's special. Born and bred at our place down near Charlottesville."

"You interested in selling him?"

Cassie Miller laughed, shaking her head. " 'Fraid not. He's been sold and resold a couple of times too often to suit my husband and me. Now that we've got him back, he'll remain with us."

Steve wasn't terribly surprised by her answer. One would have to be frigging nuts to let go of a horse like that. "Too bad," he said easily. "I'm in the market, and your Orion is one of the best looking horses I've seen in a good long while. You've already gone out of your way to prove to me he's talented, too."

"You're looking to buy, Steve?"

Steve nodded. "I'm heading down to Kentucky with my partner after the Grand Prix."

"And that would be Ty Stannard," Cassie Miller supplied with a huge grin. "That was some photograph of the two of you in today's *Times*. Nice to know romance is alive and well at those parties. My husband, Caleb, was dead set against attending—said there'd be way too many society matrons squeezed into bright pink sequin nightmares for his taste—but that photo had him regretting his decision."

Steve coughed into his fist. "Yeah, well, parties are what you make them," he muttered, still embarrassed. Though why was a mystery; he'd had hours to get used to it. Despite Steve's having practically orchestrated the moment captured by the *Times*'s photographer, it had nonetheless packed a mammoth wallop to find there, on page one of the sports section, Ty and him fused in a nuclear kiss.

Must have been a really slow day for football, he'd thought dazedly, staring at the photograph.

"Christ, I'm sorry, Ty. Didn't think we'd be quite as newsworthy as this."

Ty had looked at the picture, then at Vicky Grodecki's accompanying column and said calmly enough, "Hmm, you certainly sent my father a message this time. It's probably too much to assume he'll be overwhelmed with gratitude at not losing any more sleep over my sexual leanings. You might consider asking Sam whether he still has a bulletproof vest."

And when Steve arrived at the Garden, he discovered pretty damn quick that everyone else had been reading the morning paper, too. Bubba had gone so far as to cut the picture out, encircle it with a heart drawn in fat red marker, and tape it right above Steve's saddle tree; he and Enrique hadn't stopped laughing about it yet.

Cassie Miller didn't appear to notice Steve's discomfort. "If you and Ty Stannard are going to be down in Kentucky, perhaps you might stop at Five Oaks on your way back up to New York." Her right hand slipped inside her navy fleece vest and withdrew a white rectangular card from the breast pocket of her button-down shirt. She handed it to Steve. "We've a number of young horses you might want to look over. Two-, three-, and four-year-olds, some from Orion's sire. We've got Orion's younger brother, Limelight, here at the Garden with us now."

"You rode him in the Classic, too, didn't you?"

"Came in third with him." Cassie grimaced. "Time fault."

"Don't get cocky, kid." Steve laughed, liking her attitude. "That was a mean sucker of a course." He glanced down at the card in his hand and spoke reflectively. "Five Oaks, huh? And that's near Charlottesville?"

"Just outside."

"We might very well be calling on you, Cassie. You're heading home directly?"

"Yes. The kids are missing school this week, so we've got to get back ASAP."

"Well, it'd be interesting to see what else you've got tucked away at your farm. You put him to stud yet?" Steve asked, nodding toward the stallion Cassie Miller was riding.

"We're waiting for the spring. We've picked a few of our brood mares we want him to cover. And we're hoping to get a couple more for him before long. My husband, Caleb, and his partner, Hank Sawyer, are going on a buying trip themselves later this month."

"I'd appreciate it if you'd keep me posted on any of Orion's get."

"I'll do that," Cassie promised, leaning over to pat the stallion's sleek neck. "Well, I'll be seeing you by the ingate later. Looks like there'll be some good competition."

"Sure will. Vanguard and Macintosh here are raring

to go. We wouldn't want to make it too easy for you, Miller."

"Don't worry, Sheppard," Cassie Miller replied, adopting the same easy banter. "We work best under pressure. So long," she said with a laugh, nudging her stallion into a smooth trot.

A last glance at the business card before stuffing it into his pocket had Steve wondering whether he and Ty shouldn't simply head straight for Virginia. He was suddenly itching to see exactly how fine those other horses at Five Oaks might be.

Damned if he didn't like that woman, Steve thought as he watched Cassie Miller circle the exercise ring, guiding the big stallion effortlessly through and around the busy traffic of other riders and their mounts. Damned if he didn't like her horse, too; the touch of envy he experienced in no way spoiled the simple pleasure derived from observing prime horseflesh and fine riding paired together. A pleasure that, even after so many years in the horse business, still had the power to send excited shivers racing along his skin. Steve's only wish was to feel this way right up to the day he died.

Yeah, Cassie Miller would be tough to beat, Steve acknowledged, gathering up his reins. But that was what he loved about the game. He was eager to push Cassie Miller and her horses to the max.

The Canadian mounted police had come and gone, the crowd applauding enthusiastically as the retinue performed its precisely choreographed maneuvers flawlessly, the crisp red uniforms of the officers, the shiny coats of the horses, the bold maple leaf of the Canadian flag waving smartly, all the varied colors and textures caught and reflected beneath the bright lights of the Garden's high-ceilinged arena.

Right now there was a lull in the evening's schedule of events. Many of the spectators were upstairs, roaming around, buying expensive souvenirs and food, and seeing whether they could beat the line to the bathroom before the jumping started. Down below in the ring, a tractor was zooming around, a wide rake attached to it, smoothing out the dirt footing. A second tractor had just entered, painted jumps, poles, and wings piled on its flatbed. Workmen dressed in blue coveralls sprang off of its side as soon as the tractor slowed, ready to begin setting up the Grand Prix course. Soon the course designer would be out, doing a final measurement of the jumps, making sure the distances were right, the fences set at the correct height. And then would come Ty's favorite part, where the riders spilled out over the course, alone or in pairs, this moment their chance to walk the course. The arena buzzing with the sound of spectators' voices, the riders would be walking with that special, slightly widened gait, counting off the strides their horses would need to take from one jump to the next, anticipating what angles of approach might work best. It was the riders' final chance to analyze the challenges the course designer was putting before them. The next time these riders came into the ring, it would be on the backs of one-ton animals, the riders' job now to communicate to the horses—in the space of less than sixty seconds—how best to negotiate the sixteen fences before them.

Ty glanced over at the bank of seats to her left. Lizzie was there, in the section specially reserved for family and friends of competitors. Lizzie had urged her to go back down, knowing Ty would want to be near Steve when the jumping started. Ty had invited Sam, too, but he hadn't shown up yet. She'd caught Lizzie scanning the crowd, checking the faces of passersby, but hadn't remarked on it. Lizzie was being untypically close-mouthed about whatever was going on between her and Sam. Any other time, Ty would have been tempted to probe her friend, but tonight Ty was too keyed up.

"Hey, Ty." Enrique's voice called from behind her. "Shepp sent me to find you. He's gonna walk the course soon."

"I know. That's why I've been hiding. I wasn't sure I'd be a welcome distraction, Enrique. He's been kind of touchy since Friday night's class."

"You can say that again!" Enrique's navy-blue cap nodded in agreement. They were all—Ty, Bubba, and Enrique—walking on eggshells around Steve right now. "Sorry, boss. If I don't bring you back, Shepp's gonna bite my head off."

Steve had been livid following the qualifying class. Gordo had racked up twelve points with knockdowns on poles Steve was convinced the jump crew hadn't properly reset in their shallow cups. Macintosh had come in fourth with a beautiful round, but Steve had been too disappointed with Gordo's performance to enjoy it. He'd even lodged a complaint with the judges, demanding that the crew show more professionalism this evening, or Steve would march into the ring himself and check poles that had received a hard rub from the previous horse's round.

His protest had earned the approval of many of his fellow riders, for the National's jump crew indeed appeared to be especially casual this year. But the show of support hadn't done much to mitigate Steve's foul temper. His Kentucky drawl had gotten so bad that there were times Ty couldn't understand a word he muttered, which in retrospect was probably for the best.

Ty hadn't succeeded in distracting him from the disappointment of Friday night's jumping class until they finally returned to their suite at the Plaza. It had been midnight, hours consumed in putting the horses away, and making sure Enrique and Bubba were set for the night.

While Steve washed off the day's grime in a scalding hot shower, Ty called down and ordered from the restaurant's menu a meal that could be prepared quickly. When Steve reemerged, wrapped in one of the hotel's thick terrycloth robes, the midnight meal was waiting for him, dishes hidden under silver domes, the whole illuminated by two tall candles. Grabbing a chair, Steve had pulled her down into his lap, and there they'd sat, Ty snuggled against his chest as they fed each other bits of smoked salmon, thin slices of cold roast beef, followed by strawberries dipped in whipped cream flavored with a hint of cognac. Between bites of food and shared kisses, Ty had argued with Steve, gently but insistently, reminding him that bad rounds happened to everyone. Macintosh had done a superb job, and Gordo hadn't gotten rattled—even with the unnerving sound of falling poles following his progress. Ty was positive Sunday's Grand Prix would be his night. And Macintosh's, too.

They'd made love quietly, their movements slow and unhurried. Long after, Steve had held her, his fingers stroking her long hair as Ty's eyes grew heavier and heavier.

Steve was already showered and dressed when Ty's eyes reopened. It took only one blurry-eyed look at the window to realize he hadn't gotten more than a few hours' sleep. A second look at his closed, determined face, and Ty knew they were back at square one. Steve Sheppard was not a man to cross right now. She hoped whichever poor taxi driver picked him up was smart enough to take him where he wanted to go, and fast.

A brief, hard kiss and "Gotta go, babe. Get over to the Garden as quick as you can." Then he was out the door, Ty left muttering about temperamental athletes.

Ty followed Enrique. They flashed their IDs at the guard and skirted the perimeter of the warmup area where a few riders were taking a final practice jump. She followed Enrique through the barely controlled chaos of grooms scurrying about, horses being led this way and that, some tacked, some not, riders dressed in gleaming white breeches and dark riding jackets. Ty occasionally caught sight of a bright eye-popping red one—indicating that the rider wearing it had competed as a member of the United States Equestrian Team. She followed the groom through all the hustle and bustle back to where Macintosh and Gordo's stalls were located.

She paused, her heart bursting with love and pride when she saw him. Oh, he was handsome, no doubt about it. His hair curled slightly over his collar, a little longer than he usually wore it because she'd told him she loved running her hands through it. Those muscular horseman's thighs were outlined to heart-pounding perfection in breeches and shiny black field boots. But it was the jacket that did it, because the jacket signified so much.

Steve was wearing a dark blue riding jacket, having eschewed his other hunt coat, the red one, its left breast emblazoned with the USET's insignia. That one was still hanging in his closet back at Southwind. Seeing Steve dressed in the severe blue jacket highlighted everything she admired about him: his sense of honor, his strict adherence to a personal code. For Steve, the red jacket of the USET had been a privilege earned when he'd ridden Fancy Free. Now that Fancy Free was gone, Steve believed the right to wear the team's colors would have to be earned all over again with a new equine partner. Until that time came, Steve would wear the dark blue.

He and Bubba were going over Gordo, giving the horse a final touch-up. Bubba was hunkered down with a can of hoof polish, painting the gelding's hooves. They gleamed, dark and lustrous. Steve was using a soft towel, running it over the rich bay coat. Even from here, Ty could tell it was totally unnecessary. Southwind's Vanguard, Gordo's official show name, sported the coat of a champion. Bubba and Enrique had groomed him to a high gloss; not a speck of dust sullied him. The horse was in superb form, sleek, muscular, and set to go.

"Found her, Shepp. Hanging out with the riffraff."

"I was coming back," Ty protested lightly. "But I got distracted by the jump crew. They're setting up some pretty big fences, Steve."

"I know." Steve replied. "The course is tough. Axel Holmgeld," referring to the German course designer by name, "likes 'em high and deep." He gave Gordo a final swipe with the cloth, then handed it to Enrique. "I, uh, wanted to apologize to the three of you for being such a pain in the butt today. I really wanted Gordo to do well in the class Friday night. He's jumping too smart to settle for eighteenth place."

Enrique and Bubba shifted uncomfortably, then Bubba spoke, "Come on, Shepp, you know you don't have to apologize for anything. We're not the ones trying to go clean over courses like this. You're the man bringing home the bacon, you call the shots."

Enrique nodded as if Bubba had spoken for the two of them.

"Yeah, well, I should have let it go just the same. Tonight's gonna be different. Gordo and Mac are in tiptop shape, still full of beans. I've handled Axel's courses before; I'm not too worried about what he'll set up, even with the Garden's tightass corners—sorry, Ty."

Ty bit down hard on the inside of her lip to keep from grinning. She didn't want to spoil the mood. Something like a locker room pep talk a coach might give his players before they took to the field.

"So," Steve was saying, "if the ground crew does its job and checks the fences, I think we'll be in good shape. But if they sit on their keisters, I swear I'll . . ."

"Go marching right out there and fix each and every pole yourself," Ty interrupted, her smile breaking through. "And Bubba, Enrique, and I will be right behind you."

"I'll even bring out a rake and fill in the footing," Enrique added enthusiastically.

The four of them grinned, excited by what lay ahead. Then Ty grabbed Steve's hand, pulling him after her. "Excuse us, gentlemen, we need a quick partners' meeting before Steve walks the course."

A wide, devilish grin split Steve's face when they reached the makeshift tack room. "Ty, much as I'd like to have a quickie with you before I ride, I just don't think this is the place."

Ty shook her head, her hands thrust deep into the pockets of her camel-haired blazer. "I did *not* say quickie, Steve, and you know it." She stood on tiptoes to press her lips against his smile. Softly, lingering to whisper, "This kiss is because I love you, and this," she breathed, withdrawing her hand from her pocket, pressing the warm medallion into his palm, "is for good luck." A wistful smile crossed her features. "Good fortune is meant to be shared, Steve."

His fingers tightened around the medal at her softly spoken words. "Thanks for reminding me." His eyes on hers, he tugged the thick white tie at his neck, loosening it, undoing the top few buttons of his shirt. "Help me with this, sweetheart."

Ty stepped closer, working the clasp of the silver chain until the tiny loop was securely attached. Slipping the medallion underneath Steve's shirt, she kissed the warm skin of his exposed chest, then rebuttoned and retightened his tie. "Time to go out and win a blue ribbon," she whispered in his ear, adding, with a quick nip to his lobe, "Just so you realize what's at stake, it's the only color that will match my underwear."

"Well, then, that settles it," Steve laughed huskily, pulling her flush against him and plundering the honeyed recesses of her mouth. "To be continued, babe," a promise Ty was growing to love.

29

The jump course in a Grand Prix event combined elements of both speed and *puissance*, the French term for "power." Grand Prix fences were set higher and the time allowed set a faster pace than one encountered in other jumping classes. In show jumping competition, some classes were designed specifically either for *puissance* or for speed. Certain horses possessed natural abilities that gave them a competitive edge in one event over the other—tackling really big, monster-sized obstacles or, on the other hand, being able to gallop full tilt over a course and still go clear. That the Grand Prix demanded both strength and speed is what made it the most challenging of show jumping events.

Ty knew this. It was the kind of knowledge anyone who loved the sport absorbed early on, acquired from years spent watching show jumping, hanging out with riders, competing oneself. Indeed, the majority of the spectators packed into the Garden this evening had a solid understanding of the subtle nuances of the competition they were about to see.

That knowledge, however, didn't make the fences,

some of which were raised to the height of a six-foot-tall man and whose spreads were often just as wide, appear any the less daunting or formidable. It wasn't only that the jumps were so big. It was also that the turns horse and rider had to execute while galloping were tighter than a hairpin. And the split-second decisions that had to be made: at what angle to approach the fence, whether or not to leave a stride out (if so, asking the horse for more scope, more jump) or whether to play it conservatively, riding the line, the course, as safely as possible. A decision either way could mean the difference between a first-place ride and not even making the top ten. And while all this was happening, the electronic clock was ticking away. Classes could be won, one clear round edging out another, in fractions involving hundredths of a second. And they often were. It was a beautiful, glorious, thrilling, and unforgiving sport.

The National's Grand Prix was a big one, a field of thirty horses. The riders tonight among the best in the country, as well as Canada, Mexico, and Europe, the National being one of the stops in the U.S. horse show circuit that attracted international riders. For the rest of the winter season, the European riders mostly went back home, where their indoor circuit continued into early spring. Top American riders were faced with three choices: Europe, Florida, or California. As the Olympics were coming up next September, a significant number would be heading overseas, wanting to test themselves against the bigger European courses, while others might elect to remain in the United States and work on building their horses' confidence. For them, the choice remaining would be either to compete on the East Coast or head west. Who could say at this point which tactic would serve the riders best when the Olympic trials began in early July? But this evening's event would pro-

vide riders and spectators alike with a chance to pre-
view what the competition had going for it. Everybody
recognized the special thrill of excitement in the air.

Steve was assigned fifteenth and twenty-ninth in the
order of go, on Macintosh and Vanguard, respectively.
He wasn't the only one entering the Grand Prix with
more than one horse. Earlier, Steve had pointed out a
woman to Ty, Cassie Miller, telling Ty she'd be one to
watch. Cassie Miller had some horses under her that
were phenomenal, a big, dark bay stallion especially impressive. She was based at a farm in Virginia they might
stop by, he'd added in passing.

"Seems as though you've gotten awfully friendly
with this Cassie Miller," Ty had remarked, her eyes on
the woman warming up a flashy gray gelding. "Quite
beautiful."

"Yeah, and you should see her *other* horse. My heart
was going pitter-patter, no doubt about it."

Laughingly, Ty had promised to keep her eyes peeled
the moment Cassie Miller's name was announced, so
her heart could go pitter-patter, too.

Steve had left Ty stationed at the far end of the in-
gate while he went out to walk the course, telling her to
stay put, not to bother coming back to the warmup area
during the class—it was a madhouse with riders,
grooms, and everyone's second cousin. This way, Steve
would know exactly where she was.

Steve had said that the course designed by Holmgeld
would be tough, and it was. The fences were big and
flamboyant, the distances and approaches technically
challenging. The first ten riders in the class, most of
them veterans of the show circuit, didn't come near to a
clear round. But those ten fault-riddled rounds permitted those watching in the stands to perceive what the
riders were grumbling about among themselves: a few

spots on the course were nailing some of the riders and their mounts. The biggest threat was the triple combination. It consisted of an in-and-out and a brightly painted, tall vertical rail. Getting the distance and the pace right for the triple demanded absolute precision, because right after it, placed on an angle by the corner of the ring, was a Liverpool, a water jump with a double-oxer straddling it. In addition to knockdowns over the combination, there already had been three refusals at the Liverpool. Those were definitely problem fences.

The announcer on the PA came on, introducing Cassie Miller, riding her first mount of the evening, Orion. Ty immediately understood why Steve was so taken with the animal. A gorgeous dark bay stallion, he cantered into the ring to a collective "Oohhh" of appreciation from the crowd. Ty watched Cassie Miller rein the stallion to a halt, salute the judges, then ask him to take three showy steps backward, before kneeing him into a flowing canter. From the side of the ring, the electronic buzzer sounded, signaling the start of the timer, and Cassie Miller and her horse were off.

Ty knew it was going to be a clear round from the very first fence. Orion took the huge castle jump with twelve inches to spare, a jump so big, so assured, that for a while it appeared as if he might simply remain airbound. Forelegs stretching out as landing gear, Orion was earthbound once more, off and galloping, choosing at that moment to reveal his "temperamental" side; the outrageous buck he gave sent nervous laughter through the crowd. Unfazed by her stallion's antics, Cassie Miller had him heading straight toward the next fence, sailing over that, too, with the same awesome power. And unlike the others before him, Orion didn't so much as blink at the Liverpool. They brilliantly negotiated the course to the very last fence, the spectators rewarding

Cassie Miller and Orion with a burst of applause. Then, with Orion's ears pinned flat, they galloped to wire, finishing the course of sixteen fences in an impressive forty-eight point five seconds—the round everyone following would have to beat. Steve included.

The chances looked pretty grim, even for the experienced riders. Ty watched a rider from Canada, who'd represented his country in several World Cups and Pan American games, turn in as fault-ridden a round as younger, less experienced riders. A horrified gasp resounded throughout the Garden when his massive gray Dutch Warmblood demolished the triple spread, a jump with three sets of colored rails placed in ascending height, like a staircase. The horse had approached the obstacle a shade too flat and ended up literally walking up the fence. As the spread of rails collapsed beneath the horse's hooves, they thudded to the ground, the sickening sound filling the arena. Ty closed her eyes, afraid to look anymore, only to open them seconds later, awestruck to see the Canadian bravely continuing his round, accumulating eight more penalty points, before finishing the course.

By the time Steve cantered boldly into the ring on Macintosh, Ty's stomach was twisted into tight knots. Terrified and proud, she watched his blond head emerge from beneath his black velvet hunt cap, the flash of his smile and tilt of his head as he acknowledged the judges. The hunt cap once more firmly in place, Steve reined Macintosh three measured steps backward, as Cassie Miller had done before. With the same invisible use of aids, Steve moved the gelding into a strong canter.

It wasn't because she was in love with the man riding the deep red chestnut, and it wasn't because, through some weird set of circumstances, she had become his business partner; neither of these was the reason her nails dug deep crescent moons into her palms or why she started whispering, "Yes, yes, that's it!" over and over again, her eyes glued to Steve and Macintosh. It was because this was as extraordinary an example of precision riding as a person ever got the chance to see.

The round was flawless. Calm, unhurried, Steve rode Macintosh with the lightest touch imaginable, guiding the big, solid gelding around the course, setting him up and then letting his horse's powerful body do the rest. Silent, reverential spectators watched the exquisite display of horsemanship. A quiet so profound that the creaking of leather and the deep-belly grunt of Macintosh taking off, followed by the scattering shower of dirt hitting the wooden jumps as he landed, were the only sounds to be heard.

Then applause erupting, echoing throughout, urging Steve and Macintosh on as they galloped to stop the clock in a time of forty-nine seconds. A clear round, a blink of an eye slower than Cassie Miller's, but that was okay for now, because Steve and Macintosh had done their job. They'd earned themselves a spot in the jump-off.

Slowly, Ty unclenched her hands, all stiff and achy. Taking deep breaths, she willed her heartbeat to return to normal, only now aware that her shirt was soaked and sticking uncomfortably to her back. A good guess that she was in far worse shape than Steve, who'd looked as cool as ice out there in the ring.

But Lord, could he possibly pull that off again astride Gordo? And could Cassie Miller repeat her own fine performance with her gray horse? Would anyone else be able to challenge them?

Ty didn't have to wait long for answers. Another

American rider, based in New Jersey, who'd competed in the Barcelona Olympics, came out riding the veteran Grand Prix horse with which she'd had such great success. She, too, turned in a fabulous round, although Ty personally felt that Steve's was as yet unmatched in terms of classic equestrian perfection.

But the tide of luck certainly appeared to turn in favor of the next few horses. Despite some hair-raising distances and really hard rubs, two more horses went clear, the jumps left miraculously intact. And whatever it was Steve had said Friday night to the judges must have had an impact. After each of those wildly iffy rounds, the crew went scurrying out to confirm that poles were lying snug in their metal cups.

Just as Ty's nerves were escalating to panic proportions, the announcer pronounced Steve's name again, hearty clapping welcoming him back into the ring. It was astounding how as the evening progressed, a place as huge as the Garden had become so intimate—the people seated high above experiencing a real connection with the riders, as one after the other cantered out to test his or her mettle. A few riders already had become the crowd's favorites. From the applause Steve received, it was an easy guess he'd won some more hearts tonight.

Gordo looked superb as he cantered into the ring, his head sawing back and forth in eagerness. Like Macintosh, and some of the other horses competing, his mane was braided. The braids stood out, shiny black rolls against his blood bay coat.

Where Macintosh's character was ideally suited to the kind of precision-crafted performance Steve had turned in earlier, Gordo, as the saying went, was a horse of an entirely different color. What that gave the spectators sitting on the edge of their seats was the chance to observe Steve Sheppard ride in a completely different style, one that was an equally stupendous display of timing, balance, nerve, and athleticism.

From the get-go, it was clear that Gordo wanted nothing more than to plunge headlong into the difficult course. Steve, however, had a different idea, and tonight he was calling the shots. He held Gordo back, waiting and waiting, measuring the distance, then letting the thoroughbred go like a rocket launching from the pad. With each landing, Steve was already gathering him, holding him in check, ensuring that Gordo stayed rounded, balanced, and jumping on stride throughout the tricky course.

More than a few times, while Steve was ruthlessly keeping Gordo to a controlled canter, Ty couldn't help glancing nervously at the red numbers on the clock, worried that he might rack up a time penalty. But Steve seemed to have his own internal clock pacing him. He got Gordo to the last fence, let him fly, then had him racing flat out to the wire.

A clean round in forty-eight flat—faster even than Cassie Miller and Orion's time! The crowd went wild, cheering madly for the new first-place team.

Ty wanted nothing more than to rush to the warmup area, find Steve, and throw her arms around his neck, no doubt babbling in her attempt to tell him how proud she was of him, but remained where she was. Not for anything in the world would she muck up the works, distract Steve in any way. But as she watched the final competitors, all she could think about was getting to the last rider so the class would end and the jump-off could begin.

Out of the thirty riders who'd qualified for the Grand Prix class, a mere seven ended up going clear, advancing to the jump-off. Of that group, only Steve Sheppard and Cassie Miller shared the distinction of having gotten both their horses to jump clear. A jump-off consisted of a shortened course, but by eliminating certain fences, turns as a result became sharper, trickier. And because the jump-off represented the final opportunity for horse and rider to beat the competition, it was the moment to go all out, pull out all the stops.

The order-of-go in a jump-off was for the rider with the best time to go last. This allowed the final rider to know exactly what he or she was up against. Tonight, Cassie Miller was in what might be termed the seesaw position. She'd go into the ring as the very first round on her gray gelding, Limelight, who'd squeaked in a clear round in just under the allotted time of sixty seconds. On Limelight, she'd be setting the pace, like a rabbit in a running race. The other riders (herself included, when she rode the course for the second time on the stallion, Orion) would then try to chase Limelight's time down, bettering it. Steve was in the enviable position of having had the fastest time over all. He and Gordo would be the last round of the evening.

"Hey, Miller." Steve, like Cassie Miller and the other three riders, was already in the saddle, ready to go. He nudged Macintosh closer to the dappled gray. "Good luck out there."

"Thanks," Cassie Miller replied with a quick, nervous smile. "Got any last-minute advice?"

"To you? You got to be kidding!" Steve grinned. Though he, too, was feeling the same nervous anticipation that was making Cassie Miller's eyes as big as saucers, Steve had years more experience dealing with it. She wasn't more than a rookie, really, despite her success. He took pity on the younger rider.

"You might want to take a chance and cut your turn inside the oxer, rather than around it. Your gray looks nimble enough to handle it."

"Inside, huh?" Cassie looked out over the course, picturing the ride. "Yeah, I think he can do it. Not sure about Orion, though."

"No," Steve agreed. "And I'm not sure the other riders will try it on their horses, either. But you've got a big advantage. That stallion of yours covers so much ground, you probably won't need shortcuts. Oh, here's another bit of advice."

"Yeah?"

"Ride fast. Real fast." He gave her a wicked grin.

"Just try and catch me, Sheppard."

"Oh, I will," he called out with a laugh as Cassie Miller cantered into the ring.

Cassie Miller had an excellent round and an even faster time, thanks to Steve's suggestion, but she came away with four faults nonetheless. A knockdown at the vertical rail of the triple combination that Limelight rapped with his hind hooves was a stroke of bad luck that gave the next two riders a little breathing space. All they had to do was go clear, and they'd place ahead of Cassie Miller and Limelight. Of course, what they wanted to do was *win*. This night, however, wasn't to be the night. Both riders trotted back out of the ring with eight points apiece, each having attempted to leave out a stride in the triple combination, a distance that was already a stretch. Their horses didn't make it, chipping in a stride at the very end, their hooves slamming into the rails. The cups too shallow to hold them, the poles came tumbling to the ground. The additional four points accumulated were just one of those things—a rub too hard, and a rail dropped.

Steve was next. The other female rider besides Cassie Miller in the jump-off, the Olympic veteran, had, with exceptional generosity, offered to switch her order-of-go with Steve, thereby giving him an extra minute or so between Macintosh and Gordo.

No stopping this time to salute the judges. A brisk canter brought Steve and Macintosh into the ring. They continued down to the opposite end, circling wide, bringing Macintosh's rolling canter steadily up to pace, stoking the engine, as they headed for the first jump and the buzzer sounded for them.

Steve's mind was clear of everything except the eight fences laid out before him like a map, the turns and angles he planned to make bright dashes showing the way.

The first fence was a tall brush jump, Christmas-like with arborvitae and poinsettia clustered around its wings. Macintosh's ears were swiveling, listening as Steve talked to the horse over the pounding of his heart and the thundering of Mac's enormous hooves. Holding him steady, then loudly clucking his encouragement and driving him forward with his seat. Steve unhesitatingly asked Mac to take the jump long, because he knew Mac wouldn't disappoint. In the air, Steve already shifting his weight, his head turning, looking for that line, the sharp left inside the oxer, so Mac could shave seconds off in the gallop over to the triple combination.

And so it went, Mac listening, responding with heart, courage, everything in him. A ride so fine Steve was almost sorry to clear the eightth and last fence. But not that sorry, he acknowledged with a happy grin as he and Macintosh galloped triumphantly, Steve patting Mac's braided neck in affection and gratitude while excited applause sounded all around them.

"Nice round, Steve," "Good going, Shepp," voices called as he left the ring through the gate. Bubba was waiting for him, smiling from ear to ear. Next to him, Enrique was holding Gordo's reins. Steve went straight over to them, dropping his stirrups, dismounting before Mac had even come to a stop.

"Way to go, Shepp." Bubba gave Mac a quick pat and a kiss on his velvety muzzle before stripping Steve's saddle off. Enrique was waiting, Gordo's saddle pad already lying on the bay's back. He held Gordo's girth at the ready. The three men's movements were as efficient as those of a pit crew in the Indy 500.

Bubba handed Steve a cold bottle of water. Steve uncapped it, chugging down a few quick gulps. Gordo was already saddled, Enrique just double-checking his boots. Steve helped Bubba straighten the cooler over Mac's steaming body, then walked over to Gordo, pulling himself into the saddle with fluid ease.

"Go get 'em, Boss. Gordo wants that ribbon bad, I can feel it."

"So do I, Enrique, so do I."

Steve arrived at the in-gate just as Cassie Miller negotiated the last two fences of the course. A quick check revealed no poles down. She was going like a bat out of hell, too. *Figures,* Steve thought, shaking his head in a mixture of admiration and annoyance.

Gordo was impatiently pawing the dirt footing with his left foreleg. Through his fingers, Steve could feel the gelding's teeth grinding the steel bit in his mouth, the vibrations running up the leather reins. Gordo knew the score, all right. And Steve wanted a win for him. Badly. If only he could keep him balanced through that triple combination, they might be able to out-gallop that son of a gun Cassie Miller was riding right now. Eight perfect fences were all that stood between them and a blue ribbon and a real neat chunk of cash.

The spectators were clapping, their excitement growing, knowing Steve was the final rider of the night. But Steve wanted more, because this time, he and Gordo were going to rock the Garden.

* * *

"Damn, he's going to do it, and I was so sure I had him," Cassie Miller muttered, shaking her blond head. Standing beside her was her husband, Caleb Wells. They were by the in-gate, his arm wrapped about her shoulders. He gave an encouraging squeeze. "It ain't over till it's over, Slim."

"Yeah, but look at him go, Caleb. He's easily matching Orion's stride, and those corners he's taking! My God, do you see that? Sheppard's hunkered down like a barrel racer!"

"Yeah, but here comes the triple," her husband warned. "Maybe this is where his horse'll run out of steam. That's a long, tough line, Cassie."

Caleb had a point. The triple *had* been a bitch; it had gotten Limelight, after all. The first part of the combination, the in-and-out, was big, bigger than before, the jump crew having raised it a notch. Then came a distance of five long strides for the horses to reach the third fence, vertical rails now set at six feet. After a night of jumping, a lot of horses' legs simply didn't have enough spring left to clear it. There it loomed, huge and unforgiving.

Cassie Miller and her husband watched Steve Sheppard coming closer and closer to the in-and-out. "Up and over. That's it!" Cassie encouraged. As soon as Vanguard landed safely, she was counting the strides left to the vertical. One, two, three, four . . . a split-second hesitation, and then Vanguard was going for it, jumping out of Steve's hands, propelling himself up, his hooves skimming the top rail.

At that moment, it was as though every single person in the entire Garden held his breath. Twenty thousand eyes tracked Steve Sheppard on his horse.

He hovered, suspended, his legs no longer even touching the saddle, balancing on the balls of his feet as he threw his body forward, helping his straining horse. Hands high over Vanguard's neck.

Doubt warred with hope. Could they possibly make it? And then the thrilled, ecstatic cheer resounding throughout Madison Square Garden when Steve and Vanguard proved that indeed they could.

The crowd was on its feet, roaring, clapping wildly as Steve and Gordo cleared the final fence. Ty's cheeks were wet, glistening in the floodlights as Steve cantered over to where she stood. His eyes, too, were moist. He wiped at tears of elation with the back of his hand.

Christ, that had been a hell of a ride. He leaned down, clapping his hand against Gordo's shoulder and reined him to a trot, then a walk. He stopped in front of Ty.

"Hey, Ty, got that ribbon you wanted."

She'd never seen him look happier. "So I see." Ty laughed, wiping her eyes, her smile lit with a thousand-watt force. "That was beautiful, Steve. Look at the crowd, they're still on their feet."

Steve grinned at the fans applauding even now, then leaned over to pat Gordo's neck once more. "He put on a show, didn't he?"

"With a little help," Ty said, shaking her head, still in a state of disbelief. One didn't see riding like that very often. "Go on with you. They've got to haul out the red carpet and present you with the trophy."

"Okay, but meet me back at the stalls directly afterward. We've got some celebrating to do."

A long blue champion ribbon fluttered from the side of Gordo's bridle, the horse's body covered by the cooler that the director of the National Horse Show had presented Steve with. Ty had rushed back to Mac and Gordo's stalls ahead of Steve. Catching sight of that flutter of blue, Ty gave Enrique the signal and the cork on the bottle of champagne she'd had cooling in an extra water bucket popped out. Ty held four plastic cups ready and waiting. Two more were produced with exclamations when Sam Brody and Lizzie Osborne appeared a few minutes later.

"Hope we're not interrupting," Lizzie said, planting a smacking kiss on Steve's cheek and one on Gordo's, too. "I'd been planning on leaving before the end of your class, Steve, but you had me glued to the seat right to the very last second."

"Don't believe her. When I showed up, she was already on her feet, jumping up and down. You must have heard her, she was the one shouting, "GO, STEVE, GO!""

Steve grinned at Sam's description, at the annoyed look on Lizzie's face. "Yeah, now that you mention it, I think I did hear someone who sounded awfully like Lizzie."

Outlandish toasting and praising, mixed with hearty laughter, continued while Gordo and Mac were painstakingly rubbed down, their tired legs and muscles soothed with liniment. Ty had a bag of carrots she passed to Sam, who divided them equally between Mac and Gordo. Then Bubba and Enrique left, taking the horses to walk some more. Afterward, they'd be bandaged, watered, and fed. After that, everyone, horses and humans, could finally rest.

A voice broke into the revelry. "Steve, just wanted to congratulate you. Those were awesome rounds you turned in. The Garden doesn't see a shutout every day."

Cassie Miller was still in her breeches, with the sleeves of her rat-catcher rolled past the elbows. Her hair was unpinned. It fell in golden waves down her back.

Steve's face split in a happy grin. "Thanks, Cassie. Ty,

I'd like you to meet Cassie Miller. Cassie's that rider I was telling you to watch for. Cassie, my partner, Ty Stannard."

Ty shook Cassie's hand. "You had some fine rides yourself this evening," Ty offered graciously.

"Thanks. I consider third and fifth quite respectable, given the competition tonight." Cassie shook her head. "I really thought I had you, Steve."

"So did I," Steve laughed. "I was already cantering into the ring when you came out. You looked so good out there, I never bothered to check the clock. I figured you were the one to beat. Earlier, Ty had insisted only blue would do, and Gordo seemed to agree. There didn't seem any other way to ride it."

"I don't think anyone else *could* have ridden it like that."

Steve waved the compliment aside. "Those horses of yours will have their night to shine real soon," he predicted. "Cassie, let me introduce you to our friends. This is Lizzie Osborne, fellow equestrian. And this is . . ."

"Don't I know you?" Cassie was already saying, looking quizzically at Sam.

"Yeah." Sam smiled. "You do. I'm Sam. Sam Brody. A friend of your brother's. We met a few years ago."

"Sam Brody!" Cassie Miller cried with the same enthusiasm one might reserve for Santa Claus on Christmas Eve. She rushed toward him, and hugged him enthusiastically.

Watching, Lizzie's eyes narrowed dangerously. It nettled that Sam wasn't exactly unresponsive to this effusive display of affection, either.

"I can't thank you enough for what you did for Greataunt Grace," Cassie was saying. "It's changed our lives! All last week, the kids were e-mailing her and sending their drawings to her with a click of the mouse. And that thing you had us download . . . the game? A major hit! Who'd have thought this would be a way for two six-year-olds and a ninety-one-year-old woman to connect?"

"Mrs. Miller took to it like a duck to water," Sam replied easily.

"Well, Alex and I are eternally grateful. Great-aunt Grace means a lot to us."

"Can we offer you some champagne, Cassie?"

"Oh, no thanks, Ty, really. I've got to be running along, get back to my own horses. You'll be seeing Alex soon, Sam?"

"Hope to. Caught a glimpse of him in the stands, he looked busy with the kids. They've grown some."

"At an alarming rate!" Ty laughed. "Another reason to get back. It's an awfully late night for them." Cassie turned to Ty and Steve. "Well, so long, and once again, congratulations."

"You'll be seeing us sooner rather than later, Cassie." Steve said. "Ty's a firm believer in sharing good fortune," looping his arm about Ty's shoulders. "I'm guessing that means we'll be making a side trip to your farm next week. See how much of our prize money we can spend."

"And you'll be welcomed with open arms." Cassie Miller laughed.

While Steve and Ty were drinking what was obviously a *private* toast, staring deep into each other's eyes, totally lost to the world, Sam turned to Lizzie. "What's got your nose out of joint?"

"What are you talking about?" Lizzie demanded coolly.

"You know, the way your nose shot up in the air as soon as Cassie Miller showed up. She's a nice kid, and has had some tough breaks. Too bad you didn't say a word to her because she'd be a good friend."

"She seemed far too busy being friendly with you. Such a touching reunion, by the way."

"Lizzie! Is that a note of jealousy I detect? Impossible," he concluded, his laughter pitched low, for her ears only. "But in case I'm wrong, any time you want to show me how happy you are to see me, you go right ahead."

"Oh, Sam." Lizzie stared up at his chiseled face, her lashes batting Scarlett O'Hara-like. "Would you please, please hold your breath until I do?"

30

$\mathcal{T}$y didn't appear unbearably torn or conflicted in deciding whether to accompany Steve to Clyde Farrell's place and look at horses or to stay where she was, with his mother and sisters in the Sheppards' homey kitchen. When she opted to remain in the company of the Sheppard women, it couldn't have pleased Steve more. Ty was clearly captivated by the flow of chatter and laughter his mother and sisters shared. Steve didn't imagine she'd ever been exposed to a family this relaxed and easygoing.

Steve and his father left Ty in the hands of Olivia, Maggie, and Kerry, Steve knowing everything would be fine when he received only a distracted "See you" after brushing his lips against the shell of her ear. Ty was practically oblivious to his presence, busily engaged in the task at hand: mixing the ingredients for an apple raisin cake and listening avidly to a particularly involved story Kerry was embellishing with her usual flair for exaggeration, something about Steve and her in a cross-country race on their father's tractors.

Kerry, too, was cooking, not that she was awarded

with anything but the most menial of tasks, such as slicing carrots. Unlike Maggie and Mom, Kerry refused to
be serious about the culinary arts. She far preferred to
pilfer ingredients and gossip about horses between
bites. Give her a batch of cookies to bake, and half the
dough would be eaten before it got to the sheet. Kerry's
willingness to be stuck in a kitchen chopping a mountain of carrots was a pretty good indication that she was
dying of curiosity to learn everything she could about
Steve's new partner.

Steve's fingers had been crossed, hoping Ty would
choose the apple cake recipe and hours of stories about
his family over a trip to Clyde Farrell's. He was working
on a surprise for her, the thought having waylaid him
out of the blue. Now that it had him in its grip, however,
he couldn't wait to spring it on her.

Steve hadn't visited Clyde Farrell since Fancy's
death, only talked to him on the phone, explaining the
tragedy in halting words to the friend who'd sold Steve
the finest horse he'd ever ridden. A growing nervousness filled him, anxious how the older man would react
when they were face to face. He needn't have worried,
for Clyde pulled Steve into a long bear hug, the strength
in his body evident despite Clyde's pushing seventy.

"Good to see you, Shepp," Clyde said gruffly, stepping back, his eyes bright with emotion.

"Good to be back, Clyde," Steve returned simply, his
arm clasped around his mentor's shoulders. "It's been a
rough couple months, but I think I've turned a corner."
He swallowed down the lump that had lodged itself in
his throat. "I want you to know, Clyde, we planted some
apple trees over Fancy's grave. It's going to look beautiful when those trees bloom."

"Hardest thing to do, to say good-bye to something

you love." Clyde fished out a crumpled bandanna from his pocket and blew noisily. "Both your pop and I have been through it over the years. Still just as painful, ain't it, Steve?"

"Damn near tears you apart," Steve Sr. agreed.

The men walked on, Steve talking softly about Fancy Free, Clyde nodding his thinning gray head of hair.

Then, "I suppose Pop's told you I have a new partner."

As though suddenly interested in a group of horses being led in from a field, Steve Sr. ambled off in their direction.

"You kidding me, Shepp? Steve was on the horn with me yesterday about five minutes after you arrived, bragging about what a fine, intelligent, young woman she is. I was hoping to meet her."

"Sorry, Clyde, Ty got waylaid by Mom and Maggie in the kitchen. Mom's really taken with her."

Clyde's hand absently rubbed his belly, sighing as if he hadn't eaten in decades. "Couldn't ask for a higher recommendation than that."

"Well, Mom might be a bit partial, Ty's so polite and all. But since I came out here alone, I thought I'd see whether you have a youngster Ty might be able to bring along. It's a surprise."

"She know how to ride?"

Steve nodded. "Yeah, she's good, too. Listens well. I think she'd enjoy working with a young horse, building a relationship. Ty's patient and gentle and has good instincts. And real soft hands."

"My kind of woman," Clyde said heartily. "Tell you what, Shepp, I happen to have a couple of beauties that might be just the ticket for your lady friend."

"My partner," Steve corrected with a grin.

*   *   *

"But Steve," Ty protested, "I'm not possibly knowledgeable enough to help you select a horse."

"Time to get experienced, then, partner," Steve replied, roaring down the narrow country road whose twists and turns he knew as well as Southwind's driveway.

"All right," Ty muttered. "This is totally crazy, but all right."

She couldn't help the loud sigh of pleasure when they turned into Clyde Farrell's farm. There weren't many places in the world where horses enjoyed such beautifully maintained surroundings as in Kentucky, and Clyde's place set the standard. Ty got out of the car slowly, her head swiveling, feet following as she looked all around her, horse heaven for three hundred and sixty degrees. Before her stretched a seemingly endless white parallel line of double wooden fences, enclosing still-verdant fields. To her right were majestic white barns topped by gray roofs and gables. Near and far, horses, such horses.

"Pretty amazing, isn't it?" Steve said, standing beside her.

"I'm speechless."

"Don't be," Steve advised lightly as he took her hand. "Other than breeding horses, there are few things Clyde likes so much as talking."

"Easy to tell which one she's got her eye on. Shows fine instinct, Shepp," Clyde couldn't resist observing in an undertone, careful to move only the corner of his mouth. He'd promised Steve he'd keep his trap shut, not spoil the surprise. Though as far as Clyde could tell, Steve had no reason to worry. Ty Stannard had moved a few feet away, standing by the side of the rail, rubbing a dark gray gelding's head. Her eyes remained fixed on the horse even when, momentarily distracted, it sidled off to tear at a few clumps of grass. When its natural curiosity prompted it to return to Ty's side, she rewarded it with husky whispering and gently scratching fingers.

"What's the gelding's name again?" Steve asked, following Ty's every move.

"Silvermine. He's by Jetstreak out of Sudden Glory. Glory's still giving us nice foals. Matter of fact, the one you rode this morning, Elusive"—he pointed to a dark bay gelding playfully nipping the withers of another young horse—"is Billetdoux's and Glory's. Billetdoux is by Bellelettres, and Bellelettres was . . ."

"Fancy Free's dam," Steve finished with a smile. "I remember, Clyde." There was something in the way Elusive carried his head, the way he moved over the flat that reminded Steve of Fancy, too. His father also had noted it. Buying a young horse was always a bit of a gamble, but Steve and his father were men who were willing to follow a hunch. More often than not, it paid off.

"Can you saddle them for us? I'll just ride Elusive lightly; Ty might get suspicious, otherwise."

"But I didn't bring my breeches with me, Steve!" Ty was completely baffled by Steve's behavior. Truth be told, he was acting more than a little weird. Admittedly, she found the young gelding entrancing; he was lovely, his sleek body covered in bluish-black rosettes, the lighter gray mane and tail a striking contrast. But that didn't mean she had to try him out, for Pete's sake!

"If you hop on him, then I can judge how he moves. Look." He feigned impatience. "Much as I love Clyde, I don't really want to spend all day here. Mom's been killing herself making this huge Thanksgiving feast. I was hoping we could get back in time to shower and

change. If you don't want to ride, that's okay, but . . ."
Steve let the word dangle, laying it on nice and thick.

"I'm going, I'm going! I just don't see the point!"

The point was that Ty looked perfect astride the dapple
gray. At sixteen hands, Silvermine wasn't an overly big
horse. Indeed, he possessed the finest features in an Anglo-
Arab: the trim physique, the strong, slender legs, the beautifully arched neck, ending in a dainty, diamond-shaped
head. And shining from his eyes a calm intelligence.

Although Silvermine was three years old and had
graduated from *cavalettis,* or ground rails, to jumping
small cross bars, Clyde Farrell was of the school of
thought that didn't believe in throwing too much at a
horse too soon. Perhaps that's why Steve, when he was
in the market for a new prospect, always headed to
Clyde's first. He knew he'd find a horse still open and
willing, not riddled with the fears and bad habits young
horses sometimes had when their training was rushed
along at warp speed.

"How'd you like him?"

"He's truly lovely, Steve. Not very different from
Cantata in the way he's built, all slim and sleek, but he
doesn't feel like he's going to go slipping out from
under me, you know what I mean?"

"That's the Arab in him, Ty," Clyde offered proudly.
"A braver, truer breed you won't find."

Steve merely grunted, carefully noncommittal. Get
Clyde on the topic of Anglo-Arabs and why they were
better than any other pure or crossbreed, and they'd be
there all night. "Let me see how he moves over those
ground rails, would you, Ty?"

"And what about you?" Ty asked. "The gelding
you're on is gorgeous."

"One gorgeous horse at a time, love."

And besides, not really necessary, as Steve had al-

ready decided Elusive was coming back to Southwind.
Right now, Steve was simply enjoying the pleasure of
walking the young horse around, seeing how well he
responded to the pressure of Steve's leg. One could
learn a lot about a horse that way, its attitude, its sup-
pleness. Already, Elusive was beginning to yield, his
body flexing to the right, then to the left. Responding
without any pressure from the reins, his attitude relaxed and alert.

Steve kept walking, pretending not to notice the wistful expression that came and went on Ty's face.

Steve was happily fixated on the manner in which Ty
surreptitiously licked the tines of her fork, her tongue
darting out to capture the last remaining crumbs of flaky
crust, molasses and brandy-drenched pecans. Nobody
else seemed to notice but him. Steve's father too busy
enjoying himself, holding court, regaling Ty and the
family with the many highlights of his career in racing
and training thoroughbreds. Pop might very well go on
talking a few more hours, he being a man who appreciated an audience.

Despite the prodigious amount of food they'd all
consumed, everyone's dessert plate was scraped clean,
and only one narrow slice remained in the pie plate. Not
surprising, as pecan pies like his sister Maggie's were a
rare treat for the senses. Steve, however, was enjoying
the vicarious thrill of watching Ty finish hers even more
than he'd enjoyed his own slices.

He imagined kissing her now, his tongue tangling
with hers in a slow, sensuous wrestle. Tasting all that
dark sugary warmth. Out of the corner of his eye, he
saw Kerry's hand sneak toward the pie plate.

"Forget, it, brat," he warned, his hand settling on her
forearm.

His kid sister screwed her face in mock outrage. "You must be out of your mind. You already had two slices. And that wasn't counting Ty's apple raisin cake." Futilely, she tried to jerk her arm forward.

"Irrelevant, kid. I got plans for that pie." Steve was thinking of Ty's mouth, Ty's tongue, darting out, trailing up and down.

He only wished the slice were bigger.

Reading the expression on his face, Kerry gave Steve a knowing smirk. "I'll bet you do," she drawled, her hand trying to reach for the pie plate again. "Think of it this way, Godzilla, I'm just saving you from your baser instincts."

"Children," Olivia Sheppard admonished in a tone that had both blond heads snapping guiltily. "Will you please stop bickering during Thanksgiving? Kerry," she said firmly, "let Steve have the pie. He and Ty are only here for a few days."

Steve grinned in triumph, and his sister shot him a look of pure scorn. "Thanks, Mom," Steve replied, positioning the pie plate directly in front of him so it was out of Kerry's reach.

"Don't think I won't say anything when your clothes are covered with pine pitch tomorrow," Kerry whispered loudly, referring to the towering white pine outside Steve's bedroom window. During his high school years, it had served as his private staircase on the nights he'd snuck out of the house for a midnight tryst. Though his mother had often raised her eyebrows in suspicion at the blackened streaks covering his shirts and jeans, his parents had never been able to catch him.

Hearing Steve's burst of laughter at whatever Kerry was taunting him with now had Olivia Sheppard smiling mistily. It was good to have all the family under the same roof again. She'd adamantly refused to call their celebration this evening a pre-Thanksgiving, arguing that having all her children at home was sufficient reason to push any holiday up two weeks. If this wasn't a reason to give thanks, then what was?

Her daughter, Maggie, had outdone herself, planning this meal for a full week. And if they'd been able to make Ty feel at ease and welcome by inviting her to join in the preparations, Olivia knew that the three of them, she, Maggie, and Kerry, had also benefited. It had given them the chance to get to know this quiet and somewhat reserved woman better. Well enough to understand that Ty's initial air of reserve was nothing more than shyness, not a snooty sense of superiority.

For that, Olivia Sheppard couldn't be happier. Since he'd called to tell them of the accident and Jason Belmar's drug use, the Sheppards had been worried sick. But since Steve had stubbornly refused his family's help, there hadn't been much they could do. Watching Ty and Steve together these past couple of days, Olivia was filled with an overwhelming sense of gratitude. Ty Stannard had succeeded where probably anyone else would have failed.

She had made Steve whole again.

That they were desperately in love with each other was as plain as the nose on Olivia's still lovely face. Knowing that her son had at last found love brought such joy to Olivia, tears threatened, now as they had so often during the past forty-eight hours, whenever Olivia happened to come upon Steve and Ty. Usually, she managed to turn away before they noticed her presence. An easy feat, when two people were so wrapped up in each other. They'd be touching, Steve cradling Ty in a hug, perhaps tracing a finger down the elegant line of her cheek, or simply holding her hand. Surrounding them was an aura of piercing happiness.

Olivia Sheppard knew her son too well to think, for even a minute, this relationship with Ty might be merely a fling, a physical attraction that would fade with time. He'd always been careful, protecting himself, protecting his heart. The open affection he displayed with Ty told Olivia, more than words could, that this was the real thing.

She'd be giving Steve her engagement ring before he and Ty left. It would be wonderful to plan a wedding down here in Kentucky. But those details could be worked out later. Now it was time to put the kitchen to rights. That way Steve could do whatever wonderfully naughty thing he was dreaming about with that pecan pie.

"And did you remember to give Clyde Farrell my best?" Olivia asked, standing up and reaching for the plates. "It's a shame he couldn't join us tonight."

"Mom, if Clyde had come, we would have run out of food in the first five minutes." Steve grinned, rising to help. God, he hadn't eaten this much in at least fifteen years. "He's great, though," Steve continued. "Rory Lindemann's going to examine two of his horses for me tomorrow." Lindemann was the veterinarian his father used. Steve carried plates behind his mother into the kitchen. "If they pass, Pop said he'd ship them north for us."

"Two?" asked Ty, mystified. She was carrying a large woven bread basket in her arms; it had been filled with corn bread and homemade rolls. Nothing was left but a few crumbs. "I thought you'd decided on Elusive."

Damn, he hadn't heard her come up behind him. "Nope. Decided to take both of them," he said casually, setting the stack on the counter.

Ty nodded, as if in understanding. "They're both wonderful. It just seemed like you were really taken with Elusive. I think Silvermine has great potential. I can't wait to see you work with him."

"Actually, Ty, I'm afraid it didn't quite click with me and Silvermine."

"But . . ." Ty shook her head. "Then why?"

"Because he's for you, Ty," Steve said softly.

So this is what a surprise could do to her, make her eyes go wide with shock, her mouth open in a perfect *oh*. Even though she'd clearly loved the young horse, she really hadn't expected this, the notion tugging at him.

But seeing the tears well up in her eyes, seeing them spill over and tumble down her cheeks, had him thoroughly alarmed. His fingers felt clumsy as they brushed away her tears. When it became clear they were woefully inadequate to the task, his mouth descended, lips catching warm saltiness. "Hey, don't cry," he murmured helplessly, racking his brain for something that would stop those crystal-sized tears. "It's all Bubba's fault, really. You can blame him. He told me to buy you a present. Something beautiful. I was thinking about a new pair of shoes for you, 'cause you look really, really, um, *good* in them, but then I asked Lizzie how much those Manolo Blahniks went for." He gave a slight shake of his blond head, still unable to believe the figure Lizzie'd quoted. "For that kind of money, I'd rather buy a horse, wouldn't you?" With hands stroking her silky hair, his lips moved over her face, catching fallen tears. "Do you like him, Ty?" he whispered. "If you want something else, I'll give it to you. Anything."

"He's beautiful, Steve." Her voice was raw as if she'd been crying for hours. "But I don't deserve such a gift."

"Yeah, you do," Steve contradicted, filled with elation that she liked his present. Low laughter threaded his voice. "Think of it this way, Ty. We're in Kentucky. A place where Christmas, like Thanksgiving, comes early."

That clinched it. With a renewed sob, Ty threw her arms around Steve's neck, disjointed words of thanks mixed with tears, as she pressed kisses against the column of his neck, against his smiling, indulgent mouth. They stood, Steve's lean body wrapped around hers, Ty's soft hiccups slowly subsiding as their kisses deepened, the rest of the world forgotten. Especially the rest of the Sheppard family.

Steve's father, his index finger pressed to his lips, ushered the Sheppard women away from their posts by the kitchen's swinging door, pulling it quietly after him. He was doing his best to pretend he wasn't moved by the sight of Ty and Steve. The women were plenty sentimental and mushy-hearted as it was. The game was up, however, when Kerry caught him turning away to wipe a tear from the corner of his eye, his other hand fishing for his bandanna.

"Come on, Pop, let's break out the champagne," his daughter said with a smile, threading her arm through his. "This is a night for celebrating! Ty's got a new horse. And Steve's found himself an even finer filly. But you know why we should really be celebrating?"

"No, why, Kerr?" her father asked with a smile, never knowing what to expect from his youngest child.

"From the looks of it, that kitchen is going to be occupied for *quite* some time. Meaning you, Maggie, and I have gotten out of the washing up!"

31

$\mathcal{E}$asy come, easy go. That's what Steve had said, unperturbed by the huge amount of money they'd spent in one short week. The prize money Steve had won at the Garden, the insurance money he'd received for Fancy Free, even the money Ty had earmarked for this first buying trip was gone. Not a penny remained.

What she probably should have done was insist Steve back out of the deal over Silvermine. That would have been a lot of money saved right there. When she'd mentioned it, however, Steve had been outraged. "No way. He's perfect for you, you're keeping him. It's only *money*."

The irony of his comment was not lost on Ty.

"Money we'll need if my trust fund gets blocked," Ty reminded him evenly, knowing, however, that she was wasting her breath. The entire time they'd been arguing, Steve hadn't once taken his eyes off one of the two horses he'd purchased from Five Oaks, the farm that had bred the stallion, Orion.

Carlos was longeing the young gelding, Watermark, while Steve stood by the railing, now and again calling out instructions in a low voice to the groom.

It had been a futile hope that Steve might realize that discussing their finances deserved as much attention as watching Watermark being longed for the first time at Southwind.

Nothing was going to convince Steve of that. Not with a horse this beautiful. Cassie Miller's husband, Caleb Wells, had told them that even as a young foal, Watermark's dapple coat had blurred this way, flowing together until parts of him looked like whimsically marbled Venetian paper. Hence the name. At three years of age, Watermark was already a big horse, most likely he'd grow to be a good seventeen hands. Steve had paid handsomely for him, but Ty knew he considered every cent well spent.

They weren't the only ones who had blown some big money recently. Sam Brody's pockets were significantly lighter these days, too. But Ty hadn't heard a single complaint from Sam, either. Happily munching the hay in her new home, a roomy box stall in Steve's barn, was an all-black filly, called Cassis, the yearling sister of the stallion Orion. Cassie Miller had been delighted when Steve told her Cassis's new owner would be none other than Alex's friend Sam Brody.

Sam had driven out to meet Cassis. Standing by her stall, his thumb rubbing his cheek reflectively, "Lizzie's going to be one jealous woman."

"She still feeling all warm and fuzzy toward you?" Steve had inquired.

"I think running scared might be a better way to describe it." Sam's eyes taking in the clean lines of his new horse.

"I noticed, just in passing, of course, that Lizzie has really long legs." Steve grimaced at the sharp poke he received from Ty.

"Yeah, they are," he acknowledged, his teeth flashing

in a dangerous smile. "But mine are longer. Eventually she'll figure that out," Sam promised. With an out-stretched palm, he offered Cassis a small apple treat, which she accepted with the coy delicacy of an ingenue. "She might stop running a bit sooner, however, just to take a peek at this young mare of mine."

"Ty, hon, why don't you give Lizzie a call tonight," Steve suggested blandly. Important to keep new owners happy.

"Why wait? I have some paperwork to do, anyway. And Serena's coming by as soon as she gets out of school. We're going over all the stuff she did for the Web site and the clinic. She said the response was great. We'll need to sort through the applicants."

"I'll be in soon. Just want to check and make sure the new horses are okay."

"Bubba and you plan to tuck them in every night?" Ty teased.

Steve angled his head, capturing her lips in a long, lazy kiss. Then, with a playful wink, "Well, I can't speak for Bubba, but I got something much better to tuck in every night."

"Bye, Sam. I love your new horse."

"Thanks, Ty. I think I might, too."

Ty had left Sam and Steve with Cassis, Steve outlin-ing his training plans for the young mare, Sam seeming completely comfortable in his new role as expensive horse owner.

Which was great, Ty thought; this was exactly what Southwind needed, enthusiastic owners who were will-ing to place their trust in Steve. Ty merely wished she herself could be as sanguine. Her stomach churned, tight knots of worry.

As she walked back toward the house, she drew a deep, bracing lungful of chilly November air, willing away the knot of anxiety, of tense foreboding. Everything would be fine, she said to herself.

Watching her leave, Steve reached into his right-hand pocket, absently fingering the heavily creased stationery.

They'd made love through the night, falling asleep only as the sky was lightening. It was Monday, the barn's off day, meaning the horses wouldn't be exercised, only turned out. Steve was counting on Ty to sleep right through it. She certainly needed the rest. All the traveling of the past two weeks, along with the additional excitement of the show, had even Steve a little bleary-eyed. If one factored in the stress of meeting his family, of driving hundreds of miles cross-country, of all the work and riding Ty had been doing, it was a real testament to her strength that she could still stand.

Yeah, it would simplify things beautifully if she slept right through Steve's meeting with her father. Never learning her father had approached him, offering to buy him off. Steve could save her from that pain, at least.

After the meeting with Ty's father, he'd destroy the letter, the proposed contract, too. Both just bursting with heart-warming sentiment. Stannard laid everything out crystal clear, an eight-year-old could have grasped the implications. Without preamble, Stannard announced the fact that he'd already instructed his lawyers to file a suit that would temporarily, if not permanently, freeze the income his daughter received from her mother's trust. No further money from the trust could be used, not until the presiding judge heard the case and decided on it.

That hadn't come as a huge surprise. Ty had said that's what her father would do, and she obviously understood his twisted mind better than anyone. Sick though it was, this sort of nasty family feuding wasn't anything new. Headlines were full of wealthy families attacking each other, one member suing the pants off another. Most did it out of greed.

But Steve didn't believe that properly described Tyler Stannard's flawed motivation. Was it spite? Or was it that after wielding power for so long, Stannard had actually come to believe he had the right to manipulate people's lives—and now relished doing so?

Steve didn't know the answer. It was almost worth meeting with the bastard just to see if he could figure it out.

What did surprise Steve, however, was the rest of the Stannard's proposal. It made him think he'd been smart to infuriate the man—by making those statements to Vicky Grodecki, by having his and Ty's red-hot embrace captured on film—because the proposal revealed exactly to what extent Tyler Stannard would go to remove Ty from Steve's "evil clutches"—the words were Steve's, not Stannard's.

Stannard, while possibly nuts, certainly evil, was no fool. His letter and the propsal, were exquisitely worded, their intent to play to Steve's obvious weaknesses: his desire to own Southwind free and clear and his need for financial security.

Christ, Steve reflected. He'd changed so much in the last month, no longer the same person who'd sat in those law offices, engulfed in such self-pity that his principal goal had been to finagle Southwind from Ty. A woman who had cared enough to step forward and give him the help he desperately needed. Money, first, but the most important thing she'd given him was love, a love that had made him able to hope again.

That Steve's initial schemes had come to naught was irrelevant. The unpalatable truth was that a mere month ago, his attitude hadn't been so very different from Ty's father's. Given the chance, he would have manipulated Ty just as ruthlessly.

Thank God he'd fallen deeply in love with this brave and beautiful woman. A better man for it, he was determined not to disappoint her.

Tyler Stannard was prompt, that was about the only positive thing Steve had to say about Ty's father. Come to think of it, not even his punctuality meant a whole lot to Steve. It was other people who worked their butts off to guarantee Tyler Stannard's arrival at a precise hour. The helicopter pilot who'd flown Stannard to Easthampton, the limousine's chauffeur, sitting in it still, cooling his heels in Steve's driveway. No, Tyler Stannard didn't have a damn thing that impressed Steve. Except a daughter.

Stannard hadn't bothered to hide the faint curl of his upper lip as he'd looked around Steve's home. The king visiting the peasant's hovel. Steve had been watching from the kitchen window, cradling the last of his coffee before he went out to intercept Ty's father. He didn't want the doorbell awakening Ty.

"Mr. Stannard," Steve took the terse nod for a salutation. Tyler Stannard looked as close to apoplectic as an iceberg could be, a faint smile crossing Steve's lips when he recalled Ty's characterization of her father. Antarctica was probably too tropical for him.

"Mr. Stannard, I was just making some more coffee. May I offer you a cup?"

Stannard didn't consult the slim watch peeking out beneath the cuff of his tailored suit, but merely looked at Steve with open dislike. His eyes were the same hue as Ty's but flat, an ugly, humorless gray. "My time is extremely valuable. You indicated there were things you wanted to discuss before our lawyers met. I'm accommodating your request to come here . . ."

Steve felt his own gaze grow colder. "Well, I guess that's a no to the coffee," he drawled, letting his mouth curve around the words until his accent flowed rich and slow. "Come inside so we can talk."

He stepped back to let Ty's father precede him. The older man passed, a vision of polished money from the top of his combed silver hair to his dark flannel suit accented by a crisp white dress shirt underneath and down to the polished shine of hand-buffed shoes. Stannard smelled of money, too, catching the whiff of the crisp, subtle scent clinging to him. *Eau de moola*, Steve decided.

Stannard surveyed the house's interior and dismissed it just as quickly. A blink of those cold eyes, and Steve's home would be razed to the ground should Stannard ever get hold of Southwind. In its place, some architectural atrocity, a cottage boasting five bedrooms (not including servants' quarters, of course), each with its own Jacuzzi-equipped bathroom and God knows what else as extras.

The letter from Stannard, along with the draft of the contract, lay on top of the coffee table. Steve waited while Stannard lowered himself into the slightly worn upholstered wingback chair, then chose the sofa, himself, leaning forward, elbows propped against his knees. A blunt-tipped finger tapped the five-page draft. "I haven't sent your proposal to my lawyer yet, Mr. Stannard. I preferred to get it clear in my mind exactly what your terms are before showing it to him." Not that Jeff Wallace would ever be seeing the letter or the proposal.

"The terms are straightforward. As my letter states plainly, within a few short weeks the officers overseeing my daughter's trust will be forced to acknowledge its misuse. Meaning, Mr. Sheppard, she'll no longer be able to underwrite Southwind." He gave Steve a hard smile.

"To fight it in court will cost a considerable amount. More than you can afford."

The bastard. "Yes." Steve's tone was dry. "That part of your letter was very clear."

Stannard ignored him, continuing. "In the proposal, I have outlined two very generous options for your consideration. First, I am willing to offer the sum of ten million dollars to you. According to my calculations, Tyler has spent approximately two and a half million. To abide by the terms of your contract with her, you would need to reimburse her investment to date. That means you would walk away from the partnership owning all of Southwind and having close to seven and a half million dollars."

"And Ty and I could go our separate ways."

"Not could," Stannard corrected. "*Will.* Agreeing to either proposal entails ending all contact with my daughter. Now," Stannard continued smoothly, oblivious to the tightening of Steve's jaw, "shall we move on to the second proposal?"

Something, she didn't know what, must have alerted her to her father's presence in the house. The soft, almost droning murmur coming from the living room was pitched too low to carry up the stairs to Steve's bedroom. She didn't even hear their voices until she was at the foot of the stairs, her steps gone quiet with dread. No, it must have been something else; perhaps a particle from the scent of her father's cologne had found its way upstairs. She'd breathed it in and her innards had turned to ice.

None of it surprised her. Her father's presence, the fact that Steve had hidden the visit from her, all the careful planning involved in setting it up. Steve must have been phoning Smythe while she was out of the house;

Ty's father had never done anything spontaneous in his life.

She supposed the dull ache growing inside her was due, in part, to a sense of betrayal. But could she really fault Steve? Ty only wondered how much her father was willing to pay to buy Steve off.

Not enough, apparently. As she paused at the threshold of the living room, an uninvited audience, Steve's words rang quite clear, despite those drawn-out vowels he so loved. "The problem is, Mr. Stannard, neither of your offers really entices me. You see, I want more."

Although his back was to her, Steve must have sensed her presence. Her father perhaps too stunned by Steve's words to notice his daughter standing not six feet away.

"Ty, come in, honey. Your father's honored us with a visit." Steve had risen to his feet, smiling easily, as if everything she'd ever wanted weren't being taken away. Once again.

She swallowed. "Hello, Father."

"Tyler."

No wonder she hated being called Tyler, Steve thought. The guy hadn't even stood, let alone embraced his only child. Steve wanted to deck him. He resisted the impulse for now.

"As you can see, Tyler, your partner has agreed to meet with me privately, so we can discuss certain options." That little stress on the word *privately* was a nice touch. Stannard couldn't exactly shoo Ty away, not in Steve's house.

"Why doesn't Ty stay? I'm sure she'd like to hear what's involved."

"No. That won't be necessary." Stannard's voice was as cold as metal on a subzero day.

"But I insist."

Ty couldn't help glancing at Steve; she'd never heard him sound like this. A voice that cracked like a whip, startling even her father. For a second her eyes held Steve's, then Ty broke the contact, so he couldn't read the pain in hers.

It was over.

The only thing she wanted was to hurt herself a little more before she left. She took a seat.

Steve pushed the papers along the scarred wood of the coffee table. "Have a look." Then he leaned back against the sofa. The silence grew thick as Ty read the document. Steve just sat observing Stannard.

Did grown men get in a snit? Stannard's face was pinched even more, as though offended by his daughter's presence. If he disliked Ty this intensely, why was he bothering to buy Steve off for close to the equivalent of some developing countries' national budgets?

Or was it only that his daughter wasn't doing what he wanted or approved of that made Stannard look as if he was sucking a pound of sliced lemons?

Steve glanced again at Ty. "Well, partner." Willing to interrupt now that she was near the last page. "You see what I get if I choose option two? Kind of reminds me of that old TV show, the one where you guess what's behind curtain number one, two, or three? Your father only gave me two options, but won't I be one rich son of a gun if I go for the second?"

"Indeed you will," Ty murmured, rising from the chair. Ty now knew all she needed. Steve would be a very rich man, very soon. "If you'll excuse me, I'll let you continue with your meeting. Good-bye, Father."

She was gone.

Stannard opened his mouth to speak, but Steve raised his hand, stopping him. He didn't have much time to waste. Bubba was on the lookout, but who knew where she might decide to run?

"As I was saying, Mr. Stannard. Either offer, generous as they may be, simply isn't enough. I want more."

"Name your price."

"Your daughter."

It came out then, the seething, pent-up rage spewing forth. Stannard leapt to his feet, his face ugly and dark. "My daughter, my daughter!" he spat. "You're not good enough to lick her boots."

"Probably not."

"Don't you dare interrupt me! Look at you." His gaze raked Steve contemptuously. "Some two-bit, uneducated rider. My daughter with you? Never will I allow it. I gave Tyler everything, I *made* her what she is."

"Bullshit. Ty's a hell of a lot more than anything you could make. She made herself—despite you and every miserable thing you've done to her. She's stronger than you, smarter than you, better than you. And that humiliates the shit out of you, doesn't it? That's why you need to drag her down, keep her locked in some dungeon you've lined with cash. I may only be a dumb rider, but that's a real easy one to figure out."

"How dare you!" Stannard now so angry he was shaking, practically foaming at the mouth. "I can crush you under my heel until you're so much dust."

"I'm sure you'll do your best." Steve smiled. "But I'll have Ty. So fuck you, Stannard. And as far as I'm concerned, you can do the same to your money. Oh, and get out of my house."

Bubba was waiting outside when Stannard swept by, yanking the door of the limousine open before the chauffeur could jump to the task himself. Joining him, Steve stood by Bubba's side as the limo's tires gouged ruts into the dirt, the driver throwing the steering wheel violently.

"You want me to go run him off the road, boss? I wouldn't hurt the van, I promise. So far I don't have a police record but this, this would be worth one."

"Great minds do think alike, Bubba. I was considering something along those lines myself. Trouble is, there aren't any good cliffs for him to go flying off. So thanks, but no. If he comes back, though, we can always reconsider. Where is she?"

"Don't know. I took all the keys, like you said. She came into the barn, spent a few minutes in Silvermine's stall, but then she went back out. My guess is she went to the ocean. Must be a soothing place for some." He grimaced, rubbing a stomach that lurched at the mere thought of an unsteady horizon.

But Steve didn't hear, already running, following the line of fence that ended a few hundred yards away from the Atlantic Ocean.

No tears. Not now, not later. The spreading ache of emptiness persisted, though, causing Ty to curl into herself, her arms hugging knees folded tight, while the wind whipped about her. Her ears were ringing from the wind and cold, one more hollow ache.

She stayed immobile, watching the waves come roaring, one after the other, crashing close, the spume racing toward her. The damp cold of the sand was seeping through her jeans, chilling her skin, ready to penetrate her very marrow.

She hugged herself tighter. Had he said he loved her? Not really, not in so many words. And if he had, so what? He'd loved horses and Southwind for far longer. Could she blame him for succumbing to so powerful a lure? His farm and his horses were his life. She'd seen that, understood it even better during their visit to the Sheppards' home in Kentucky, a family where horses were the beginning and the end. And no one knew better than she how hard it was to escape the influence of one's family, Ty thought, her lips pressed in a bitter smile.

Well, now he'd be free, able to run Southwind precisely as he wished, no longer needing to accommodate finicky owners or demanding partners. Her usefulness had been her money. It was gone. Why should he have to put up with the rest?

Her throat clenched in a sudden tight spasm. Dropping her head down upon her upraised knees, Ty forced her muscles to her will, swallowing, pushing back the infinite sadness that threatened to overcome her.

He kneeled beside her, his approach too quiet to be heard over the windy battle roaring in her ears. Feeling his body brushing hers, she made to rise, but his arm detained her.

"Don't." Her voice sounded harsh, foreign even to her. But his hand remained, only gentling its grip. She ignored it, it meant nothing. "Has my father left?" To be heard over the crash of waves and the howl of the wind, she had to speak more loudly than she wanted. Already her throat felt strained and raw.

"Yes."

"I'll go pack my things."

He was looking at her; she could feel the weight of his eyes.

"Really? Before you've seen it through, Ty? Before we've even held the clinic? Before you know whether we can make it, you'll go, leaving it all?"

"Don't," she repeated, as her head whipped around, the strands of her hair lashing her face. Her eyes were glittering dangerously. "Don't pretend to me that what I do matters. I'd sign over my half of the partnership right now, and it wouldn't matter. So don't lie to me."

"That's where you're wrong. Everything about you matters." His hand reached out, carefully raking the tangled hair from her face. "By all rights, I should be angry as hell with you for doubting me, for not trusting me. After meeting your father, though, I can see why it might be hard for you to trust." Something in the tone of his voice had her eyes searching his. "Ty, I told him to go fuck his money."

She stared, too shocked for words.

"I know; he was a little surprised, too. This is probably only the second time in his life anyone's had the nerve to tell him to take a flying——hike." His hand reached for hers, the beginnings of a smile playing over his lips. "You were my shining example, Ty."

"But the money . . ."

"Christ Almighty, what *is* it with money?" he asked, exasperated. "We're doing fine. We'll get clients. I'm damned good at what I do, and you're an eagle-eyed businesswoman. To tell you the truth, I hope to hell your father does block your trust, 'cause then he'll have shot his last round. We're going to make it, Ty. That is, once we renegotiate."

"I'll sign the contract over to you as soon as we get back. Bubba can witness it," Ty said quietly. "I should have done it long ago."

But Steve was shaking his head. His laughter drifted on the wind. "No, Ty, that's not what I meant. I'm talking a whole new contract. A big one, package deal. You and me, fifty-fifty."

"I don't understand." Confusion was plain on her face.

"A new partnership, Ty." His hand lifted hers, bringing it to his lips, warming her cold skin. "You get me, and I get you. Forever." Feeling the band of metal sliding up her finger, Ty looked down. A diamond twinkled back at her.

"Mom gave this to me last week. I wanted this show-down with your father over before asking you. Marry me, Ty. I love you. Let me give you babies. Let me give you a family, a real family. Let me give you love."

Steve's lips found hers, drinking in her tremulous smile, her whispered "Yes."